# SINGAPORE GIRL

Also by Murray Bailey

Singapore 52
Singapore Boxer

Map of the Dead

Black Creek White Lies

I Dare You
Dare You Twice

# SINGAPORE GIRL

## Murray Bailey

Heritage Books

First published in Great Britain in 2018 by Heritage Books

3468643

copyright © Murray Bailey 2018

ISBN 978-1-9997954-3-6
e-book ISBN 978-1-9997954-4-3

Printed and bound in Great Britain by Clays Ltd, Elcograf S.p.A.

Heritage Books, Truro, Cornwall

For Kerry—my wife, my girl.

# ONE

In my experience, many soldiers like to show off their war wounds like badges of honour. I suspect the psychology is about the relief of survival. Something akin to: *look how close I came to death.*

But I was no longer in the army and my injury was nothing to be proud about. I had been shot in the leg. A bullet had passed through my right calf muscle. It wasn't life-threatening; it was merely an annoyance.

It was early morning but the sun was a purple haze against the ominous clouds. I sat on my porch and watched the lightning far out at sea. The timing of the rumbles told me it was coming this way.

My apartment was on Beach Road, just down from the famous Raffles Hotel. I'd enjoyed staying at the swanky hotel for a couple of nights, but my meagre government pay packet forced me to find this place. It was simple and clean and the views out to the South China Sea made it worth every penny.

When I did my training regime every morning, I finished with a run along the coast, usually out towards Changi in the east.

Early morning, with the air still cool and the breeze from the ocean, was a great time to run. But of course I hadn't run for almost a week. I still trained though. It

1

was in my blood, having been an amateur boxer for almost half my life.

Forked lightning danced on the horizon and I breathed in electrically charged ozone.

I leaned back in my chair and opened my book. *The Art of War*. The English translation. It had been delivered to my home on the day after the incident at Singorah airfield, where I'd been shot. There was no accompanying note, no suggestion of the sender. But I knew.

I'd already read the book twice and each time found more insight in the words. I wondered whether anything was lost in the translation, because one thing I had learned, in almost eight months here, was that the Chinese loved double meanings. Words and numbers on their own meant one thing, but read in combination could mean something totally different.

"Morning, boss!"

A voice I recognized called from the road below. Sergeant Dave Hegarty, better known as Hedge, on account of his bushy eyebrows, leaned against a military police Land Rover and waved.

I pushed up and stood at the balcony railing. "Good morning. Everything all right?"

"Something's happened."

I waited for him to tell me more. I'd already guessed this wasn't a social visit.

He said, "Are you back at work?"

"Depends." I wasn't officially. The doctor had signed me off from work for ten days and I was halfway through. I was also supposed to use a walking stick, but the wound was healing nicely and, providing I took it slowly, I could walk just fine.

"Could do with your experience," Hedge said, leaving the jeep and coming closer.

"What's happened?"

He lowered his voice. "An incident."

It was always an incident. He was being deliberately vague and I wondered why. Probably because he'd been told to pick me up.

I shook my head and smiled. "You'll have to tell me more, Sergeant."

"There's a body."

"A body?"

"At Woodlands Crossing."

"And you need me because...?"

"Can I update you in the jeep?"

I shook my head again. "Tell me first. Like I said, it depends. I'm supposed to be resting and keeping an eye on the thunderstorm."

Hedge laughed. It sounded like relief, and I figured he was allowed to explain if I wasn't immediately persuaded.

He said, "Can I come up and talk?"

"Meet me at the top of the stairs."

"The body," he said a few minutes later outside my door, "it's on the causeway."

"Civilian?"

"Don't know. Could be army. Could be anyone."

"Anyone?"

"Male anyway. That's the point. He's dead. He's naked and we have no idea who it is." He paused and took an awkward breath. "Boss, it's not a pretty sight."

Now he had my interest. "Tell me more."

"The body... the hands have been cut off... and there's no head."

3

# TWO

Sergeant Hegarty drove me towards Woodlands Crossing, the northern tip of the island.

"I haven't seen you for a few months," he said after we had left the city. Once in the jungle, red laterite stones flicked up under the Land Rover's wheels. We bounced and splashed through ruts and puddles from last night's rain.

"The wet season—don't you just love it?"

He was being ironic. Although, with his Welsh accent that rose in pitch at the end of sentences, most things sounded ironic.

It rains a lot in north-west England. I'd grown up in Manchester, so I know. However, Singapore's wet season was a different kind of rain. Heavy, unrelenting, merciless downpours. The temperature varied between hot and very hot and the humidity could make your clothes damp even without the rain.

So why was I still here? The answer was complicated. I was working for the government secretary responsible for internal security for two reasons. The first was due to my past activities in the Middle East. I didn't believe the secretary would use the information he had against me, but there was always a risk.

The second reason was more compelling. Singapore was a colourful city of many facets, surrounded by exotic jungle and the sea. Of course, the beautiful women had a part to play in the allure of this tropical paradise.

Probably because I hadn't responded, a few minutes later he tried again: "What's it like, boss?"

I was thinking and didn't answer straight away. I figured he was angling for information about police operations. The sergeant was a talker, and I knew his boss, Major Vernon, would love to know what I was up to.

I said, "Wet."

He laughed. "I don't mean the weather. What's it like... being shot, I mean?"

"Painful."

"It was a Chinese gang, right? You were on a drugs case?"

"Something like that." I paused and half turned towards him as he fought with the wheel. "Look, sorry, Hedge, it was just a police matter." In other words, it wasn't a military issue so I wouldn't be sharing. My job working for the secretary was intelligence, particularly about anything that was a threat against the state. It meant working with the civilian police and military police but I wasn't a liaison officer. They had their own people for that and Secretary Coates believed in sharing only what was necessary. He'd used the old Second World War expression: "Loose lips sink ships." It was unlikely to be true, but he was in charge. What I did understand was that my job required trust, so I only shared information judiciously. I never gossiped about work and I remembered who I'd told what.

"I get it," he said. "Don't let the cat out of the bag."

"Not really..." I started to say and then realized Hedge was doing his old trick of dropping clichés into conversation just so he could explain them.

"Is that a new one?" I asked.

5

"In medieval times people would go to market to buy a piglet. The vendor would let them select the animal and put it in a bag for them to take home. Only, con artists would switch the bag for one with a cat inside."

"So the expression literally means finding out there's really a cat in the bag. Discovering the truth."

Hegarty grinned. "Good, isn't it?"

"One of your better ones."

"I have more."

"I'm sure you have, but let's save them for another almost appropriate expression."

We drove in silence for a while except for the rattle and bump of the suspension. After Bukit Timah, we passed through a particularly waterlogged region where water ran across the road.

"You didn't ask me a critical question," Hegarty said.

"What was that?"

"Nationality."

I laughed. "He's dead."

"I mean colour. You know, Chink, Malay…"

"He's white."

Now it was the sergeant's turn to take his eyes off the road. "How did you…?"

"Deduction. *Could be army*, you said. Many British soldiers are white and most of the whites are army. Plus, I don't think you'd be so excited if he wasn't white." I'd also wondered why Hegarty had been sent to get me. Why did they want me involved?

As we approached Woodlands I realized there was no traffic coming the other way. We overtook a long queue of vehicles and saw why. The crossing barrier was down with four sentries blocking the way, clearly signalling that the causeway was closed.

One thing I'd learned about Singaporeans is their patience. Yes, they worked hard and for long hours—

often frenetically so—but when confronted with something they could do nothing about, they waited. Men leaned against their vehicles and smoked or chatted.

They paused, watched us pass, and then returned to their business.

When we reached the front of the queue, the soldiers stepped aside and the barrier was raised.

Forty yards wide and a thousand yards long, the crossing to Malaya was a busy trade route. A rail track ran alongside, but since there was no train held at the border I figured they weren't impacted by the closure.

At the far end of the causeway I could make out people and vehicles queuing to enter Singapore. About halfway along were two vehicles, both Land Rovers, both military police. One was just parking.

Hedge drove cautiously. In places there were sections missing and I knew pedestrians had to walk in the road. There were also potholes and the repairs were constant. The bridge had been destroyed in 1942 to slow the Japanese advance, and although it was now fully operational, there was always work being done to reinforce the stone thread that connected Singapore to the peninsular mainland.

As we approached the parked Land Rovers, the officer in charge greeted us. I recognized him: Lieutenant Cole from 200 Provost at Gillman Barracks. He had unfortunate features with small eyes that earned him the name Polecat Cole behind his back. However, despite the appearance he seemed to be a good MP.

"Sir!" he said as I got out. I discouraged the men from referring to my old status. Hedge got away with calling me boss, but otherwise I preferred Ash or Mr Carter.

Behind Cole stood two more MPs, both wearing gloves, and another man I recognized: Doctor Kishan Thobhani from Alexandra Hospital.

I shook the lieutenant's hand and waved to Thobhani. "How are you, Doc?"

I wasn't sure of his heritage. His usual swarthy skin looked grey but it may have been the light. The thunderstorm would have reached landfall by now and the clouds danced with violet and grey.

"Just got here myself," Thobhani said, grunting, and then pointed to the roughhewn boulders beside the road. Beyond them was the choppy dark water of the straits.

We left the road and stepped onto the rocks.

Just as Hegarty had described: a naked male body, white, but with a tan except for where his underwear would have been. He was face up, or at least would have been if his head was still attached. The hands had also been removed.

"Has it been moved?"

Cole responded, "Just from the edge of the water. He was partially in."

There was no sign of blood on the rocks. "He didn't die here," I said.

"Nope," the doctor said. He was squatting beside the body looking at the exposed meat and bone of the neck. He stood up.

"Did he wash up?" I asked.

"Dumped in the water, you mean?" Thobhani pursed his lips. "No, I would say decomposition hasn't gone far enough. It's unlikely he'd float yet."

Cole said, "So he was dumped here."

The doctor said, "He didn't fall from a train. Too far to roll." The body was on the opposite side of the causeway to the rail track. "Nor could someone have thrown him this far."

8

Cole shook his head. "No scrapes on the body either, so wasn't dragged far."

I noted that comment but turned to the doctor. "Time of death?"

He shrugged. "It's hard enough in these temperatures, but this level of exsanguination…"

"Best guess?"

"More than a day. Not more than two. I'll have a better idea when we look at the level of decomposition."

I bent down, careful not to stretch my right calf, and looked at the body. The cuts were clean.

"Axe?"

Thobhani grunted, "I don't know. Almost looks surgical. Perhaps garrotted or a guillotine, no?"

"Any guillotines around here?"

The doctor shook his head and shrugged at the same time.

Back to the lieutenant I said, "When was it discovered?"

"First thing. First truck across reported it to the guys on the Singapore side. They closed the crossing straight away."

"And you were here first?"

"Not me. Major Vernon was the one to close the crossing. He arrived soon after the body was discovered."

Major Tony Vernon. I knew he regularly went to Johor Bahru on the other side of the straits so wasn't surprised. It also explained why I'd been picked up so soon after the body had been found.

Hegarty was probably reading my mind. "It was the major who asked me to fetch you." Then to Cole he said, "Could they have dumped the body and then reported it, sir? The first truck to cross, I mean."

9

Cole shook his head. "Unlikely. Once the barriers were raised there will have been a stream of vehicles."

"Then too many witnesses and too risky," I said. "What time was the causeway closed last night?"

"Nine o'clock."

That was earlier than it used to be but I knew concerns over smuggling had tightened customs regulations and increased checks.

"Heavy cloud cover, so it would have been pitch-black," I said. "It's unlikely to have been the last vehicle because it's too obvious, but you should find which vehicles crossed after nightfall."

"That'll be hundreds."

I shrugged. "Focus on the last hour and any covered trucks travelling from Malaya. Work back from the last to cross."

He frowned at me.

The body was lying with its toes pointing to Singapore, which might suggest a vehicle travelling to Malaya. Maybe subconsciously laid it the same way. But this was well planned. The blood had been drained, the identity surgically removed. My gut told me the direction of the body was no accident. I figured it had been laid the opposite way around.

The sky lit up and it felt like the rain was imminent.

The doctor beckoned to the soldiers, who lay a stretcher on the ground.

"Before you take him," I said, "what else can you tell us, Doc? Now or later, I'm keen to know what he died of."

Hegarty laughed. "His head was chopped off."

"Unlikely to be the cause, no?" Thobhani said. "Hard to saw someone's head off if they're alive—unless they're unconscious, of course. I'll have a better idea after the autopsy."

"How long?" I asked.

"To get results? Depends what else I've got on. Maybe a couple of days."

Undeterred by the previous put-down, Hegarty said, "One thing we know for sure."

We all looked at him and then the body, where he was pointing. "He wasn't a Jew."

"Thanks," Thobhani said with sarcasm. He said something else but his words were lost in the thunder.

Cole said, "All right, let's roll him over—if that's OK, Doc?"

Thobhani nodded. "Onto a stretcher. And carefully."

Cole waved to the two soldiers. "Go ahead," he said.

I stood back and the two men placed a stretcher on the ground and walked around to the far side of the body.

I heard one mutter, "Again. And always us that gets the dirty work."

"Get a move on," Cole said, and the two men put their hands under the body, lifted and rolled it onto the stretcher. There were dark marks on the skin, about four inches long between the shoulder blades. Writing maybe.

The doctor and I crouched to take a better look.

"What do you think?"

Thobhani shrugged. He licked his finger and touched a section, rubbing it back and forth. He looked at the tip and placed it in his mouth.

"Blood, I would say."

I looked again at the marks and tried to make sense of them. The sky crackled and flashed and a second later the raindrops started.

"Numbers," Cole shouted against the dying rumble. "It looks like the numbers two, two and one, to me."

11

# THREE

The rain lasted less than an hour and fresher air now blew off the sea. I stood outside the Georgian property in the government sector and knocked on the shiny black door.

The Malay butler always answered but never spoke to me. He just turned and I followed.

Secretary Coates was in his library-styled room. Although still early, the air was heavy with blue smoke from his cigar. Coates was sitting in his big leather armchair wearing his usual black suit and white, wing-collared shirt.

He was ex-army—Second World War—and it was rumoured he'd been in a special unit called Force 136, who had operated behind Japanese lines. He liked to talk but he'd never shared personal information with me; never talked of his past. I had come to think of him as a disapproving headmaster.

He had his false leg crossed over the other and made no move to stand or shake my hand. When he spoke, his fingers kept hold of his chunky cigar and I figured he was in a foul mood.

"The incident at Singorah."

I had half expected him to ask how my wound was. After all, I'd been signed off work for another week, but Coates had a single-track mind. Allegedly it was the security of the island, but I knew there was a personal angle at play.

I said nothing and watched the smoke swirl between us.

"It was a bloody disaster," he said.

"Yes, it was."

"That's not what I pay you for!" He had raised his voice and gripped the chair's arms. "Tell me what happened."

Of course, he would have received reports, but I humoured him anyway and recounted my version. I said that the police had been monitoring a group of Chinese for a week following a tip-off. One night, they were observed loading a truck and were followed to the airstrip. By the time I got there, the road out had been blocked and twenty police were stationed around the field. I joined the officer in charge.

As he updated me, the doors of the hangar rolled open and we could see a small aeroplane that someone identified as a Cessna. The Chinese were pushing it out manually and clearly intended it to get onto the runway before firing up the engine.

The smart move would have been to get them as they came out of the hangar. But they were out in the open before the OIC announced by megaphone that they were surrounded.

For a minute the gang froze and looked around. But it was too dark. Maybe they thought he was bluffing, but they started firing and heading back for cover. The police returned fire and it was chaos. Four cops were injured and may have been shot by their own men. I'm also sure that I wasn't shot by a Chinese bullet. Eventually the shooting stopped and we found that all but one of the gang members were dead. Although he was mortally wounded.

13

They also forgot about the plane because, in the confusion, it took off and got away with the real evidence. The intelligence said that they had drugs in army crates. The police found no drugs, although they did find empty crates marked with "British Army" and "Medical Supplies".

Coates said, "And the survivor denied he worked for Andrew Yipp."

"That's right, although the man died on the way to hospital."

"It was our first big chance to catch Yipp red-handed and it was a balls-up."

"But you just said—"

"That they weren't working for Yipp?" Coates flung his cigar at the wall. "Of course they were working for him! You have one simple job and that's to show Yipp for what he is. Eight months and bugger all to show for it."

I shook my head. "With respect, sir. There has been no evidence."

"You've found no evidence. That's not the same thing, son."

The truth was, the police hadn't found any evidence either. Coates said Yipp was guilty of major criminal activity but what he really wanted was evidence of sedition.

I decided there was no point in arguing any further. After a minute's silence, he sat back and seemed to calm down. The fan in the ceiling turned slowly.

"Tell me about the body on the causeway."

"Naked man with no head or hands. Probably dumped there before the crossing closed last night, though the MO at the scene thought it could be up to two days old."

"Signs of torture?"

14

"Hard to say. If you ignore the obvious, then no."

"In the war, the Chinese Reds decapitated traitors. Did I tell you they fought on the same side as us back then? We always knew there'd be a problem after we beat the Japs, but during the occupation they harboured us and we trained them." He laughed bitterly at the irony. "They were always on edge, always wary of betrayal. So they cut off heads and occasionally removed the heart and liver."

"The body was intact. Although there was something painted on the back. Probably in blood."

He considered this and frowned. "Like a message?"

"Maybe."

"Chinese?"

"I don't think so. Lieutenant Cole wondered if they were numbers—two, two, one."

Coates thought for a moment and shook his head. "Any ideas?"

"None."

"Why on the causeway?"

I had an idea but I waited for Coates to voice it himself. For the first time, I noticed that he had a glass of something—a stengah, watered-down whiskey most likely—on the table beside him. He took a sip before speaking.

"No man's land," he said. "Singapore control ends on the Woodlands side and Malaya control begins at the other end."

"Army jurisdiction," I said. This wasn't a police matter. Not unless it could be linked to either Singapore or the mainland. In the meantime, 200 Provost Company were in charge.

"Quite," Coates said, his voice dropping. "And I want you to stay close."

15

Thinking about the case, I walked down to the river. Why was the body on the causeway? Was that relevant? Could he have been a traitor of some kind?

I crossed halfway on Cavenagh Bridge and watched the stream of bumboats and the larger tongkangs carrying wares out to waiting ships. There was often the pungent smell of fresh rubber but today I could also smell cinnamon.

Suddenly I felt hungry and realized that I'd missed breakfast. The thunderstorm had passed and I judged from the clouds that it wouldn't rain for a while, so I continued across the pedestrian bridge to find somewhere for an early lunch.

That's when I saw her.

Su Ling, Andrew Yipp's translator cum personal assistant, was sitting in the passenger seat of a Bentley, watching me.

I must have hesitated, because she smiled and nodded.

Su Ling was Eurasian and easily the most attractive woman I had ever met. Her almond-shaped eyes were green and her skin almost golden. Her black hair was swirled atop her head and held with a silver needle that matched the trim on her red cheongsam.

"How are you?" she said, opening the door and stepping out.

"Still here, but I prefer the dry season."

She flashed a smile and then glanced at my leg. "I heard you were injured. Is it better now?"

"Just a flesh wound."

"Good." She nodded towards the Bentley. "Have you got a few minutes?"

For a second I thought this was about me and her but then she clarified: "Mr Yipp would like to see you."

16

# FOUR

In 1952, the Cathay Building, with its sixteen floors and radio mast, was by far the tallest on the island. It was the only building to have air-conditioning, and Andrew Yipp had his head office on the twelfth floor. Unlike other Chinese businessmen, Yipp enjoyed his high profile.

Su Ling and I travelled up in an elevator, the bellboy keeping his eyes averted the whole time.

As the doors opened and we stepped out onto the floor, the buzz of human activity stopped. The staff looked at me and then away again. All, that is, except for one. A man called Wang was standing in an office and glared at me through the glass. I knew he was Yipp's henchman, his bad boy, a man known for his violence and aggression.

I gave a friendly wave and hoped it annoyed him.

Su Ling showed me into another room and said that she would let her boss know I was here.

I stepped over to the broad windows that faced south and took in the breathtaking view. A stone's throw away was Fort Canning, the HQ for the British Army in the Far East. Beyond that I could see the jungled islands of Pulau Brani and Blakang Mati, the South China Sea gleaming in the sunlight that broke through the clouds.

The room itself was minimalist. I'd been in a similar room months before: a wooden tiled floor with a large silk rug. Along the edge of the rug were cushions. Yipp preferred others to be seated in his presence, and I wanted to show respect, so I selected a cushion facing the windows and waited.

Ten minutes later, he stepped silently into the room. The last time I'd seen him, Yipp had worn a silk suit and performed tai chi. Now he was the consummate, immaculately dressed oriental businessman in a suit. Although small and impossible to age, he had charisma, and fire in his dark eyes.

He nodded to me and sat opposite.

"I think you are hungry, Captain Carter." He paused with a slight smile and I wondered how he knew. I suspected he'd had me followed. Probably knew where I'd been that morning and arranged for Su Ling to pick me up on the far side of the bridge.

He said, "Please join me for a meal."

Without waiting for a response, he clapped his hands and a woman in a white silk gown floated in and placed a square black plate and chopsticks in front of us. She returned with an array of small dishes and I recognized prawn dim sum and a chicken dish.

A fine china cup and a teapot were also placed on the floor and the lady poured me green tea.

I waited. After a respectful pause, Yipp used the chopsticks to transfer a morsel to the square plate and then to his mouth. I copied the move and then we both took a sip of the tea.

"I am impressed, Captain," Yipp finally said. "Not only have you mastered the chopsticks, but you show me great respect."

I inclined my head. "Is not all warfare based on deception?"

Yipp clapped his hands with delight. "Sun Tzu's *The Art of War*. Very good."

18

I'd guessed the book had been a gift from Andrew Yipp and now I was certain of it. "Thank you for the book," I said. "It's helped while away the hours."

"And how is your leg? I heard you were shot."

"It's an inconvenience."

"Because you cannot run?"

"Hopefully I'll be able to run again very soon."

We ate in silence for a while. When he set down his chopsticks, I did likewise. He fixed me with his bright eyes and, as though our conversation had been uninterrupted, said, "I think you now understand why I have used you. It is through the information brought by the converted spy that we are able to seize the enemy."

I shook his head. "With respect, I believe Sun Tzu was referring to enemy spies, rather than the enemy itself."

"It is owing to his information, again, that we can cause the doomed spy to carry false tidings to the enemy," Yipp quoted.

He was assessing me so I said nothing.

"You are of course correct, Captain. You were my doomed spy in Sun Tzu's terms. The enemy, however, was not whom I feared it to be. And you are not my enemy now."

I said, "I'm not?"

"No, but I fear that you think I am *your* enemy. You have been watching me. The police—your spies—have followed me. You have been watching my operations. For many months you have found nothing, could act on nothing, until a few nights ago. In fact, I am partially grateful for your intervention."

I didn't bother arguing that the police didn't work for me, that they had a reporting line into Secretary Coates, my boss. I waited for him to explain.

19

He said, "The men who were killed at Singorah airfield were not acting under my orders, Captain. They were stealing from me. They were acting on their own, taking my drugs to Malaya."

"So you don't deny that they were your drugs?"

"No, I don't deny that, Captain. I also don't deny that they were in British Army medical crates. Fakes. Just like we use US-marked crates, we need to mask the contents for fear of theft. Deception again, you see, Captain."

That triggered a question that I'd wondered about: "Were the drugs bound for a British Army base?"

Yipp held my gaze; dark brown eyes locked with my grey ones. The corners of his mouth curled up slightly. "How would I know where the drugs were headed, Captain? The men you shot were stealing from me. Where the drugs were headed, I cannot say."

I nodded.

He said, "Who told you about the operation?"

"The police had an anonymous tip." I was surprised that he hadn't been aware of the activities of these men. After all, he admitted they worked for him.

As though reading my thoughts, he said, "I had a man at the airfield. I suspected what was happening."

I said, "One of the policemen."

He said nothing. It must have been a policeman since there was no one else there. If it were true, he was telling me he had someone on the inside of the police force.

There was no point in asking Yipp about him. Instead, I said, "And yet, you let the men continue. By one estimation they got away with hundreds of pounds' worth of drugs."

"You are right. But there was no need to act because you and your men had things under control. The skilful leader subdues the enemy's troops without any fighting. In this case I relied on you to act for me."

20

Unless it was all deliberate.

The businessman picked up his chopsticks and we ate again. The chicken was in a delicious black bean sauce.

"This is good food," I said.

"This room...," Yipp waved his empty hand at the walls. "This room was once the office for your Admiral Lord Mountbatten. After the war he made the building his headquarters of South East Asia. His role was to oversee the transition from military to civilian rule. He believed that the West could be the friends of Asian nationalists."

He paused and I waited for him to finish.

"And yet the British continue to rule Singapore, the very place from which he worked. That is irony, as you British like to say."

I didn't comment. I knew that the governor had arranged elections and that a legislature had been appointed. However, I also knew that there was disquiet about who had a right to vote and the role of elected members. I suspected there was self-interest at play. Officials like Secretary Coates would do as much as necessary to prevent revolution, but no more. Internal security didn't just mean protection against the communists in Malaya.

"Possibly you have no opinion or you keep your views to yourself. Either way, you are very wise, Captain Carter." He paused for effect before adding: "This should not be personal."

I took a sip of tea and waited a respectful time before changing the subject.

"Do the numbers two, two, one mean anything?"

"Why do you ask?"

"The body at Woodlands Crossing had what looked like numbers on its back."

His eyes didn't stray from mine, and if he was thinking, he masked it well. After a few beats he replied, "They do not mean anything to me."

"The body was decapitated. Is that something that Chinese communists would do to traitors?"

"During the occupation there were communist groups called 'mobile squads'. They murdered thousands of people suspected of collaborating with the Japanese, however I never heard of them removing heads. That was more likely to be the Kempeitai."

"I've heard of them."

He smiled. "As an ex-military policeman, I expect you have. They were the Japanese equivalent, although they had more sweeping powers." He paused for a moment and I wondered if he was remembering an incident. "They decapitated. They would also stick the head on a pole to deter others."

"And leaving decapitated remains?"

"As a consequence, of course. But it sounds like you need to find the head."

The silent woman came in and whispered into his ear.

"I'm afraid my next meeting has arrived. Thank you for visiting me." He stood and surprised me by bowing low to show respect. "I hope you do find the head. And please continue to study Sun Tzu. Choose your battles carefully, Captain. Only fight the battles that you can win."

I returned his bow.

As he was about to leave the room, he hesitated and turned back to me. "Please remember that we need not be enemies."

# FIVE

Su Ling accompanied me to the ground floor. We didn't speak and stood side by side. A couple of times her hand brushed against me. I wondered if it had been deliberate, and in the elevator she stood closer than before. Her ylang-ylang perfume reminded me of the night we'd spent in each other's arms, and the thought of her quickened my heart.

On the ground floor was the biggest cinema on the island. I knew nothing about the latest film but it starred Gregory Peck and Ann Blyth. A romance, I guessed from the poster. Not my kind of film.

My mouth was a little dry as I pointed to the advertisement. "Fancy an evening..."

The look on her face stopped me. At first she just regarded me. The room was silent except for the rush of blood in my ears.

I said, "Just the cinema. That's all..."

She inclined her head and gave a coquettish smile. "That would be nice. Perhaps next week?"

If it weren't for my injured calf, I would have had a spring in my step as I walked back to my apartment. I knew who she was and what she represented. And she knew me. What could be the harm? I asked myself. She was a stunning beauty and, after all, it was just the cinema. And maybe dinner afterwards.

There was a letter from the secretary waiting for me when I opened the door to my rooms. It said: **Get over to Gillman. Major Vernon has a theory.**

I hailed a cab and instructed the driver to take me to the barracks. I asked him to follow the scenic route, although he didn't understand. So I directed him over the Anderson Bridge, past the docks and Keppel Harbour, and up the coast road to Pasir Panjang.

Gillman Barracks was home to 200 Provost Company, with buildings scattered around a small hill.

At the security gate, I paid for my ride and introduced myself to the guard. He knew I'd been many times but still pointed to the office, a white single-storey building with square pillars that wouldn't have been designed by any self-respecting architect.

As I walked up the drive, a naval car came the other way and I recognized the passenger: Commander Alldritt. He was in charge of Keppel Harbour and didn't like me. He was Vernon's friend, and I briefly wondered what he was doing here on a military police base.

I continued into the building and knocked on the acting CO's office door. I waited. I could hear Vernon shouting, and when he called "Come!" I saw he was on the telephone.

As he berated someone, I sat at the other side of his expansive desk with its worn leather inlay. There was a long credenza behind him and an array of filing cabinets. I knew he kept his records there; every report, every message was written down and filed away. I knew because I'd been through them in the past.

Major Tony Vernon had small, cold eyes and a signature hairstyle. He was balding and shaved it at the front, leaving a straight line over the crown. I found it

24

hard not to stare, though it was better than looking into his piggy-eyes. He gripped the telephone so tightly in his left hand that his fingers were white. I noticed he had plasters on two of them.

Vernon swore at the person on the other end and slammed down the receiver. Clenching his teeth, he now fixed his eyes on me.

"Mr Carter."

He pointedly didn't use my old rank but I didn't mind. I'd long given up caring, just as I didn't want to wear a uniform or brassard. I especially didn't want to have to salute Vernon. And he didn't bother to ask me to.

He said nothing for a count of ten and I knew it was part of his power game. In fact, I suspected there had been no one on the other end of the phone. He did that to intimidate.

I smiled. "I hear you have a theory."

"What do you think about the body?"

"He was dead."

Vernon glared at me. "What about the number? Two, two, one, wasn't it?"

I said, "I'm not the one with the theory."

"He could be a soldier."

"Is there anyone missing?"

"Everyone from Singapore is accounted for. There are three men unaccounted for in Malaya. Two British, one Gurkha."

"The body was white." Which meant we could rule out the Gurkha.

"I'd like you to investigate."

That surprised me. The major and I didn't have a good relationship. It was probably best described as a mutual lack of respect. I said, "Why me?"

"Because I think something is going on and my theory is that it's bigger than the British Army—if it is a soldier."

"Explain."

"Drugs," he said, raising his eyebrows. "Someone supplying drugs."

"Is this more than a hypothetical?"

Instead of answering, he said, "I understand that the drugs *you missed*"—he emphasized that, like it was my fault—"at Singorah airfield were in army crates and destined for Malaya. You were a detective. Join the dots."

"You'll have to join them for me."

He showed his teeth in a beatific smile. "Drugs going out disguised as army supplies. Suspect drug activity at the camp in Johor Bahru. A gang-style murder."

"Gang-style?"

"What else could it be?" He sat back. "I've seen this sort of thing before, and I spoke to Secretary Coates. He thinks it might help with your job here in Singapore."

"Why me?" I asked again.

"Firstly, this could be huge. This could be bigger than an army-related issue and Coates agrees. Secondly, you aren't an MP, so the men are more likely to open up to you."

I said, "There's another reason."

He stared into the middle distance and then looked back at me. For a moment he let his mantle of aggression relax. "Look, all right, you are a damn fine investigator and you are more likely to get results."

I said nothing.

"I'd like you to start by talking to Colonel Underwood at Majidi Barracks."

"When?"

"No time like the present. Sergeant Hegarty will be your driver. He should already be waiting outside."

A thousand thoughts were going through my head but I just nodded.

He actually stood and offered his hand.

"Thanks," he said. "And I assumed you won't want to billet at Majidi so I took the liberty of booking a room for you at the King George Hotel."

# SIX

I was about to get in beside Hegarty when Lieutenant "Polecat" Cole ran over and swung into the back of the Land Rover.

"Thought I'd be of use," he said as I joined him. "Major Vernon..." He stopped himself and shook his head slightly.

I figured I knew what he was thinking. "We're all friends here, Jim." I said it quietly so Hegarty wouldn't overhear. "If you want to say something about Vernon, I'd appreciate it."

Cole seemed to think about it for a long while but he may have been waiting for the road noise to increase.

"I just think you'll do better with official support."

"As an MP."

"Right. It's almost as though Vernon wants you to... you know, fail."

That made sense to me. My legal status outside of Singapore was nil. I could probably use my contacts to gain influence, but with Cole's presence that wouldn't be necessary.

Hedge drove me back to my apartment so that I could grab an overnight bag. I thought about wearing my Browning revolver but decided the gun in my ankle holster would suffice. The Browning was official whereas I'd been given the Beretta by a gentleman called Pope.

28

He seemed to think he owed me a favour and I liked that my boss didn't know about it. So I stuck the Browning in my bag.

Back on the road, and beyond the city limits, to break the silence, I said, "The marks on the body's back. Why didn't you tell me about them straight away? Why did it rely on me spotting them?"

Cole pulled at his lip and looked at the trees.

He said, "How did you know?"

"The men had already moved the body. You'd already seen it. And you showed no surprise when we flipped him over."

"Vernon said it was best to wait for the pathologist's report. Thinking about it now, maybe that was also Vernon being difficult. Giving you half the picture. But then you saw the marks—I shouldn't have blurted what I thought they were." He smiled awkwardly. "Sorry, Captain."

"For goodness sake, call me Ash."

"Yes, yes, of course. Have you been to Malaya before?"

"No."

"I can't say you're in for a treat." He went on to tell me about the history of the conflict, most of which I already knew. But I let him talk and he seemed to relax.

After a while of nothing but green jungle rumbling past, we arrived back at Woodlands Crossing.

The queue was only four vehicles long and the guards straightened up as we approached the checkpoint. Hegarty slowed but didn't need to stop as the barrier was quickly raised.

We passed the spot where the headless body had lain and were soon driving under the barrier on the mainland side. Here the queue was longer and there were more pedestrians and cyclists. There was also a much larger

29

Customs office, and everyone appeared to be thoroughly checked before passing through.

I spotted an MP I recognized from Gillman. "Any luck with the register of vehicles last night?" I asked Cole.

"Ah, you saw one of my men. I've got four on the case, checking the register and questioning people. Many of the lorries do this crossing regularly. With a bit of luck, by closing time we might get a witness."

The road through Johor Bahru was known as Route One. It went all the way through the country into Thailand. Although the town was two miles away, the whole roadside was like a ribbon of shacks and bashas, which were basic lean-to shelters.

The town itself was about a third the size of Singapore city. And like the island city, the streets were crammed with people, rickshaws and animals. The sultan's palace stood on a hill, majestically overlooking the town.

At the centre of Johor Bahru, the streets opened up to a square with grand white buildings similar to Singapore's government sector. And then we were travelling north again on a narrower street with shabby houses. Hedge sounded his horn to manoeuvre until the traffic and houses thinned to nothing. Briefly.

"Majidi Kampong," Hegarty shouted over his shoulder as we came to a village. In the near distance, left and right, we could see rolling hills. Beyond them, the jungle created a wall of green.

The sergeant turned off the main road and I had my first sight of Majidi Barracks. A head-height white wall stretched around an area that looked the size of four football pitches. Although low, it was huge in comparison to the village close by.

30

The entrance appeared more oriental than British military, with what I thought was a Chinese-style roof over the portico.

Hegarty explained to the guard that we were here to see the CO and seconds later we were inside and driving past white breeze-block buildings. They had wooden stakes supporting corrugated tin roofs. The pitch was clearly designed to handle torrential rain, although the noise must have been tremendous.

The buildings were all single-storey except for the officer's block. We parked outside.

Colonel Underwood turned out to be a lieutenant colonel. He had a ruddy complexion and a deep frown.

"Is this what it takes to get 200 Provost out of their holiday camp?"

I held out my hand. "Ash Carter. I work for the Governor of Singapore."

He looked at me like I was something unmentionable he'd stepped in. "What the bloody hell do I need a politician for?"

"State security," I said, and as he scrutinized me I added: "I'm particularly interested in whether there are any bandits—"

Before I could finish, he snapped, "CTs! We're to call the bandits communist terrorists now." He turned his attention to Cole. "Are you going to investigate the drugs problem or not?"

I tried my disarming smile. "Could we start at the beginning? Would you mind telling me about the drugs problem."

Underwood looked back at me and I saw the anger in his eyes reduce.

"I requested an investigation months ago. And the MPs finally show up when there's a body on the crossing. Is it even drugs related?"

31

"That's what I want to find out. That and whether it's connected to CTs. So, tell us about the drugs. Are we talking about cannabis?"

"We've found a few stashes and handled it appropriately. We've also had to arrest men for possession of heroin, but again it's all within normal tolerances. Personal use rather than anyone out and out dealing in the stuff. And more importantly, no one using to the point of addiction."

"Amphetamines?" Cole asked.

I knew the history of amphetamines. Heavily used by the Japanese invasion force. In fact, they were sanctioned and used by many armies during the Second World War—before we understood the damage they could cause.

"Undoubtedly amphetamines," Underwood said. "The locals call it *shabu*. I know men take it, but we've only had a couple of problem cases. And they were dealt with. No, that's not my main issue. That's not why I wanted an investigation. It's something else. Something that changes men's behaviour. Fighting and aggression." Cole looked like he wanted to say something and I guessed he was thinking those weren't bad attributes for a soldier. But Underwood explained: "It's among themselves. I've seen men under stress many times. They can get ratty as hell, but this is different. This is extreme violence from men who are meek by nature. I've got more men in the brig for disorderly conduct than ever in my career. And they're just the tip of the iceberg."

"What do the men say?"

"They deny it. In fact, a day in a cell seems to sort them out. They soon become meek and apologetic again. The men have started calling it the *Crazies*. It's like it's

32

the norm. Like it's all right." He took a breath. "But it's not normal and I want it stamped out."

I looked at Cole.

The lieutenant said, "It's the first I've heard of it. We'll definitely investigate."

Underwood shook his head in disgust. "First you've heard of it..."

I leaned forward. "I understand your frustration, but we're here now. Can we loop back to the body—?"

"Not one of my men."

"I was told you had three potential AWOLs."

"All back now and under twenty-four hours late. Delayed on the train from Penang, which was attacked by CTs. No, my men are all present and accounted for. In fact, I haven't had an AWOL for the nineteen months I've been here."

"Does two, two, one mean anything to you?"

Underwood frowned at me. "Two hundred and twenty-one? You mean the numbers two, two, one? Like an army unit..."

I could see his mind processing.

"Could it be that? You asked about missing soldiers. There's an AWOL from the RAOC. BVD 221."

# SEVEN

Hegarty followed directions and we were soon on Route Three heading north-east. The road curved left and then right, following the path of least resistance. We couldn't see very far due to the elephant grass that lined the road. It was taller than a man and hid the rise and fall of the land around us.

About ten miles outside Johor Bahru, we saw a military sign. It said: Base Vehicle Depot. Another beside it said: Tebrau Airfield and FTC. We turned and drove up a gentle hill. At the top the road split. BVD 221 to the left, Tebrau and FTC to the right.

We could see them both. The BVD section appeared to be a large fenced enclosure. The "airfield" looked more like a proper airport than the usual temporary field. It had numerous buildings and hangars and a runway as long as the one at Changi.

Outside the gated compound were two young men in jungle fatigues. They were sitting on giant stones outside the entrance. Some kind of informal guard, with their rifles lying across their thighs.

It took them a moment to realize there were MPs in the Land Rover. They leapt to their feet, awkward and unsure how to behave, but Hegarty didn't stop. He drove straight into the enclosure. Amid the clutter of trucks and cars, I recognized a Scammell tractor used as a rescue vehicle. There was a garage unit and prefabricated blocks. Right at the back was the only solid-looking construction: offices.

A sergeant stepped out of the building as we drove up to it. He stopped midstride and snapped off a salute.

"Help you, gents?"

Cole was first out of the jeep. "Your CO available?"

"No…" The sergeant looked uncertain. "Maybe I can help, sir. I'm the chief clerk."

By this time the three of us were on the steps in front of the sergeant. Cole led the way towards the door. "All right, let's go inside."

We passed two offices. One had another clerk working behind a desk; a young guy in a turban who looked up and watched us walk past.

The sergeant took us into the next room and stood nervously behind his desk. We crowded in on the other side. Again, Cole spoke first: "We're investigating the headless body found on the crossing this morning."

Now the chief clerk's eyes showed surprise and then looked calculating. "What's that got to do with us?"

"You're missing a man," I said.

"Who told you that?"

"We've just come from Majidi Barracks."

The clerk said nothing.

"The CO there told us you had a man AWOL."

"Oh cripes that was yonks ago! Sergeant Gary Bender disappeared, what… ten months ago maybe."

"Describe him."

"White, five ten-ish, black hair, skinny. Can't remember his eye colour I'm afraid, if that's important."

"Anything else you can tell us?"

"Arrogant sod and I never liked him. He went off in a 'three-tonner' and never returned. Your chaps investigated. No sign of him or the Bedford truck."

The three tonne Bedford's were the very common army trucks, used for most transportation including troop movement. I could imagine the difficulty of finding a lost one.

I looked at Cole, who shook his head. "Drugs?" he said. "Any problems here?"

The calculating look returned. "None," the clerk said after a pause.

I said, "We're investigating the possibility that the killing is drug related."

The clerk said nothing.

"The number two, two, one has led us here."

Still the clerk said nothing.

I said, "Who's your CO?"

"He's never around. The man you want would be Major Chris Broom."

"When will he be back?"

"I don't know." He paused uncomfortably. "Might be around tomorrow, if I can get a message to him."

I nodded to the others. "Then we'll come back tomorrow."

We left him there and returned to the Land Rover. The fresh-faced Indian guy came out—the one from the other office. He glanced at us as though about to say something but then walked past. Hegarty turned the key and the engine fired throatily.

As we were halfway out, we passed the guy in the turban. He turned and raised a hand.

"Someone should take a look at that," he said in a gruff voice that belied his young looks.

"What?" Hegarty asked, bringing the Land Rover to a rolling stop.

"The engine." His tone sounded a bit off and I wondered why he seemed concerned. "We could tune it for you."

Hegarty grumbled, "It's fine."

The soldier looked at me, patted the door and smiled.

I was still wondering about the strange young man when Hegarty stopped beside the road, hidden from the BVD entrance.

He turned around and held out a piece of paper.

"That kid slipped me this note."

# EIGHT

The note said, **Check out Ulu Tiram**.

"What's Ulu Tiram?" I asked.

Cole said, "It's a wild goose chase, that's what it is. We should go back—"

"Seriously, Jim, what is Ulu Tiram?"

"A town. It's a place where some of the soldiers go for R and R. It's not far from the jungle, if you're into nature, and bars and girls if you're into something else."

Hegarty said, "There's also some sort of base north of there with the jungle training guys."

I hadn't heard of either place. "How far from here?" I asked.

Hegarty shrugged. "Maybe five miles. Isn't it worth going back in and questioning the kid?"

I noticed he directed this at me. "No," I said. "He'd just clam up. There's a reason why he gave us the note. He heard us talking to the sergeant. If it was all right to talk, he would have."

Cole nodded. "I agree. We pick him up now and we might never find out what he knows. Let's investigate this village."

We came to the split in the road. Right to Route Three and then north to the village. Left was the airfield.

I said, "Transportation is a key requirement for a drugs operation, right?"

Cole looked at me. "Right."

"Let's take a look at this airfield."

"The note said Ulu Tiram."

"We aren't in any kind of rush. We may as well do this now since we're already here."

"Fine," he said after a pause. "Let's pay the FTC a visit."

Hegarty turned left and we headed down the road beside the runway. Close up we could see that it wasn't an airfield at all. It was a proper runway that had once been tarred. Poor upkeep meant weeds pushed up along its whole length.

The buildings had offices and common rooms. The largest had RAF written above the door and a sign beside it. This was the squadron leader's office.

Hegarty parked outside and Cole knocked on the door.

A clerk invited us in and moments later we were being introduced to Squadron Leader Alex Kennedy. Unlike all of the RAF men I'd ever met, Kennedy wasn't young or slim or bright-eyed. Maybe he had once been all of those. Too long behind a desk, too long at this base, I supposed. However, despite his weary eyes, he gave me a big smile and a firm handshake.

"Welcome to the 656 Squadron, Tebrau airfield," he said.

After introductions, Cole said, "What is this place? FTC specifically, I mean."

Kennedy looked at the lieutenant askance, as though he should know, and then smiled. "MPs. Well I guess you don't normally come across us. FTC stands for Flight Training Corps. We train pilots."

"Out here?"

"Jungle flying isn't the same as flying back in Blighty. Easy to get lost over the central regions in particular.

Unless you're trained, one bit of jungle looks like another. Plus, the Highlands suffer from a lot of fog. Anyway, we're mostly about recon and surveillance." He looked from Cole to me and back. "So how can I help you, gentlemen?"

Cole provided limited information, only that we were following up a lead about drugs.

I came straight out with it: "Could your planes be involved at all?"

Kennedy laughed.

"What's funny?"

"Ever seen an Auster T7? Great little plane, for the job it does."

I was no expert on planes and had to admit I didn't know what one was.

"Come on, let's walk," Kennedy said.

He was out of the door and striding towards the hangars. The others followed almost as quickly but I trailed slightly behind because of my leg.

The first hangar had no doors and we went inside.

"There you go," Kennedy said. "The illustrious T7."

In fact, there were two in the hangar.

"They have a de Havilland Gipsy Major 7 engine. 145 horses and a larger prop than wartime Austers. And external non-retractable aerofoil flaps." His tone said he wasn't really impressed. I figured 145 horsepower wasn't much for a plane.

I was looking at a small, over-wing monoplane. But the most important thing was the obvious lack of cargo space.

Kennedy said, "Two seats and twin controls."

I said, "So not ideal for running drugs."

"Not only that, but all the flight logs have to be filed. No way could anyone be diverting to pick up and drop drugs."

"Anything else?" Cole asked after circling the nearest plane.

Kennedy smiled. "Well we have four of these, but let me show you what else." He took us into the next hangar past two more T7s and then into the next. This one had a single plane. Although it was like no aeroplane I'd ever seen before. The first thing I noticed was that it had no wings. Then I spotted a giant propeller above the fuselage. I doubted it could fly.

"Avro Rota autogyro," Kennedy said. "We just have a couple of pilots who can really fly this funny thing. But it's the future, at least something like it. You don't need a hundred-yard strip to take off and land. These things can land in a jungle clearing."

Cole said, "The future?"

"Search and rescue is what it's all about. Our role is changing. Less training in surveillance and more operational. A couple of months ago one of the lads rescued the wife of the main bandit leader down here—a district committee member, no less. Took her to hospital." He shrugged and shook his head. "Sometimes I think the world has gone crazy. It's all because of this new hearts and minds thing."

He walked us around it and kept talking. "The latest incarnation has been developed apparently. They're calling them helicopters."

"It means spiral wing," I said, "Like Da Vinci's invention."

"You got it. Some of the first ones are being shipped here to us—little old us—here in Malaya. We'll switch to training pilots to fly those new things."

This was getting diverted. Although interesting, I realized we were just an audience for the squadron leader. This wasn't helping our investigation.

41

"Any other planes?" Cole asked, looking towards the next hangar door."

"There's another Auster that the humanitarian aid unit use—"

"Who?"

He laughed. "You know, the sick, lame and lazy squad. No good for anything else. So... they have an Auster for running aid goods back and forth, but you'll be amazed at what else there is here." Kennedy strode off again and this time took us outside and across to bigger, older hangars. The door creaked open and we stepped inside.

I saw nothing but ghostly outlines until he hit a light switch.

It was like a museum. Before me was a row of old planes, but something was off. These weren't British and yet they were painted in RAF colours.

"Japanese," the squadron leader said. "This used to be a Jap airfield in the war. This is where they were all brought at the end of the war with the intention of taking them back to Blighty. Some made it. Most didn't. I don't know why. Maybe the cost. They were just left here to be scrapped. But as you can see, we've not had the heart. There are four more of these units with as many planes in each."

I said, "Can they fly?"

"A couple of us have been in out in the Dinah." He pointed to one of the smallest planes: a sleek twin prop with low-set wings. It was a few feet longer than the Auster, with a canopy in the middle of the fuselage.

We walked along its length and Kennedy ran his hand under the nose.

"Proper name is the Mitsubishi Ki-46, and it was used for reconnaissance. Awesome machine. I'd love to fly it officially... we both would... but politics forbids."

He continued to lead us around and spoke like a museum curator relaying facts about the various planes. I was vaguely intrigued but the details passed over my head. Cole seemed more interested.

When I could get a word in, I said, "The other side of this is whether you have anyone missing."

Kennedy stopped and looked at me and I realized this little tour had brought life back to his weary eyes.

He said, "Who's missing?"

"We don't know," Cole said, and then explained about the body.

Kennedy led us through the hangar's pedestrian door and outside.

"Squadron Leader?" I prompted.

"There are only thirty of us—me, six pilots and the rest are engineers." He shook his head. "Every single one accounted for, thank God. It's not one of my men."

"What do you know of the BVD?" I asked, walking faster than I was comfortable with.

Thankfully, he stopped. He said, "They're on our site."

"You're not happy about it?"

He shrugged and started walking again back to the office. "They've been here a couple of years. The RAF have been here since the end of the war. It just feels a bit of an imposition. Why on my airfield?"

"Are they a problem?"

"Just the noise and the traffic. It's totally changed the dynamic. And, if we are expanding with search and rescue, they'll be in the way."

Since the helicopters didn't need the runway, it struck me that Kennedy's argument was flawed.

Cole said, "We understand that they had someone disappear a while ago."

43

"Wouldn't surprise me," Kennedy said. "But we keep ourselves very separate and I try to ignore them." He opened his door and gave us the original friendly smile. "If I can ever be of further assistance, please feel free to visit again."

Back in the jeep, Cole said, "Waste of time."

"Maybe." I watched the road and the ditches and the tall grass and thought about what Kennedy had said. I wondered if his information might come in useful later.

# NINE

It wasn't five miles, it was more like eight.

Hegarty said, "Know the origin of the phrase 'wild goose chase'?"

"Trying to chase geese?" Cole suggested.

"It was an old English horse race where the lead horse followed a complicated route."

"Sounds like a funny sort of race," I said.

Hegarty shrugged. "But there you have it."

We passed a World War Two pillbox, half consumed by undergrowth, before rounding another hillock. The village appeared out of nowhere. Tall grass and then a strip of shops and bars that seemed out of place and too modern. One called Sin Sin was the most prominent.

Hegarty laughed. "No need to guess what they sell there!"

He drove to the end of the strip and noted there weren't many soldiers in sight. A couple stared at us long and hard, the MP markings possibly flagging us as "trouble".

Following Cole's instructions, Hegarty turned around and parked at the end of the strip.

We walked back along the shopfronts and looked in. Local shopkeepers looked back, first expectantly and then with caution. Were they worried about us? MPs normally prevented trouble and yet I definitely saw concern on a few Malay faces.

The first place that had any customers was called The Coke Café. Inside, there were five young soldiers drinking Coke. They may have been drinking beer for all the raucous noise they made.

There wasn't much space inside so I waited on the street. Cole and Hegarty approached the group, who immediately fell silent.

I could see Cole speaking and occasionally the men would answer. Short and perfunctory, providing minimal information, I figured.

Cole and Hegarty came out.

"Nothing. Let's keep going."

We continued past a grocer's and then a camera shop with a Kodak sign outside. This really was the modern world! Then we came to a decent-sized bar containing a group of squaddies, a few locals drinking beer and a soldier on his own.

Cole and Hegarty headed for the squaddies. I walked to the bar. The solitary man had a three bottles of Tiger Beer lined up in front of him. I ordered a bottle from the bar and, when he returned my nod, I walked over to his table.

It only took a second to realize he was drunk and barely able to string two words together. I managed to establish he was a corporal from a camp he referred to as Holland Road.

I asked if he knew where I could get drugs, but he was no help. I left my beer on his table.

Outside, Cole said he'd also drawn a blank, and we walked towards the most prominent bar on the strip: Sin Sin. When we passed a butcher's shop, I hesitated.

Hedge said, "Hungry, boss?"

I shook my head. It wasn't food I was thinking of. The meat shop had given me an idea.

Cole led the way into Sin Sin. Inside, the lighting was appropriately dim and a stage suggested entertainment. However there was no sign of the immorality promised by the name. There were two Malay barmen, who looked like they could take care of themselves. On either side of the room were two groups of squaddies. I counted seven to the right and six in the one on my left. They chatted among themselves and showed no interest in me or the other man who sat alone at a table. He was RAF.

This time I decided to hold back.

"Get anywhere?" I asked as they came out a few minutes later. I could tell by Cole's face that he hadn't.

"I'm getting nothing," he said. "I really think this is a waste of time."

"What do you want to do?"

Cole checked his watch. "I'm going to get back, just in case there's any news either from Doctor Thobhani or witnesses."

I said, "Check the last ten, maybe twenty vehicles that went across the causeway. We saw Customs on the JB side. They check everything, don't they?"

"Thoroughly."

"Look for a vehicle that could have carried a naked, headless body without arousing suspicion."

Hedge laughed, thinking I was joking. I wasn't.

"Like a butcher's van," I said.

Cole raised his eyebrows and nodded. "Aren't you coming with us?"

"I'll stay here. Maybe I'll get better results as a civilian. Maybe something will happen later on."

47

Hegarty laughed again. "Oh it will! The boys back there said Sin Sin puts on quite a show at night. You'll have to wait until after nine though."

Cole said, "You're sure?"

"Yes. I'll root around here and find my own way to the hotel."

"I'll come back and pick you up," Hegarty said.

I glanced down the road hoping to see a taxi. I didn't. "I'll work something out."

Hegarty gave me the address of the King George Hotel in Johor Bahru and we agreed they would pick me up in the morning. We'd travel back to the BVD and question the Indian kid who slipped us the note.

"Let me have my bag as you pass," I said.

"We can drop it off," Cole said. "Not far out of the way and easier for you."

I thanked him and watched them walk up the road and get in the Land Rover. When they approached in the jeep I put my hand out to stop them.

Cole was in the passenger side and leaned towards me. "Changed your mind?"

I shook my head. "The butcher's van. You're looking for three men. At least three."

"Why three?"

"A driver and two others."

"Why?"

"The driver is obvious. The body was placed. Deliberately. It would have been difficult to handle. It was dark. It would need two men. And it wouldn't be the driver because if he stopped too long it would have aroused suspicion. So he kept going. There were probably three in the van at the Malay Customs check and only a driver on the Singapore side. The other two could have walked off in either direction."

Cole nodded and they drove away. I wanted to delay returning to the bar so I strolled to the butcher's. Inside, I could see carcasses hanging from meat hooks at the back. I went inside. There were two Malays. Men. Probably father and son. Probably owner and future owner.

I asked if they had a van.

They understood me. The younger man told me they didn't have anything other than a couple of bicycles. He offered to show me, but I declined.

He said they didn't need a van because all their meat was delivered. He gave me the name of the firm in Kuala Lumpur.

"That's a long way. How do they keep the meat fresh?"

"Ice," he said.

I thanked them and walked back and entered Sin Sin.

The pilot was still eating. He glanced up, registered my entrance and returned to his meal.

I ordered a beer and headed for his table.

"Mind if I join you, mate?" I asked, trying to sound casual, just one of the lads.

He assessed me for a second before inclining his head. "Of course. Providing you don't mind if I finish my meal."

We sat in silence while he ate and I sipped my beer. Eventually he set down his cutlery and held out his hand.

"Flight Lieutenant Robin Turner."

I told him my name.

"Well, Ash Carter, if you're thinking about eating here, be careful. Unless you're used to it, you'll probably get the trots."

I waited a beat and then lowered my voice. "Know where I can get any drugs?"

"Why did you pick me?"

49

"Because you're on your own, which I figured meant you were more likely to talk to me."

"What sort of drugs are you looking for?"

"Amphetamines?"

"You aren't sure?"

"*Shabu* or anything stronger?"

He shook his head. "The only time I came across drugs was in Hong Kong. We were in the Kowloon district. An old Chinese guy sat cross-legged inside an open-fronted shop, puffing away on a hubble-bubble. His eyes were glazed and bloodshot red. I've not heard of any opium since being here. The only drugs that the men get are for curing gonorrhoea."

I said nothing.

He said, "And even if there was some kind of dealing going on here, how would you find out?"

"I'd ask?"

"Like you were a user rather than a cop?" He took a swig of beer. "You're not a user and you don't look like you're here to have a good time. I've experience of these things. My little brother screwed up his head taking drugs. You aren't the sort. You're fit, probably a health nut and aren't even a drinker. You've hardly touched your beer. You aren't going to convince anyone."

"So I'm wasting my time?"

"Are you an MP?"

"Used to be."

"So you were with the MPs that came in just now."

I nodded.

"I don't have a problem with MPs." He glanced in the direction of the squaddies. "Not like that bunch. No way would those MPs get a soldier to talk."

I said, "That's what I figured."

He said, "You aren't in uniform."

"As I said, I'm not an MP anymore." He looked intrigued so I added: "Long story, but I'm helping out. What can you tell me about the others?" I nodded towards the squaddies. "Are they from around here?"

"You've got one group from jungle training and I guess the other one is from JB. You get some coming out here because it's as close as you can get to the kill zone without being in too much risk of meeting a bandit."

"Apparently they're called CTs now."

He smiled and seemed to be appraising me again.

I said, "I visited Tebrau airfield. You based there?"

"Too long. FTC 656. Wish I could fly Spits down at Changi, but once a flight trainer always a flight trainer."

"I met Squadron Leader Kennedy. Nice chap."

"Alex's great, if…"

"Go on."

He shook his head and I guessed he'd decided his comment was inappropriate.

He switched topic: "Seriously, I would help you if I could but I don't know any drug suppliers or dealers." He paused and finished his drink. He was probably ending the conversation.

I offered to buy another but he refused.

I said, "I'm more interested in a drugs trade via Singapore. A possible Chinese connection."

I had his interest again. He asked, "Then why *shabu*? Shouldn't you expect opium or heroin?"

I had to agree. As far as I knew, Andrew Yipp wasn't involved with amphetamines, but a job is a job. For now anyway.

"So what's the long story?" Turner asked, again switching subject.

"I was an MP for seven years and then left."

"But that's not the whole story."

"The whole story is dull. I was a captain in the Special Investigations Branch."

"Serving where?"

"Middle East."

"I hear it's a mess."

"Those would be my words too."

He nodded. "So what happened?"

"I'd had enough. A man can only push a rock up a hill for so long."

"Sisyphus," Turner said, referring to the Greek myth. "He was a sinner, wasn't he? Seems an appropriate bar for you then."

I smiled. "You're taking my analogy too far. I was frustrated by politics and lack of progress."

"So you came to Malaya?"

"Singapore. I officially work for the government."

"More politics."

"It's the way of the world I'm afraid. Although I get more freedom now I'm out of uniform."

He studied me again, thinking. "There must be a reason why you chose here, though. Why come to this village?"

"A lead. When an investigator has nothing else, he follows what he does have. Sometimes we have to backtrack, but so far it's brought me here. Does two, two, one mean anything to you?"

"BVD 221," he said. "But then you knew that already. You've been to Tebrau."

"You're right, but I don't know the connection."

He said, "Let's, for arguments' sake, say that the military is involved somehow. It could be anyone, and if it's on a commercial scale then it could involve any transportation base."

"Like an airfield."

"It's possible. Though I can't see how our training unit could be."

"Kennedy is convinced it isn't."

"I could check the flight logs."

He stood and I walked with him to the door.

Outside, I said, "Are you aware of anyone who's gone missing in the last few days?"

He shook his head. After a moment's thought, he said, "You know, if I wanted to kill someone it would be in jungle training. Sure, they only get five bullets each, but they are live rounds."

"Heard of anyone shot or missing from there?"

We were walking south on the road now. I guessed he either had a vehicle or a long walk back to the airfield.

He said, "No, but doesn't mean it hasn't happened. They're a funny bunch by all accounts. You should go there. Talk to them."

"Where's the base?"

When he answered, I blinked in surprise.

"Here. Well, just outside. It's a vast area called Camp Kota Tinggi." He stopped and pointed to a Land Rover painted in sky-blue RAF colours. "I'll drop you, if you like?"

I climbed in beside Turner and he drove up the strip and past where Hegarty had parked.

Less than a mile later we turned left, following a hand-painted sign. There was a guardhouse, the usual boom barrier and a white picket fence either side.

The boom was raised without question and the road went from smooth to bumpy. Compacted sand had been converted to ridges and made the jeep rattle and jolt.

At the top of a rise, I got my first sight of the Kota Tinggi camp.

# TEN

The view opened up to show a vast area with four distinct but spaced out sectors.

Before us were white buildings. They were the usual for a large base: latrines, First Aid, a NAAFI. All white, all concrete, all ugly. I also saw a cinema called the New Globe. The name was probably an attempt at humour, although I seriously doubted any Shakespearian plays would be shown here.

Apart from this built-up area, the rest had a temporary feel. We'd passed limited security and there was no perimeter fence. It was as if the army had found a reasonably flat area and decided to set up camp. Then over the years, the facilities had become bricks and mortar and it had become permanent.

The road ended in a turnabout and Turner stopped the Land Rover. He pointed to a group of *attap* buildings that could have been a Malay village.

"They're the quarters," he said. "You have all sorts staying here. I think you'll find they're the various support units, engineers, ordinance… I don't know."

"The BVD guys?"

"Definitely."

He pointed to the left and a series of large tents that reminded me of a scout camp. "That's the humanitarian aid unit." Then he pointed the other way and I saw the glint of curved metal roofs. "That's the operational part of the Jungle Training Corps. I can drive you over, if you like."

Although the Land Rover was built for off-road, I declined the offer. He shook my hand, and again there was something in his eye that I couldn't judge.

"What's your plan after this?"

"Back to the village when the bars wake up."

He shook his head. "Like I said, good luck with that! If I find anything on the flight logs, I'll look for you in Sin Sin." He grinned, gunned the engine and jolted away in the direction of the highway.

I walked across the fields towards the JTC buildings. They were at the edge of the camp, just before the bushes and long grass started. Not far behind that was a wall of jungle. I could just about hear birds and the occasional whoop of monkeys.

As I neared, I could see that the curved metal roofs were Nissen huts, like mini aeroplane hangars. Six of them. I guessed they were training rooms and maybe common rooms for the instructors.

Suddenly there was a shout and a volley of gunfire. Instinctively I crouched and drew my revolver. Then I felt foolish because there was another shout followed by gunshots. I walked to a ridge and spotted the source: a firing range. Fifteen men were lined up, firing at targets.

A couple of men, I took to be instructors, walked behind the line. One of them turned and looked my way.

"Oi!" he bellowed, like the best drill sergeant I'd known. "Get the bloody hell down!"

I stepped back and headed for the training rooms.

Inside the first I saw a corporal with JTC insignia. He was bent over a map. He had a radio and wore earphones.

He looked up, smiled initially and then looked concerned.

"Can I help?" he said uncertainly. "No civilians allowed here."

I always carried my old warrant card in case of such challenges and flashed it to him. I didn't bother saying I was no longer an MP.

He told me there was one unit here doing weapons training—the guys at the range. There was also one unit out in the jungle north-east of Kota Tinggi village—he pointed to the map before him. Although they had the same name, the camp and village looked about ten miles apart.

He told me his job was to stay in communication with the unit in the jungle. He said there was a third unit but they weren't operational today. I figured they were the staff I'd seen in the village earlier.

I could have waited for the sergeant major to finish at the firing range and talk to him, however this corporal seemed open and knowledgeable enough.

I asked him whether there had been any trouble.

"What, like fighting bandits?"

It seemed the new CT terminology hadn't reached this far either.

"Anything over the past few days?"

"Nothing. In fact, nothing for the past couple of years we've been here. The bandits don't come out into the open down here. They're in the jungles around here"—he circled a large area north and north-east before the Highlands began—"but we keep the men away from known bandit locations. That's my job, see." He tapped the headphones and was clearly proud of the responsibility.

I nodded. "You're obviously doing a great job. So no one hurt in the past few days?"

"No. Definitely no."

"Anyone lost?"

"If they get lost they have the radio but they also carry a flare gun."

"I mean an individual. You know, disappeared?"

"No."

The radio crackled and the young man urgently took the message. It was just an update on the unit's location and he placed a marker on the map as they spoke.

I mouthed "thank you" and went back outside.

Maybe Cole was right about this being a wild goose chase. As I walked back towards the white buildings, I thought about Hegarty's explanation of horses running a complicated race. And then I replayed our conversation with Squadron Leader Kennedy. The humanitarian aid unit used the airfield.

The humanitarian aid unit—the ones Kennedy had described as sick, lame and lazy—were in the tents at the other end of the camp.

I reached the rutted, sandy road still deep in thought. If the body had 221 written on the back, did that relate to the RAOC at BVD 221? Could the body be that of Sergeant Bender, the AWOL?

I wouldn't try and confront anyone from 221 here. I'd wait until we questioned the clerk with the turban tomorrow. For now, I'd have a chat with the aid unit to kill time before returning to Ulu Tiram.

I walked past the NAAFI and turned towards the tents. And that's when I heard him.

"Hey, College Cop! Is that you?"

It was a voice I never wanted to hear again. It was a voice I would never forget.

# ELEVEN

"College Cop!" the voice barked.

I stopped and stared. There was a group of men coming out of the NAAFI. At the head of them was a large man.

His name was Stevenson. Slugger Stevenson.

I couldn't believe it. The man walking towards me was surely not still in the army? The last time I'd seen him he looked like a pirate with a black eyepatch.

Now he had no patch, looked like he was in the humanitarian aid unit and wore three stripes on his sleeve. He'd been a corporal the last time I'd seen him.

He strode quickly and stopped right in front of me. The other men formed up behind him. More than ten, less than twenty. I didn't count them because I was too focused on the man who was now toe to toe with me. I could smell his coffee breath, he was that close.

We were the same height, around six two, but where my build was athletic, he was solid with heavy muscles.

Neither of us said anything. Neither of us moved. It was like a playground staring game. I sensed the crowd gradually moving around me. I don't know what they knew, but I could feel the tension in the air.

Finally, Stevenson spoke. "Nervous, College Cop?" There was taunting aggression in his voice.

I realized my heart was racing. Fight or flight? The body's natural dilemma in stressful situations. I tried to relax and said nothing. I remained unblinking, my eyes fixed on his good one. Flight wasn't an option because of my injury. I was running nowhere.

"This is the man!" Stevenson announced to the crowd. "This is the man who blinded me."

"It was an accident," I said.

Stevenson was still playing to the crowd. "This is the military pig who poked my eye out. Got promoted to captain as a reward."

The other men began to grumble and hiss.

My mind started to process options. How would I fight this mob? At the same time, I said, "Two things. It was an accident. And I'm no longer an MP."

Slugger threw a rude hand gesture that could have been an attempt to make me flinch.

The crowd "Oo'd".

Again the tense silence. I should hit first. An uppercut would deal with Slugger, but then I'd be exposed to the rest. Would they attack or back down?

Stevenson pointed to his right eye. It looked cold and stared straight ahead, independent of its twin. "Glass," he said. "Looks almost natural don't you think?"

I could pull the Beretta out. But how would that look? They'd know for sure I couldn't use it. So it wasn't a threat, just a weak gesture. And I couldn't show weakness. Instead, I decided to try and talk him down.

I said, "You may be a sergeant now, but you haven't changed, have you, Slugger? You know it was an accident. I didn't mean for you to lose your eye. I'm sorry for what happened. I haven't fought in the ring since."

It had happened more than three and a half years ago. We had boxed in Palestine for the title of services heavyweight champion. Stevenson had a big rep as the Slugger. He was expected to win, but that was before people had seen me fight.

I was fast whereas he was strong. Most of his fights ended in a knockout, which worked well for him since his opponents entered the ring with a single expectation: that they would end up on the canvas.

Army fights are short and most pugilists aren't trained. So the man nicknamed the Slugger pummelled them until they went down—sometimes deliberately.

In the final round I had caught Stevenson in the eye with a left roundhouse. I still don't understand what happened. He spun and face-planted one of the ring's corner posts. He staggered and then screamed. He dropped to his knees, his face covered by his gloves. I'd never seen aqueous humour before. It was smeared on his face and gloves.

The medics said there was no way to save the eye. It had just popped.

It wasn't the way I wanted to win. When the adrenaline subsides, no boxer really wants to hurt his opponent. The fight was over. And it was the last time I had entered a ring.

I repeated the message. "I retired after our match."

Stevenson scoffed. "You were an idiot then and you are an idiot now, Carter. You won by default. So you were ahead on points, but it was only a matter of time. I'd have had you down."

"We'll never know." I turned as though the conversation was over, even though there was nowhere to go unless the mob parted.

Stevenson grabbed hard at my arm, pulling me off balance. Again the crowd excitement increased.

He said, "I want a rematch, College Cop. We have a ring here."

His cronies cheered.

I pulled my arm out of his grip.

He said, "I may not be good enough for the regulars anymore, but at least I can box. This humanitarian crap doesn't take much time in a day, so I train. You know what? I train because I imagined one day I'd get another crack at you. And look what we have here. College Cop has come to visit."

And then I became aware of the chant. "Fight, fight, fight." It was like being back at school.

The chanting got louder and someone nudged me in the back.

Stevenson took a step away, gauging his reach probably.

"Fight, fight, fight!"

Someone pushed me again and I almost fell towards Stevenson.

He grinned and raised his fists.

The adrenaline coursed through my blood. Fight or flight? Block out the other men. I clenched my fists. Slugger Stevenson grinned.

Fight.

A horn sounded. And then again.

"What the hell?" The men scattered as a pale blue Land Rover bumped over the verge and almost hit me.

"Get in!" Turner screamed.

I looked at Stevenson. Backing down wasn't an option.

"Get in!" Turner yelled at me again.

Stevenson laughed. "Run, College Cop. Or should I call you Chicken?" He dropped his hands. "Run, Chicken, run!"

I took a breath and climbed into the passenger seat. The other men were laughing and clucking like chickens.

I clenched my hands harder against the adrenaline.

61

Turner bumped back to the sandy road. I looked back and saw Stevenson with his arms in the air, raised in victory.

The men cheered.

Turner said, "Good job I came back."

I turned away and focused on the rutted track.

"Why did you come back?" I asked after a few more breaths.

"We found something. Well, actually, the Squadron Leader found it in the flight logs. You'll want to see."

# TWELVE

Squadron Leader Kennedy was on the steps as we drove up and he beckoned us into his office. We sat opposite his desk and he spun a ledger around so that it now faced us.

I recognized it as a flight log. At the top of the page was an aircraft number. Below was a grid with headings, some of which meant nothing to me. They were: Check; VOR; Course; Altitude; Wind (dir and vel); Temp; CAS; Others with + and -, then; Time off; GPH and Fuel.

"A busy little plane," Kennedy said.

"What am I looking for?" I asked, shaking my head at the meaningless columns of figures.

"Well I don't know if all these destinations are correct, but let's look at another Auster's records. Let's find one with the same destination." Kennedy pulled another log from the pile on the desk and ran his finger down it. "There," he said. "If we compare two flights to this place up north, one for this plane and one for the first, what do you see?"

I compared the two lines. Much of the detail was different, but the one that shouldn't have been too different was Fuel. Same distance but about fifteen percent more fuel.

Kennedy pointed to another destination and again I saw the first plane was using more fuel.

"Could it be a less efficient engine?" I suggested.

Kennedy nodded. "Yes it could, but if it was then the difference would be proportionately the same each time, roughly. It's not. Proportionately more fuel is used for shorter distances. Look, here's another example."

This time the fuel consumption was similar.

I said, "The first two records show the plane diverted. That last flight didn't and proves our case."

"Exactly," Kennedy said. He stood and walked outside. We followed him to the small single hangars. We walked past the first, the second and the third. At the fourth he stopped and pointed. "That's the second plane."

"Mine," Turner said beside me.

Kennedy walked past the gyro-plane. He walked past the next hangar too. It was empty. At the final hangar he went inside.

"The first of the two planes," Kennedy said.

This one was another Auster but was different. It was tan with non-RAF markings. In fact, I didn't recognize them, although they were clearly British with a red cross on the tail but also the Union flag.

Kennedy had his hands on his hips as though waiting for me to understand.

I shook my head.

He said, "Not one of ours."

Turner said, "Humanitarian aid unit's plane."

I took a closer look.

"Virtually identical to the T7," Turner said, "but without the twin controls. Still a two-seater but more space." He opened a hatch and showed me a small hold.

Of the crates I'd seen at Singorah airfield, I figured you could get at least three of them in the space. Packed without the crate, maybe you could get a whole lot of drugs in the fuselage.

Kennedy said, "Like I said when you were here earlier, not one of my men and not one of my planes."

We walked back to the office. I noticed the light was fading fast.

Turner said, "Want a lift back to Kota Tinggi? Now that you know the plane is the aid unit's, I mean."

"Better that I go back with my two MP friends," I said.

Kennedy shook my hand and left us outside his office door.

Turner looked at me and cocked an eyebrow.

I said, "I'll head for my hotel."

"In JB?"

I responded that it was the King George. He said I would have to wait a while for a taxi or he could drop me there. And so we were soon heading back down Route Three into Johor Bahru. He put the headlights on and the elephant grass became a blur.

If the pilot expected good company he was surely disappointed. My mind was on the case, and more specifically the humanitarian aid unit.

Turner must have read my thoughts because he started talking.

"Hearts and minds," he said. "Bloody ridiculous. You know the original strategy was containment—the Briggs Plan. So now it's about winning them over, winning their hearts and minds, about being on their side rather than being at war with them. As if they'd forget, right?"

Although I was thinking about Slugger Stevenson, I must have nodded because Turner kept talking.

"We reckon it's why this is an Emergency and not a war," he said. "Look at Korea. Bloody Americans go in there with hobnailed boots on. They've trampled on the very people they were supposed to be fighting for. Instead of a fight between North and South, it has become a war between the US and Communist China. Korea won't be the end of it, mark my words."

I must have been half listening because it reminded me of *The Art of War* translation. There was nothing in it about the general population, although there was a passage about not fighting all the time. Sometimes it was better to defeat the enemy by breaking down their resistance.

Turner carried on and told me the same story about the Chinese Committee member's wife who had been airlifted and taken to hospital.

"And then there's the humanitarian aid," he said. "On the one hand our boys are fighting but on the other we're giving food and medical supplies to the needy." He laughed. "But who are the needy? The bandits, that's who. My point is, we don't know. They get instructions where to deliver the supplies and off they go. Hearts and minds and a bit of food. And maybe you've also discovered that there's a bit of quid pro quo."

I looked at him, registering the words about food and drugs. "What?"

"Maybe, just maybe those dodgy aid chaps are trading the supplies for drugs." He stopped the jeep. "Here we are, though I'm surprised you aren't staying at the European and Oriental."

"Why?"

"It's much nicer."

"Hold on," I said, and went inside. A minute later I was back with my bag.

"European and Oriental, sir?" Turner said, grinning.

"That would be marvellous."

A few minutes later he stopped at the end of the drive rather than the steps of the splendid-looking hotel. It was

British colonial from before the war, I reckoned. Large windows glowed with orange warmth. Much nicer than the other hotel. Undoubtedly more expensive, but then the government was paying.

A porter in full uniform, hat and white gloves that picked up the light, stood on the steps and looked our way.

Turner coughed.

I faced him and saw that same quizzical look in his eyes that I'd seen before. Previously I thought he'd been appraising me.

He said. "I just wanted... I don't suppose you go the other way?" A smile flickered on his lips, and that's when I realized what he meant. It was illegal so I guessed he was always careful how he broached the subject.

"No," I said.

"Oh." He looked nervous. "Please don't—"

"Not a problem," I said, shook his hand and thanked him for the ride.

The porter took my luggage from me and guided me to the front desk. I was introduced to the receptionist, who said there was an available room.

I was just signing the register when I heard a commotion. A young woman in uniform was remonstrating with a member of staff.

"I'm sorry about that, sir," the receptionist said to me. "I'm afraid it's because she's missed the sitting for dinner."

I focused on the young woman's words, listening to her complain.

"I've travelled for hours to get here," she said. "I've walked bloody miles and I've been bashing my head against a brick wall. All I seem to get are officious prigs like you!"

I looked at my watch. We'd missed the sitting by less than fifteen minutes. I walked over to the member of staff who was blocking her way.

Another staff member—who I figured to be the manager—joined them. He said, "If you don't desist this instant, madam, then I shall be forced to expel you from the hotel. You are disturbing the other diners."

"Other diners? How can they be *other* diners—you aren't allowing me—"

"Excuse me," I interrupted. I showed the manager my government ID and glanced into the dining room. "It would appear that your customers are being served their starters."

The manager flushed with nerves and looked in. "Hmm, yes, Mr Carter."

"So I would be grateful if you would allow me and my companion to have a table and skip the starter."

The manager blinked twice, swallowed and said, "Please come this way, Mr Carter."

I may hate working for Secretary Coates, but there certainly were advantages. Especially since the young lady was rather good-looking.

# THIRTEEN

Jane Dobson was a nurse; a WRAC based in Penang. Her strawberry-blonde hair was short with a curl and she had an energy about her that could either be called vivacious or feisty. Her brown eyes were quick and bright, although the way she collapsed into her chair at the dinner table told me she was exhausted.

The maître d' had put us on a table tucked away from the other diners. After he lit a candle and left us, Jane said, "He thinks we're a couple."

She then introduced herself and wanted to know all about me. Lots of questions that made it hard for me to find out even the basics about her.

There was no choice of meal, and I ordered a bottle of white wine from the menu as the main course was served.

I let her taste the wine. After a sip she pulled a face and laughed. Then she stopped herself. There was something wrong. Something in her life that wasn't a laughing matter. I smiled encouragingly but received no explanation.

As we ate, I managed to learn that she was from Hastings originally, been a military nurse for four years, the last two of which had been in Penang. It wasn't hard to figure her for about twenty-two and engaged. Twenty-two based on her time in the army. Engaged because of the ring on her finger. She was at the hotel alone, so I figured she was here because of the boyfriend; perhaps he was in the army too. Maybe they were having problems and she was here to confront him or possibly track him down.

I couldn't have been more wrong but it took a long time to get the story.

It wasn't until the dessert had been served, and she had drunk most of the bottle of wine, that she finally told me why she was here. She had already learned I was a detective of sorts and about my strange case. I wondered why she was so interested about my reach and influence.

She poured herself the final glass after offering to top up the one I'd hardly touched. Then she took a gulp and began. "Six weeks ago, one of the girls from the orphanage connected to the hospital was adopted. She came down here to a new family. She was a lovely girl. Half Dutch, half Malay. Looks unusual because she had blonde hair and light brown skin." She trailed off, staring into the middle distance as though picturing the girl.

"You said 'had blonde hair', like something's happened."

Jane looked at me with tears welling in her eyes. She blinked and they ran down her cheeks. When she spoke, her voice was very small and choked. "I can't find her, Ash. That lovely little girl. I can't find her!" She wiped her eyes. "Sorry, I was doing so well, holding myself together and all that. No point in getting emotional."

"It's all right," I said. "Do you have her new address?"

"No, I don't have anything. I thought she would be easy to find. You know, go through the adoption organization, check the paperwork. There *is* no paperwork! No one has any. It's as though she never existed."

Jane said that the girl's name was Laura van Loon. She pronounced the first part of Laura as Lau as in cow, the Dutch way. They had become attached while the girl was at the hospital for a kidney problem.

"I was so pleased Laura was to be adopted, but then it happened so quickly. When I asked for details I was fobbed off and then it was too late. She had been transferred via Johor Bahru's adoption centre to meet her new parents."

Jane finished her glass and I called the wine waiter over to bring another bottle. She composed herself while the bottle was brought, opened and poured into her glass.

She smiled awkwardly at me. "You must think me so foolish. Sorry to have spoiled your meal."

"Not at all. Tell me the rest."

She said, "I hadn't even seen her off, hadn't said goodbye, but at least I knew Laura would write. But she hasn't. Six weeks and no word."

"How old is she?"

"Twelve."

"Virtually a teenager then. She'll write eventually."

"No, we were close. She would have written straight away. She'd want me to know she was all right."

"So you've spent the day looking for her."

"I had to wait until I could use my leave. I've been to the adoption centre here and got nowhere. I didn't even manage to see anyone of importance."

"I'm sure everything is fine, Jane. You know how it is with bureaucracies. My guess is that they're rushed off their feet and didn't understand the importance of it. After all, you're not related to Laura, just knew her from Penang. They probably have a hundred and one things to deal with and she's just another statistic to them."

71

We talked some more, the discussion going in circles. The dining room emptied as people adjourned to the lounge or bed. We stayed at the table. The staff cleared up around us and eventually we were alone.

She was quite tipsy now. I finished my single glass and she had the rest. I turned the conversation to other things and for a while we talked about England and childhood. Then she came back to my more recent history.

She asked about the Middle East and then: "After your science degree, why become an MP?"

I shrugged. Sometimes I asked myself the same question. "General science was fine, although I was more interested in astronomy. I just decided academia wasn't for me. Why the army? Well, remember the war was coming to an end, but it was by no means over. Plus I came from a long line of military men."

"Your father?"

I didn't want to get drawn into what my father had been responsible for during the war. Hero or villain was a matter of perspective. I also didn't want that to lead on to my mother's suicide. It was too personal for this conversation despite her appeal and the enjoyable company. So I switched the topic away from it.

"I became an MP because no one in the family had ever been one."

She looked at me knowingly. "Like you were thumbing your nose at your ancestors."

I laughed. "Maybe. Maybe a shrink would analyse it that way. For me, it seemed logical. Science teaches you to process problems in the same manner needed to solve crimes. That's the story I'm sticking with anyway."

Now it was her turn to laugh. Then she stood up, unsteady on her feet. "Thank you. You've cheered me up. I didn't think…"

I stood up as well. "What's your plan—for tomorrow I mean?"

"I've failed to find Laura in JB. I've a few places to visit in Singapore tomorrow but then I need to get back to work."

"I'm sure she's fine. Bureaucracy..."

"Yes," she said unconvincingly, and took a step. I reached out for her as she wobbled. "Did the room just spin?" She laughed again, more of a giggle now, then said, "Would you take me upstairs?"

"I'll help you to your room."

She smiled weakly and took my arm, leaned heavily on me. She stumbled a couple of times and I needed to put my arm around her. She giggled, but it was the wine, not her. Not really.

At her room, she opened the door and looked at me in a way that only a woman can. She didn't need to say anything.

I gave her a kiss on the cheek. "Take care, Jane Dobson."

She pulled away and the door closed quickly behind her. I was left standing in the hall feeling I'd handled it badly when the door opened again.

"Thank you," she said. "For... you know..."

Then she handed me a piece of paper. It had her name, and an address: Minden Barracks, Penang.

"You'll find me there," she said.

I nodded.

She blinked as though trying to stay in control, to stay focused.

On the other side of the paper was more writing. Laura's name and other personal information.

She took hold of my hand and looked into my eyes. Hers were starting to look bloodshot but the vitality was still there. And the sadness.

"Find her, please. You can investigate... because of who you are."

"I'll do what I can," I said, unsure that I should promise anything. "If I hear anything, I'll be in touch."

Then she kissed me, full on the lips, and was gone.

# FOURTEEN

My room was clean and nicely decorated with a period feel, like Georgian, I figured. The bed was queen-size and comfortable. But sleep eluded me.

I briefly thought about Jane's mission to find the young girl, but that was a distraction. In fact the whole evening had been a distraction from what was really troubling me. I hadn't told Jane about Slugger Stevenson. I hadn't told her that I had backed down from a fight. For the first time in my life, I had walked away from confrontation.

I recalled Andrew Yipp's words, quoted from *The Art of War*: "Choose your battles carefully, Captain. Only fight the battles that you can win."

It was sound advice but it stuck in my craw. It wasn't me. I faced up to bullies. I didn't walk away. You can't fight your own nature. Maybe Sun Tzu understood that. Maybe he didn't. Maybe his wisdom was just academic.

Images of my boxing match with Stevenson flashed in my mind. It had been a gruelling fight. I knew about Slugger's haymaker right. I'd seen earlier bouts where men had been lifted off their feet with its power.

I was agile and fast. I was well coached and could jab to score points and move to avoid the big blows. I was also a southpaw, which gave me an advantage. Most of the men had never been trained, and a lefty caused them problems. Fighters tend to act on instinct. They have their favoured punches and combinations. Especially as tiredness sets in, they stop thinking, stop expecting the blow to come from the left glove.

Most of my powerful punches were counterblows; I'd wait for the opponent to strike, to commit themselves, and then bam.

The approach served me well. Although amateur boxing in the army wasn't the same as being a regular pugilist. Most of the heavyweights had broken noses within a year. Stevenson's nose was squashed like it had been broken many times, whereas mine was undamaged. Boxing seriously from the age of sixteen. I'd gone on to box for Cambridge for three years and then a further three in the army. Through my agility, I managed to avoid the big punches. That is, until I met Stevenson.

I could smell the canvas, the chalk and the sweat. I was there, my adrenaline was pumping. I was focused. I was thinking. I was moving. But the big guy kept getting me with body blows. He wasn't stupid. He must have seen me fight and knew I was fast, that I'd avoid the power blows. So he got in close and hit me hard, like a punchbag.

I remembered the surge of energy I'd found, how I'd danced back and let him come for me. He thought he had me in the corner. I sensed the ropes at my back. And then I sidestepped. That's when I threw the roundhouse and caught him in the eye. The left glove, when his brain expected the right.

I felt the impact. I saw the distortion of his face and the sweat spray off as he spun. I saw him hit the ring's post. And then it was me. My face. My eye hitting something on the post. The pain. The shock. Blinded. Liquid cold on my cheek.

I woke up covered in sweat. And I knew what I had to do.

# FIFTEEN

After my exercises there was no shower, only a bath. I improvised by throwing water over my body—careful not to get my bandages wet. I dressed and was about to put on the ankle holster but then stopped. I didn't need it for what I had planned. In fact, it was better that I didn't have it.

There was no sign of Jane at breakfast. But then I didn't expect her. I figured she'd get up late and drink a lot of water until she felt better.

I rang Gillman Barracks from the hotel phone and got put through to Lieutenant Cole.

"Find out anything last night?" he asked without preamble.

"Nothing," I said. I'd decided not to tell him about what we'd learned about the extra fuel being burned by the humanitarian aid flights. Not yet.

"Like I said, just a wild goose chase."

I said, "Any news from the crossing?"

"We have a couple of leads. One's described as a meat wagon. Pig carcasses bound for Singapore city. Three men inside."

"And the other one?"

"A hearse."

"How many?"

"Two people."

I nodded to myself. It was the butcher's van.

I said, "What's the news from Doctor Thobhani?"

"Massive internal injuries. Looks like he was severely beaten before he died."

"I didn't see the bruising."

"The Doc says it's there but not as pronounced as you'd expect. He thinks maybe death occurred as a result. Beaten to death, like someone went crazy. There are two broken ribs and extensive internal damage: haemorrhaged bowel, ruptured kidneys and spleen, collapsed lungs."

I shook my head, trying to dispel the image.

He continued: "Last meal was noodles and chicken. Blood still in the abdomen due to the haemorrhaging but the rest totally drained. So no real bruising on the skin."

"Real bruising?"

"There are some skin changes that he says are telltale. Like if he was kicked to death, apparently a pathologist can get a read on the shoe size and shape."

"And in this case?"

"He hasn't decided yet."

I said, "What about the numbers on the back?"

"Definitely blood."

"OK. And time of death?"

"That's puzzling him. He's saying there are mixed results. Most suggest under twelve hours, but the blood in the abdomen is thin and black, which suggests longer. Although he can't say how long."

I thought for a moment. The butcher's van. The conversation I'd had with the butcher about ice from Kuala Lumpur.

I said, "Has he thought about cold storage? The body might have been packed in ice."

"I'll tell him."

One of the reasons for my call was about the clerk at BVD 221—the one in the turban who'd slipped us the note. I wanted to delay going there.

But before I managed to give an excuse, Cole beat me to it. He said, "What do you want to do today? I gave the major a debrief and he wants us back at Majidi Barracks. Thinks we need to talk to the men there—the ones Colonel Underwood suspects of taking drugs."

That surprised me. "What about 221? What about the Indian clerk?"

"Maybe later."

"What aren't you telling me, Jim?"

There was a pause on the line. Then he said, "The Doc's not sure about 221. Might not be anything. Might be random. He said the body had been on its back and maybe that's how the blood got there."

I guess that made sense. It was a shame that the lead seemed to go nowhere. Except that Cole didn't know about the Kota Tinggi camp. Where the ROAC unit from BVD 221 billeted and where the humanitarian aid unit was. I didn't like coincidences.

"Wild goose chase," I said, echoing his previous words.

"So, what are you going to do?"

"Oh I don't know," I said, trying to sound casual. "I'll have a poke around here. Maybe I'll do a bit of sightseeing."

"And come back to Singapore later? We could pick you up."

"Sure," I said. "Seventeen hundred hours at the hotel, all right?"

"Sure," he said, echoing me.

I put the phone down. There was still no sign of Jane, so I left her a message at reception, wishing her a more successful day and a safe journey home.

Then I requested a taxi and asked for Camp Kota Tinggi.

# SIXTEEN

I felt wonderfully calm as I walked along the bumpy, compacted sand road. There was cloud but the sun was out and the air had that morning freshness that made me think of a late English summer. Maybe the smell of warm grass helped.

The birds seemed to be more confident this morning too.

Past the NAAFI, I stepped onto the grass and walked across the scrubland towards the tents.

I could see aid workers. Some were sitting in the sun on deckchairs. There was a group at a couple of benches eating. I could smell sausages and figured they had their own little cookhouse going on.

As I got closer I could see that some of the tents were actually huts under awnings. Inside them I spotted bags and crates: flour, biscuits, blankets, buckets, a whole panoply of hardware that was probably ex-army.

I don't know who whistled, but a moment later all eyes were on me. Then someone shouted, "Slugger!"

I kept walking, heading towards the largest tent, more like a marquee than a scout tent. I figured this was effectively their HQ, if the humanitarian aid unit had such a thing. A man emerged carrying a plate of food and an enamel mug. He stopped, looked at me and then over my shoulder.

I reckoned I had a following. I could hear the mutters and footfall.

"Over here, College Cop," Stevenson shouted from my right. He was standing, hands on his hips, with a grin on his face.

I turned towards him. The men behind me got closer.

Stevenson said, "Has the chicken changed his mind?"

I said, "I've come to deal."

Stevenson laughed. The men behind me began a chorus of guffaws.

I said, "Talk in private first. Then you can have your fight."

Stevenson stopped laughing. He nodded towards the marquee and headed for it. There were four men now standing outside, two wearing aprons.

Stevenson told them to clear off.

Inside and alone, I said, "I want an honest answer first. Then I'll fight you. If that's really what you want."

"What's your question?"

"Who's the pilot of your plane?"

Stevenson looked puzzled by the question. "Jeevan. Why?"

"Is he running drugs?"

Stevenson laughed. "No, and that's two questions." He pushed past me, knocking shoulders. "Come on then, let's go."


The boxing ring was the far side of the HQ tent. I guessed it was deliberately hidden from the rest of the camp. The men stood around the edge of a bare patch of earth. There were no posts and no ropes.

A tall chair overlooked it and I was told this was for the referee. It was more like an umpire's chair at a tennis match.

Stevenson had removed his top and quickly put on his gloves. I was given a worn, brown pair that felt heavier than I was used to. They were longer than modern gloves, were laced at the wrist and filled with straw. Stevenson wore soft boxing boots. My shoes were my usual brogues. They were less than ideal for quick footwork in a ring, but then my leg injury was going to hamper that anyway.

Amid the general buzz of excitement, I heard someone running a book and generating high betting interest. However, it wasn't about who won. They were betting on how long I'd last.

The referee nominated a second for me. This man would hand me a stool and water between rounds. Stevenson's would give him advice, whereas my guy looked like he'd never been in a fight in his life.

The referee climbed on the stool and the men cheered. In a thick Geordie accent, he said, "In the blue corner we have the Slugger"—the men cheered heartily—"and in the red corner we have the military pig!"

I heard pig-like grunts amid the boos.

"I want a good clean fight," the referee shouted above the noise. It was without much conviction and the crowd jeered. "Five rounds of three minutes. There will be a count of ten for a knockdown. Three knockdowns and you're out."

Was I supposed to complain? Army bouts were traditionally three rounds of two minutes. I didn't care. These were probably camp rules, and there was no debate.

The referee continued: "I will determine a winner of each round based on points. The winner of the bout will either be by knockout or by winning the most rounds."

84

Stevenson grinned. "Don't worry, College Cop, you won't make it to five rounds."

The crowd was pushing and getting restless. "Get on with it!" someone shouted.

The referee continued: "No punching below the belt. No holding, no kicking, no biting." He waited for us both to nod our agreement before finishing with the obligatory: "May the best man win."

I couldn't see it, but a gong sounded nearby. I went to tap gloves with my opponent but he threw a jab. The crowd immediately started chanting, "Slugger! Slugger! Slugger!"

I back-pedalled around the ring to much derision. Ordinarily I reckoned I could beat Stevenson for brains and speed, but I couldn't match him blow for blow. His strategy, and I assumed he had one, would be to crowd in, hitting fast and heavy.

I kept moving. Ordinarily I would have been lighter on my feet. I tried to move faster but my injured right calf screamed.

Stevenson had a piledriver right hook that could knock a man to the floor. His right uppercut would lift a man off his feet. He had ten, maybe fifteen pounds weight advantage over me and would use it if a blow landed.

We did a couple of circuits. Whenever I neared what would have been the ropes, hands pushed me back. After a sustained series of blows to my arms, I received a push from the crowd and Slugger caught me in the ribs.

He thought he had me then but I threw a quick right that he couldn't duck or block. After rocking his head back three times, Stevenson quit the attempted body blows and tried to mix it up.

The gong sounded the end of the round and we went to our respective corners. My stool came out and I sat down feeling pretty good. The blows that Stevenson had landed hadn't been with full force. In turn, I'd made some good contact and, counting the blows, I was up on points.

The referee stood up in his chair and pointed to Stevenson's corner. "The first round goes to the Slugger."

There was a huge cheer.

I shook my head at Stevenson, who grinned at me.

At the sound of the second round gong, Stevenson stepped quickly to the referee's chair and said something gruffly to him. Then he turned and came at me swinging. I bobbed and weaved and the pushes went wide.

We settled down into the cat-and-mouse routine of before. Mostly, I back-pedalled.

Stevenson had a nice combination: straight left to the face and straight right to the body. I paid little attention to the left, knowing there was no real force behind it. I pulled my head to one side and at the same time shot a left to Stevenson's ribs, beating his right hand.

Stevenson tried again and again to make contact with my solar plexus. I kept my elbows in, blocking. In return, my longer reach caught him with a few straight rights. Finally he cottoned on and dived under it, sinking a hammer blow into my midriff.

I clinched him to catch my breath and immediately hands from the crowd pulled us apart. Stevenson threw a punch as I was held and caught me on the cheek.

"Lucky that was just a tap." He grinned, mocking me.

"Cheating," I said. "Is that the way you win?"

He closed in and we traded blows until the end of the round. I ducked and rode everything and not a solid punch landed. But then I made little progress in return.

"The second round goes to the MP!" the referee screamed above the noise and was immediately drowned out by boos.

Again that felt wrong, but maybe he was making up for the previous bad call.

Stevenson stood in his corner like a tethered beast desperate to get out again. My stool didn't appear so I also stood.

At the sound of the third round gong, Stevenson lunged forward. I stepped in to meet him and then moved to the side. My signature roundhouse made contact with his temple. It was a crunching blow that made Stevenson stagger. When he turned and looked back, his good eye had a fire in it.

After trading blows, I realized Stevenson had spotted that I favoured moving right. I pushed off with my left and protected my bad calf. My opponent started feinting with the left and driving a straight right, left combination at the place where he guessed I would move to.

I tried a trick of shooting my right to the face, dropping into the ribs and then jerking up towards the jaw in a kind of half uppercut. That took Stevenson off balance and my left would follow like a piledriver.

He twisted and took the big blow on his shoulder.

I landed an uppercut and followed it with a blow to Stevenson's belly. The man merely howled, bloodthirsty and angry. In reply, a whistling left hook glanced off my temple and flung me into the crowd's pushing hands.

Someone lashed out with a kick to my calf.

I staggered and Stevenson ripped a blow to my heart. He followed up with an immediate straight to the face. It drove me back on my heels with a grunt.

Stevenson pounced, the slugger that he was, but I was ready. I sidestepped his charge, hooking him viciously on the ear as he shot past. Then I ducked, just as Stevenson slewed around, and threw a right hook.

I backed away, shooting a right jab to Stevenson's face just as the gong sounded.

"Third round goes to the MP!" the referee tried to shout, but it was lost in the crowd's frenzied yells.

Stevenson sat and drank water from a cup. I had nothing. He glared at me from across the ring. We were both tired, but I judged myself to be the fitter man.

He won most bouts by knockout and I could see him building himself up for an explosion of power.

If the gong sounded, I didn't hear it above the noise. I just saw Stevenson leap up and charge towards me. I felt hands propel me forward and then the excruciating pain.

I still don't know what happened, whether it was natural or caused by someone else. All I know is that it was like I'd been stabbed in the calf.

I staggered right just as Stevenson began his onslaught: left, right, left, right. He swung away, ignoring the jabs I replied with.

It must have looked like a schoolyard scrap, Stevenson flailing his huge arms and me unable to dance away. I blocked and counterpunched.

He caught me a flashing right hook to the head. I staggered but immediately answered with a left hook to his ribs.

Head down and chin in, he bulldozed forward, driving me into the crowd.

Again the shooting pain in my right calf. I must have glanced away, maybe instinctively looking to see if someone had kicked me. It was all the opening Stevenson needed. From the corner of my eye I saw a straight left. I dodged it. But he had planned for the move and his right hook took me off my feet.

The thwack of leather, driven hard against my jaw, reverberated through my skull.

I tried to keep my balance but my right foot landed awkwardly. I slipped on the dirt.

For a second I was down, my right leg on the edge of the ring. But it was long enough for someone to take the opportunity. A boot stamped down on my calf.

I yelled out, gritted my teeth and forced the pain from my mind. I heard the referee start to count and I forced myself to my feet.

I expected a moment to recover, but there was to be no respite. Stevenson immediately rained blows at me and all I could do was back away, arms square in front of my face and body, blocking the punches.

I backed into the mob and was pushed back towards my opponent.

They were braying now. They could see an end in sight. "K-O! K-O! K-O!" they screamed, willing the Slugger to knock me down again.

I straightened my arms against the blows and managed to push Stevenson back, giving myself time to get my posture and footing right. I tried to dance right and weave, but my injured calf didn't want to move.

I stumbled and Stevenson lunged, catching me with a glancing blow to the head. My right leg crumbled and my knee hit the ground.

Slugger closed in, winding up a haymaker.

The thought briefly passed through my mind that I could go to ground and end it. But quitting wasn't in my nature. If I were to go down, it would be fighting.

I tried to push up with my leg but it was weak and I hardly moved the knee off the ground.

Time slowed. I saw Stevenson's grin, sweat dripping from his nose. I saw him wind up and draw back his right, ready for the knockout.

I raised my arm as a block. I tucked in my chin. And prepared for the blow.

# SEVENTEEN

The punch never came. Instead of landing it, Stevenson grabbed my arm and pulled me up.

"You're hurt," he said, and I heard real concern in his voice.

The bottom of my right trouser leg was scarlet. Blood ran freely over my shoes.

"You're hurt bad!" he said to me. And then to the mob he bellowed: "Get back, you scum! Give him space! Cranny, get me a jeep!"

There was still a wall of noise from the crowd, but for a moment all I could hear was the rush of blood in my ears.

Stevenson put me onto the stool.

Using his teeth, he tore out his laces, removed his gloves and then attended to mine.

I heard an engine, and the men parted as it pulled up beside me.

As Stevenson helped me into the passenger seat, a soldier asked, "Who won the fight?"

Stevenson ignored him.

"I bet good money. Did you win?"

Stevenson swung around and poleaxed the man. "Any bugger else?" he yelled. "The fight's over. Nobody won."

The driver, Cranny—real name Matt Cranfield—bounced us across the scrubland to the main buildings. He stopped outside First Aid and Stevenson insisted on offering his arm.

I hobbled into a small room and sat on a bench. Stevenson and Cranfield stayed outside watching through the door.

The man who looked at my leg wasn't a doctor. He probably had field training at best. After cutting away the bottom half of my right trouser leg he hesitated at the sight. Perhaps the sodden bandage made it look worse.

"It's just a flesh wound," I said.

He carefully unwound the gauze and looked hard.

"Stop the bleeding," I said.

"Yes, but I can't fix this. You need to get to the hospital."

I tied a strip of my trousers above the wound to stem the flow. The man nodded.

"Right. Right. I'll clean you up and we'll get you to hospital."

Five minutes later I was back in the jeep with Cranfield driving. Stevenson was beside me in the back. I had the front seat folded forward so my injured leg was raised.

We followed the twisting road south, elephant grass on either side.

Stevenson said, "You should have told me you were injured."

I didn't respond straight away. My arms ached and my ribs hurt from Stevenson's punches. He was undoubtedly the strongest opponent I'd ever fought.

"You beat me," I said, "injury or no injury."

"Your injury made a big difference. You've still got lightning quick hands."

For the first time I saw a different side to the man. He wasn't the Slugger. He wasn't just a bruiser in a boxing ring out to win at any price.

I said, "Your eye... It was just an awful accident."

I think Stevenson gave a slight acknowledgement.

"Your injury put me off boxing for life," I continued. "That was my last time in the ring."

"I always knew you were a damn fool, College Cop." Stevenson grinned. "But I guess you're not quite the pussy I thought you were."

I hadn't been paying attention to the route. We'd come off Route Three, and Stevenson said, "Where you going, Cranny?"

"Majidi Barracks. The medical centre there."

"We need to get my friend to a hospital."

"What, the Alexandra?" Cranfield responded with surprise, referring to the one in Singapore. It was probably almost an hour's drive away.

"The local one," Stevenson said. "The Sultana Aminah Hospital. Let's get him there."


I insisted that they didn't wait for me at the hospital. But before they went, I asked Stevenson again about the drugs.

He looked at me, up close, so I could see his honesty. "It may not be the proper army but in the aid unit we do a good job."

"What about the flights?"

"Jeevan again?"

"He's deviating, probably landing someplace else. The FTC squadron leader showed me the flight logs. Your Jeevan is up to something."

Stevenson shook his head. "Not Niroj. If you met him, you'd understand. Niroj isn't running drugs. He

93

was busted out of Fleet Air Arm for making a mistake. No way would he make a mistake again. Definitely not drugs."

"You're sure?"

He shook my hand. "As sure as I am that my face hurts," he said with a grin.

"You probably cracked my ribs," I said. "If it weren't for the leg, I'd be here for the ribs."

He laughed. "The name's Scott."

"Ash," I said.

"A pussy name." He shook his head. "No, I think I'll keep calling you College Cop."

We were from different sides of the track but he wasn't the one-dimensional thug I'd taken him for. We would never be friends but I figured I could respect him as a fighter and a human being.

The Malay doctor, on the other hand, seemed too busy for a show of humanity. He cleaned the calf and swabbed the area with iodine. Then he restitched the wound. There was no gentleness, but I trusted that he knew his job and it looked neat enough.

He gave me some Aspirin for the pain.

"Anything stronger?" I asked.

He just smiled like I was making a joke.

"Walk on it as little as possible," he said by way of conclusion. "Use a stick. In two weeks' time, come back and have the stitches removed." And then he bustled out.

A nurse gave me water and I gulped it down with a couple of the pills. Then she handed me a walking stick and helped me to the door.

I decided I'd jump in a taxi back to the hotel, get changed and then head for home. The drugs investigation could wait—if there even was a drugs problem.

I stopped and stared in disbelief. Parked outside the hospital, in a VIP space, was a pale blue Bentley that I recognized. It was one of Andrew Yipp's cars.

# EIGHTEEN

I wandered the corridors looking for the Chinese businessman. When I passed a sign to Adoptions, an idea struck me.

I smiled at the middle-aged lady behind the desk. Her dark forehead showed years of worry or stress, or maybe both.

"Adoptions?" I asked with a smile.

She looked at me suspiciously.

"I'm looking for someone."

She took a breath and pushed aside a ledger as if to demonstrate that she was being diverted from important work.

I said, "I'm looking for a girl. Twelve years old, blonde hair, brown eyes. Her name is Laura van Loon."

The lady did a slow blink. "No."

"No what?"

She pulled her book back.

"No twelve-year-old girl." She looked up at me with hard eyes and I wondered what was going on in that worried head of hers.

I said, "Laura is missing. My friend thinks she came to the adoption centre, here."

Again with the slow blink. "Not here."

"Could you check your records please?" I took out my government ID.

She didn't bother looking. "Babies only here," she said. "No twelve-year-old girl. You need the adoption centre."

I looked up at the sign that said "Adoptions". "There's another adoption centre?"

"This is the adoption department. You need the adoption centre." She scribbled something barely legible on a piece of paper and handed it to me, then jabbed a finger at the writing. "The address of the adoption centre. Ask for her there."

"Ash?"

A woman's voice behind me made me turn. Su Ling was standing in the corridor, curiosity etched on her face.

"What are you doing here?" And then she glanced down at my torn trousers and bandaged leg. "Ouch!"

I walked towards her and she met me halfway. I hoped for an embrace but got a cool handshake.

"You've been fighting," she said.

"You should see the other chap."

"Really?"

"No." I smiled and she smiled back. "Get a cup of tea?"

"I can't. I'm waiting for Mr Yipp."

"What's he doing here? Not fighting as well I hope?"

She laughed and I remembered how much I liked it, whether it was genuine or not. "No, no, no. He's a patron here," she said. "He's in a board meeting."

"A patron of this hospital?" I knew he was described as a philanthropist but I wondered why here. Why this hospital.

"One of his many investments."

"Investments?"

"Of his time. Though I think he donates as well. The public hospitals are pretty basic, you know."

I did know. The doctors were clearly overstretched and they'd given me Aspirin as a painkiller. I'm sure the MO at the barracks would have provided morphine. Only a lack-of-drugs problem here then.

"Let's walk," she said, and I wondered why her tone sounded off.

After a turn into a new corridor, she opened a door and we entered a storage room. There were shelves and brooms and buckets.

She shut the door behind me.

I said, "What—?" But before I could finish, she pushed me against the wall. She pressed her body against me and kissed me hard. I felt my loins stir and she responded by gripping my buttocks and pressing even closer.

I was lost in the embrace and didn't notice the door open. But Su Ling did. She kicked against it and shouted, "Occupied!"

We held each other tightly, listening, panting.

The door stayed shut.

She pushed herself away, keeping one hand on my chest. I could feel my heart beating against it. Fast.

After a moment she seemed to relax and let out a small laugh. "That was a bit foolish."

I grinned. "It was nice—while it lasted."

She straightened my shirt and then smoothed down her dress.

"Where are you staying?"

"European and Oriental Hotel."

"I'll come to you later... If I can get away." She nodded at the door. "Now, if you don't mind, you should leave first. It wouldn't be seemly..."

I nodded, kissed her and slipped out into the corridor. She shut the door behind me.

At the hotel, the receptionist handed me a letter. It was from Jane. She started by apologizing for being drunk last night and thanking me for not taking advantage. She mentioned how much she enjoyed our conversation but thought she hadn't made much sense.

She wrote: You were a scientist. You said yourself that science teaches you to look for evidence. I remember you said that there was a similarity between that and detective work. I can find no evidence of what happened to Laura van Loon. Please, please, please help. I think the lady at the adoption centre will talk to you. Because of who you are. And you are a detective, so you will know what to ask, what to look for.

She included the address of the adoption centre. The same one I'd been given at the hospital.

Please help me find Laura. With Love. Jane Dobson.

I already had the description of Laura. Jane had given it to me last night, but the letter included it again. She also gave me her contact details at Minden Barracks, Penang. I figured she'd forgotten or maybe she was worried I'd thrown the note away.

In my room, I cleaned myself up and got re-dressed. My face glowed unnaturally in places and my left eye was bloodshot and puffy. I guessed it would be a couple of days before the swelling went down.

I had been intending to visit Majidi Barracks and find out how the interrogations were progressing. If there was time later, I'd continue to search for Laura.

My plans changed when I got downstairs. Hegarty was waiting for me.

"Boss!" he called out.

He took in the walking stick and facial bruising.

"Wow! Are you all right?"

"I'm fine. Have you come to take me to the barracks?"

99

"No. The opposite in fact. Pole... I mean Cole has been and gone; finished at Majidi and now back in Sinagpore."

I heard disdain in the sergeant's tone.

"Does he think that's a wild goose chase too?"

"Didn't say as much. He interviewed four men and said no one was talking."

"So where does that leave the investigation?"

"Nowhere." He shrugged. "I thought you'd want to know, so I've come to take you home."

"I was thinking of staying. Another night at least." I paused and could see he was intrigued.

"What happened? Did you get into a fight at Ulu Tiram? At the Sin Sin bar?"

I shook my head. "I have a favour to ask. Would you be my taxi?"

"You're onto something?"

"Maybe, but I have a personal matter I'd like to deal with first. I made a promise... to myself at least."

I told him about Jane Dobson and the missing girl.

After a moment's thought, he agreed. "But only on the grounds you tell me about the fight."


The adoption centre was an inauspicious building on the eastern fringe of the town. In the reception, there were pinboards with photographs of children. I scanned them and estimated at least three hundred photographs.

"That's not all of them." A woman who looked Chinese, late forties maybe, stood at my shoulder. "I'm in charge here. How can I help you?"

I introduced myself and she said her name was Miss Liang.

"I'm looking for a child."

Her eyes narrowed, suspicious maybe.

100

"She's a friend of a friend and has gone missing. Her name is van Loon, Laura van Loon."

"Half Dutch, half Malay," the woman said. "Twelve. Though looks younger. Blonde hair and brown eyes, so I would recognize her, right?"

For a moment I couldn't tell whether she was mocking me or giving me good news.

"You know her?" I asked.

"Your friend came in yesterday. She asked me, now you've asked me." She smiled without humour. "I don't know her and, as you can see, I'm very busy." She pointed to an office where I could see piles of boxes on the floor and an open one on a desk.

I took out my government ID. "Can we just talk for a minute, please?"

Miss Liang led me into the office, avoiding the boxes. She sat at the desk and I took the opposite chair.

"Moving out?" I asked.

She sighed, and for the first time she seemed to let down the barrier. "Trying to sort it out. It's very disorganized. Not like how I'm used to running things."

She pulled a ledger from the open box and ran her finger down a column. I guessed she was scanning a list of names.

She went through a few pages before saying, "I have to tell you that she doesn't ring a bell. But then I've only been here for a couple of days so it could be she was in and out quickly."

"Is that usual?"

"I don't know." She stopped searching and closed the ledger. "I've checked the past six months. The name van Loon isn't there. I'm sorry."

"Could she have been registered in the adoptive parent's name?"

101

"I very much doubt it... although based on how disorganized this place is, it could have been or maybe she was never recorded. I have no idea how thorough my predecessor was. I am trying to sort it all out. Trying to rehome these poor kids."

I felt sorry for the woman. She clearly cared and worried about the orphans. I said, "What about other orphanages. Could she have been transferred?"

She shook her head. "Then we'd at least see her name come in and go out again. I should also have an address. Although..."

"Although the records aren't all complete?"

"Right. You could try the one just outside the town. It's in Pasir Gudang."

She wrote down an address and I thanked her. I also gave her my office address and said she could call.

"Is this a military police matter?"

I realized she was looking over my shoulder. Sergeant Hegarty was standing in the reception area. I'd asked him to wait for me and assumed he'd stay in the Land Rover.

"Government in Singapore and military police?" For a brief instant I thought she seemed concerned. Maybe I'd been wrong about her before. She continued: "Is this something more? Is your friend really looking for Laura or are you investigating something bigger?"

I said nothing for a moment and watched as her composure returned. I said, "Is there something you want to tell me?"

Her eyes told me she was flip-flopping between saying something and not. Finally she just said, "No."

I said nothing. The old interrogators' technique: wait and they will fill the silence. She did.

"I was just interested, that's all," she said, looking uncomfortable. "Just wondered if there was more to this than looking for a girl from Penang. If you don't mind me saying so, it really doesn't seem to be a Singapore government issue."

I stood and shook her hand. Leave her guessing, I thought.

# NINETEEN

Much of the road to Pasir Gudang was really a well-worn track through a heavily wooded region. The smell of the straits rose up and I knew the water was beyond the trees to my right.

I'd told Hegarty about my fight with Stevenson of the humanitarian aid unit. I also told him that I'd found nothing in the village but returned to the airfield where I'd been shown the flight log of the aid unit's plane.

"Is it coincidence?" he asked me.

"I don't believe in coincidences."

"And what about the pilot. Why haven't you confronted him?"

I said, "And how did Cole get on at Majidi?"

He looked at me askance and then got my point. He said, "No point in just asking him, right?"

"No, there isn't. If I just confront him he could clam up."

"What are you going to do then?"

I was going to wait. See what happened next. But before I could respond, we suddenly came out of the trees. There was scrub and then there was a golf course. One second semi-jungle and the next an affluent enclave with British colonial properties and manicured lawns.

"Wow!" Hedge said, looking from side to side, taking it all in.

I gave him the address of the orphanage and he soon saw a sign for it and we travelled up a long drive. At the end was an *istana*. I learned this was the term for a house built for royalty. Not a palace but something pretty special. Only, this *istana* was well beyond its glory days. All the woodwork needed painting and I could see cracks in the render.

Huts in the grounds gave the impression of a refugee camp. We saw kids playing, and others sitting on benches receiving instruction—maybe lessons, although the teachers looked barely older than children themselves.

A lady came out onto the veranda and watched us approach and park.

She introduced herself as Lady Eden Hage-Dando. She had a ramrod straight back, was six feet tall and looked about sixty, in my estimation. She had long grey hair in beautiful condition and wore small half-moon glasses. Her face was craggy with age, but she presented herself well and spoke with the lilt of the British upper class.

Hegarty waited in the Land Rover but she suggested I invite him in to join us for sandwiches.

Five minutes later we were in a sumptuous lounge with a servant pouring tea. He also brought thin white cucumber sandwiches with the crusts cut off.

"Now, young man, enough of pleasantries. You are here for a reason." Her voice was a little prim, but it wasn't unfriendly.

I told her about Laura. As soon as I mentioned the blonde hair, she shook her head. "There is no one like that here, nor has there ever been. I set up the orphanage after the war, damned terrible time then. Not so bad now, you know, but there are so many children without families."

"How many children are here?" Hegarty asked.

"In my orphanage there are seventy-two. But there are orphanages all over. Some of the children find new families, but it is getting more and more rare."

She peered at me over the straight edge of her glasses and for the first time I suspected that her eyesight was poor even with the spectacles. In a conspiratorial voice she said, "I think there is something going on at the hospital."

I leaned forward.

"Parents prefer young children. Ideally babies, but we rarely get any babies for adoption and lately the number of adoptions has fallen and fallen. Our biggest opportunity is either with family members or Singaporeans." Her voice dropped a level. "Babies are being sold from the hospital to childless parents in Singapore. I'm certain of it. I've been here long enough to know how things work. More babies are being adopted straight from the maternity ward. My contacts tell me that mothers are paid for their baby and it is then sold for ten times the amount in the name of adoption."

"Do you have proof?"

She sat upright once more. Her demeanour switched back to one of military camp commander. Her voice was no longer conspiratorial. "No, but I will get my proof. Mark my words."

I nodded, certain that Lady Hage-Dando would do as she said. Then she twitched her head and I wondered if she wasn't a little batty. Living under these conditions would be enough to turn anyone slightly mad. I wondered then whether she had been interned here during the Japanese occupation. Life during and after the war must have been a world away from what it was now.

"What can you tell me about the adoption centre in Johor Bahru."

"A shambles."

"I met Miss Liang."

Lady Hage-Dando frowned. "Really? She's there? I thought she was at the Sultana Aminah Hospital. She runs—perhaps I should say was running—the baby adoption department. It's funny."

"What is?"

"Her name is Yiqing Liang"—she pronounced the first name as Yee-Ching—"It means: she is sunny. She's anything but sunny, in my opinion. And I don't trust her."

"Because they're selling babies?" Hegarty asked, as though just catching up between mouthfuls of sandwich.

"That's right!"

The way the elderly lady said it was like a revelation. Now I really did suspect her mind was going.

I said, "If an adoption has been prearranged for a child and the documentation was completed somewhere else, not Johor Bahru, but the child comes to Johor Bahru, where else could the child go?"

"Directly to the parents of course." She shook her head. "That really would be unusual. Alternatively, the child could go to a boarding school. Petersen would know."

"Petersen?"

"The young man at the adoption centre."

Hedge gave me a look: *she's nuts.*

I said, "The adoption centre in Johor Bahru?"

"That's right."

"Was Petersen the one in charge there? We met Miss Liang."

Lady Hage-Dando seemed confused and then understood. "Petersen isn't there anymore?"

I shook my head.

"Then you should find him!"

Hedge pulled a face again. I could see he'd had enough but I persevered.

"Where might he have gone?"

She thought for a moment before brightening. "Yes, now I remember. Major Rix will know. Major Rix was his friend. I think they were in the army together."

She paused, and I was about to ask where I would find Major Rix when she spoke again.

"You asked about schools, didn't you? Well there's a coincidence: Major Rix runs the boarding school at Bukit Zarah. Perhaps you'll find young Petersen there."

# TWENTY

Back in the Land Rover, Hegarty said, "Mad as a hatter. Did you see the way she kept twitching?"

"And you're about to tell me the origin of that phrase, I guess."

"Yes, but after you tell me where next. Ready to pack up and go back home?"

"Not at all."

"So it's another runaround."

I looked at the darkening sky. We hadn't reached the forest yet. The golf course was on either side of the road and I saw men on a green also looking up.

"Shall we put the cover on?"

"Cripes, yes!" Hedge said, stopping.

We clipped on the canvas roof and set off again.

"Mad as a hatter," Hegarty said. "Hat makers used mercury to remove animal skins and of course mercury is poisonous."

"It was mercury nitrate, but you're probably right."

The first raindrops began to fall, thudding on the canvas roof. The wipers smeared insects across the windscreen.

Hegarty said, "So, back to Singapore?"

"You're forgetting something."

"I am?" The sergeant swivelled in his seat. "To do with the missing girl?"

"No, to do with the body and the drugs. We had a lead that we didn't follow up."

Hegarty nodded. "The Indian chap at BVD 221. But didn't we agree that questioning the men wasn't going to get us anywhere."

"That was elsewhere. This man slipped us the note. He wants to tell us something."

"All right. Back to BVD 221."

It was still early afternoon and I figured we were in no rush. "Not yet," I said. "We've got time to kill."

Hegarty drove through the forest, the windscreen clear now the pounding water had cleaned off the muck.

I said, "Let's pay Major Rix a visit."


The deluge continued. We left Johor Bahru and then travelled north-west a short distance to a place called Pulai Perdana. A local man, sheltering under a giant *Cola* tree, haltingly gave us directions that took us west and then right, up a hill.

The school at Bukit Zarah was another *istana*, though from this distance it looked bigger and in better shape than Lady Hage-Dando's orphanage.

Stone eagles, mounted on top of the brick gateposts, glared down at us. The closed gates were over ten feet high and very grand and I could see an equally tall wall running around the perimeter.

Hegarty offered to get out into the rain. The gates dwarfed him as he pulled a handle that hung to the right-hand side. After giving it a tug, he ran back to the shelter of the jeep.

A man appeared on the other side of the gates. He was bent over by the force of the rain. He had a huge raincoat, like those that Australian farmers wear.

Fumbling with the lock, he opened the gate a crack and came to meet us.

He looked in through the window and seemed oblivious to the rain cascading off his nose.

Hegarty wound the window down.

The man said, "Can I help you?"

I leaned across and smiled. "Just visiting." I could see him better now. White, and from his accent probably British.

"We don't take visitors," the man responded.

I held up my government ID. "I'd like to see Major Rix."

His eyebrows went up. He hesitated and then turned. "Follow me."

Just inside the gates I saw a guard hut and a dog kennel. Both were empty.

The man in the coat walked along the drive towards the grand schoolhouse. We trundled along behind him in the Land Rover.

The gardens on either side of the drive were immaculate: mowed grass with box hedging. As the drive swept around, there were impressive stone steps leading to an entrance. The gateman opened the door and we left the car and ran inside. He stayed on the doorstep but pointed to a side room and said, "Please wait there."

The room was plush, with rosewood furniture and two burgundy chesterfields opposite one another, a rosewood coffee table between them. We took one sofa each. Hegarty leaned back and relaxed. There was a pile of brochures on the coffee table. I picked one up. It was about the school, describing it as an exclusive boarding school. So exclusive they boasted only twenty places. There was no mention of fees, but then I'd been at a private school myself and I was pretty sure they were all discreet about the cost. Based on the description, I figured the number of places was also a reflection of the price.

"You are here to see Major Rix."

A tall young woman stood in the doorway. She appeared mixed-race Chinese, Eurasian maybe, late twenties, good-looking, although not in Su Ling's league. Her voice was soft and charming.

I stood up.

"Please follow me." She gave a slight bow and we followed her down the hall, past a broad panelled staircase, to the rear of the school.

Watching her turn and walk, I reassessed her as a lady rather than a woman.

There was a door on the left and one on the right. The one on the right had a sign that said "Head".

She stopped outside the door on the right and smoothly turned to face me.

"The major will see you for a minute, but just a minute, you understand. He is a very busy man."

I nodded.

She knocked on the door and opened it for us to enter. Major Rix stood behind a desk and walked around it to meet us. The first thing I noticed was his black hair, which was clearly dyed. He had a couple of inches advantage over me but was thin, and when I shook his hand I thought of piano fingers.

"How can I help you gentlemen?" he said. His voice was clipped, almost British upper class, and yet I heard a slight Australian accent underneath.

Whereas my boss, Coates, reminded me of a headmaster, Rix was more like a thespian. I imagined him saying: "I'm an actor, darling", although his title suggested otherwise.

I smiled. "Were you here in the war?"

"Certainly. The Australian Twenty-Second," Rix responded with pride. "I was billeted around these parts before the Japanese came."

I noticed the decor. He had some ancient-looking oriental artefacts. Based on the kimono on a dummy, a black fan with a red dot on the wall and a mounted samurai sword, I figured they were all Japanese. I'd met many people who hated the Japanese for what they had done during the occupation, but I'd met an equal number of collectors, not least of whom was Arthur Pope—my contact who'd sold me the Beretta.

I nodded at a brass paperweight. It looked like a stubby pagoda.

"Also Japanese?"

He inclined his head. "An antique."

"You're a collector then?"

He looked at me quizzically.

"It's just that I have a friend…"

Rix said, "You didn't come to talk about Japanese artefacts. And I don't believe you are interested in—"

"No. Another friend asked me to look for a twelve-year-old girl."

Rix glanced from me to Hegarty and back, clearly not understanding our roles. But he smiled and said, "You have a lot of friends it would appear."

"I've been led to believe that a chap called Petersen might know her."

"What's the girl's name?"

"Laura van Loon. Half Dutch, half Malay."

He shook his head and his lips pulled tight. "Not a name I've heard, I'm afraid."

"Do you know how I can get in touch with Mr Petersen? I understand he's a friend of yours."

"He served under me in the war."

"Do you know where he is?"

Rix looked quizzical again. "Isn't he at the adoption centre? But then I suppose you've already checked there."

"We have and he isn't."

"Then I'm sorry." Rix gave a heavy shrug. "I don't know. Although he was always terribly unreliable. Probably just buggered off someplace—if you'll excuse the expression."

I said, "It makes you sound more Australian."

"Something I try to avoid, you understand?"

I said, "May I ask what age you take your pupils from, Major? I didn't notice it in the school brochure."

"From fourteen to eighteen. It's a finishing school, you understand. Very exclusive."

I nodded. "Is it possible that Laura was adopted and sent straight to a school like this?"

"If she had wealthy adoptive parents then it could have happened. However, I find it highly improbable and I can assure you it wasn't this one." He paused. "Look, I suggest you try in Singapore. Half Dutch, half Malay, you say. Yes, I recommend you inquire at the boarding schools and adoption centres in Singapore."

I nodded. "I may do just that. Anywhere in particular you would suggest?"

"I'm afraid not. Now, if you'll excuse me, gentlemen, I have a busy schedule." Rix stepped back behind his desk and picked up the telephone. He nodded goodbye to us and asked for the operator.

The elegant lady, whom I tagged as his personal assistant, walked us through the hall. From upstairs I could hear music—an opera.

She said, "We teach our young ladies the finer things in life." She opened the door for us and we left her standing in the doorway.

It had stopped raining. Our Land Rover was no longer alone. A big black car was parked on the other side of the steps. Beyond them I could see a garage and workshop.

I stood by the jeep for a moment. Where was everyone? Admittedly this was a school rather than an orphanage, but the atmosphere couldn't have been more different. Maybe that was down to exclusivity. We'd seen lots of children at Lady Hage-Dando's place. Here, at the Bukit Zarah school, we'd seen just three adults. Then we saw a fourth. As we drove to the gate, I spotted a man clearly on patrol with a German shepherd dog by his side.

Although he had an actor's temperament, I was left with the impression that Rix ran his school like a military operation.


I wanted to arrive at BVD 221 at the end of the day. Most men would finish by six so they could get back to their digs for the evening.

I asked Hegarty to drop me outside the compound and sent him in to have the Land Rover looked at. Meanwhile, I chatted with the two guards at the gate and wanted to make my presence obvious.

Civilians employed in the depot left first at five o'clock. I watched as the initial batch was searched at the gates, and then walked slowly up the track towards the airfield.

I stood and waited.

The army men began to leave soon after, and most left in Bedford trucks. I hoped the Indian clerk wasn't on board.

Inside the compound, I could see a mechanic under the bonnet of the Land Rover. Hegarty stood over him, no doubt encouraging him to finish before he left for the day. We needed that Land Rover.

And then I saw the clerk with the turban. He came out of the little office and walked towards the Land Rover. Hegarty gave a nod towards the gates and the young man seemed to understand. He took out a cigarette, lit it, took a long pull and used the time to look around as he walked. When he glanced in my direction he hesitated and then continued. But instead of walking up the hill towards me, he turned away, down to the main drag.

I gave him a head start and then followed, only I had my stick and was limping. The corporal was getting further ahead.

Around a bend I lost sight of him and was relieved to find him sitting by the track as I caught up.

"You slipped us a note," I said.

He held out his hand. "Navdeep Sethi."

I shook it. "The note?"

"Do you smoke?" He held out a packet.

I declined. "You said to go to Ulu Tiram."

He nodded.

"I went there. Was it any bar in particular?"

"I meant the camp."

"Kota Tinggi?"

"Right, only we call it Ulu Tiram because that's really where it is."

He swallowed and I guessed he was nervous.

I said, "It's all right, you can just tell me."

He said nothing.

"You heard me asking your sergeant about drugs. Is anyone from your unit involved?"

"In trafficking, you mean? No!"

"All right," I said, trying to remain patient. "Is it the humanitarian aid unit?"

116

"Yes."

I nodded. "So you know about the plane and the diversions?"

"Plane? Diversions?" he said, as if I just didn't get it. "No, it's the trucks you need to follow."

# TWENTY-ONE

The young man from BVD 221 wouldn't say anything else. It was like his exposé released him from a burden.

"What now, boss?" Hegarty asked when he picked me up.

"Hungry?"

"Me? Always." He grinned. "What do you have in mind?"

As we entered the village of Ulu Tiram, I think he expected us to eat there. But we didn't. We continued the short distance to Camp Kota Tinggi.

He parked beside the New Globe cinema and we went into the mess hall.

There was limited choice: chicken, mash and peas, or nothing. We opted for the chicken. Maybe a dozen other men ate the same meal and I spotted three in aid unit uniforms. Two sat together. One sat alone. He was all angles and bones and his skin was dark, although I didn't place him as Indian. He looked at me and nodded, respectful.

All three aid guys finished shortly after we arrived. I ate slowly, thinking. Hegarty gobbled his food down and followed it with tapioca topped with a blob of strawberry jam. At least, the cook claimed it was strawberry. Hedge said it was sweet and red but tasteless.

We drank tea and I managed to drag it out for an hour.

The quick transition from day to night had happened as we ate, and we emerged from the mess in semi-darkness. Pools of light were shed by the central buildings. I saw groups of men walking down the road and I figured they were heading for the village and a better food selection.

"What are we doing?" Hedge asked as I walked towards the cinema.

"Checking what's on."

Pathé News was currently running. The main feature didn't start for another hour and a half. I studied the poster of John Wayne in a usual pose: tough cowboy comforting a pretty young woman. *Angel and the Badman* was the title. I guessed she was the angel. Maybe he was the bad man, though why they had made that one word was beyond me.

"Have you seen it?" a voice asked behind me.

Stevenson.

"No," I said, without turning. "In fact, I'm not into westerns."

"You're missing out on a treat."

I couldn't tell whether he was being sarcastic.

"How are you?" he said.

"The face and ribs still hurt."

"Why have you come back?"

Now I looked at him. "You know why."

"Humour me. Imagine I don't know."

I asked Hegarty to give us a minute and he retreated to the Land Rover. Once there, I could see his face at the window.

Stevenson and I walked out of the light. I said, "You lied about the drugs."

"I didn't."

119

"I've a source—"

"Well he's wrong. Look, honest it's not drugs. It's hooch is what it is."

"Hooch?"

"Samsoo."

I'd heard of samsoo. It was an illicitly distilled alcohol that the Thais and Chinese drank.

I said, "So, are you telling me you're brewing it or distributing?"

"Neither. The chaps pick it up on the route. You know we're not supposed to have it, but it's all hearts and minds. They're all heart and we don't mind." He laughed at his own joke.

"You said 'they'. Who are they? Who are your suppliers?"

"Hey, I don't know. There's a fine line between an insurgent and the people. I'm not really a soldier anymore. I just help the people, and if the people don't shoot at me, then I help them."

We walked some more.

I said, "So you pick it up. But what's the trade? What do these people get in return?"

"The guys just give them some of the supplies." He shrugged. "Nothing big, just a simple trade for the hooch. Like I said, we're supposed to distribute the stuff anyway—just this way we get a benefit."

"And what about the body on the causeway yesterday?"

"Don't know anything about it."

"You don't know who it is?"

He shook his head.

"Scott, I need you to be honest with me."

"I am. I seriously don't know of anyone who's missing. It's nothing to do with us."

"And what about Jeevan, your pilot?"

Stevenson shook his head. "Seriously, no. You saw the guy in the mess hall. He told me. He's the skinny darkie. He's as timid as a mouse. If the records show he's not straight then I'd look at who did the records."

I said nothing.

He said, "So are we cool about the hooch?"

"I'm not interested in the samsoo."

"Thanks, Ash," he said, and shook my hand. "If there's anything…"

"Sure."

He grinned. "And when you're fit again we should have a rematch. I'll whip your arse for real, then."


Hegarty dropped me at the hotel. The guests were having dinner and I stood and watched them for a moment. My focus was on the little table where Jane and I had sat and talked. I'd enjoyed her company. Yes she was sad, but she'd also been fun. Su Ling was more attractive but there was an edge to her. I couldn't read her, and there was always the niggling doubt about her motives. Whereas Jane was open to a fault.

But Jane was now in Singapore before she returned to Penang, and Su Ling was in Johor Bahru. Su Ling might walk into the hotel at any time.

There was a businessman in the bar and I joined him. His company seemed a better prospect rather than wait in the quiet of my bedroom. I sipped a Tiger Beer while he knocked back brandy. He was an engineer working for a private company who built propellers for passenger ferries. I didn't expect there to be much call for those, but apparently I was mistaken. He referred to them as propulsion systems and explained that ferries had specific requirements. Weight, roll, pitch, manoeuvrability were all specific to a heavy goods ferry.

"You wouldn't put car tyres on a tractor now, would you?" he said.

He'd recently been in Penang, where his firm had sold a few for the big ships that traversed the mile crossing between the island and mainland. Of course, talk of Penang made me think of Jane and my failure to help.

I kept glancing at the entrance. Each time someone entered the hotel, I looked up in case it was Su Ling. But it wasn't. The businessman eventually excused himself and retired to bed. I killed another hour, dipping in and out of articles in the *Straits Times*.

Finally, I decided she wasn't coming and went up to bed.

I don't know what time it was but I'd been asleep and opened my eyes. The darkness was almost absolute. Grey light framed the curtains.

For a second I imagined someone in my room, and I thought: Su Ling.

And then it was confirmed. A floorboard creaked.

And I saw a shape move by the curtains.

# TWENTY-TWO

But it wasn't Su Ling about to get into my bed. The shape moved and bent over where my bag was on the floor.

Damn! My gun was in there. But my walking stick was beside the bed. On the opposite side to the intruder.

Rolling out of bed, I snatched up the stick and yelled. The words didn't make sense. They were animal-like and wild. I stood and slashed in the darkness.

A wooden chair crashed. The intruder grunted, and then, after two quick steps, the bedroom door banged open. I lunged for the door but it closed as I reached it.

There were no lights on in the corridor. I scrabbled against the wall until I found the switch. As the light came on, I saw a dark figure disappear around the turn at the end.

I gave chase as fast as my leg would allow. At the turn, I half expected them to attack, but the corridor was empty. However, a window was open. Below the window was a roof and then the driveway. I heard nothing except cicadas. I flicked off the lights and strained to see, but it was too dark out there.

Then, above the insect noise, I heard the crunch of feet on gravel. Running. The sound grew distant and stopped. An engine fired up and a car drove away into the night.

When I got back to my room, I stood in the doorway with the light on. The wooden chair was on its side. My bag was open and my clothes were on the floor.

A quick check told me the intruder hadn't touched the gun. In fact, nothing had been taken from my bag. Maybe I disturbed them early enough. However, my trousers had been on the chair and my wallet in a pocket. I picked them up. My wallet was gone. And so was my government ID.

I folded my clothes and was just placing my shirt on the chair when I noticed a folded piece of paper on the floor.

I opened the paper and stared at the two red Chinese characters written on it.


Boat Quay was heaving with lunchtime trade. Across the Singapore River, the odour of spices and rubber competed with the mouth-watering smell of cooking from the myriad of small restaurants that occupied the short stretch opposite the godowns.

I leaned against a wall and watched a young Eurasian woman. Su Ling was sitting at a table with two friends.

As soon as Hegarty arrived in the morning, I asked him to take me back to Singapore. I didn't tell him about the break-in or the Chinese note I'd been left. I'd had it translated by a member of hotel staff. He had said it meant "vicious knife". It also had a double meaning. The combination of the two characters created a third word: "death". It was a clear threat, and I wanted to think about the implications first.

My explanation to Hegarty was that I wanted to speak with Lieutenant Cole. He'd been in with Major Vernon when I arrived at Gillman Barracks so the three of us talked.

"Update?" Vernon asked me.

I told him what I'd learned about the humanitarian aid unit, the samsoo trade and the odd flight logs of their plane.

"It's a good lead," Cole said. "Better than the progress I made at Majidi. Maybe Colonel Underwood is mistaken. Maybe it isn't drugs, it's dodgy alcohol."

Vernon said, "Let's go in and bust them."

My instinct was to contradict him but instead I played the diplomat. "We could do that. Or we could tail them. Find out who they're dealing with."

Vernon thought it over. "The body... Could it be one of them—the aid chaps?"

"They know nothing about it."

"And you believe them?" His tone was scornful.

"I do. A sergeant admitted to everything else and I see no reason to doubt him."

"Progress on the body?" Vernon directed this at Cole.

"Well the 221 does seem connected. It led us to the BVD and then the Kota Tinggi camp—which is where the aid unit are."

I asked, "What about the meat wagon?"

Vernon looked at me and frowned.

Cole said, "Customs couldn't give me any details except for the driver and two passengers. They couldn't remember any logos on the side but one chap thought it was a blue van. Then again, it was pitch-dark except for the spotlights from the Custom's building, so he couldn't be sure."

"Did you tell Doctor Thobhani about the ice?"

"I did, and he said it explained a lot. Explained why he was confused about the time of death. He now estimates more than sixty to seventy-two hours but said it was impossible to be precise."

"What about the internal injuries?"

Vernon looked surprised. "Internal injuries?"

Cole said, "Sorry, thought I'd told you. He didn't die from the decapitation. Looks like he was badly beaten and that's what killed him. Lots of internal damage. 'Probably with a cricket bat' was what Thobhani said. A vicious and prolonged attack that probably went on after he was already dead."

Interesting. So it appeared we were looking for a cricket bat-wielding maniac. No one said anything for a while. I was waiting for a decision since I didn't want to do this alone.

Finally, Vernon looked me in the eye. "Right then, we'll do it your way. Let's follow these aid chaps. As Secretary Coates thinks, Andrew Yipp's probably at the end of this."

I said, "There's no evidence of his involvement."

"Yet," Vernon said, and waved towards the door. The meeting was over.

He was right. There was no link to Yipp at the moment, but I didn't like the note, and seeing him was next on my list of things to do.


Su Ling left the table and I spotted her ride. I climbed in the other side of the trishaw as she got in and deliberately left a space between us.

"Oh, Ash! You made me jump." She glanced at the gap and then at me. "Is everything all right?"

"No," I said.

"Because I didn't make it to the hotel last night? I didn't get the chance and—"

"It's not that," I interrupted. "I'd like to see Mr Yipp."

She looked at me askance, her beautiful features distorted with concern for a moment.

"Why?"

I handed her the piece of paper from the hotel.

She shook her head. "Oh my!"

"Vicious knife," I translated. "And death. It's clearly a threat."

"You're right, it is a warning. In English you would be more blunt and say, 'back off or die'."

She instructed the rider to start, and we headed for the Padang.

I said, "Do you know anything about it?"

"What are you saying, Ash?"

"Just that." I was probably being too blunt, because her eyes told me she was upset at the implication.

She said, "How would I know…"

"I told you where I was staying. Someone broke into my room and left it for me. It was a double message. One literal and one that they could just walk in and leave a note in my pocket. The implication was that they could have killed me then and there."

Her eyes looked moist and she placed a hand on her heart. "I had nothing to do with it."

I noticed we were circling the Padang rather than heading for Yipp's office. I nodded and smiled, although I knew she'd see it as fake.

"I'd like that meeting with your boss now, please," I said.

# TWENTY-THREE

I stood on the steps of the General Post Office. Fullerton Square was busy and congested. For such a small island there were far too many cars. They were parked all around the square, blocking the flow of traffic at one of the main junctions in the city.

Su Ling had dropped me at the Padang rather than taken me to the Cathay Building. She said that Yipp would meet me at four o'clock, and I'd been waiting for almost an hour. I decided to allow just ten more minutes.

Before coming here I'd been to government administration and obtained a replacement for my stolen ID. I made a call to General Gaskill, Commander-in-Chief, Far East. I was sure one of the reasons for being on Secretary Coates' staff was my direct access to Gaskill. Once I was put through to him, I asked for a favour. He said someone would call me back.

While I waited, I visited Coates and gave him a quick update. He didn't mention the body on the causeway once. He was only interested in the possible Chinese connection, which in his mind meant a link to Andrew Yipp.

Our meeting was interrupted by the phone call Gaskill had promised. Army Service Corps. I asked the guy about future humanitarian aid missions. When I knew the schedule I requested a variation. Gaskill must have said something because the guy on the other end agreed without question.

And now it was almost five o'clock and I was hanging around outside the General Post Office thinking I'd been stood up by Yipp.

I spotted a black car looking for a parking space. It was familiar. A large Ford. And then I had it. It was the car I'd seen at the school in Bukit Zarah.

My breath caught in my throat as Commander Alldritt got out of the Ford. He strode purposefully towards me. For a second I thought he was going to speak to me, but as he approached he assiduously avoided eye contact.

Should I ask him what he'd been doing at the school? I doubted he'd tell me. He was Major Vernon's friend and didn't like me.

While I was wondering whether Alldritt's presence at the school was one connection too far, I spotted a Chinese driver waving at me from a limo.

Descending the steps, I walked towards the car. As I drew nearer I realized it was Wang, Yipp's bad boy, at the wheel.

He stepped out and opened the door for me like he was a chauffeur rather than a thug. We exchanged no words and I climbed into the rear. The car was otherwise empty. No Yipp. Wang shut the door after me and set off.

He drove east for about two miles to an industrial estate at Kallang. I knew Yipp had a warehouse nearby and wondered whether he had chosen the site deliberately. Was he reminding me of a previous incident I'd been involved in? Maybe. I judged that he was all about symbolism and nuance. However, I didn't care. He may have guessed what I'd done but he couldn't use it against me.

Andrew Yipp stood with his back to the warehouses, looking along the river to the sea. Wang loitered fifty yards away and observed.

There was an acrid smell of sewage and oil that rose up from the river. Industrial and dirty, it was an extreme contrast with the Singapore River in the centre.

I walked over to Yipp and stood by his side, looking in the same direction.

"It is a beautiful sight," he said without turning. "I never tire of gazing out to sea."

I said, "You honour me with this meeting, sir."

Yipp nodded slowly and took a long breath of the less than refreshing air.

I said, "When we last met, you suggested that we shouldn't be enemies." Then I handed him the warning note.

Yipp looked at it and handed it back. "How did you get it?"

"It was sent to me." I paused and then told him about the unit at the camp near Ulu Tiram. I said they were trading with locals who could be bandits.

"What are they trading?"

"The army men get alcohol. Samsoo. The men they trade with get aid supplies."

Yipp continued to stare out to sea. In places I could see where it was raining. Clouds streaked down into the water.

I said, "Do you know anything about this operation?"

I realized I was being abrupt and direct but he answered straight away. "I do not. If there is such an operation, then I fear that they may undermine my legitimate business."

"Samsoo?"

"I'm not interested in any illegal alcohol."

I wanted to say "drugs" but knew he wouldn't confirm or deny any such trade.

He said, "What can you tell me about this group, the ones who may be bandits?"

"Nothing yet. My plan is to follow the army unit and learn what's happening and who's involved."

"That will be very dangerous. Will you take many men?"

I let the question hang for a moment before saying, "Just a driver."

"Why?"

"Because if I take too many men, I risk warning the people I'm looking for."

He nodded. "And the other reason?"

"Because then I know whom I can trust."

He let out a small guttural laugh.

I said, "I may need some help."

Yipp finally turned to look at me and held my gaze for a few beats. "I think you English have a saying about making a pact with the devil. However, I prefer the Chinese proverb, Captain Carter: it is good to strike the serpent's head with the hand of your enemy."

"And you are not my enemy," I said, replaying Yipp's own words from our last meeting.

"Indeed." Yipp laughed again. "Now, Captain, tell me the detail of your plan."

# TWENTY-FOUR

The British Army truck left Kota Tinggi base at six in the morning. The Bedford "three-tonner"—snub nosed with a cab that was slightly wider at the bottom and a grill that gave the impression of a mouth—was a common sight on the roads.

As were army Land Rovers. Hegarty and I were waiting in the village, not far from Sin Sin. There was no sign of life from the shops and bars, and rain thudded on our roof.

With the hood pulled tight and the windows closed, condensation started to mist the windows. But we still saw the Bedford roll past, the Humanitarian Aid letters bold and white in the grey morning.

Hedge waited until they were out of sight before pulling away and following. He stayed well back and left the lights off.

The route took us across the north of Johor Bahru. Rain had been falling for a couple of hours and sat in pools. Every few hundred yards the jeep's wheels would slip. However, after a couple of miles we reached Route One, heading north towards Kuala Lumpur. Red stone laterite kicked up under the Land Rover's wheels and the bump and slip stopped.

Elephant grass beside the road soon gave way to trees and then jungle, black and foreboding in the pouring rain.

Every mile or so tracks led off the main road into the jungle. We passed small settlements. Mongrel dogs stared at us with no enthusiasm to run or bark. Children played in the rain and we saw adults going about daily chores like feeding chickens, paying no heed to the weather.

Hegarty had started an annoying whistle that was probably tuneful in his head but less so to my ears. Finally he stopped.

"So what's in the truck?" he asked.

"Salt, grain and medical supplies bound for Malacca. From there, they'll be distributed throughout the region by the local guys."

"And you know that because...?"

"Because I requested it."

"And you're expecting them to do some kind of drugs deal on the way?"

"Let's see," I replied. However, we could see less and less as the storm intensified. The wipers washed water from side to side, and the rear lights of the Bedford blinked with the changing visibility.

"I should put the lights on," Hegarty said.

I took a long breath. He was right. The heavy clouds, the close-in trees—it was like evening out there.

"Fine. Don't lose them but keep well back."

The headlights burst into life but only served to light streaks of rain.

The Bedford's tail lights disappeared.

We rounded a corner and the red lights began their on–off rhythm in time with the wipers again. Then we lost them as we approached another bend. It was long and then it switched the other way.

"Where are they, Hedge?"

We came out of the second bend.

"I don't see them."

He put his foot down and we splashed and bumped for a few miles. Finally, a red blinking light gave us hope and the sergeant squeezed out a little more speed.

He closed the gap quickly and we realized the lights were different. It wasn't the aid truck.

I said, "I've been thinking. They can't have got this far ahead. They must have turned off."

"Into the jungle?"

I shrugged. "I don't see any other possibility."

We turned around and took it more slowly, looking for side roads. We passed one and shone the lights along the narrow track. It was muddy and rutted but I couldn't see recent tyre treads.

"Keep going," I said, and Hedge resumed our southbound journey, checking left and right.

The thudding rain stopped suddenly, the wipers swooshing nothing for a moment before Hegarty switched them off. We saw the trees ahead light up and then sunlight broke through around us. Immediately, the ground steamed like a thousand boiling kettles.

Now when we found a side road, I got out and looked for tracks. We identified four potential routes the Bedford may have taken but we couldn't be sure. Then we came to the switchback, the long bend left and the long bend right. We'd reached the point where we'd last seen them.

Hegarty U-turned, bumping over a soft verge, and then the Land Rover juddered to a halt. Steam rose from the front of the car.

He got out and looked under the bonnet.

"Radiator leak," he said, his Welsh lilt making it sound amusing, like it was good news.

"We'll have to get a tow."

"I can do better than that, boss," he said with a grin. "An old trick my father taught me."

There was a cluster of *attap* huts about a hundred yards away, and Hegarty set off walking.

When I reached him he was already trying to speak to the Malays who lived there. An old man sat outside a hut and watched us. Finally a lady understood and fetched him an egg.

"Water?" he asked her. "In a can?"

All of these little hamlets were by streams. It made sense. The woman called out and, a minute later, a child appeared with a mug of water.

He thanked her but tried to explain again that he needed something larger. But even miming didn't seem to make sense to her.

The old man got off his chair and hobbled towards us. His dark, craggy face was inscrutable as he looked at us hard.

When he spoke, he put out his hand, palm up.

"You're looking for the girls?"

"No," Hedge said. "Water. War-ter."

I was intrigued. "What girls?"

Again, the hard, unreadable eyes.

I fished in my pocket and put two notes in his palm.

He flashed a mouth with only a few teeth. "Five days ago. The three girls." He pointed north. "They went that way."

I said, "You think we're looking for three girls?"

He shrugged. "You aren't with the others." It was a statement rather than a question. "I'll get you water."

Like the woman, he called to someone, and this time we received a large plastic bottle so heavy with water that the child staggered with it on their head.

135

Back at the jeep, Hedge took off the radiator cap, cracked the egg and poured it in.

"The egg will seal it." He grinned. "Clever, no?"

"Let's see if it works first."

He emptied half the water into the radiator and turned the engine over. Moments later, we were on the road again.

When we reached the first of the four possible off-roads, we turned. The early sun created long shadows where it broke through the trees. The puddles were like muddy goldfish ponds and we bounced and splashed along. After a few yards I signalled that we should go back.

"No tracks," I said. "They didn't come this way."

The same was true for the second, but the third was promising. Like the others, it was a narrow track running off into the jungle. But this one was well used and had fresh tyre ruts caused by a heavy vehicle.

Hegarty turned onto the track and bumped the jeep into the wet ruts.

The jungle quickly degenerated into swampland. The tree cover became thinner, and I was concerned about being seen.

Hegarty had a different concern. He said, "I don't know how long my radiator trick will last. If we get stuck out here..."

I reluctantly agreed and Hegarty reversed the Land Rover back along the track. He bumped and swerved over the ruts and puddles, the jeep much harder to reverse on the difficult terrain. He got us to the road without crashing, although the air was blue with his curses.

I asked him to return to the second track but I wasn't planning to go down this one. I wanted somewhere to wait. I wanted somewhere we could hide and watch for

136

the Bedford coming back down the track. He parked behind the trees and we walked back to the road. We found a couple of rocks, sat in the shade and waited. A troop of macaques watched us and we heard insects all around.

Hegarty seemed to be miles away for a while before he spoke. "It's odd."

"What is?"

"Not having a monarch. George is dead and Elizabeth hasn't taken the throne yet. She seems nice. Do you think she's up to being a queen?"

"I don't know."

"What if she does a runner like her uncle? We could become a bloody republic!"

An army troop carrier went past and we got strange looks from the tired-looking men inside. I guessed we must have looked curious; two white men just chewing the fat beside the road in the jungle.

Hegarty said, "It's one step closer to communism."

"What is?"

"Being a republic."

"I think Americans would disagree."

"But what would happen to the empire? We can't have the British Empire without a queen."

A local cycled past, his bicycle piled so high with plastic bottles that he could barely see over them.

I said, "We should ask him. I'm not sure Malaya likes being part of the British Empire."

"Rubbish! Er... with respect, sir."

"When the Japanese were here in the war, it was an occupation. And yet we're an occupying army too."

He thought for a while. At least, I guess he was thinking, because he didn't say anything or whistle. I continued to watch the junction where I figured the aid truck had gone.

Vehicles travelled south to Johor Bahru and vehicles travelled north to Kuala Lumpur beyond. But nothing came down the track.

The shadows shortened and the insects gradually fell silent. We could hear birds calling and the macaques finally got bored and moved away.

Hegarty stretched. "Why is it an Emergency? Why not the Malayan War? It's the Korean War but the Malayan Emergency."

The same thing had struck me when I'd first arrived in Singapore. Coates had explained it to me.

"It's all about insurance, dear boy," he'd said. "Lloyds of London wouldn't provide compensation in a war. But an Emergency... well that's totally different. A wealthy landowner loses part of his rubber business, then insurance pays out."

I explained it to Hegarty.

"Always serve the rich," he scoffed.

I laughed. "Are you sure you don't want a republic?"

The macaques came back. Or maybe it was a different troop. A couple had quick sex only yards in front of us. Like a display or a challenge. Hegarty chuckled like a schoolboy.

He said, "What do you think?"

"The grin from the male isn't actually a smile. He was showing us his sharp teeth."

Hegarty laughed again. "I meant the aid workers."

"They're not coming. Maybe they've already gone. Maybe there was another way out."

Hegarty nodded. "So what now?"

I knew where the aid unit was supposed to go. After all, I'd requested it. Plus I'd had enough of hanging around waiting.

"Malacca," I said. "Come on, we're going to Malacca."

# TWENTY-FIVE

Hegarty took up whistling again once we had passed Kluang and turned west towards a town on the coast called Muar. The closer we got to the coast, the thinner the jungle became.

We turned north onto the coast road. Trees became sparse and the landscape changed to one of farming and paddy fields. Paired bullocks pulling long carts became as common as trucks. The carts had grass roofs shaped like the winged bonnets worn by Swiss nuns.

We stopped and Hegarty refilled the radiator. We took the covers off and enjoyed the fresh wind in our faces.

It was ninety-odd miles from Kluang to Malacca and, at a steady thirty-five miles an hour, the sun was well past its zenith by the time we drove through the centre of the town.

Chinese banners adorned buildings and I thought it looked like a dilapidated version of Singapore's Chinatown, but with wider streets.

To our left, I could see a large working port with long godowns. There was an overpowering smell of rotten fish, and we wound up our windows and hoped it would ward off some of the evil stench.

Ten miles later we turned off on a side road that led to the large military complex known as Terendak

Barracks. On the edge of the barracks was a row of shops and bars, clearly catering only for the army. London Bar, Wellington Bar, Sydney Bar, said the crudely painted names outside, and I figured that soldiers chose their watering hole along partisan lines.

This was repeated inside the barracks walls, with three distinct sections for the British, Australian and New Zealand regiments who shared the same base.

It was a sprawling complex, maybe twice the size of Majidi Barracks in Johor Bahru.

Of the buildings near the entrance, the NAAFI was the most prominent. Another large building dominated the rear. The red cross painted on the tower told me this was where we were heading. Terendak Military Hospital.

However, before we went there, Hegarty spotted a motor pool and garage and he took the Land Rover in there to get the radiator fixed.

"It'll take about an hour," he said, joining me as I walked towards the hospital. Although the building in the shadow of the ugly white block of a hospital was actually where I wanted to go. It was a small one-storey building with a triangular, orange-tiled roof. A sign above the door said, "Aid Distribution."

There were boxes and sacks piled up outside and a couple of men were carrying them through the open doors.

One of them, a lanky sergeant, was in charge.

As we approached, he froze and looked at us wide-eyed.

"MPs?" he said uncertainly, looking me over.

I said, "The aid truck from Kota Tinggi's been then?"

"Not long missed it. Why?"

Hegarty said, "Name?"

"Goodwyn."

We let the man sweat for a moment. Not only was he as thin as a rake, but he was pale and his eyes were sunken with dark shadows around them.

He glanced into the storage area behind him, maybe hoping for support, but the other guy couldn't be seen.

I said, "Show us the paperwork for the shipment they delivered."

Goodwyn took us into a room and handed me a piece of paper. "All signed and accounted for," he said, trying too hard to sound relaxed.

"Show us," Hegarty said. I handed him the paper and he took out a pen. "Every item, Sergeant Goodwyn. If you'd be so kind."

While the aid worker walked around with Hegarty, I poked around in other areas. Goodwyn kept glancing at me, and I liked the signals he was giving. I could see the worry in his eyes the closer I got to whatever he didn't want me to find.

"Boss!" Hegarty called. "Medical supplies."

I walked over and looked at the crates. They were the same boxes I'd seen at Singorah airfield.

"Open them," Hegarty said.

Inside was a packing list. I picked it up and checked the contents off against it. Nothing extra. Nothing missing.

"Shall I open some more?" Goodwyn asked helpfully.

I said, "No need. I can see that everything on here is present and correct."

Goodwyn breathed out. A smiled briefly played on his mouth before he hid it.

I said, "The problem is, I have the original shipping list."

Goodwyn blinked.

"I know what was in the truck because I arranged it."

I heard a door close at the back of the building and figured it was the other aid worker. He'd heard enough and wasn't staying for more.

Goodwyn cleared his throat. "Well the paperwork…"

"Has been changed," Hegarty said. "This is only half of it."

I said, "So half has gone. What came in its place?"

"I don't know…"

"But you do."

Hegarty said, "Shall we just rip the place apart, boss?"

"No need. Let's walk this way."

I headed towards the far right-hand corner. Goodwyn's eyes had told me he was nervous about this spot, and then I saw them. Boxes with sacking over the top. Everything, except for the new shipment, had dust on it. Or maybe sand or salt or flour. Whatever the coating, it was a sign that things hadn't been moved for a while. These boxes had no dust. In fact, the floor around the box also showed a lot of activity.

"Open them," I said.

Goodwyn sighed and pulled back the sacking. He picked up a crowbar and prised open the top box.

Upon first inspection, the contents looked innocent enough. Twenty-four canteens on a layer. There were two layers.

Hegarty picked one up, opened it, sniffed and wafted a sweet, sharp smell towards me.

He replaced the cork. "Samsoo?"

Goodwyn bowed his head and then held his hands out in a gesture of contrition.

"Anything to say for yourself?" Hegarty asked.

"It's just hooch?" Goodwyn said hopefully.

"You're trading in illegal alcohol."

"Not trading. Just buying for our use."

I looked at the number of boxes. Three hundred and eighty-four. A delivery every couple of weeks, maybe. Not *only* for personal use, that was for sure.

But I wanted more than samsoo.

I said, "Move the boxes aside."

Goodwyn stared at me.

"Move the boxes!"

He only had to slide three boxes out of position to reveal what I'd suspected: a trap door.

When it was open, we could see a short ladder to a storage area below.

Hegarty went down with a torch. He found a light switch, and a second later he called out excitedly, "A drum."

I heard a noise like a lid being prised off.

"More samsoo. And empty bottles. They're emptying the canteens in here and rebottling it."

I looked at Goodwyn, whose face had sweat lines. The sweat must have been sticking to dust on his skin.

"Ah!"

"What is it?"

"I've found our amphetamines. I think they're mixing the samsoo with amphetamines."

Goodwyn hung his head.

I said, "Who's the supplier?"

Goodwyn said nothing.

"Is it Stevenson?"

Goodwyn shook his head.

"Someone else in the aid unit at Kota Tinggi? Come on, man. You can't get in deeper trouble, and I'll be able to find out who the driver was."

The light went out and Hegarty started to ascend the ladder.

"You don't get it, do you?" Goodwyn said. His voice was brittle, like he would burst into tears at any moment.

"It wasn't the Kota Tinggi boys who delivered here today."

Hegarty handed me a long thin case. Inside was a row of ampules, each one labelled "Morphine".

I said, "So who was it?"

Goodwyn looked away.

"Talk!" Hegarty said.

The aid worker shook his head, and now tears really did flow. "If I talk," he spluttered, "I'm a dead man."

# TWENTY-SIX

Sergeant Goodwyn refused to say anything except that the morphine was for medical purposes. There was a shortage. I suspected he was a user, but I wasn't an expert in this, as Flight Lieutenant Turner had guessed when I'd met him in the Sin Sin bar.

I'd arranged for the shipment to Malacca and I'd also arranged for a pick-up from Penang. My plan had been to find the supplier en route but we'd lost the aid truck in the jungle. Had there been some kind of switch? Is that what Goodwyn had been telling us?

The Penang connection was a trap for Jeevan. Better to catch him red-handed than confront him with no evidence at his home base.

I'd asked General Gaskill to arrange transportation so I could be at the airport in Penang by tomorrow morning. I regretted not being more specific.

The Dakota was loaded ready for its propaganda mission. The twin engines rumbled and thundered as it taxied off the airstrip north of Terendak Barracks. It was based at Kuala Lumpur but had been diverted to Malacca, and this was my organized ride. Thanks, General!

Dakotas were nicknamed the "biscuit bombers" because they were favoured for dropping supplies to active troops. They were also used for broadcasting messages and dropping leaflets in the jungle. The idea was to convince the communists they wouldn't succeed. Of course that would work! Tell the enemy they can't win and give them a leaflet.

One saving grace was that it wasn't as cringeworthy as the Americans in Vietnam dropping giant condoms to intimidate the Vietcong. Some US general somewhere had believed the enemy would be worried by the size of GI Joe's penis.

A flight would get me to Penang much quicker than a car or train. And it wouldn't involve travelling through bandit country.

At least, I thought it was safer, until I experienced how these guys operated.

The pilot, co-pilot and navigator took up their comfortable seats. I was alone in the hold and found a box to sit on. The co-pilot had given me headphones and, with the cock of an eyebrow, wished me luck.

The headgear muffled the sound but I could still feel the vibration from the lumbering engines as we took off.

Once the plane was airborne, I settled down for the long flight and looked around. By the hatch was a huge metal frame, as tall as a man and stacked with the small white leaflets. On either side of the fuselage were banks of speakers. There was little additional room in the hold; enough for a man to walk the length of the plane but that was all.

I figured a direct flight to Penang should take a little over an hour. However, I was warned that the Dakota would take more than two. I looked again at the leaflets and knew the flight wasn't just for my benefit. This was an operational run too.

As I waited, I wondered how Hegarty was getting on. I'd left him filling in the relevant forms. Goodwyn was in the barracks jail and could stay there for a long time. Court martial was the likely outcome. But he didn't interest me. He was the end of the chain. And he was afraid. More afraid of someone than of being charged for dealing with drugs. I gave this person a label: Mr X.

Was the body on the causeway another Goodwyn? Was it someone Mr X had dealt with? Was it a message to other Goodwyns?

The co-pilot interrupted my thoughts. He opened the cockpit door, squeezed over and signalled that I should lift one of my ear protectors.

Over the juddering engine noise, the co-pilot shouted, "Go up front!" He leaned closer. "I'm about to do the first drop."

I manoeuvred past him and then the navigator. As I stepped through into the cockpit I felt air being sucked out. The co-pilot had opened the hatch door.

Sitting beside the pilot, I exchanged nods and looked out of the window.

I knew we'd been descending but was surprised we were so close to the treetops. We were in a valley between mountains. I could see breaks in the jungle and clusters of huts.

"How high?" I shouted.

"Five hundred feet," the pilot mouthed back, or maybe he shouted, but I couldn't hear him. The navigator patted him on the shoulder and he did a thumbs up.

Seconds later, a thin cloud of leaflets sprayed from the Dakota like out of a crop duster.

The leafleting stopped as suddenly as it had started and the pilot took the plane higher. The rush of air ended abruptly as the co-pilot closed the hatch. But he didn't come back to his seat up front.

We continued north and I noted that the tree-clad mountains were becoming higher and more frequent. In the distance they became purple then violet before fading to a pale blue.

People described the jungle as both beautiful and terrifyingly vast. I could see why.

I watched the altimeter slowly tick up to twenty-five hundred feet. In the co-pilot's comfortable seat and with the incredible view, I was starting to think this extended journey wasn't too bad after all.

That was until the navigator patted the pilot on the shoulder and pointed. A few seconds later and the Dakota was turning in a wide circle. The navigator checked I was strapped in and made a thumbs-up sign to the co-pilot in the rear before buckling into his own seat.

The co-pilot opened the side door. Suddenly there was no air in the cockpit and at the same time a wall of sound hit me. Two thousand watts of loudspeaker boomed through the aircraft. Then the pilot cut the engines.

The Dakota stalled.

Initially, I felt no change, the booming bass of the speakers much greater than the rumble from the engines. And then it was as though the plane suddenly realized that the engines had been cut. Like something out of a cartoon.

The plane started to lose height quickly. My stomach lurched. I gripped the seat. Cold prickles of fear covered my neck and I looked desperately at the pilot. He smiled at me and gave the "OK" hand gesture.

*OK? We're falling out of the sky, for God's sake!*

And then it was over as quickly as it had begun. The pilot pressed the starter and the engines kicked into life again. He took control and we rose and levelled off.

"It's so they can hear the message without the engine noise!" he shouted.

I was about to shout my gratitude that it was over when he repeated the procedure, cutting the engines again.

The speakers boomed, the plane went into free fall and my heart froze.

Over and over, the pilot repeated the manoeuvre. By the fifth time I realized the stall lasted for less than thirty seconds. Although it seemed like minutes.

I'd been on the rollercoaster in Blackpool as a child. I didn't enjoy it but I knew the trick. If you tensed up, it was worse. Relax and you could enjoy it. Like the pilot seemed to be enjoying himself.

I tried to imagine I was a bird and focused on what the recording was saying, but it was too distorted. It was the same message repeated over and over.

Finally the rollercoaster ride ended and the side door closed. A tap on the shoulder by the navigator told me to switch places again.

As I passed the co-pilot I lifted his earphones. "What was the message?"

He lifted mine. "Simple message to the bandits, 'Come out and go back to a better life'."

"Does it work?"

He pulled a face, *who knows?* and patted me on the arm.

I settled back on my uncomfortable box and stared at the speakers.

I could no longer see anything but I felt the Dakota climb. My vague sense of the geography told me we were going north over the Central Highlands. When we

149

were bumped and buffeted by turbulence for about half an hour, I figured I was right.

Worrying about turbulence seemed pointless when you've plummeted a thousand feet without engines. However, when we finally touched down at Penang's airport, I was relieved.

I also knew I could never fly in a Dakota again.


Minden Barracks was four miles north of the airport, just outside George Town, the capital. A driver met me and drove his Land Rover quickly on tarmac roads.

The low sun gave the clouds an orange tinge that made the buildings look warm.

My immediate impression of Penang was one of wealth. Well-spaced British colonial mansions had beautiful grounds with attractive palms and ferns. Singapore's colonial buildings were mainly in the city centre where the original settlement had been. The houses in the suburbs, north and west, were pretty and grand, but not on this scale.

I didn't know the colonial history of Penang, but based on the company names along the wharf it was an easy guess that it had revolved around shipping rubber and tin.

After reporting to the commanding officer, my driver showed me the officer's quarters and my room. Gaskill had arranged the room for me. I showered and changed and then headed out to have a look around.

The main barracks could have been purpose-built, but it had in fact been a plantation house. Except for a central block of three storeys, the barracks were only two high, with offices and officers' rooms downstairs and men's quarters above. There were six smaller barrack blocks, all grey concrete, but partially hidden by the numerous palm trees in the grounds. There were married officers' houses away to one side and other smaller buildings including a school.

On three sides I could see rubber trees. The fourth side looked out to sea across playing fields and open grassland. Beyond, I could see a white sandy beach.

Unlike the bases in the south, there was no high fence or walls. I figured the bandits weren't expected here. It was an island with one port and much further from the mainland than Singapore. And there was no causeway here.

I remembered the businessman at the European and Oriental telling me about the giant ferries and his equally massive propellers. I made a note to visit the port and see the behemoths for myself if I had time.

I spotted the building I was looking for: the Minden Military Hospital.

Penang had so far given me the impression of tranquillity. However, inside the hospital, the illusion was shattered.

Injured soldiers, mainly from fighting in the north of Malaya, were brought here for treatment and safety. The wards were crammed. Beds lined the walls. There were no curtains for privacy, just a mobile screen used when a patient died.

A ward sister bustled past and I managed to catch her attention.

"Where can I find Jane Dobson?"

"Off-duty," she said without stopping. "You'll find her at the bar."

# TWENTY-SEVEN

The sister scurried away before I had chance to ask where the bar was. I walked back into the barracks' grounds and found a soldier having a sneaky cigarette against a wall.

"Tuckers?" he said. "Outside. Opposite side of the road."

I left the barracks and looked at the row of wooden shacks with palm-leaf roofs opposite. A badly painted sign informed me of the bar's full name: Tucker's Bar and Grub.

I could see darkness rushing in fast from the east and Tuckers had gas lamps hanging outside. There were tables to the front and side with palm-leaf parasols. Most tables seemed occupied by off-duty men and women. I saw no sign of food. I saw no sign of Jane.

I crossed the road and saw more of the side tables. And there she was, chatting with another woman. Jane's hair shone in the light from the lamps, the usual strawberry-blonde looking more flame-orange in the light.

"Hello," I said as I approached.

She looked up, startled. "Ash? Ash!"

"Just the one Ash will do."

She gave me her awkward smile and I remembered how much I liked her mouth. Her kiss.

"Mind if I join you?"

The other woman stood. "Kate. Kate Williams," she said in a broad Australian accent. She grinned and then walked away saying she'd get us a waiter.

I sat at an angle to Jane and a man plonked a bottle of beer in front of me.

"Don't mention it's not Australian. Tucker—the owner—is a bit sensitive about it. We call it chemical beer." She smiled at me again. "But then you aren't much of a drinker as I recall."

I took a sip. It was cold and welcome.

She was still looking at me. "I didn't expect to see you again... It's nice though... seeing you, that is."

"I was passing through." Which was sort of true. Yes, I'd arranged for Jeevan, the aid pilot, to fly to Penang tomorrow, but the truth was I could have picked somewhere else. I chose Penang because of Jane.

She said, "Well I'm glad you did. Have you eaten? Tucker starts serving grub soon."

I said I hadn't and added: "I assume you're here because it's better than the mess?"

"Not really." She laughed, light and relaxed. "And the beer's no good either. It's just good to get outside the barracks. Plus I like Kate."

"And there's the great view." I was looking at her rather than the coast but fortunately she didn't pick up on my corny line. Instead she looked out into the gathering dark.

"You should have been here half an hour ago," she said. "You could see the mainland then."

I checked the menu and Jane ordered a bottle of Australian wine. I could smell the cooking, meat on hot griddles, and decided to gamble on the dish of the day. Which was meat on a hot griddle. When it came, it looked like beef, although I noted Tuckers suspiciously

153

avoided any reference to a specific animal. It oozed with a rich, peppery juice and was served with a chunk of bread.

We were one of the first to be served and I noted that there wasn't a sitting time. Food came out when it was ready.

I said, "We were lucky we didn't have to wait."

Jane grinned. "That's because Tucker is a mate of mine." She nodded over to the bar and Kate Williams waved back.

"Ah, Kate is Tucker."

"Her father set this up and Tucker is her maiden name."

"Not bad," I said, after a bite of bread soaked in sauce. "I went to the adoption centre and met Miss Liang."

She ate a chunk of meat and washed it down with a slug of wine. "I hope you made more progress than me."

"I persuaded her to show me the books. Laura's name wasn't there."

"Do you think she was lying?"

"I found out she was new. She used to work at the hospital in the town, responsible for baby adoption."

"Makes sense, I suppose."

"A lady at an orphanage told me she didn't trust Miss Liang, but I don't think she was lying. I think she was just stressed. It seems her predecessor just up and left and wasn't as organized as Miss Liang would have liked."

When I started talking about Laura, Jane must have hoped I had good news. I had nothing for her. All I could say was I'd tried.

"What about the predecessor then?"

"A chap called Petersen. The lady at the orphanage thought he might know. But I couldn't find him. I went

154

to a school over on the west. Bukit Zarah. A finishing school apparently."

"Apparently?"

"I don't know. I just had an odd feeling... You know how some buildings give you the creeps and you don't know why? But anyway it was a dead end. The man who runs it didn't know where Petersen was."

"Thanks for trying." She touched my hand and left it there. "How's your investigation going? You didn't come to Penang to tell me you'd failed to find Laura."

I finished my beef-like meat and realized I'd also drunk a whole bottle of beer. Jane poured me a glass of wine.

"Beer then wine, you'll feel fine," she sang.

"What?"

"Just a little rhyme to remind myself which order I can drink things. Wine then beer makes you feel queer." She removed her hand and pointed at my leg.

"Your leg is worse."

"I got in a fight," I said. "The following day. I was foolish, but then it gave me the time to check out the adoption centre for you."

"The investigation?" she prompted.

"I'm no closer to finding out who the causeway body is. But I'm making progress on the drugs connection. The man I fought was part of the humanitarian aid unit—"

"The sick, lame and lazy," Jane said.

"That seems unfair. They have a job to do."

"It may be unfair, but from what I've seen it's generally true."

"It looks like they're trading aid shipments for illegal alcohol. Whoever produces it is also producing amphetamines. I followed a shipment to Malacca and found another army group mixing the two, creating...

155

Well I'm no expert on mixing drugs and bad alcohol, but it can't be good news."

She flashed me a naughty smile. "Oh I don't know…"

"You're telling me…"

She touched my hand again. "Ash! I'm pulling your leg. No, I haven't taken drugs and alcohol. Never together anyway." She laughed her light laugh again and I couldn't tell whether she was joking or not.

She took another slug of wine and watched as I took a mouthful. It wasn't too bad.

Her hand was still on mine.

I said, "You haven't mentioned the lucky man."

"Lucky man?"

I nodded towards the ring.

"Oh that." She winked. "That's to ward off unwanted attention." She slowly and deliberately removed the ring and put it in her pocket. Then she placed her hand back over mine and I swore she raised an eyebrow.

She said, "So why are you really in Penang?"

I told her about Jeevan. I didn't know how he fitted in but he was a lead I needed to follow.

She said, "Any other reason?"

"I wanted to see you again."

She smiled and stood and kept hold of my hand. "Where are you staying?"

"I have a room in the OQ."

"Good," she said lightly. "I've never stayed in officer's quarters before."

# TWENTY-EIGHT

Jane sneaked out of my room in the early hours. "No false promises," she said, kissing me hard. "No long goodbyes either."

I'd told her that I was only staying one night, that I would confront Jeevan and return home. And she'd said that she had an early start at work.

She had dressed in the dark and then reached out for me.

I held on to her for a moment.

"It was nice," she said.

"Nice?"

She laughed. "All right then, very nice. Maybe we'll do it again."

I pulled her back towards the bed and an outside light, through a gap in the curtains, lit her pretty face.

"Another time." She pulled away and then kissed my cheek. A second later I was alone in the room.

I could have spent another hour in bed. Instead, I performed my exercise routine and stretched my injured calf. The stitches looked sound and I felt it was healing again quickly.

It was still dark when I left the barracks, and once outside I felt the full force of a south-easterly wind. I flagged down a cab and got in just as the rain started. My driver slowed and then stopped after a few hundred yards. A torrent struck the windscreen and I couldn't see anything outside. Eventually he started again but only marginally faster than jogging pace.

I limped and splashed from the cab to the airport office and dumped my things inside. I found an office clerk, who seemed barely awake. He was surprised at my interest in flight arrivals and said there'd be nothing coming in for at least a couple of hours due to the storm.

He may have been dopey but at least he lent me an umbrella and told me where to get breakfast.

I killed a couple of hours in the canteen with a newspaper. The sky got lighter, but not much, changing from indigo to pewter. It was still raining when I returned to the office and the dopey clerk offered me a chair and cigarette. I accepted the chair.

He was interested in why I was here and not at the airport over the water. Butterworth on the mainland was the main RAF base and I would see fighters like Hornets and Tempests and bombers called Brigands. He said Penang airport mainly saw Dakotas and Austers.

I explained I was waiting for an Auster—the humanitarian aid plane. The guy nodded and shrugged. I expected him to ask me why, but he didn't. He just checked a register and said, "It's not called in yet. If it's on its way, I'd say you've got at least another half hour to kill."

He made me a cup of tea and talked about football as he smoked another cigarette.

The rain finally stopped completely, although the sky remained leaden. A fire crew practised an emergency drill beside the main runway, racing to a plane through the puddles and putting out imaginary flames.

Ten minutes later I saw something silver cut through the clouds like a graceful bird. I recognized it: a Dakota like the one I'd hitched a ride in. And never again.

I saw another Dakota, and then at ten fifteen an Auster appeared out of the low, dark clouds and landed heavily. It taxied, tracking back along the runway towards the office.

Nothing happened for fifteen minutes and I wondered what was going on. Finally the hatch opened and the pilot climbed out. By this time I was at the door and then walking towards him.

"Jeevan?" I called.

The pilot stopped and removed his flying cap, shook his head.

Not Jeevan. I took a closer look at the plane and realized it wasn't the one I'd seen at Tebrau airfield. A slightly different design and it didn't have the humanitarian aid markings or colours.

I returned to the office and waited. There were lots of staff and ground crew but no sign of the clerk I'd chatted to earlier.

At midday I returned to the canteen and ate a quick lunch. Outside once more, I stopped in surprise. There was a plane I recognized. Not an Auster. RAF colours but sleek with something oriental about its design. A Dinah. The one Squadron Leader Kennedy had shown us in the giant hangar at Tebrau.

I walked over.

"Ash?"

I turned to see Flight Lieutenant Turner approaching from the office block.

"Robin. What are you doing here?"

He pumped my hand and grinned. "I could ask you the same thing."

"Waiting for the humanitarian aid pilot."

"Ah."

We continued towards the Dinah but he didn't elaborate.

159

I said, "I assume you arrived in the Dinah."

"Took a sneaky opportunity to take her out. Sorry."

"Sorry?"

"You were expecting Jeevan but I came instead. It's just a little job so I took the opportunity... He's a lazy bugger and more than happy to let me do a shift."

I wondered why we were now at the plane. Was he about to leave? He opened the hatch and I saw four boxes marked as medical supplies. He smiled awkwardly.

After a pause he said, "I assume you want to take a look. I haven't opened them myself. I picked them up first thing from Changi and brought them straight here."

I opened the first box. Medical supplies. Nothing unusual. Nothing extra. Nothing missing.

All four boxes were the same.

He breathed out. "For a minute there I was worried."

"Everything's fine." I looked around. "So who takes delivery of these?"

"The humanitarian aid chap here. I just went to find him but he's late. But then so am I, so maybe he's been and gone. Have you had lunch?"

Of course I had, but I joined him in the canteen and drank tea while he ate.

"The more I think about it," he said between mouthfuls, "the more I don't think Jeevan is your problem. Two reasons..."

I waited for him to continue.

"One, he's a nice, quiet chap. And two, there's nothing he could be doing. Just a few boxes of medical supplies. There's no big smuggling thing going on with that."

I'd pretty much come to the same conclusion. Maybe it was all about the aid trucks and Mr X in the jungle.

When we went outside again, the sun had broken through and the dark, wet airport was transformed.

There was a covered Land Rover parked by the Dinah.

"Great. Lippy's here."

"Lippy?"

"Oh, his name's actually Lipscombe but that's a bit of a mouthful."

A man climbed out of the Land Rover and nodded to me. It was the dopey clerk from earlier.

I said, "I thought..."

He grinned and held out a hand. "Richard," he said. His hand was soft and limp.

"Four boxes of medical supplies for you," Turner said.

"And I've just got one for you today."

As the men loaded the four boxes into the Land Rover, I studied the crate in the back. It was a solid-looking wooden box, three feet high with less depth and width. It took the two of them to lift it out and place it on the ground.

Turner said, "Open it up, Lippy, there's a good chap."

Lipscombe undid a latch and lifted the lid. Inside I saw a pile of clothes and blankets.

"Would you mind emptying it, please?" I asked.

The aid worker didn't hesitate. Leaning on the side, he tipped it up so that the items could be pulled out. He was relaxed, so there was no surprise when nothing unsuspected came out. I helped him scoop the items back in and righted the crate.

Turner and Lipscombe lifted it into the hold, where it just fit, then locked the hatch.

He offered us a limp handshake once again before driving off.

"What now?" Turner asked me.

"Back home," I said. "Give me a lift?"

"Sure."

Twenty minutes later we were smoothly in the air. The cabin was warm and the monotonous engine drone soon sent me to sleep. At first I dreamed about Jane Dobson and hoped we'd meet again, although I couldn't imagine returning to Penang any time soon.

Later, as we approached Johore, I realized I was replaying my recent experiences. My mind kept returning to the airport and the exchange between Turner and the aid worker. My gut told me there was something odd. I just couldn't put my finger on it.

# TWENTY-NINE

A week went by with little happening except it rained a lot and Major Vernon came to the government office where I was working. He made a big thing of praising me for the identification and arrest of the aid guy at Terendak Barracks for dealing in amphetamine-laced samsoo.

Goodwyn had confessed to supplying soldiers in the region and so Colonel Underwood at Majidi was also satisfied. Vernon had also arrested the two men who had traded with the unknown supplier—Mr X—in the jungle. They claimed that they didn't know who Mr X was and that they just looked out for mile markers in the wrong place. Mr X's men used them to signal where to meet.

When I asked about the body on the causeway, Vernon said he was satisfied the case was closed. The man hadn't been identified as a missing soldier so it wasn't a military matter anymore.

During the week Secretary Coates was preoccupied by political wrangling and complained about the SPP— the Singapore Progressive Party—taking more control. Andrew Yipp was on the outside and appeared less of a threat to colonial rule than the alleged conservative Chinese businessmen within the legislature.

I was happy at Coates being distracted but troubled by the unexplained body and Vernon's quick dismissal. However, I settled back into daily routine.

And then two things happened on the same morning. The first was a letter from Jane. It was like the note from the hotel but this time included the photograph of a pretty girl: blonde hair, brown eyes and a golden complexion. I'd already figured it was Laura van Loon before I saw her name on the back. She looked about ten in the photo, although Jane had said she was twelve. I realized Jane was desperately trying to keeping her search alive by sending the letter and picture. Which was fine. I put the photograph in my wallet just in case.

Later that day I received a phone call from the Army Service Corps. I hadn't updated General Gaskill and so no one got the message that I wasn't officially interested anymore. Underwood's drug problem was solved and Jeevan, the humanitarian aid pilot, seemed to be a red herring. Slugger Stevenson—I still couldn't think of him as Scott—was certain the pilot was innocent. In addition, I struggled to see how he could get anything substantial in the hold of his little Auster T7.

The call came from a junior clerk who informed me about the humanitarian aid unit at Kota Tinggi. They were scheduled to make a small delivery tomorrow. Destination: a place called Batu Pahat.

I looked it up on a map. About sixty miles north of Johor Bahru, south of Malacca.

All I had been doing for a week was case reviews. Secretary Coates had asked me to read through all the police reports for the past year and provide a summary. He wanted to know if there were any patterns that the police hadn't spotted. Could it be that there was insurgent activity that had gone down as a normal crime? The main focus was on anyone who had left-wing

164

tendencies, anyone who might be a communist sympathizer.

Wang, Andrew Yipp's thug, had been mentioned twice, although never arrested. In the first case he was classed as a witness to a murder, although his statement proved too general to help find the perpetrator. In the second case he provided the tip-off that a group of shopkeepers were paying for protection. I couldn't be certain but I suspected the protection racket was being run by Yipp's arch rival, Chen Guan Xi. I'd met the man earlier in the year, although he wasn't officially in the country.

I found it ironic that Secretary Coates was out to get Yipp but had already banned Chen from returning to the country. I had no doubt they were both heads of illegal Chinese Secret Societies and yet we couldn't prove Yipp was doing anything wrong. To all intents and purposes Yipp was an upstanding businessman and philanthropist who despised the communists and his rival Chen. I knew Chen's mistake had been to openly criticize the colonial system and then visit China. Yipp had done neither.

For about a minute, I pondered the phone call regarding the humanitarian aid schedule. I looked at the pile of police reports I had yet to read and thought about the aid trucks. I still didn't know the source of the samsoo and amphetamines—my Mr X. I figured I'd also not rest until I knew the link to the body on the causeway.

I'd had enough of this tedious work so I picked up the phone and asked to be connected to the Cathay Building and Andrew Yipp's office.

I spoke to two people before being connected to Su Ling.

"Ash, for what do we owe the pleasure?"

There was something off in her tone. I figured someone inappropriate was within earshot.

I said, "How are you?"

"I'm fine." She stayed with the formal tone. "Unfortunately, Mr Yipp isn't available to take your call."

So, this was personal rather than the need for formality. "Have I done something to offend you, Su Ling?"

The line was quiet for a moment. I heard the faint electronic clicks the wires made and some background noise from the office.

When she spoke she said, "Mr Yipp isn't available. Can I pass on a message?"

I told her about the aid delivery scheduled for tomorrow then added, "Are we still on for the cinema?"

"No," she snapped, and the line went dead.

I stared at the black plastic handset before replacing it in the cradle. Maybe I deserved that. I'd been back for a week and hadn't been in touch.

Oh well. I returned to the monotony of reading reports written with no style and in clumsy English. As I had all week, I took a lunchtime walk to find something to eat, and mid-afternoon I took tea and biscuits from the tea trolley. The day passed and I found nothing interesting. And then the phone rang.

I picked it up tentatively, expecting Su Ling, but it wasn't. The operator said I had a call from Penang.

# THIRTY

Palpable excitement came down the phone line. "Ash," Jane said, "Something's happened."

"What?"

"I sent a memo out to all the hospitals in the country," she explained. "I know I shouldn't have but it was worth the risk. You know, they all deal with orphans and, like ours, have an adoption department."

"OK."

"Well, I just thought it was worth providing them with details of Laura. Just in case. You know, she must be somewhere. She was supposed to be at the adoption centre in JB, but as you discovered, there's no trace of her there. Maybe, just maybe, she's turned up somewhere else."

Although her tone didn't sound encouraging, I said, "And you've had a response?"

"The hospital at Kuala Lumpur. It's not Laura but another girl. There's another girl there."

"I don't understand."

"Monalisa Cardoso. She was also from here and was transferred to JB over a year and a half ago. And yet she's turned up in KL. A nurse said Monalisa recognized Laura's name."

"That does sound promising."

"I need your help, Ash."

I was expecting this. "You want me to go and ask her about Laura?"

"Would you? That would be fantastic!"

What the hell? I thought. After checking out the aid delivery I could go to the hospital and question the girl.

I packed away the police reports, left a note on the desk for Secretary Coates, and headed for home.

Sergeant Hegarty shouldn't have been my driver since my investigation was no longer sanctioned by Major Vernon.

"I told the night clerk where I was going," he said as we drove north in the darkness towards Woodlands Crossing. "Vernon may be annoyed but he hadn't arrived by the time I left."

"You could have checked last night when I asked you."

"Oh, was that last night? I thought you just called." He grinned. "I trust you don't mind that little lie?"

"No trouble getting the gun?"

We were both armed. Like me, he had on a Sam Browne with a holstered Browning service revolver. I looked like a plain-clothes cop, which in a way I guess I was.

He said, "Lieutenant Robshaw approved it."

We drove through the jungle, the headlights bobbing in the darkness.

I said, "There's something about the body that bothers me."

"The dead chap on the causeway?"

"Why there? Why was he headless?"

"I don't know."

"If it was a warning, then, based on tradition, it should have been a head on a pole."

Hegarty nodded. "I guess."

"So why no head?" I waited to see if he'd respond but he didn't. "No head so we can't identify the man. Why do that?"

"I don't know," Hegarty said again.

"The hands were removed too. Again, that's so we couldn't fingerprint and work out the victim."

Hegarty said nothing.

I said, "Because if we knew the victim it could lead to the murderer."

"Blimey!" Hegarty stopped short of the barrier. "I get it. But..."

"But?"

"I don't get it. If it's a warning then who is the warning for?"

"Someone who knows what it means."

Hegarty spoke briefly to the guards and got them to let us onto the causeway. Army business.

And that was another thing that bothered me. As we passed the spot where I'd seen the body, I said, "Who is responsible for this no man's land?"

"The army."

"The army," I intoned.

"Blimey! Are you saying this really is an army matter?"

"I don't know what I'm saying, Hedge. It's just all very strange. Vernon has said it's no longer an army matter, but it just doesn't sit right with me. The body was placed. It was deliberate. The only other explanation I can come up with is the warning was for someone they knew would be crossing. No point in a warning if the right person—or people—don't see it."

We went through the barriers into Malaya. There was already a van and truck waiting for Customs to open. I hoped one would be a meat wagon but neither was.

169

The rain started and we splashed our way to the village of Ulu Tiram and our parking spot near the Sin Sin bar. We sat and waited, the wipers flicking the water left then right across the windscreen.

He said, "It's my birthday today."

"Happy birthday. How old are you?"

"Twenty-four. I'm celebrating with the lads tonight. Will you join us?"

Normally officers wouldn't fraternize with "the lads", but since I was no longer an MP and I liked the sergeant, I agreed.

Like before, the lights of the aid truck appeared just after six and we pulled out behind it. Every now and then our lights picked out a logo on the tailgate. A face appearing over a wall—a character called Mr Chad. It was a different Bedford from last time. That one had the outline of a naked woman on the tailgate. I'd seen another with a skull and two burning cigarettes, like a comedy pirate symbol.

The rain continued as we strained to watch the rear lights. The sky lightened but we were now heading north through the jungle.

I said, "What will you do after the army?"

"I can't imagine there is an after. I'll still be in at thirty-four, forty-four. Maybe sixty-four."

"Why?"

"Because I love it... and I don't know what else I'd do. What about you?"

"I'm no longer in the army."

"I know, but did you know what you wanted to do?"

"No," I said, and I guess I still didn't know.

We passed the small kampong where we had stopped and asked for an egg and water. There was no sign of the old man, but other people were around the huts and further afield. I briefly wondered where everyone else had been when we'd stopped here before.

I also thought about what the man had said about looking for girls.

"They didn't turn off," Hegarty said, breaking into my thoughts.

We drove passed the sidetrack where the aid truck must have gone last time.

Hegarty said, "Maybe this one is legit. Maybe we're going straight to Batty Parfat."

"Batu Pahat."

We continued north, the rain eased and Hegarty dropped back to a safer distance.

"Do you think they've given us the slip?"

Maybe they had, but there was no point in worrying about it now so we just settled back and followed. Thirteen miles before Kluang we came to a crossroads. Batu Pahat was to the left. About twenty-five miles west. The Bedford turned right.

Ten minutes later, at a small village, the truck turned right again. It was another jungle track. I signalled for Hegarty to slow and wait a moment. Livestock wandered on the road. Children ran out and shouted at us so I nodded and Hegarty continued.

We bumped off the laterite onto wet mud. The tracks of the Bedford were clear as day and we followed. There was only one way to go, no turnings into what quickly became swampy.

With the windows down we couldn't hear any other traffic. Either the truck was too far ahead or had stopped. There was the constant chatter of monkeys and the loud mournful call of a hornbill cut the air. We passed trees with slender white trunks and the jeep was filled with a sherbet-sweet scent. Then the jungle closed in, and overhead, orchids flowered high under the green canopy.

We pulled up a hill and saw how the Bedford had dug its wheels deep in the ground. Hegarty slowed as we crested the rise. The track swept left and then split. Both routes fed into dark jungle.

Hegarty edged forward. "Left or right?" he said.

"What?" I was looking at the trees. Did something move? "Stop. Just stop."

Hegarty stopped.

"Listen." I waited a beat and drew my Browning. "It's gone quiet."

"Silence is golden," he said. "You know where—"

But he didn't finish the explanation of the phrase. He slumped forward and a split second later I heard a gunshot. Then another and another and bullets pinged off metal.

"Get out!" I shouted, opening the door and rolling. But even as I said it I knew Hedge wouldn't be getting out. His eyes stared blankly, half his face a scarlet mess.

# THIRTY-ONE

The firing ceased and for a second there was a surreal calm. I don't know what happened or where the blow came from because one moment I was peering around the front tyre and the next I felt pain explode in my head.

I remember the smell of the damp earth and tyre rubber and blackness.

When I came to I was in the back of a short truck, tied to a bench. My head throbbed and my wrists ached from the restraints. Apart from that I seemed unharmed. I opened my eyes.

It was dim, because the dark green cover of the rear was pulled down and tied shut. Pinpricks of bright light flashed along the seams as the truck moved from shade to light to shade. I swallowed air that was both stiflingly hot and humid. Sweat dripped from my face.

There was another man in the dark, trussed up like me. His head was down and I briefly thought he was unconscious. Until he spoke.

"Stay calm. Take shallower breaths. And don't struggle. It's too damned hot in here and there's no way these bindings will come loose."

"Who—?"

"Jack Smith."

"Not army?"

"No. You?"

I decided against an explanation and opted for: "Not me. I was with an MP though. Any idea what happened to him?"

"Dead, I'm afraid. Single shot to the head. Who was he?"

"Just a friend." I looked at the spots of light for a moment and then back at Smith. "How long was I out for?"

The truck bumped over rutted ground and we moved with it, our bindings so tight that there was no way to dampen the jolts.

"An hour maybe," he said after the bumps stopped. "We've been bouncing around like crazy. It might not seem like it but this is the first semi-decent road we've been on. I'm surprised you stayed unconscious for so long."

I said, "Who are they?"

"I don't know."

"So why have they picked you up? What's your story?"

"Story?" He cleared his throat. "One minute I was hiking through the jungle, the next I was being confronted by this Chinese gang. I thought they were bandits but, I don't know, maybe it's because we aren't soldiers."

"What the hell were you hiking in the jungle for?"

"Freddy Spencer Chapman. Name ring a bell?"

"No," I said, although I had heard of him. It was easier to let this other guy speak and he seemed to like talking.

"Stayed behind enemy lines when the Japanese took Malaya. Survived the whole war running guerrilla campaigns. He was the Malayan equivalent of Lawrence

174

of Arabia. Well, basically, I'm a fan and I just wanted... you know... I was following his footsteps."

I nodded, though he probably couldn't see me too well.

He said, "What were you doing with the MP?"

I said nothing.

"I mean, are there other MPs around? Could we be rescued?"

"No."

Then he was quiet and I could hear his breathing over the rattle of the truck.

"Take shallower breaths," I said, replaying his earlier words to me.

"I'm worried."

I said nothing.

He said, "I'm worried about what's really going on. Why were you following them?"

"Who said I was following them?"

"But you were, weren't you? Why else were you out there. Me, I had a reason. Freddy's first main camp used to be around here. You... you were travelling with an MP. You were looking for someone or you were following them."

I said, "I told you, I'm not a soldier. I work for Internal Security in Singapore."

"Internal Security?" His tone was almost mocking but then it changed. "But... then... You think they *are* bandits. You think they're planning an attack."

I said nothing.

"You think they're going to attack," he said again. "Where? Who?"

"Where would you attack?"

"The camp at Ulu Tiram."

"Kota Tinggi. What makes you say there?"

175

"Easy target, not well protected and there's them stores there. We have a shortage of food here in Malaya. It's not like Singapore over here you know!"

I felt the truck steer left. I'd felt it steer left more than right. "I don't know about you," I said, "but I get the distinct impression that we're going round in circles, always turning left."

I could hear his breathing get louder.

"What are they gonna to do with us?"

I shook my head. I had no idea.

The breathing quickened, panic building. He started to mutter, "Oh my God!"

I said, "Stay calm. We'll be all right."

"Oh my God, they're gonna kill us!" His voice was hysterical now. Then he shouted: "Help! Somebody help!" He thrashed around as much as the tight bindings would allow and banged his feet on the metal floor.

The vehicle stopped suddenly and the jolt made me grunt.

Blinding light burst in as the rear flap was pulled back. Two wiry Chinese guys swung up carrying machetes. Smith wailed but all they did was chop at the ropes tying us to the bench. My legs were free but my hands were still locked tight behind my back. A sacking hood went over my head and I was dragged and then pushed. I took a couple of steps, was jabbed in the back again, and fell forward into space.

The ground hit me hard. I tried to roll, expecting the impact, but my shoulder jarred and my ribs felt like they'd been punched again by Slugger Stevenson—though without boxing gloves this time.

I lay still for a moment and heard Smith thud beside me. Dirt and dust stuck to my sweat-damp clothes and skin.

Smith whimpered. I could also hear the tromping of many boots. How many men where there? It was impossible to tell from the noise, but there were a lot more than the two I'd already seen. Somewhere close by, I could also hear the metallic sound of machinery.

There was something sweet in the air. I could smell it through the earthiness of the sacking. This wasn't the sherbet smell of citronella trees we'd smelled earlier. This was more chemical.

Without warning, I was jerked upright and pulled backwards by my bindings. I stumbled and slid for about a hundred yards. Then the pulling stopped. I was spun around and pushed.

Again I fell onto my face only this time the ground was soft, maybe dry grass. Sounds were now deadened and I figured I was inside—a hut maybe.

After a minute of no sound I tried to stand. My head bumped into a ceiling; a thatch of some kind, probably palm leaves.

I manoeuvred around and felt the back wall. In the centre, there was a thick branch supporting the roof and I used this to rub the sacking until it was off my head.

It was good to breathe the air properly, even though the sweet chemical smell was even stronger than I'd thought.

The hut was small and circular, about ten feet in diameter. A heavy animal hide covered the entrance. I gently shouldered the flap to look outside.

No chance. Something hard jabbed me in the face and I staggered back. There was a guard outside and I was going nowhere.

The walls looked solid, clay in a kind of wattle. The roof was palm leaves, but branches radiating from the central support would prevent me climbing through.

I sat against the support and closed my eyes. As a child I'd been locked in confined spaces. My disciplinarian father thought isolation was the best punishment. Maybe for some people, but I learned to use the time. I focused on something like a mathematical problem. I learned all my times tables before most of my class had mastered the fives.

Staying calm and relaxed, that was the trick. As an adult I used the skill to think through cases. The body on the causeway caused me the most difficulty. I started replaying the events of the first day. The body had led to the BVD unit, which in turn led to the aid unit at Kota Tinggi. I got to the point of following the truck this morning when a scream broke my concentration.

Smith was being tortured, I thought. The screams got louder and louder, broken by sobs and pleading. Then the screaming stopped and was replaced by whimpering. It got closer until the flap opened and Smith was pushed into my hut.

He lay prone on the floor and moaned for a few minutes. Then gradually he eased himself up, moving like every muscle in his body hurt. The shirt on his back was shredded and his face was covered with grime and blood.

I watched him.

"Oh God," he mumbled. "I thought they were gonna kill me, I did. Oh God, I hope that's it. I hope they don't do that again. I don't know anything. I told them I don't know anything but they beat me anyway. God, I really thought I was gonna die." He looked at me, exhausted and deflated. "They'll do you next. Tell them whatever they want to know—tell them! Maybe it'll save both of us."

I said, "What do they want to know?"

"Just what you were doing following them. How much you know about their operation." His eyes flashed briefly and he added: "You do know what they're up to, don't you?"

"Pretty much."

"What?" Smith pleaded. "What's going on?"

"I'll tell you," I said. "But first let's stop this charade. Untie my hands and I'll tell you what I know."

# THIRTY-TWO

Smith's mouth dropped open. I was impressed at how quickly he got it. He shook his head like a dog shakes water from its body. One minute he was poor tortured Smith, the next he was… well, someone else entirely.

"How did you guess?" he said.

"Your story was all over the place. You said you'd been in the back of the truck from before I was picked up and yet you knew about my friend. You knew he'd been killed with a single shot to the head, which implied you'd witnessed it. And yet you didn't know he was an MP. If you'd seen him you'd have seen the Land Rover. You'd have known."

Smith nodded.

I said, "And that whole thing about Freddy Spencer Chapman."

"That's true. In fact, this is really where his first camp was—although it was never his camp. It was the Chinese bandits he worked with. Ironic isn't it how we trained them in guerrilla tactics, marksmanship and bomb making. And it's true he was Malaya's version of Lawrence of Arabia. It's just that he never got the recognition."

I said, "Why am I still alive?"

"We're not murderers." He gave me a sad smile and shook his head. "The shot that killed your driver was a freak. An accident. The last thing we want is trouble."

"Too late. Killing a soldier—not least an MP—will bring you a whole heap of trouble." I locked eyes with him and used the voice of command. "Untie me, soldier."

For a second he looked uncertain and I thought he might actually untie me. They had taken my Browning but I could still feel the Beretta in my ankle holster. They hadn't thought to check.

Eventually he shook his head. "How did you know...?"

"Stands to reason you'd either be serving or ex-army."

"What else do you know?"

"Untie me first."

"Tell me what you know and then I'll untie you."

I thought it unlikely but I had little option. So I said, "Your little gang is producing illegal alcohol and drugs. You distribute via the aid workers." I was thinking as I spoke. "But the transaction doesn't happen here, does it? You don't want them here so you meet at prearranged spots, different each time. You use misplaced mile markers so the driver knows which jungle track to take. You exchange samsoo for their goods. You add the drugs and alcohol and deliver on their behalf. Oh, and the exchange is easy. You have your own Bedford. You have an aid truck. This way, they leave in one and return in yours."

Smith nodded. "How did you figure that?"

"There's a character on the tailgate of each of them. The aid unit have two trucks but I've seen three different ones. Who were you dealing with at the camp?"

181

"No one in particular. Anyone." I could see he was proud of the arrangement.

"And you set this all up?"

"Yep," he said again. "So you see, we're no problem really. We're just providing a service."

"With amphetamines and opium?"

"Not opium. Morphine. Do you know the price of morphine? It's like liquid gold. We produce the amphetamines but just get as much morphine as we can lay our hands on. It's not much, but when we get it we sell it on to the hospitals."

"And some users," I said, thinking of Sergeant Goodwyn in Malacca.

"Can't help if they use it themselves."

I said, "Where does Sergeant Gary Bender fit in?"

Smith just stared at me.

I said, "AWOL about ten months ago from BVD 221."

Smith said nothing.

"Thirteen days ago there was a body on the causeway."

"I heard."

"What do you know about it?"

"Nothing."

"Connected to BVD 221," I said, watching him closely.

He looked surprised. "Really?"

"Is it Gary Bender?"

Then he laughed. "No. I can categorically tell you it's not him."

"But you said you didn't—"

"It isn't Gary Bender because he's alive and well."

And then I got it. The missing truck. It was here. I said, "You're Bender."

He grinned. "Much more lucrative outside the army, but I have no complaints because it gave me this opportunity and lots of contacts."

"So who was the body?"

"Like I said, I've no idea."

"Were you responsible for the warning?"

"What are you talking about?" Suddenly he was serious.

I said, "I received a note in Chinese to back off my investigation."

"Nothing to do with us."

"Why should I believe you?"

"Because..." And then he shouted, "Guards!" before turning back to me. "Because, my friend, you aren't a problem."

Two Chinese men burst into the hut, grabbed me and dragged me into the sunlight.

We were still in the jungle but it was a broad clearing with fifteen huts built from a mix of *attap* and corrugated iron. There was a large dust bowl area in front of the huts and then a corrugated iron building big enough to park three Bedford trucks. But the aid lorry was parked with other vehicles: jeeps and a smaller truck that looked like a Japanese hangover from the Second World War. I figured that was the one we'd been in earlier. The one that had brought us here.

The large building had a smoking chimney, and I guessed this was their distillery. It looked temporary and able to be taken down and moved with little notice.

There was a cluster of saplings and a large dead tree trunk, sad and grey against the dusty red ground.

I counted twenty-four men, all Chinese, all armed. They wore the clothes of peasants. There was no sign of the light green uniform of the insurgents. These men weren't communist bandits.

In the centre of the dust bowl was a Chinese man, taller than the rest and smartly dressed. From the way Bender and the Chinese spoke, I figured Bender wasn't in charge here. The other man was.

Bender raised his voice to the man and received a backhand to the face for his insubordination. I wondered if he'd argued in my defence. But then he just walked away.

With a bark from the Chinese leader, I found myself forced to kneel.

In reasonable though flat English, the leader said, "He doesn't think I should kill you. He thinks maybe you could work with us."

I bowed my head deferentially. "Untie my hands and let's share tea."

"I don't think so. You have served your purpose and told us what you know. Alive you are a liability. Dead you are another problem gone away."

He had a pistol in his hand and raised it. His men gathered around to witness the execution.

I took a breath and looked at the barrel. I saw his finger twitch.

"Andrew Yipp," I said.

His finger eased.

"What about him?"

I had no idea. I was simply scrabbling for an excuse to stay alive. "Untie my hands…"

"What about Mr Yipp?" I sensed he wasn't just intrigued but also afraid or at least concerned.

"I know him and…"

The leader tossed back his head and laughed. For a second I was focused on his neck. His face looked young but the loose skin on his neck said older. Much older.

And then the neck turned red and the laughing was choked off. Blood splattered around me and the air was filled with a thousand gunshots.

# THIRTY-THREE

I was moving before the Chinese guy hit the ground. I got down and rolled, kept low and assessed the situation. People were scattering and shooting. I couldn't see the assailants. Gunfire came from the jungle and the defenders shot wildly into the trees.

There were two bodies close by so I rolled to them, partly for protection and partly because I needed to get the ropes off my hands.

I found a knife and started squirming on the ground, cutting the cords. Bullets whizzed overhead and rattled on the metal huts.

Another gang member went down in front of me. He was immediately on his feet again, screaming and firing blindly. Multiple shots spun him back to the ground.

In the dust bowl we were exposed and survival looked unlikely, especially since the attackers still hadn't shown themselves.

Most of the gang members still alive had made it to the cover of the huts. Others were firing from the corrugated iron building.

No way was I going to make it to the huts, so I lay for a minute and finished cutting through the ropes. The Beretta was soon in my hand and I took a breath.

The closest hut was less than thirty yards away but the dead tree was closer. Bender lay on the ground beside it, firing judiciously into the jungle. Unlike most of the gang, Bender appeared to be conserving his bullets, firing only when he saw a target.

I didn't fancy my chances running towards the gang members defending the huts. I didn't fancy my chances running at all.

Bender looked at me and beckoned.

With a fast crawl, I covered the twenty-yard gap. I lay on the ground, partially protected, and watched.

There were three remaining men in the centre and they died seconds later. Of five by the closest huts, two had survived so far. They ran for the cover of the large building. And then, for the first time, an attacker appeared. The man walked brazenly out of the jungle, his Sten gun ratter-tatting its message. The running men fell.

The defenders in the factory building now had a focus and a volley of shots rang out. The guy with the machine gun sank to his feet, a startled look on his face. He continued to fire until the gun went down, shooting the ground.

I realized that the man had been a lure. As soon as the defenders changed position, a swarm of men came out of the jungle and blasted the building with a sustained and awesome onslaught.

Two men danced grotesquely as they tried to escape and a hundred bullets tore through their bodies. The attackers closed in. Now that they were in the open, I could see that they were also Chinese.

"Chinese Reds!" Bender moaned. "They don't take prisoners." He raised his gun ready to make a final stand.

"Don't shoot!" I snapped at him. "They're not commies. Watch."

Bender lowered his aim.

More Chinese came out of the jungle. The attackers swept into the main building and the shots became more sporadic and then occasional as the last men were despatched.

A shout from inside stopped the shooting.

They came out of the building and formed a semicircle at the edge of the dust bowl. They were looking at us but their weapons were pointed at the ground. I had the sense they were part of a well-trained army, though I was certain they weren't bandits. They had no uniforms and I could see no sign of the red star that communists usually wore.

"OK," I said, "get up slowly and deliberately drop your gun."

We stood and raised our hands.

It was then that I realized that the Chinese gunmen weren't looking at us, but past us.

I turned to see a man walk out of the jungle. He pointed his gun at me and grinned with the smile of a reptile.

"Mr Carter."

"Wang," I said. For a second I thought he was going to shoot, but he lowered his gun arm.

"Mr Yipp sends his regards," Wang said without any pretence at friendliness. Yipp sent his regards but Wang was just doing his job. And it was one he'd rather not have done.

I said, "Thank Mr Yipp for me, please. But you were almost too late."

Wang grinned again. "I wasn't sure how long to leave it. But then decided Mr Yipp would rather you stayed alive."

As I suspected, Wang and his men had been here a while and deliberately left it to the last minute.

Bender said, "You led them here!"

188

Wang lifted his gun again but this time pointed it at Bender.

"Who is this?" The gun was cocked.

I raised my hand. "He's my prisoner. He's needed for questioning."

Wang glared. "Is he a member of this gang?"

Before Bender could speak, I said, "He's army. He's an AWOL. Like I said, he's wanted for questioning."

Wang waited a couple of beats, probably trying to assess the situation. Was he willing to challenge me further? Then with a begrudging nod he shouted at his men. They immediately dispersed and started to douse the huts with gasoline. Seconds later flames began to lick the air.

Wang turned his attention back to me "Your jeep is parked on the track, Mr Carter. About a hundred yards away. If you would like to be accompanied, I would be happy to escort you wherever you are going. Or if you need help walking..." He showed his teeth in a kind of smile again.

I shook my head. "Pass on my gratitude to your boss," I said, and picked up my Beretta.

"Now you owe me, Carter."

I stopped and snorted derisively. "Wang, Wang, Wang. What a pleasure it is to deal with you. But I don't think so. And I don't think Mr Yipp would appreciate you taking credit."

The henchman spat. "In that case, you had better keep one eye open for me, Carter. You don't impress me one little bit."

I smiled, gave him a four-fingered wave, and started to walk to where he said the jeep would be.

Bender shuffled up beside me. "Thanks," he muttered, his head hanging like that of a beaten dog. "Thanks for saving me back there."

Before we reached the jungle's edge, a loud explosion rang out. I turned to see flames shooting upward, smoke belching from the factory. A wall collapsed. Dead gang members were being carried and flung into the flames.

I started walking again. "We've both been lucky today."

The Land Rover was tucked beside the track, hidden behind a rhododendron bush with scarlet flowers. Hegarty was no longer at the wheel. His body had been dumped in the rear and my first task was to wrap him and lay him down.

But I didn't get that far. Bender staggered against the jeep and moaned. He clutched his side where his shirt now looked like the colour of the blossom around us.

He looked sick and I saw sweat on pallid skin.

"How bad is it?" I asked.

Bender pulled back his shirt and showed me a stomach wound.

He said, "I'm gonna die, aren't I?"

"Let's get you to hospital."

"I've seen stomach wounds before. If blood loss doesn't do it, septicaemia will."

I manoeuvred Hegarty's body so that I could get access to the first aid kit and swabbed Bender's wound with iodine and gave him a bandage to wrap around his body.

While he was finishing off, I removed the canvas roof to get better access and disconnected the rear seat. Now I had room to lay Hegarty down. I tore a section off the roof and covered him with it. All the time, explosions and pops filled the air.

I held his shoulder for a second and in my head asked for his forgiveness. I suspected following the aid truck would be a big risk but I shouldn't have gambled with his life.

With my help, Bender climbed into the passenger seat. He closed his eyes.

"Don't go to sleep... for two reasons," I said. I turned the key in the ignition and gripped the blood-smeared steering wheel. "Firstly, if you go to sleep you might not wake up. Secondly, I need you to help me get out of here."

Bender opened his eyes, took a ragged breath and nodded. As we came to the first fork in the track, he pointed the way.

After a mile, to keep him alert, I said, "You were planning to let me go, weren't you? That argument with the gang leader..."

"I just thought we were scaring you. I really thought your friend's death was an accident. But I guess not. Min wanted to know what you knew before killing you. He's always been afraid that a rival would find him." He coughed repeatedly but then calmed himself. "Ironic that one did."

I drove again and the noises from the burning camp diminished until I could no longer hear anything but the sound of birds and screeching monkeys.

"Were you telling the truth back there?" I asked. "You don't know whose body it was on the causeway?"

"No."

"And you don't know about the message I got."

"No."

I believed him but it created a problem for me. The body had led me here and yet Bender claimed there was no connection.

Finally we came out onto a proper road and I had to nudge Bender awake.

"Where are we?"

He blinked and took a faltering breath. "South-east of Kuala Lumpur," Bender said. "At least we should be. Only about twenty miles to KL."

# THIRTY-FOUR

Bender shut his eyes for longer and longer periods. I suspected he wouldn't make it to Kuala Lumpur.

Just to keep him awake I said, "Tell me about the drugs."

He opened his eyes and tried to focus.

I said, "Amphetamines and morphine. You were dealing in those."

"I've told you about the drugs... nothing more to say."

"Tell me about the warning. The message in my room."

He shook his head. "Not me."

"Tell me about Jeevan. Where does he fit in?"

"I don't know... I don't know any Jeevan."

The aid pilot's involvement still bothered me but I moved on.

"Who are your contacts?"

He stared ahead, his eyelids flickering open and shut.

"The names. Who do you deal with?"

He coughed then said, "One condition."

"What?"

"A letter for my mum. Promise... promise you'll post it." He coughed again with the effort of speaking, and this time blood speckled his chin.

"Stop the jeep," he said quietly.

I pulled into the long grass verge and switched off the engine.

"Promise me," Bender said.

"I promise."

He looked at me for a long time, his eyes changing focus. Then he put a hand inside his vest and pulled out an envelope. He handed it to me. It was addressed to a woman in Mile End, London.

Bender then told me five names, including Goodwyn in Malacca. I didn't know any of the others and there was still no mention of the pilot.

"What about Jeevan?" I asked again.

Bender leaned back, his eyes struggling to stay open. He looked as though the energy was draining out of him quickly. Eventually he shook his head.

"The body on the causeway. Who was it really? One of those men?"

Bender didn't answer. He closed his eyes.

"You promise?" he said.

I started towards the city again, and for a long time Bender said nothing. His breathing became more and more shallow. He let his head flop sideways and took a shuddering breath.

He said something inaudible.

"What?" I stopped the engine. "Bender, what did you say?"

His blood-encrusted mouth moved and he said something that sounded like: "other plane and promise."

"I'll make sure your mum gets the letter. I promise."

Bender's head dropped.

"What about the other plane?" I asked, but he was gone.

★ ★ ★

194

Niroj Jeevan awoke in a good mood. He thought the government man called Carter knew what was going on. He thought he was in trouble again, but nothing had happened. Turner had gone to Penang in his place and Turner had been cool. There really was nothing to worry about.

He'd been told about the message in the hotel, how Carter had been warned off. Maybe it had worked. Maybe Carter was happy with the samsoo angle.

It was a good misdirection after all.

All Jeevan needed to do was keep mum. Don't say a word. Like he hadn't admitted to anything last time. Nor did he point the finger at the real culprits. Sure he got busted out of Fleet Air Arm, but he was still a pilot and was still flying.

He sat alone in the mess tent and ate breakfast. He had been born in England, but his name and skin colour meant that he hadn't made any real friends in Kota Tinggi. Some were OK, like Slugger Stevenson, but most of the men were racist bigots. It had been the same in Fleet Air Arm. It was probably the same the world over.

He didn't do much wrong. Not really. He was the scapegoat really, and in the beginning he hadn't understood the big picture. He'd thought the arrangement was more innocent, but the payments he had received made him realize that this was something much, much bigger. He had laughed at the simplicity of the arrangement, at its audacity. It was blatant and yet secret at the same time.

He found out the initial route had been by the train that ran the length of the country. It had worked for a couple of years, starting small and building into the big operation it was today. But trains were dangerous, too restrictive. The Man had been involved in the early days and had seen the risk of using the stations. Which, after all, were in the centre of the towns. The one in Johor Bahru was next to the hospital, which was handy. When they stepped up the operation, the use of the trains had to stop.

He jumped on a ride to Tebrau airfield, arriving before the aid truck with his cargo. As he watched them draw up alongside the Auster, he thanked God that the Man had approached him. He would retire rich. His plan was to get as far away from Asia as possible. Maybe he would go to India. There, he'd be a very rich man.

He strode over. Stevenson, the beefcake of a sergeant, watched him approach from the comfort of the Bedford's cab. Stevenson pretended to be a friend but he wasn't really. He just felt sorry for him as an outsider.

Jeevan had been the only man on camp who hadn't watched the fight between Stevenson and the ex-MP government man. Everyone else wanted the Slugger to win. Jeevan hadn't cared; he would have been happy for both to lose.

He arrived at the plane early and watched as the final boxes were loaded into the hold by a couple of men. "Any decent drugs?" Jeevan asked the two aid workers.

"Piss off!" was the reply he received. These stupid grunts have no sense of humour, Jeevan thought. He picked up the manifest and checked it off against the boxes in the hold. The engineer handed him his gear and told him the plane was fuelled up and good to go.

The guy performed his usual ritual of patting the pilot on the back for luck and took up his position at the front of the plane.

Jeevan fired up the engine and the chocks were removed. He gave the ground crew the thumbs up and taxied out and onto the runway.

It would be a long ride, almost two hours over some of the worst areas of fighting, but he would feel safe at four miles up. It would be another bumpy ride, but he was a damn good pilot and turbulence made otherwise dull flights more interesting.

He made one last check of his instruments.

There was a crosswind and, as he accelerated along the runway, he felt the tug to one side. The poor condition of the tarmac didn't help.

Shy of seventy miles an hour, the wheels left the ground and the Auster lurched hard left as Jeevan fought against a gust of wind. He rapidly gained control and the plane lifted into the air and towards the heavy sky that promised another wet day.

Just before he reached the cloud ceiling, he felt a judder. It didn't feel like the wind. This was different. The plane juddered again and alarm rushed through his veins. It felt like he was out of fuel.

The engine spluttered. He checked the fuel gauge. It said "full". For the first time he smelled something: the sharp acrid scent of an electrical spark.

In the hold, the fuel had pooled towards the tail. The small electrical device had been clicking for some time, its battery almost spent, but the sparks continued. As the Auster started to level out, the fuel moved back along the body of the plane.

When the sparks ignited the fuel, the explosion was instantaneous.

# THIRTY-FIVE

On the outskirts of Kuala Lumpur, I crossed a small river and stopped. My clothes were caked in sweat, blood and dirt, and my exposed skin was dirtier still. I splashed my face and set off once more.

Both Hegarty and Bender were now in the rear and I must have looked a terrible sight as I drove into the city.

My first impression of Kuala Lumpur was of a run-down Chinese market. The streets were lined with vendors calling for customers and shouting at thieves. Now and again the smell of sewage rose and fell and combined with rotten fruit and vegetables.

In one street I found the way blocked by the sheer weight of people. The sound of my horn was barely audible above the cacophony of street sellers.

The first person to react was an elderly woman. She stared at the bodies in the rear of the Land Rover and started to scream.

Within seconds, the whole crowd was shouting and waving their arms. But they parted, pulling children and animals out of my way.

Eventually I neared the centre, where the streets were exceptionally wide and colonial buildings lined either side. Here the city seemed very similar to Singapore, British-run and wealthy. I stopped by an alarmed policeman and asked for the main hospital.

I'd assumed the Kuala Lumpur hospital would be near the centre but was wrong. It seemed I must have been close before and was directed back to the edge of the city.

I've never heard the simile "as pretty as a hospital" and doubt I ever shall. However, Kuala Lumpur Hospital was about as ugly as one could be, characterless and like an office block.

When I arrived at the gates, the immediate assumption was that I was here because of the bodies. I was here because of Jane's phone call. She'd sent a memo to hospitals about Laura van Loon and another patient had recognized the name.

I explained to the guard that I was also here to see a patient. When I parked, I asked a couple of orderlies to get the bodies inside. Although cloudy, it must have been eighty degrees Fahrenheit, and the sergeant had been dead for almost three hours.

Shrouds were placed over them and, one at a time, they were taken from the Land Rover.

Once inside, I spoke to the receptionist and explained. I repeated the explanation to a male administrator who agreed that the bodies could be taken to Singapore. Having sorted that, I asked where I would find the Cardoso girl.

"Please take a seat, Mr Carter," the administrator said. "I'll find the doctor for you."

I guessed this meant something had happened. Perhaps the girl was no longer at the hospital. I was given a cup of water and sat and waited.

Half an hour passed before a doctor came to find me. He introduced himself as Shaheen Meah. Although his eyes showed signs of extreme tiredness, he had a bright smile and a shiny scalp. However, as soon as the smile faded, I knew there was bad news. He drew me into a private room.

"I'm afraid the young lady died last evening," he began.

If I'd been able to speak to the girl I might have obtained news about Laura.

I grimaced. "What did she die of?"

"Typhoid. She was also terribly malnourished and barely coherent. If you drove from the south you will have gone through some of the worst-affected areas. We have a typhoid epidemic in the shanty areas."

I nodded. That explained why I'd caused so much panic as I drove through the city. I looked a state and I had two dead bodies in the back. They thought we had typhoid.

The doctor continued: "We think it's under control, but the people are paranoid. The disease is spread by the polluted water, but most of the people think you can catch it directly off someone infected."

I said, "What can you tell me about the girl?"

The doctor had a folder but he didn't need to look at it. "Female, white skinned, dark hair, five two, five stone eleven. All skin and bones. Very underweight and weak. Said she was sixteen."

I said, "I understand that the girl recognized Laura van Loon's name. She's really the one I'm looking for."

"Yes, one of the nurses asked the Cardoso girl. She thought the girl recognized the name but, like I said, the girl was incoherent. She had a raging fever and was delirious. She kept saying something about a poisonous flower, but we couldn't make sense of it. Maybe she thought the fever had been caused by a flower she'd eaten. She also said there were three of them—three girls. Maybe the van Loon girl was one of the others.

200

However no one similar has turned up. So where she came from and who she was with is a mystery."

He had no more information, and when I asked, he gave me the file. "I had a copy made," he said. "When I heard a government man from Singapore was interested, I knew you'd want a copy."

I said, "How did you know?"

"The memo we received. The one saying that you were looking for Laura van Loon."

I nodded although the memo had come from Jane not me. I opened the file and saw that the first thing was a photograph of Monalisa Cardoso's naked body on the mortuary slab.

The doctor said, "Did you know her?"

I shook my head.

"Despite her claims of poison, there was no evidence," Doctor Meah said. "Just typhoid, although we didn't do a full autopsy. My theory is that she's walked a long way. She was starving and probably caught typhoid from a dirty stream."

I didn't expect an autopsy, not when they had a typhoid epidemic. I'm not a doctor and I wouldn't know poisoning when I saw it, but still I said, "I'd like to see her."

He blinked. "Oh, I thought you knew."

"What?"

"She was collected a couple of hours ago. A private ambulance, I think."

"Which hospital? Could I see the details, please?"

He said he'd get me the sign-out sheet. It would take a few minutes and he asked if I'd like to clean up. A minute after he left, I was brought a shirt, trousers, towel and a bar of soap.

I had to wash in a sink, but hot water and soap did the job. Dirt and blood swirled down the plughole as I emptied the sink and refilled it again and again.

The shirt was white and fitted OK. However, the trousers needed a few more inches and I decided my grubby pair looked better than ones that revealed my socks and ankle holster.

There was a phone in the room and I picked up and asked the operator to put me through to Gillman Barracks. I spoke to Lieutenant Cole and recounted what had happened.

"Oh my God," he said when I told him about Sergeant Hegarty. "No one in the history of 200 Provo has ever been killed before."

I said, "I'm sending him back, and tell Major Vernon that Hedge deserves a commendation. There won't be much evidence left, but he helped in the destruction of an illegal alcohol and drugs factory. It was probably funding the bandits, and Hedge went into that jungle without fear."

"I'll pass it on," he agreed.

I gave him the names that Bender had provided and said I'd provide a full report when I got back. Ending the call, I asked the operator for Minden Barracks hospital.

When the call was put through to Jane Dobson, I said, "You used my government credentials when you sent the memo out."

"I'm sorry." I heard her swallow. "Are you mad at me?"

"It's fine," I said. "I'm at the KL hospital now. Unfortunately the girl has died, so I couldn't find out anything. There's also concern that maybe she was too delirious to really recognize Laura's name."

Jane said nothing.

"You said she was also transferred to JB."

202

"Monalisa? Yes. The same adoption centre."

"You didn't ask the lady—Miss Liang—there?"

"I didn't think to ask about others. I should have gone armed with the names of all the children who had been transferred. All the ones I knew of—"

"Could you get that list?"

"The guy here is a pain. And officious. Looks down his nose at the rest of us."

"Try him again. In fact, insist he gives you the list. Use my name—something you don't seem to have a problem with."

She laughed but there was little humour in it.

"Thanks, Ash. What are you doing next?"

"Back to Singapore."

The doctor returned with a piece of paper. "Got to go," I said, and I ended the call.

The doctor handed me the sign-out sheet. I saw the last name said Monalisa Cardoso, although her name was misspelled. It was today's date and just over two hours ago. There was a staff member's signature and then the signature of the person taking charge of the body. I could read neither.

I pointed to the staff member's name. "Could I speak to this person? I'd like to know more about where the girl has been taken."

"Ah, that's a problem." Doctor Meah looked awkward.

"Yes?"

"The reason I took so long coming back is because I don't recognize the name and none of the staff will admit to signing her out. I'm afraid I can't tell you where the body has gone."

The doctor apologized as he explained about the ease with which bodies could be signed out. A dead body meant having the expense of storage and disposal.

"A hospital willing to take a body? Well, we don't ask too many questions. Although we should at least know where it went."

I said, "But it was an ambulance."

"Yes. There is no way it could have been taken otherwise."

"How many ambulances will have left here in the last couple of hours?"

He shrugged. "Four, maybe five. But that's a complete guess, although one will have been yours. I understand you asked for two bodies to be transferred to BMH Alexandra."

I didn't say any more. I left the building and drove back to the entrance gates. There, I got out and questioned the guard.

"How many ambulances in the past two hours?" I asked him.

He thought for a moment. "Three. Yes, definitely three, if you include the odd one."

"The odd one?"

"Private, they said. Had the red cross but was more like a van."

My blood froze. "What colour was it?"

"Blue, sir. Dark blue."

# THIRTY-SIX

I had no idea which way the blue ambulance had gone but I put my foot down and raced along Route One. After an hour I passed a white ambulance and guessed Hegarty and Bender were on board.

I recognized where we'd come out of the jungle, Bender dying in the passenger seat, Hegarty's body rocking and bouncing about in the back.

Later, I spotted the mile marker that shouldn't have been there; the one used as a signal by the gang.

The clouds lowered and darkened. I was driving without a cover. It could rain at any moment and I'd be drenched.

I was over halfway by the time the first raindrops fell, and as soon as I spotted someone sheltering under a *Cola* tree, I decided to do the same.

The guy was a Tamil—at least that's what I figured based on his simple skirt, naked upper half and white turban. He spoke no English, but I guessed he laboured on a rubber plantation—a tapper. We sat together under the great tree and watched the rain pound the road.

It reminded me of the time below the hill to the school at Bukit Zarah. That time it had been a Malay sheltering under a similar tree because of its plate-sized leaves.

The Tamil smoked and offered me a cigarette. I don't smoke. I never have.

And then Hegarty's ambulance went past.

I accepted the cigarette and he lit it from his own. We sat with our backs to the *Cola* tree and I took a puff.

I watched the rain and I thought about Sergeant Hegarty. His birthday. Twenty-four.

I thought about his silly jokes and the way his thick eyebrows moved. I thought about his smile and good company, his fascination with phrases and his Welsh lilt that meant I was never sure if he was serious or not.

He was a real character, a nice guy and I'd miss him.

I realized he didn't deserve a medal, but his parents should be proud of their son. Unlike Bender's. I still had Bender's letter but I wouldn't post it. He didn't deserve the respect. He was also partly to blame for Hegarty's death. Of course, the other part was my fault. I didn't need a driver. I could have gone alone.

Thinking about Bender's letter made me wonder whether Hegarty had done the same. I knew he came from a little town on the Gower Peninsula, beyond Swansea, in Wales. In that moment I decided I would write to them.

The cigarette burned down. I stood up and thanked the Tamil guy. He seemed to understand and placed his hands together like a prayer for me.

It was still raining. I got into the Land Rover and drove away. The seats were already wet and getting wetter by the second, but it felt good. It felt like the rain could wash away the guilt I felt for Hegarty's death.

By the time I reached the small village where Hegarty had asked for eggs, I'd had enough of the rain.

I pulled off the road and parked next to the hut where the old man had been sitting. Two bedraggled dogs watched me as I climbed out. The chickens pecked the ground.

206

I couldn't see anyone but there was smoke coming from one of the huts. It was fairly central to the tiny kampong and twice the size of the others.

Inside, I found the whole family sitting around the edge of the room. They had bowls of soup and tea. The old man was there and he nodded to me.

I was offered tea and sat by the door.

The old man scrutinized me for a moment. "You aren't like the others," he said.

"Which others?"

He looked away and shrugged. "Not the same."

I wondered whether he meant the English generally or something more specific but couldn't get any more explanation from him.

"Thank you for the eggs and water," I said, filling the silence. "We managed to get all the way to Malacca because of you."

The old man nodded.

"You mentioned three girls," I said.

He scrutinized me again. One of the ladies said something to him and his lips tightened.

I was holding the folder from the hospital. The cover had damp patches but the contents were still dry. I took out the photograph of Monalisa Cardoso.

He took it and I saw his hand shake slightly. The woman who had spoken glanced at it and then away.

The old man said, "She is dead?"

"Yes."

"Did you kill her?"

I was horrified. "No! I was trying to find her... well, I am trying to find the other girl." I took the picture back. "I hoped this poor girl could help."

The old man narrowed his eyes, maybe assessing me.

I took out my wallet and his eyes bulged before realizing I wasn't about to hand him cash. I showed him the photograph.

"This is the girl I'm looking for," I said, pointing to Laura. "You saw three girls?"

"Yes."

"Was she one of the three you saw?"

"No."

"Are you sure?"

The old man exchanged words with the woman, who no longer appeared agitated.

I said to her, "I really need to find this girl. Her name is Laura."

The woman's accent was difficult to understand as she spoke. "They stayed here three days. Then a man came and they ran. They said they go to Penang. They very afraid of the man."

I nodded and pointed to Laura's picture. "And she definitely wasn't one of them?"

"No."

"The men that came looking. They were like me, yes? White?"

"Yes."

"Their vehicle... like mine?" I pointed to the Land Rover.

"Yes, and the other. The van."

"Van? What colour was it?"

"Blue."

"Dark blue?"

"Yes."

Traffic passed every minute or so, I figured. On average. Sometimes two or three together, sometimes nothing for five minutes. I pointed to the road. "Have you seen the blue van today?"

The man spoke to the others and I saw shaking heads.

"No."

I realized it was a long shot but I also figured these people were so used to the traffic, maybe they didn't take notice all the time.

"Did you see a white ambulance go past in the last hour?"

Again the question and the shaking heads.

Hegarty and Bender's ambulance had definitely passed here and they hadn't noticed it.

I finished my tea and thanked them. I was offered more eggs and found them pressed into my hands, unwilling to accept my refusal.

The rain hadn't eased, but I got back on the road and headed for the crossing.


I jumped the queue as I approached Customs at the northern end of the causeway. Once at the front, a Customs guy jotted something down and waved me through.

On the Singapore side, I pulled over to the guardhouse, shook off the rain and stepped inside.

"Can I help you, sir?"

I recognized the sergeant before me. I'd seen him at Woodland's crossing before.

I said, "You were here on the morning the body was found, weren't you, sergeant?"

"And you are?"

I showed him my government ID, but he already knew who I was.

I said, "Any progress at your end? Any ideas on the blue meat wagon?"

"No, sir."

"Have you seen a dark blue van or ambulance this afternoon?"

He looked uncomfortable.

"What's wrong?"

"Sir, previously you were with Lieutenant Cole…"

"And I'm working with the 200 Provost Company. What about the meat wagon or blue ambulance?"

He shook his head.

"All right, at least tell me about the timings. When the body was found… When did the crossing open and when was the body found exactly?"

"Sir," he said again, only this time there was confidence in his voice. "My orders are that this matter has been investigated and is closed. The RMP aren't investigating anymore."

I said, "But I am."

"Well, sir… Respectfully, you will need to take that up with Major Vernon."

# THIRTY-SEVEN

Still feeling frustrated, I arrived at Alexandra Hospital, where my bedraggled state drew disapproving glances. It had stopped raining but I looked like I'd just stepped out of the sea.

When I could get the receptionist to acknowledge me, I discovered that Doctor Thobhani wasn't available. I left Monalisa Cardoso's damp folder with a brief note and asked that it be passed along.

Before leaving, I confirmed that the ambulance had been and gone. Hegarty and Bender were now in the morgue.

I felt like confronting Major Vernon. After all, Gillman Barracks was but a stone's throw away. However, based on the looks I'd been given, I decided to go home and bathe and change.

By the time I arrived at Gillman I was feeling refreshed and more calm. I left the Land Rover with the motor transport boys and apologized for its condition: missing the back seat and cover, and soaked through.

As I walked into the office, I could feel the sombre mood. The air seemed heavier, thicker than usual.

The duty clerk walked me to Vernon's door, knocked and walked away.

The major stood by the window with his back to me. "What the hell do you think you were doing, Carter?"

"Doing my job."

He turned and glared at me. "And now a man is dead. One of my men is dead and it's your fault."

I said, "We found the source of the illegal alcohol and drugs. Sergeant Hegarty is a hero and I recommend him for a commendation."

Vernon's jaw rippled with tension. "One, you aren't an MP anymore so your recommendation means nothing. And two, Sergeant Hegarty was acting against orders. If he wasn't dead he would be looking at a charge right now."

I shook my head. "His last orders were to act as my driver."

"That was over a week ago!"

"The orders weren't revoked and my understanding is—"

"I don't give a bloody damn"—he was shouting now and leaning towards me, hands on the desk—"about your understanding!"

I returned his stare and counted to ten. "Why have you told the men at Woodlands Crossing that they can't talk to me?"

"This is no longer a military issue."

"But someone has been murdered."

"This is no longer a military issue," he said again as though I hadn't heard the first time, and his voice became patronizing. "You know yourself that we can't waste our time on civilian cases."

"So you've handed the case over to the police? Which jurisdiction? Singapore? Johore?"

Again he spoke with a mocking tone. "The body was on the causeway, not in Singapore. Not in Malaya. I can see that I need to spell it out: military jurisdiction. No one is interested."

"I'm interested."

He scoffed. "Get out, Carter. And don't think you've heard the last of this. Secretary Coates will get a full report from me... and this time it won't be so glowing."

I walked out and left his door wide open.

Lieutenant Cole was waiting for me and accompanied me down the drive.

I said, "I'll write everything up for you."

"I heard Vernon refuse Hedge a commendation."

I nodded. "Any news on the meat wagon?"

"It's over, Ash. There's no point—"

"It's not over. The start of this was the body. It led to the drugs and five military personnel dealing. And because of Hedge's help it uncovered the source and stopped it."

Cole said nothing.

I said, "It's not over and I feel I owe it to Hedge."

We reached the barrier and he placed a hand on it.

I looked back at the office and could feel Vernon watching us. "The body," I said. "It was the start and yet seems unconnected. And Vernon thinks it's unconnected."

I thought I heard Cole sigh. I turned and looked into his eyes. "What?"

He shook his head. After a pause he signalled for the guard to raise the barrier. I walked under it. He stayed put but his next words stopped me in my tracks.

"Oh, did you hear about the incident at Tebrau?"

"No."

"A plane exploded after take-off. I think it was that pilot you were interested in."

"Jeevan?"

"That's the fellow."

I flagged down a taxi and left Cole watching as we sped away.

213

Squadron Leader Kennedy was in his office, head in hands. He looked up as I entered and his weary eyes seemed to have aged ten years since I was last here.

"What happened?" I asked.

"We don't know, and I have never had anything like this happen on my watch before. Never."

Turner came in and shook my hand. He looked even more pale than the squadron leader. "Awful," he said, "just awful."

"What happened?" I asked again.

"He took off, got to about a thousand feet and it exploded. Poor bugger didn't stand a chance."

"Anything flammable in the cargo?"

"Nothing according to the manifest."

"Where was he headed?"

"Seletar. It's in the north-east."

"Fuel issue?"

Kennedy said, "That's all we can think of. But there were no problems in fuelling her. A blockage or leak maybe. We just don't know."

Turner nodded. "And we've checked all of our Austers and there isn't a problem."

"Just a freak accident," Kennedy said, lowering his eyes. He seemed to switch off for a while, staring at the papers on his desk.

"Just a goddamned freak." Turner looked at me. "How did you get on... you know... questioning him?"

"I didn't get the chance," I said, now regretting that I'd planned to catch him in Penang.

"And how is your investigation going?"

"We traced the source of the drugs. It was a Chinese gang operating in the jungle south of KL."

The squadron leader looked up from his desk again and reached out to shake my hand. "Good," he said, though I don't think he'd been listening. "If there's anything more…"

Turner added, "Just ask. Happy to help in any way."

Both men forced smiles as I left and I asked the taxi driver to take me to the camp at Ulu Tiram.

The sun tried a final valiant effort to break through the clouds before giving up close to the treeline.

"Drop me here," I instructed the driver, and I signed a chitty so that he could reclaim the fare. Then I walked up the sandy track into the Kota Tinggi camp.

# THIRTY-EIGHT

There was a buzz in the canteen that made a welcome distraction from my solemn mood. Scott Stevenson sat opposite me and ate dinner.

I'd told him what had happened, how we'd followed the Bedford into the jungle and been ambushed by the gang.

"The boys didn't know," he said, fixing me with his one good eye so that I'd know he was being honest. "They really just made the switch. The Chinese took our lorry and we took the spare one back—and never with anything other than the hooch. Trust me."

"I do."

"And we never knew where their factory was. Each time it was a different meeting place."

I said, "How did Jeevan fit in, really?"

Stevenson shook his head. "Seriously, he didn't. I told you he'd been busted out of Fleet Air Arm and he didn't really fit in. Partly that and partly because of his colour."

"Why was he busted out of Fleet Air Arm? You didn't tell me that before."

"Something happened in Changi. He claimed he took the fall for someone else but wouldn't say. I think he was partly afraid."

"And the other part?"

"Money. I was suspicious he got paid off. Paid to keep quiet."

I ate in silence for a minute, processing the information.

Stevenson said, "What was the link to the headless body?"

"I don't know."

He looked at me surprised. "But I thought..."

"Precisely." I then told him about the blue van and blue ambulance and my visit to the Kuala Lumpur hospital." It was good to talk it through, although I was still no closer to making sense of it.

He said, "Aren't you suspicious that the meat wagon and the ambulance might be one and the same?"

"Absolutely! I don't like coincidences."

"Why would a private hospital send an ambulance to collect that girl?"

I finished my meal and set down the cutlery. "I don't know," I said, but my mind was whirring.

He said, "If the meat wagon was actually an ambulance, then..."

"Customs definitely said meat wagon... but not butcher's van. Wouldn't that be the usual expression? Meat wagon sounds like a vehicle that you wouldn't expect meat in."

"Like an ambulance."

I shook my head, "But then they'd have said ambulance and the old man in the jungle said blue van not ambulance." The girl was somehow connected to the body on the causeway, that's what my back brain was processing. But how?

The last vestiges of the sunset left a purple glow in the west. I hitched a ride in a troop carrier back to Orchard

Road, where they turned right towards Tanglin Barracks. I hailed a trishaw and headed for Alexandra Hospital.

This time, the good doctor was available, although he apologized that he only had a minute.

"I'm sorry about your friend," he said.

I hadn't thought of Hegarty as my friend before, but Thobhani was right. There weren't many people I thought of as friends but likely lad Hegarty should be counted among them.

"He died instantly," I said. "So we can be thankful for small mercies."

"Indeed, but you aren't here to talk about him, no?"

"The girl. Did you get a chance to look at her file?"

"She was malnourished and severely underweight but died of typhoid. Who was she?"

I knew he didn't mean her name, so I said, "I don't know. I think she's important but..."

"Important to what?"

"Connected somehow to the body on the causeway." I shook my head. "Do you know of any private ambulances that are dark blue?"

"No, but then I can't say I know of any private hospitals. Then again I'm army, and like most army men I keep my head down and do my job."

"That's kind of what Major Vernon wants."

"I get it," he said.

I, on the other hand, didn't get it. Investigation was in my blood. I was no longer RMP but I would always be a detective. Surely Vernon should feel the same way? Then again, he was never Special Investigations Branch, so maybe he didn't. Maybe he really thought the job was about keeping the regular soldiers in line. The difference between us, the difference between regular police and a detective.

I switched back to Monalisa Cardoso and said, "What about poisoning? Apparently the girl kept talking about a poison flower."

He shook his head. "There's nothing in the file… Without a full autopsy I couldn't…"

I nodded. Of course not. But he hadn't finished.

"But there's something else. I don't know if it's relevant, and it's not in the notes… which doesn't surprise me. It's sensitive and I think some hospitals have a policy on being discreet."

A nurse called him and he said he had to go.

I gripped his arm. "Quickly. What is it?"

"From the photographs," he said. "A young girl like that… it could be put down to early… you know… activity but I think it was worse."

The nurse called him again, concern in her voice.

"Doc, what are you saying?"

"Early sexual activity. But I think it's more likely sexual abuse," he said, turning to run. "I'd bet my meagre pay packet on it."

# THIRTY-NINE

I considered telling Jane but then dismissed the idea. She'd put two and two together. Anyone would. Monalisa was being abused, Monalisa and Laura were transferred to Johor Bahru and so Laura was being abused. I thought back to my meeting with the doctor at the KL hospital. He had seemed awkward. He'd wanted to tell me but maybe policy or decency had prevented him.

By the morning, I'd decided to say nothing. But that isn't the same as doing nothing. Ordinarily Hegarty would have driven me, and I thought of him as I travelled in the back of a taxi.

The adoption centre in Johor Bahru was just opening as I arrived. Miss Liang stood at the door and I could see worry on her face.

Without preamble, I said, "Where's Petersen?"

She walked into her office and sat behind the desk, like she wanted a defensive barrier between us.

Her face was set firm now. "I told you before that I don't know. He left this place in a mess."

"Monalisa Cardoso…" I said, leaning over the table.

She moved back. "Not a name I know."

"Why not? She was also transferred here from Penang."

"We can go through the books—like we did for that other girl."

"Laura van Loon."

Miss Laing masked it well, but her eyes told me she had remembered the name before I said it.

"Why are you here?" she asked.

"Tell me what's going on. Tell me about the girls."

"I'm not telling you anything. You work for Andrew Yipp. You know what's going on at the hospital."

One of Sun Tzu's sayings came to mind: *attack is the secret of defence*. I thought about what Lady Hage-Dando had said.

"The sale of babies," I said, like I knew.

She just looked at me with hard eyes. Her diminutive body seemed to expand, like she wanted a confrontation.

I said, "Tell me."

"Ask Andrew Yipp."

A long silence between us told me I was getting no more on the subject so I switched back. "The girls were transferred here," I said, as though I knew this too. "Where did they go?"

She said nothing.

"Where is the private hospital—the one with the blue ambulance?"

No response.

"Has Petersen got something to do with this?"

"Go!" she said, and I could almost taste the venom. And that was it. I tried more questions and got nothing in return.

As I travelled back to Singapore I was cross with myself for thinking I could make Miss Liang talk. She knew what was going on, I was sure of it. I also thought about the adoption department at the Johor Bahru hospital—the Sultana Aminah—and of Andrew Yipp.

221

Was Miss Liang guilty of something or was she afraid to talk? Was she afraid of Yipp?

We approached the city and I instructed the driver to drop me at the Cathay Building. I travelled up to the twelfth floor and asked to see the Chinese businessman.

Su Ling came out to see me. Her eyes were cold and formal. "He's busy," she said.

"I need to see him."

"You are forgetting your manners, Captain Carter." Only Andrew Yipp called me by my old rank and it felt wrong now hearing it from the woman who had once been my lover.

I said, "Would you be so kind as to ask your esteemed employer if he would meet with me." It was over the top but she accepted it and told me to wait by the Padang.

"The bench outside St Andrew's Cathedral," she added.

I knew which one she meant. I also knew I could be waiting a long time. Which was fine providing it didn't rain.

An hour passed. There was a rugby match at the sports field end and it provided a distraction. They were by no means professional and it reminded me of my schoolboy days. Rugby in the autumn meant wet ground and a plastering of mud. At least that was preferable to frozen ground and hard impacts.

A pale blue Bentley caught my eye as it drove past. It was pre-war and in great condition. It was also one of Yipp's fleet. It turned the corner into Coleman Street and was out of sight around the cathedral.

I got up and walked to the junction. The Bentley was parked a short distance ahead. The rear door opened.

Like before, I expected Wang would drive me somewhere to meet Yipp, but I was wrong. Yipp was in the back of the car.

I closed the door behind me and the Bentley pulled away.

I nodded to the businessman, remembering my manners this time. There was nothing to be gained by confrontation.

"I am grateful for your intervention in Malaya," I said.

"I am not your enemy," he said, as he had told me before.

I wanted to say, "But we both know that the gang could have been your rivals." They were Yipp's enemy. Instead I nodded and said, "It is better to capture an entire army than destroy it."

He nodded, recognizing Sun Tzu.

I continued: "It would have been beneficial if some of the gang had been spared. They could have provided valuable information. They may have had connections with the communists."

He shook his head, a wan smile on his lips.

I said, "But Sun Tzu..."

"Captain Carter, you are naïve. Of course Sun Tzu's words are incredibly wise and a strategist would be a fool to ignore them. However, there are other wisdoms in the world."

I waited for him to explain. Through the window I saw we had left the city and were heading east.

He said, "Who defeated the great Chinese empire?"

"The Mongols."

"A young man called Temujin. If I find a serpent's nest and cut off the head of a few, what do I have left?"

"A serpent's nest."

He nodded. "And in time it will grow and be stronger. Temujin defeated the Chinese because he believed in total annihilation. At least that's how it seemed. He knew it was about the spirit. As his army swept through the

223

Great Wall and into the villages, his men killed everyone. Except one. That survivor would be sent to the next village, not to warn them, you understand, but to instil fear in their hearts. A man who is afraid will lose a fight."

I appreciated that from boxing. Respect for your opponent was one thing, but if you feared him, you would undoubtedly lose. I knew it was why Slugger Stevenson had tried to intimidate me before our bout. It was the same principal whether Slugger knew it or not.

Yipp continued: "Eventually the enemy did not fight Temujin's army and he became one of the greatest leaders the word has ever known."

"Genghis Khan," I said.

"Annihilation is a tool, a means to an end. Genghis Khan won the ultimate victory. Measured by population, he ruled the largest empire in the history of mankind. Greater than the British Empire." He paused. "Sun Tzu was correct. The greatest victory requires no battle, however this does not mean that this is achieved without extreme actions beforehand."

"I understand," I said. "But then let us not pretend that you did this for me."

For a moment I thought I'd offended him with my directness, but then he laughed. Then he spoke to the chauffeur and the car turned around, returning to the city.

To me he said, "This wasn't what you wanted to talk to me about, was it, Captain?"

"I need to understand what is going on."

He waited for my explanation.

"The body on the causeway, the missing girls... the private hospital."

"Private hospital?"

I told him about the blue ambulance and the girl in Kuala Lumpur.

224

He shook his head.

"Please tell me about the hospital in Johor Bahru. What is your interest there?"

"The Sultana Aminah Hospital. I am a patron," he said, confirming what Su Ling had told me.

"Women are paid and their babies taken away."

He studied my eyes for a moment and I thought he wasn't going to comment, but he did. "A service," he said.

"A business."

"Of course it is a business, but these women do not want those babies and there are wealthy families in Singapore who do."

"And are willing to pay for the privilege."

"Of course. It is not illegal, you understand."

"Is the private hospital connected in some way?"

Again he held my gaze and I believed him when he said, "I do not know of this private hospital."

We re-entered the city: the shanty town, the industrial sector, the shop-houses, the offices and hotels, and finally the colonial centre.

"Just tell me one thing," I said as we stopped beside the cathedral. "Where does Miss Liang fit in?"

He frowned and considered his response. "She used to be at the Sultana Aminah. I think she disapproved of the service."

"And her connection to the missing girls?"

He shook his head. "I cannot help you."

As I watched the Bentley drive away, I realized Miss Liang had been very clever. She had not only used attack as a form of defence but misdirected me. I knew then that I needed to go back armed with the full list of children transferred to the adoption centre.

* * *

I rang Jane from the office and had to wait until she was free to speak.

"Did you get the list of names?" I asked.

"No."

"You used my name and position?"

"He was uncomfortable. He's normally so dopey but that really riled him and he got aggressive. He said you didn't have any authority."

That rang a bell. "Dopey, you said? What's his name?"

"Lipscombe. Richard Lipscombe, I think. But everyone calls him Lippy."

# FORTY

I told Jane that I'd be in Penang as soon as I could. Without bothering to go home and pack, I just got in a taxi and headed for Woodlands Crossing.

Like the day before, I directed the driver up Route Three to Tebrau airfield.

"You said you'd do anything to help," I said to Flight Lieutenant Turner when I arrived.

He looked surprised and uncertain. "Yes?"

"You have my authority to fly the Dinah. Get her ready, I'd like you to fly me to Penang."

He disappeared inside to tell Squadron Leader Kennedy and was longer than I expected.

"Filing the flight plans," he said when he emerged. "And Alex is fine with it."

After giving the ground crew instructions, we had to wait for the plane to be pulled out of the hangar and prepared. And finally we were taxiing and punching a hole through the clouds.

We didn't speak much, and I watched the vast jungle bubble and swell beneath us. The light bled from the sky and it was dark when we finally touched down.

Jane was waiting. She ran from the office block and leapt at me, wrapping her arms around me so tightly that I could hardly breathe.

I thanked Turner and asked if he'd fly me back in the morning. He'd told me he didn't like flying over the jungle in the dark so I knew he'd stay over.


Early evening and the hospital at Minden Barracks was still busy. However, the adoption centre was locked up. Jane said she'd seen Lipscombe leave the barracks just after six and he wasn't expected back until his office opened at nine.

In a taxi she asked me for more details about Monalisa. After I told her what I knew, she said, "Before we eat, I'd like to speak to the doctor at the Alexandra."

"Of course," I said, although my voice betrayed my uncertainty.

"I need to know," she said. "How sure is he? If Monalisa was abused"—she had difficulty even saying it—"then how likely is it that Laura was too?"

There was no point in me commenting. Doctor Thobhani couldn't express a view on Laura's condition and what Jane needed was a hundred percent confirmation of abuse.

She found an office and I picked up the phone and asked for the Singapore hospital and then the doctor.

"Sorry, I was so rushed earlier," Thobhani said when he came on the line.

I explained that Jane wanted to hear about Monalisa and I handed him over. Jane listened and asked questions and listened. Eventually she said, "So you're sure." And then: "Thank you."

She handed the phone back to me.

"Sorry," he said. "I told her as gently as I could. She's all right, no?"

228

I thanked him for his help, but before I put the phone down, he said, "Is this connected? I meant to ask you earlier but, you know, I was needed…"

"Connected?" I wondered which piece he was thinking about.

"To the letters RZ?"

"Pardon?"

"RZ. You know, the letters on the cadaver on the causeway." His voice trailed off. "You didn't know?"

"Tell me."

"I told Lieutenant Cole. It wasn't 221. To be honest I never really saw that myself. Cole didn't tell you?"

"What did you tell him?"

"Well you know it was written in blood. By a finger I think. But I don't think it was originally 221. It was like the letters had been written, washed off, and the numbers gone over the top. Like I said, I wasn't so sure, so I used ultraviolet light. It did look a bit like 221, but upside down. The number 21 looks like a broken R, no? When I got a close look I could see the fainter areas. And it wasn't a 2 but more like a Z. Yes, it had definitely been RZ. Is it connected?"

"I don't know," I said.

"And there's the other marks."

"Tell me."

"Again they must have been washed off, but there were two chevrons—you know, arrows—one up and one down."

"Meaning?"

"I have no idea, you're the detective. But I can tell you they were also washed off."

"Could it have been natural—water from the straits?"

"Not a chance," he said. "My opinion, for what it's worth, is that someone tried to remove both and deliberately tried to make RZ look like 221."

"And you told this to Lieutenant Cole?"

"Yes."

I ended the call frustrated that Cole hadn't told me. RZ was clearly important, and it looked like 221 had been a diversion. What did RZ mean? Could it be the initials of the dead man? And then there were the arrows.

Jane was looking at me quizzically.

I shook my head. Too many unknowns.

"Let's eat," I said.

We went to Tucker's and ate the same meat and bread meal we'd had before. We sat side by side and talked and I went over everything again. It had only been ten days but it seemed an age. So much had happened: following the aid truck, Hegarty dying beside me, capture by the Chinese gang and the subsequent rescue by Yipp's men.

"Was it worth it?" she asked.

"My friend getting killed in exchange for stopping the alcohol and drugs trade? Definitely not."

She hugged me then and we sat in silence for a while. I could see lights dancing on the water of the straits. Given a bottle of wine, I think I could have finished it easily, but we'd agreed to stick to water.

When we started talking again it was about what I'd found out at the hospital, that Monalisa had been with two other girls. She'd recognized Laura's name apparently but that couldn't be verified. She'd also repeatedly referred to poison flowers and yet there was no evidence of poisoning.

Jane wanted to hear about the private ambulance and the mystery of who had signed out the body and where it had been taken.

I told her about the villagers who had seen Monalisa and two other girls but were sure Laura wasn't one of them.

"The blue van again," Jane said.

"Too much of a coincidence," I said.

She wanted details of my second meeting with Miss Liang and how she had deflected me back to Andrew Yipp.

"She's clever," Jane said.

"Or scared."

Jane checked her watch. It was just before the hospital went into night-mode at ten. That meant reduced staff and reduced lighting.

"Still too early," I said.

"We should wait a few more hours," she said. "We should get some rest."

I didn't have officer's quarters arranged this time so we snuck into her small room. We lay in each other's arms on her single bed.

We kissed and talked about trivial things.

She said, "I don't do sad sex."

I held her closer and said I understood.

An hour later she'd torn my clothes off and decided it wouldn't be sad sex after all.


At three in the morning, feeling refreshed and more positive, we snuck back out of her dormitory. We walked into the hospital and up a flight of stairs and along two corridors and passed no one.

As expected, the adoption centre door was locked.

I checked left and right and barged it with my shoulder. The door jamb splintered and we slipped inside.

For a few beats we listened in case someone investigated the sound. But no one came.

Jane switched on the light.

It was a cramped room with a small window. There was a desk, a filing cabinet and a storage cupboard. I opened the cupboard and saw that it was stacked with children's clothes. Donations, I figured.

When I turned back, Jane was already forcing open the filing cabinet. It had four deep drawers and each was packed with hanging files. Each hanging file had a child's details.

They were in alphabetical order and Jane checked both V and L before declaring that Laura's file wasn't there. Monalisa's file wasn't there either.

"There will be a record somewhere," I said.

There was a draw in the desk and I kicked it open. Inside I found a ledger. It was similar to the one I'd seen at the adoption centre in Johor Bahru—the one Miss Liang had shown me the first time. That book hadn't had Laura's name in it, however this one did. There was a date of arrival and a date of transfer. Seven weeks ago she'd transferred to JBAC—Johor Bahru Adoption Centre.

It was just like the other children. A date in and a date out. Only Laura's record was different. Against the entry was a faint tick. I found the entry for Monalisa Cardoso. Transferred to JBAC eighteen months ago. Tick.

In a list of maybe a hundred names there were twenty-two with ticks. All girls. None of them had an Asian name.

"All mixed-race," Jane said.

"Looks that way."

"So, what now?"

I sat in the chair and put my feet on the desk. "Now I wait," I said. "He's coming back to get this ledger and I'll be here to greet him."

# FORTY-ONE

I persuaded Jane to go back to bed and get some sleep. I waited until I was sure she'd gone before I picked up the telephone. For the early hours of the morning, the operator was far too perky. Perhaps my call had broken the monotony of the night. She was called Deborah and said she enjoyed working nights.

We chatted briefly and then I asked her to place two calls, one to Gillman Barracks and the second to the Kota Tinggi camp. There was a process at Gillman for night calls and I wasn't kept waiting long before Lieutenant Cole came on the phone.

I talked and he listened and agreed.

My second call was more frustrating. It took Stevenson over half an hour before he spoke on the other end.

Deborah kept asking if I wanted to keep holding. I said I did. She said, "You have a nice voice."

"So do you," I said.

"Are you single?"

"Yes."

"But you are probably short and fat, right?"

"And ugly," I said.

"Just my type, then," she said, and we both laughed. Then she switched back to her professional voice and said, "Connecting you."

Stevenson's voice was instantly on the line. "No one calls us at night," he grumbled.

I said, "You want to help?"

"Do you think I can get my two men out of clink?"

"They were trading in illegal alcohol."

"But they were just driving that time. We're all involved."

I thought it over for a moment before saying, "I'll see what I can do, but this is linked to Jeevan's death."

"You think he was murdered?"

"I'm sure of it."

"Then I'm in. What do you want me to do?"

"Just meet me at RAF Changi in the morning."

Stevenson ended the call and Deborah said, "Anything else?"

"No," I said and thanked her.

She said, "Anytime, sweetheart. You know how to reach me."

I resumed my pose, feet on the desk, leaning back, and closed my eyes. I figured I could sleep for a few hours before anything happened. However, with too much going on in my head, I gave up after an hour and a half. I left the office light on and went outside.

The clouds had gone and the night sky stretched spectacularly overhead. Cassiopeia and Perseus were bright but I could see faint constellations that I could never see from my home in Singapore.

Since I had time to kill, I decided to walk the three miles into George Town and enjoy the majesty of the early hours.

When I arrived at the port I found the port security office and was offered a chair and a cup of tea. I had over two hours before the first ferry left. The office was warm and the chair comfortable. Within minutes I must have been asleep.

Richard Lipscombe waited until an hour before dawn before moving. He'd pulled the files of the girls and destroyed them but he'd forgotten the summary ledger.

When he arrived outside the hospital he realized the office light was on. Someone was up there. Probably the Singapore government guy. He'd find the evidence, which was bad, but at least he was here.

Must be waiting for me, Lipscombe thought. *Good.*

Instead of returning to the main gate, he cut across the base towards the trees on the perimeter. From there, getting onto the road was simple.

He came out about four hundred yards from the main gate. As he glanced that way, he watched a six-wheel Austin Gantry pull out and turn towards him. It would be heading for George Town and the ferry, and it would provide the perfect cover.

He flagged the truck as it approached.

"Room for one more?" Lipscombe asked as it slowed.

The driver nodded and Lipscombe headed for the rear. Hands reached down and hauled him inside. There was plenty of room since the Austin Gantry could comfortably cope with twelve men, probably more. Lipscombe manoeuvred to a seat and counted figures in the dim light.

Although he could barely see, he nodded to the soldier sitting opposite.

"Where you headed?"

"Just west of Betong," the guy replied. "There's a bridge out that we've got to repair by tomorrow. Fat chance of that!"

They were sappers—engineers, which made sense since the engineers tended to use the four-wheel-drive Austin Gantry Trucks for towing and lifting.

235

Lipscombe had planned to catch the train in Butterworth and head south. Now he considered staying with the engineers; it would be dangerous but he could go north through Thailand.

"Perfect," Lipscombe said, and settled back.

They made good progress for ten minutes before he felt them slow. He figured they'd reached the main congested streets of George Town. Soon after, he smelled rotten fish and the diesel from the docks. They slowed more and then stopped.

They'd be in the queue for the ferry now.

Nothing happened for a good quarter of an hour except it got lighter and the noise outside increased.

Eventually the rear flap lifted and a face appeared.

"Sorry lads, there appears to be a hold-up."

Men grumbled and Lipscombe asked, "What do you mean?"

"A hold-up. I don't know. We just aren't moving, OK?"

Lipscombe didn't need to hear any more. He pushed back to the tailgate and climbed out. Peering around the truck he saw that the ferry was docked and some vehicles had boarded. The Austin Gantry was only a hundred yards short of the barrier but it was down.

He spotted the other queues, one just with pedestrians and bicycles and one with animals and carts. Neither of these was being held up.

There was no sign of Carter. Maybe this delay was just routine.

The barrier raised and the vehicles started to load again.

Lipscombe made a quick decision. He walked smartly away from the cover of the truck and headed for the pedestrian line. Ten strides later and the realization struck him. Vehicles were being checked on board the ferry. If he got on then he'd be trapped. If Carter was around, maybe that's what he was planning.

The smart move would be to wait, sit it out and catch another ferry.

Lipscombe turned sharply away and kept his head down. He glanced casually about as he walked away from the port. At first he used the cover of trucks and people and then he cut away and pushed between pots and fishing nets until he reached the first godown. Now he had good cover. He looked back towards the port. There were people everywhere but no one seemed to take any notice of him.

There was a fish market beyond the godowns and he headed straight across it. After the market the town began. He reached a building that had a shaded corner and hesitated. He looked back.

No one there.

Then a woman's voice, close by and intense with emotion, said, "You bastard!"

As he swivelled back, the last thing he saw was a metal pole as it crashed into his face.

# FORTY-TWO

I didn't see Lipscombe get out of the Austin Gantry but I figured that was where he'd come from. He first headed towards the ferry and then stopped mid-step.

He turned, made his way out of the docks and I tracked him all the way. At the godowns I almost lost him as I moved parallel. He disappeared between them and it was only when he crossed the fish market that I knew I had him again.

He made good progress without being too obvious. His only failing was to assume I'd be behind. And then he stopped. Rather than enter the shadow of a building, he swung around and then back.

As soon as I saw the pole hit him, I started to run.

Jane stood over the prone body, ready to strike again.

"Jane! Stop!"

She looked at me. The pole shook because of the adrenaline.

Her pause gave me time to reach her and grab the pole.

She let out a breath, her eyes wide.

"I... I was going to kill him."

"I guessed."

Lipscombe started to groan. I bent down, confirmed the injury above his eye wasn't life-threatening, and slapped on handcuffs.

Jane's eyes were still staring. I wrapped my arms around her and felt the aggression slowly ease away. I felt her tears on my neck.

"I'm sorry I didn't tell you," I said.

"I guessed. I realized you wouldn't wait for him at the hospital. It was too risky."

"I figured he'd try and catch the first ferry off the island."

She said, "I was waiting outside the barracks. I saw him get in a lorry and had my taxi follow. I wanted him on his own... I was going to kill him."

Lipscombe started to rise and I put my foot on his back to stop him. I thought of sending her away before interrogating him but changed my mind.

I said, "Bring the metal rod. If he doesn't tell us what we want to know, you can break his legs."

I pulled him to his feet and into the shadows. There was a locked door in the building's wall and I kicked it open. We went in and Jane found a light.

It was a kitchen, probably for a restaurant. There were benches and sinks and metal utensils hanging from hooks.

I pushed Lipscombe against a bench, where he squatted, his eyes bulging with fear.

"Tell me what's going on," I began.

Lipscombe swallowed but said nothing.

I nodded at Jane and she raised the pole.

He said, "I just supply the girls."

"To order?"

"Yes."

I said, "Who to? Who are you supplying?"

Jane twitched the pole.

Lipscombe looked at me and then Jane. "I don't know."

"Of course you do."

239

He swallowed. "I just liaised with the pilot."

"The pilot?"

"Jeevan," he said after a hesitation. "The pilot from the humanitarian aid unit at Kota Tinggi. I gave him details. He confirmed the Man wanted them. I did the paperwork. He took them."

Jane said, "Is Laura alive?"

"I don't know what happens to them."

"They go to the adoption centre in Johor Bahru."

"That's what I'm told."

I said, "Who's *the Man*?"

Lipscombe said nothing.

To Jane I said, "Break his right leg."

She took up position, lined up the pole and drew the backswing.

Lipscombe bit his lip and closed his eyes. Jane struck his thigh. It wasn't hard enough to break a leg and certainly not on his thigh. I'd figured her blood lust must have eased and it had. But the blow must have hurt.

I said, "Who's the Man?"

He said, "He'll kill me. I can't talk."

"I'll protect you."

His eyes looked pleading for a second. "You can't help me."

I thought about the warning I'd received. The one at the hotel. "Is the Man Chinese?"

"I'm not telling you anything."

"Is it Andrew Yipp?"

He said nothing.

"Is it Petersen?"

He looked at me with hard eyes, like he was assessing how much I really knew.

"What's Yiqing Liang's role?"

He looked away.

I said, "The girls ran away. Monalisa Cardoso is dead. The others are probably dead."

Lipscombe looked shocked. "I didn't know. Honestly. I just send the girls to the adoption centre."

"To Petersen."

"I guess. I don't know what happens after they leave."

Jane said, "For God's sake, you know it's not innocent!"

Lipscombe dropped his head, couldn't make eye contact with her.

I said, "Who was the body on the crossing?"

He shook his head. No idea.

"What does RZ mean?"

"I don't know."

"Is it someone's name?"

"I don't know."

"Is it a warning?"

"I don't know." He was almost in tears now. There was nothing left. No fight, no lies, just an obstinate refusal to tell us.

We tried more questions and threats but learned nothing more. Lipscombe was genuinely terrified.

I dragged him out into the sunlight and we marched him to the port security office where I got an MP to take us to the airport.

Turner jumped up when we pulled outside the office block. He stared long and hard, eyes as wide as saucers.

"You've got him," he said.

"We're taking him back to Singapore. You and me."

"What's he said?"

I shook my head. "Best we don't talk about it. Have the Dinah prepared and log a flight to RAF Changi."

Turner stared at me.

I said, "Don't worry. I've cleared it for you to fly the Dinah. You won't get in trouble but you will have to

241

leave it there for scrapping, like it should have been years ago."

Turner scurried away and I pushed my captive to the floor, where he sat, head down.

Jane said, "So you really are excluding me again."

We'd already talked about this in the Land Rover. I'd told her I was flying back with Lipscombe. She wanted to come with me but I just couldn't do it. However much I'd like her company, her emotion would get in the way. She'd almost lost it near the fish market. Lipscombe could be dead already.

There was another reason. I didn't want to risk Jane's life. Lipscombe was terrified of someone and that meant someone who wasn't afraid to kill. I suspected he was responsible for the body on the causeway and Jeevan's death. In addition, I'd already lost Hegarty and I didn't want to risk losing Jane.

We talked about it again and I asked her forgiveness.

She shook her head and fixed me with her eyes. Finally, I think she could see I wasn't changing my mind and she reluctantly nodded.

Her kiss on my cheek told me she was still mad, but she accepted she wasn't coming.

"Find Laura," she said, looking away and then back. Her voice became harder. "And if someone *has* hurt her, I want you to make them pay. Do that for me."

"I will."

# FORTY-THREE

I said I wasn't going to talk about the case and Turner didn't ask me anything. I sat in the co-pilot's seat again and Lipscombe was handcuffed behind us. There was another seat but I made him sit on the hard floor. It only seemed fair.

I closed my eyes and used the time to think. The 370-mile flight south passed quickly and we were soon descending into Changi.

There were two Land Rovers parked near the runway and I saw the way Turner looked at them.

"Taxi away," I said, pointing. "Let's go over there."

Turner frowned but complied.

As the engines died, I said, "Are you RZ?"

"Pardon?"

"I know, Robin, so just answer the question before the MPs get here."

He unclipped and placed his hand on the hatch lever. I pulled out my gun.

"You aren't going anywhere."

"How did you know?" He glanced behind at Lipscombe. Yet more confirmation.

I said, "Jeevan was just a patsy, wasn't he? He was a misdirection, just like implying that you favoured men. How could I suspect a homosexual man could be involved with teenage girls?"

He said nothing.

"Jeevan's plane could have taken a girl in the cargo but it would have been cramped and I think someone would have noticed. The Dinah is much bigger. You probably even let the unsuspecting girl have the navigator's seat."

Turner looked out of the window. He could see the Land Rovers approaching and the MPs' red caps.

I said, "But the real indictment was the flight records. I don't think Jeevan's showed any deviations until after I'd visited. You had access to the logs and you edited them. You set him up again to ensure the focus wasn't on you."

"Circumstantial evidence at best!"

"But we both know it's true. And then you killed him."

Turner's eyes implored me to believe him. "I didn't. Honestly!"

The MPs were outside now. Waiting.

"Are you RZ?" I asked again.

"No!"

"But RZ is the Man, isn't he?"

Turner nodded.

I swivelled and looked at Lipscombe. "Is Turner the Man? You don't need to be afraid of him now." I didn't think so, but I had to ask.

Lipscombe shook his head.

I hadn't thought so but could have been deceived by Turner's friendship. He'd known which hotel I was staying in, so he either left the warning or told someone else.

I said, "Where did you take the girls?"

"A tiny airfield north of JB."

"Who met you?"

I signalled to the MPs and the hatch opened. Lieutenant Cole climbed in and I asked him to remove Lipscombe.

When they had climbed out, I pointed my gun at Turner, the muzzle close to his temple.

He closed his eyes, a long slow blink, preparing himself.

I said, "Just an accident. Like Jeevan's crash."

He shook his head with resignation. "It wasn't me."

"I've been debating whether to hand you over to the MPs or Slugger Stevenson. I'll tell him you killed Jeevan and you won't last five minutes when he gets his hands on you."

Turner shook his head, defeated.

I needed information and I wasn't getting it. So I tried a different tack and lowered the gun.

I said, "Tell me about Jeevan. What happened here and why was he drummed out of Fleet Air Arm?"

"You know what happened. He was suspected of smuggling."

"Right," I said, bluffing because I hadn't known the reason.

"They needed a pilot for the aid unit so he took that."

"You're forgetting your part in that." Turner had said he wanted to fly Spits at Changi but was stuck in the training corps. My call to the RAF at Changi had told me a different story. Turner had flown at Changi and volunteered for Tebrau shortly after Jeevan had left. He'd deliberately switched to the FTC."

Turner looked awkward.

I said, "He took the fall for you, didn't he?"

"Yes."

"What were you smuggling?"

"Just contraband at that point. Not much, just enough to see us by. But also enough to get us into trouble. He

245

was caught and said it was just him. You see, I had to make it up to him."

"So you found a way to earn more money. You helped transport the girls."

He looked down. "They weren't so young at first."

"But still, they didn't know what was in store for them."

He said nothing.

"And when I got too close, you killed him."

His eyes said otherwise. "No! I wouldn't do that."

"But you altered the flight details that implicated him."

"I panicked. I thought it would help you focus on the aid unit and what they were doing. You'd soon realize it couldn't be Niroj in his Auster and I knew he could cope."

"Is the squadron leader involved in this?"

He scoffed. "What, and murder my friend? Not a chance. No, Alex is innocent. He's a good guy."

"All right, so who's the bad guy?"

Turner clammed up again. I'd been doing so well but he just refused to say.

I raised the gun again. "Who is the Man?"

He shook his head. "Shoot me or hand me over to the MPs. Make your choice."

We sat in a tense silence for a moment. He was afraid of the gun but more afraid to talk. I'd assumed that Turner had been responsible for Jeevan's death. But now I had it. Jeevan was killed as another warning.

I said, "The Man killed Jeevan, didn't he?"

Turner nodded.

"A warning to you, so that you wouldn't talk?"

"Everyone is afraid of him. They say he's evil."

"Who is he? Come on, Robin, it's just you and me now. The Man killed your friend, for God's sake."

246

"I mean, I'd like to tell you, I just can't."

"Why not?"

"Because I never met him."

"But you dealt with someone."

"Petersen."

"He's the man who took the girls from you?"

"Yes," he said. "Petersen was my contact."

"And where is Petersen?"

"I don't know."

"I'm sick of people claiming they don't know. Frankly I don't believe you." I looked out of the window. "Maybe I should hand you over to Slugger Stevenson."

"I'll tell you one thing. If I give you some information I want your protection, OK?"

I raised my eyebrows and waited.

He said, "The airfield. Find that and you'll find the Man's plane. If he tries to run for it, he'll use that plane." And then he described where I'd find the airfield.

247

# FORTY-FOUR

The Land Rovers took both prisoners away but I asked Cole to stay with me. I was just starting to think that Stevenson had let me down when he arrived in one of the humanitarian aid Land Rovers.

"You're late," I said.

"Better late than never," he said with a grunt. "Now, who murdered my man Jeevan?"

"I'll tell you on the way."

I pointed to the passenger seat and asked Cole to get in. I sat behind them.

"Where to?" Stevenson asked me.

"Woodlands Crossing," I said. "And let's not go the scenic route."

As we drove, I told them what I knew. Lipscombe was identifying teenage girls through his adoption centre and Turner had flown them south. He used Jeevan as his fall guy because of their history.

Turner delivered to Petersen but where Petersen was taking them wasn't clear and three girls seemed to have escaped. One had made it as far at Kuala Lumpur. The other two probably died earlier. Doctor Thobhani suspected that Monalisa Cardoso had been sexually abused.

Cole said, "You spoke to Kishan?"

"Yes."

We approached the crossing and Stevenson jumped the queue. When we got to the barrier the guard saluted Cole and we were immediately on the causeway.

Stevenson said, "Oh to be an MP!"

I said, "Stop about halfway along."

As we slowed, I said, "Men were searching for the missing girls on Route One heading for KL. They used a blue van and Land Rover. An ambulance picked up the dead girl from the KL hospital. It was also blue."

We stopped and got out.

I continued: "We think the body found here two weeks ago was dropped by a blue meat wagon."

Cole nodded.

"It bothered me that Customs described it as a meat wagon rather than a butcher's van."

"Does sound odd," Stevenson said.

"It was odd because it was just a blue van," I said. "There was meat packed in ice, because they needed cover for the dead body. They knew Customs would check so they made it look like a butcher's van. I think they used the same vehicle as the ambulance."

"Same people," Cole said.

"I'm certain of it. The only problem is, I was looking for a drugs problem."

Cole said, "There was a drugs problem."

"But the murder relates to the girls." I glanced at Stevenson and nodded.

The aid worker was standing behind Cole. He looped his arms under the MP's and then locked them behind the man's neck.

Cole struggled briefly. "What the hell are you playing at?"

"What did you know?" I asked.

"None of that!"

"Who was the body?"

"I don't know!"

"You lied to me. Why should I believe you now?"

Cole shook his head vehemently. "I've never lied to you, Ash."

"You said the markings were 221."

"That's what I thought. And no one disagreed with me!"

"What about RZ?"

"Kishan... the doc thinks it was RZ."

I laughed mirthlessly and Stevenson lightened his grip. I was sure passing travellers must have wondered what was going on—two men threatening an MP—but no one came to his aid.

I said, "Why didn't you tell me?"

"Because you found the source of the drugs—the Chinese gang. Vernon said the case was over. And you know Vernon. I didn't think it was important anymore."

I said, "Let him go, Scott."

Cole stepped away and rubbed his neck. His reaction could have gone one of two ways. If he was aggressive now, I'd know he had something to hide. He wasn't.

He said, "Sorry."

I said, "You're an investigator, Jim. We had a body and no explanation. You shouldn't have given up—despite Vernon."

He shrugged. "But it was no longer a military issue. It will have been passed on to the civilian police."

I signalled to Stevenson and we got back into the Land Rover. I sat in the passenger seat.

Cole placed a hand on the rear, ready to climb in. "What now?" he asked.

"You can walk back," I said.

He removed his hand and looked sheepish. "What can I do?"

"To make amends? You can start by making sure no one gets at our prisoners. And try and get more out of Turner. He may know more than he realizes. Secondly, you can find out which police are dealing with the body on the causeway now that Vernon has rejected it."

Stevenson pulled away and we headed for the Malayan boarder. I imagined Lieutenant Cole watching us but didn't turn back.

"That felt good," Stevenson said.

"Because you hate MPs."

"Is it that obvious?" He laughed. "So where now?"

"The adoption centre," I said. "Petersen is the key to this and we need to find him."


The adoption centre was locked up and Stevenson shouldered open the door.

We wasted thirty minutes searching the records for anything about Petersen. I also checked for the names of the girls with ticks in Lipscombe's ledger. We found nothing.

Miss Liang hadn't been lying when she'd said there was no record of Laura or Monalisa. And yet I couldn't help feeling she was hiding something.

When I'd questioned Lipscombe at the port in Penang, his eyes had told me something. He knew the names Petersen and Yipp but he hadn't recognized Liang. Either she wasn't involved or she was one step removed.

I remembered thinking that Miss Liang was either clever or scared. Which was it?

"What now?" Stevenson asked. "Shall we wreck this place?"

I stared at him.

251

He said, "From what you've told me, it's dodgy as hell. Let's trash it."

"No," I said, and walked out of Liang's office. "We go back and follow the trail," I said.

"Cop speak?"

"Petersen is the link so we're going to the school. The chap who runs it is Petersen's friend."

"So he should know where the bugger lives."

"Right."

Stevenson grudgingly kicked the Land Rover back into life and followed my directions north-west of the town until we came to Bukit Zarah and the drive up to the school.

"Wait outside," I said as we stopped by the heavy metal gates.

The sun beat down directly overhead, casting shadows under the stone eagles. I realized they were a contrast—out of keeping with the *istana*. In fact, the whole surrounding wall was ugly compared to the old Malayan property. This time I also noticed a plaque by the gate bell. It said: Rafflesia.

"It's like a fortress," Stevenson said.

"And run like one."

I rang the bell but no one came. After trying again without response, Stevenson sounded the horn.

Eventually a man came out of the front door and walked to the gates. This wasn't the Brit I'd met before.

"How can I help you?" he said with the hint of an Australian accent.

"I'm here to see Major Rix."

"You came before," he said, like it meant I should only visit once.

"Is that a problem?" I smiled. "I really need your boss's help."

252

He glanced at the house and I wondered if he was looking for instructions but then he immediately pulled out a key and unlocked the gates.

I left Stevenson in the Land Rover and the gates were shut behind me. As we walked to the house, I noticed the distinctive bulge of a gun under the man's jacket.

"Expecting trouble," I asked.

"You can never be too careful," he said, then added, "Bandits, mate."

"Australian?" I asked. "Did you serve with Major Rix?"

"I did."

When we reached the front door it was opened by another man. They exchanged nods and I was passed over like a relay baton.

He said, "This way please." His Australian accent was less pronounced but he also had a concealed gun. He took me to the same waiting room as before, the one with the chesterfields and rosewood. I wasn't kept waiting long before the elegant assistant collected me. She knocked on the headmaster's door and we entered. This time she followed me in.

Rix stepped smartly forward and shook my hand with his piano fingers.

"What a surprise to see you once more, Mr Carter. How can I help you again?"

"I really need to find Petersen."

"You asked me last time."

"I appreciate that, but last time he was just a piece in the puzzle. Now I know he's critical."

"Critical?"

"As in, important to the case."

He looked quizzical. "Which case? I heard you'd cracked a big drugs deal."

"How did you—?"

253

He laughed. "Goodness, it's a small community really. I hear things on the grapevine. Especially when they are so big."

I glanced towards the lady. She stood silently in a corner watching intently.

I said, "It seems the case is bigger or maybe different. And it looks like Petersen could really help."

Rix looked me in the eye. "I told you last time I didn't know where he was."

"You haven't seen him since?"

"No."

"But you know where he lives?"

Rix hesitated. "No. Well, not really. Somewhere in JB. I don't know the address. Perhaps the adoption centre can tell you?"

I looked at his Japanese artefacts: the kimono, the sword, the brass paperweight. I picked up the paperweight, solid and heavy. A good weapon. I glanced at the papers that had been weighed down.

I said, "Ironic, isn't it?"

"What?" There was an edge of doubt in his tone.

"This fascination with the Japanese. You must have lost thousands of men in the war."

"I don't like what they did, but I respect them as warriors and strategists." He cocked an eyebrow. "I just remembered you had an MP with you last time. On your own now?"

"Someone is waiting at the gates for me."

"I thought the RMP wasn't interested anymore."

I said, "It seems the grapevine was wrong this time."

He nodded and glanced at the paperweight still in my palm. I replaced it on the desk.

I said, "Why have your men got weapons?"

"You know the answer to that, Mr Carter. These are still troubled times. The parents who send their children

254

do so in the knowledge that security is one of the highest priorities."

I said, "I'd like to see your register. Who boards here?"

He smiled. "That's private."

"Was Monalisa Cardoso a pupil?"

"I don't know that name."

He took a breath and I could see I was testing his patience.

In her precise English, the lady said, "This Petersen fellow... what's he done?"

"Buying young girls for the sex trade. At least, that's what I think."

"Oh!" She placed her hands to her face and swivelled to look at Rix. "It would be a disaster... If the parents thought there was any scandal linked to the school..."

Rix raised a hand to placate her. "Don't worry, Sarah. I haven't seen him and there is no connection."

Now the lady looked at me. "There has been a finishing school here for over fifty years, Mr Carter. We are well respected and produce fine young ladies. If there were a scandal... Well, please, all I ask is that you don't drag us into this."

I said, "You've nothing to fear."

She nodded and smiled for the first time.

I nodded at Rix. "If Mr Petersen does make contact or you hear of him, please would you ask him to contact me?"

"You have an address?" He picked up a pen.

I gave him the name of the hotel in the town—the King George—and he wrote it down.

He said, "Now, if you'll excuse me..."

When I exited his office, there were now two men to escort me, one on either side. The guard with the German shepherd was also at the gate.

255

As we walked, I said, "Either of you know Petersen?"

Neither of them looked at me. Neither of them responded.

The dog pulled tight on its lead. It didn't bark but I reckoned it could attack on command.

"Nice dog," I said to the guard.

He nodded and stepped aside so that the man on my right could open the gate.

I walked through. The gate clanged shut behind me. The key was turned.

I raised my hand in a friendly farewell and got in beside Stevenson.

"Well," he said. "Find out about Petersen?"

In a voice loud enough to be overheard I said, "Major Rix has been a great help. Let's go."

Stevenson turned the vehicle around and headed down the hill.

"What's going on?" he said.

"The good major isn't being totally honest."

"He knows where Petersen is?"

"Maybe, but he seemed at war with himself. He was trying to be nice but didn't want to be."

"Those men were armed."

"Because of bandits, they said."

"There isn't a problem around here."

"No, but like I said before, he runs it like a military operation. However, I noticed something else this time. The windows all have bars. What kind of school has bars at the windows?"

Stevenson didn't answer straight away.

I said, "I told Rix I was staying at the King George Hotel."

"Are you?"

"No."

We reached the outskirts of Johor Bahru. Stevenson was still thinking.

Eventually he said, "We should go back and challenge them some more. This time let me ask some questions."

"No," I said.

He shook his head. "I don't understand. I thought you followed the trail."

"Oh, I do." I gave him some directions before adding: "I'm going back. Only next time, it'll be after dark."

# FORTY-FIVE

Someone should pay for Jeevan's murder and that was why Stevenson wanted action. But I needed more evidence. The hobnailed boots approach only got you so far.

We arrived at the King George Hotel in the town and this time I checked in. The room was on the first floor and smaller than my room at the European and Oriental had been. But it was clean and practical and most importantly had a window that opened out to a backyard.

After rejoining Stevenson, we took a stroll around the local shops. I bought a dark shirt, black trousers and a pair of gloves.

We had lots of time to kill, so after changing into my new outfit, we sat in the hotel lobby and bounced around a few ideas.

Stevenson grumbled because he didn't like waiting.

"All right," I finally said, "we'll do something. You can take me to Tebrau airfield."

"To punch Squadron Leader Kennedy?"

"No. I'm going to ask for his help."

Stevenson wasn't happy but he drove anyway, and when we got there I asked him to interview everyone about the explosion.

"What am I looking for?" he asked.

In all honesty, it was a distraction, but maybe he would find something. So he dropped me outside the office and I went in to see Squadron Leader Kennedy alone.

He sat at his desk looking depressed as I told him what I knew.

"I can't believe it," he said, rubbing his eyes. "Are you sure? First the plane blowing up and now you tell me Robin—"

"Turner confessed he'd altered the flight logs."

He looked at me long and hard, and I saw worry in his eyes. He said, "I have two questions for you."

"Yes?"

"Jeevan... Can you be sure Robin didn't cause the explosion?"

"Turner is afraid of someone they call the Man." I studied his face as I said this and saw no recognition. "This man is likely to be the cause of the explosion and also the body on the causeway. He controls people through fear. That's not your man. Turner is guilty of trafficking, but not murder."

Kennedy let out a long breath, like I'd eased his biggest worry. Then his face creased with concern.

"Trafficking?" He shook his head trying to process the word. "Trafficking not smuggling? That's an odd word."

"Girls," I said.

His eyes went wide. "What do you mean?"

"At one point—when he was at RAF Changi—he was a small-time smuggler, but since he's been here, it's been young women."

"Prostitution?"

I nodded. "It seems likely."

He said, "I never saw any... girls."

I said, "The second thing? You had two questions."

259

"Me. Do you suspect I'm involved?"

"Are you?"

He looked horrified. "Good God, no!"

"I didn't think so," I said, "but I do need a favour."


I hadn't appreciated how confined an Auster training plane was. My head almost touched the overhead window. I was so close to the windscreen that I felt exposed as Kennedy took off into the easterly wind.

He curved around through over 180 degrees and we were soon over Johor Bahru. In the air, my sense of direction was useless. I could see houses and roads and grassland and forests. I spotted Majidi Barracks, but that was the only thing I recognized.

The sky rapidly darkened with heavy clouds. "We probably have under thirty minutes before it chucks it down." Kennedy had to shout above the engine noise. Then he pointed ahead. "There's your Bukit Zarah."

I got the sense of the hill, but only just. I spotted the road up to the school and then the school itself. From above, the grounds looked bigger. I also noticed that the garage units behind the main building were maybe twice the size I expected. There was another building off at an angle.

Around the perimeter I could see treetops. The forest stretched mainly north and north-east. To the west was a square of land.

"What's that?" I asked.

"Farm, maybe?" He turned the plane around. "Pigs, probably."

I took a good look and then pointed north.

Kennedy knew what he was doing. He swept towards the coast, around and back inland. His pattern formed a tight, repeating wave, all the time looking below and around.

"It's like search and rescue," he shouted over the thrum of the engine.

I nodded. The ground rushed past and I had to keep looking up for fear of vertigo.

He said, "Helicopters are the future."

"You said, before."

"Robin's a great pilot. Will I get him back?"

I looked away from the ground again. "I doubt it."

He nodded.

I said, "How big will this thing be?"

"At least a hundred yards, probably two. It should be as obvious as..."

"What?"

"There at nine o'clock."

I could see tracks through the jungle, some straight, most curving, all narrow. And then a swathe cut through the trees. Clear from the air. Probably hidden from the ground.

Kennedy turned towards it. "Want to land?"

"Fly on," I shouted. As we went over, I checked for anyone watching but saw no one. Nor did I see a hangar.

"It's tight," Kennedy said. "Not many could land there."

"Except Turner."

"I could land in this but not the Dinah."

"Back home?" he said, circling a finger.

"Back home," I said.


Stevenson shook his head at me when I climbed out of the confined space.

"No luck?" I asked.

"Waste of time," he said. "What about you?"

261

I was about to tell him about the jungle airstrip when a clerk ran over, breathless.

He looked at the squadron leader and then me. "Mr Carter?"

"Yes."

"Urgent call, sir. In the office. Life or death, he said."

# FORTY-SIX

The man on the other end of the phone was Major Vernon.

I said, "Life or death, Major?"

"Yours," Vernon said with venom. "What the hell are you playing at, Carter?"

"Investigating a crime that remains unsolved."

"Really?"

I let the question hang.

He said, "You have one of my vehicles."

"Lieutenant Cole let me borrow it."

"You've stolen it. I want it back."

I said, "Have you spent the last few hours trying to track me down just to ask for your little jeep back?"

He didn't respond straight away and I figured I was right. He'd been calling around unsure of where I'd gone. But then he surprised me.

"Stealing an army Land Rover is one thing, Carter. Impersonating the RMP is a serious offence."

"I'm not impersonating anyone."

"That's not what I've been told."

"By whom?"

"It doesn't matter."

"It does if you're pressing charges."

I heard him breathing and imagined his jaw muscles moving the way they did when he was irritated.

He said, "You went to the school at Bukit Zarah, posing as RMP."

"No I didn't."

"They say you did."

"Who?"

He breathed again. "Bring the Land Rover back now."

"Who told you?"

"Bring it back immediately and I won't press charges."

I said, "Why was Commander Alldritt at the school?"

"What?"

"When I was there almost two weeks ago, I saw your buddy Alldritt." His car anyway.

"I don't know…"

"Does he have a daughter at the school?"

"Carter, bring my Land Rover back. You have four hours. After that, all bets are off."

I was about to ask him what he meant by that but he slammed the phone down.


Stevenson and I killed some more time by eating at the Kota Tinggi canteen. Rain pounded on the roof, and as men came in, their clothes steamed.

Dinner was beef stew and dumplings. As we ate, I told Stevenson about the flight and he told me what he'd found out.

"I spoke to everyone who was there that day. The man who fuelled up the plane insisted he'd done nothing wrong, but I reckon he feels guilty. You know, just in case it was his fault." He shrugged. "Everyone was putting it down as a freak accident. And no one saw anything suspicious."

"No contradictions?"

"You mean did someone say something that didn't tally with what someone else said? No. Everyone was in shock. I don't think they really knew Niroj. To them he was just the humanitarian aid pilot, but an exploding plane... well it's affected them."

"Who else was there that day?"

"Apart from Niroj, they saw the aid lorry come in. I got the names of the chaps who dropped off." He shook his head. "Straight as dies. No way were they involved."

I couldn't be so certain but waited for him to finish.

"There was one other thing that a couple of ground crew mentioned." He shook his head. "But it was nothing."

"Tell me."

"Just someone lost. Happens occasionally, they said, on account of there being no gates. People come in looking for the BVD but miss it. Or drivers take the wrong turn and end up on the airfield."

I said, "Tell me about this one."

"Two people, a man and a woman. Only description I could get was she had grey hair."

"Vehicle?"

He froze, mouth open. "Shit! It was a blue van. I didn't think."

"It's all connected," I said.


It was dark but still too early when we left the canteen. A group of men were going into the cinema so we killed some more time.

The crowded room soon filled with cigarette smoke, which masked the smell of damp clothes. Like most army cinemas, the experience was more about interaction than the quality of the film. When the good guys appeared, everyone cheered. They booed for the bad guys and catcalled whenever the heroine spoke.

It was hard to follow, but maybe that was the point. The mismatch of the criminal gunslinger with the beautiful Quaker girl made me think of my relationship with Su Ling. Only I knew she wasn't an angel.

At the end, the men, including Stevenson, howled with derision. On the way out, he said, "I've seen that film three times this week and it doesn't get any better. No way John Wayne could become a Quaker—no matter how pretty the girl."

I said, "The bad man falls in love with someone apparently too good for him. Proves he's not such a bad man after all."

"What do you think of the final line?"

"Only a man who carries a gun ever needs one?"

"Right," he said, and then answered his own question: "It's nice in theory but John Wayne handed in his gun at the end, after confronting the rustlers. In the real world those men would have shot him. He was only saved by the gun of the marshal."

As we walked outside, I said, "What are you saying?"

"You have a gun and I don't."

I used to have the service revolver but now I just had the Beretta on my left ankle. Stevenson must have spotted it.

I said, "You don't need one for what I have planned."

"See," he complained, "you sound just like the marshal."

# FORTY-SEVEN

We came upon the school from the west. I pictured the lanes I'd seen from the air and located the farm. We were downwind and could smell the pigs.

After the farm we came to the woods, beyond which was the school. We parked and headed for the school's perimeter wall.

The rain clattered through the trees. Stevenson had given me a coat and a torch. He had a rope wound over a shoulder and an eight-inch knife on his belt. He also had two folding stools and a small bag.

I had a bag too. Mine was empty, his wasn't.

When I asked him about it, he'd said, "You won't get me a gun. I need to defend myself."

"Not the knife, I mean the bag."

"So do I," he'd said and laughed.

I picked my way through the wet undergrowth, the Beretta in my belt. Our torches flashed up and along the wall.

It was ten feet high all the way along. Smooth with no handholds. There were also no trees close enough to climb.

"Thorough," I said.

"There'll be glass on the top, I expect."

I didn't doubt it. That's why I had the gloves.

When we neared the entrance, we retreated in case anyone was at the gate. Light spilled through the metal bars from lanterns along the drive. The gardens were lit too, like they were on show.

Open late then. It was after midnight.

I could see three large dark cars parked where I'd seen Alldritt's car previously.

We eased back into the trees and I exchanged looks with Stevenson.

"We wait," he said, and opened up the stools.

I pulled up my collar but the rain still managed to get down my neck.

Stevenson opened a tin. "Want a smoke?"

I declined.

"I don't know why I smoke them. Free tins of Players. I keep getting them and it's become a habit."

He went through four and a slow hour passed. I started to wonder whether the lights would ever go out. Surely they didn't keep them on all night?

It was another fifteen minutes and another cigarette before there was movement at the gates. After unlocking them, one of the staff swung both wide. The three large cars left, one after another. The gates clanged shut and the key was turned.

"Not staff," I said, referring to the three vehicles. "Too grand."

"Hopefully the staff will leave soon then."

I shook my head. "I don't think so. The gates were locked again."

The garden lights went out.

We left it another ten minutes and took a peek. As expected, there were no more cars, but light slid through the cracks of the garage door and at least two rooms inside the main building had lights on.

We left the stools where they were and made our way back through the wet undergrowth. It wasn't until I broke cover and stood by the wall that I realized the rain had stopped. Under the trees, water still dripped down, thudding on branches and leaves.

We were a third of the way around. I stopped, removed the coat and put on the gloves. Stevenson laced his hands together and boosted me up. He suppressed a grunt as I stood on one shoulder and then the other. Perhaps I should have invested in some soft-soled shoes as well.

I rested my hands on the top and felt wicked shards of glass. The gloves would protect my hands but I needed more, so I folded the coat and placed it on top of the wall.

From my position I had a good view of the grounds. The building I'd seen from the air was closest. It was smaller than the garage and if there was light inside I couldn't see it. I could still see the garage maybe fifty paces away. The school was about two-thirds of this distance and I could see two downstairs rooms had lights on. Someone briefly appeared at the window on the left.

There was a part-glass back door and a dim light came from there too. Upstairs was in darkness.

I scanned the grounds for movement in case someone was patrolling, but I saw nothing. The gates were on the far side of the school from my position and I supposed there might be a man in the gatehouse.

Without warning, the back door opened.

A man came out followed by a female. From this distance I couldn't judge her age, but she was smaller than Rix's assistant so I figured she was a pupil.

The door closed and they walked towards me, led by the man. He had a torch that lit a path I hadn't noticed before.

Because of the darkness, I saw less and less as they came my way.

I ducked my head down in case the guy swept his torchlight towards me but he didn't. I couldn't see the front of the nearby building and they disappeared. They must have opened a door and gone inside. The garden lit up briefly and went dark once more.

The man appeared moments later. This time he was alone. His torch bobbed along the path back to the school and he went inside.

The grounds became still once more and I jumped over the wall. My landing would have been more elegant if not for the box hedging I stuck one foot through. The crunch sounded loud to my ears so I stood still and waited.

I first approached the smaller building nearby. There were bars at dark windows. I placed my ear to the wall but could hear nothing.

On either side of the path was more box hedging. It formed a maze-like pattern across the grass. I crouched and then crawled, zigzagging as I followed the line of hedging. The grass ended and a couple of yards of shingle filled the gap from border to wall.

I was about to step onto the stones when the click of a door made me duck down once more. This time it was the garage. The silhouette of another man appeared in the doorway before the garage lights went out. I heard the door close and he jogged across the garden towards me.

As he approached, I flattened myself to the ground and drew my gun. But he wasn't heading for me because the next sounds I heard were his feet on the stones and the back door opening and closing.

A dog barked, the sound coming from the direction of the gates. It gave two bursts of three barks and was then quiet. No one called the dog. No one came outside to investigate. Maybe it had seen a rat or a squirrel or monkey.

I waited for a few beats just in case the situation changed, before stepping lightly across the shingle.

Here, beside the main property, there was pale light and faint shadows. I figured I could be seen if someone were looking for me.

I found a nook in the wall and stood and looked around. The windows had bars, so the only way in was the door. There were at least two men inside and they were undoubtedly armed.

I wanted to get into Rix's office, to go through his desk and find anything that would point me to Petersen.

I edged to the nearest window and peeped in. Rix and two other men were at a table, talking. As I watched, a fourth man came in. I'd seen a total of four men before. There could be more, but maybe not. I'd also met the Chinese, mixed-race assistant. Maybe she wasn't even here. Maybe she'd gone home before we'd arrived and watched the gates.

I slipped past the back door and glanced in through the panelled glass. The light came from the front of the house rather than the hall itself. Maybe there was another room with an open door.

Next I came to the room that had been lit. The door was slightly ajar and I could see a paperweight on the desk—the brass Japanese house.

I returned to the back door, checked no one was there and carefully opened it. As I closed the door behind me I noted a key in the lock.

To my right was the room with Rix and his men. I could hear them talking, relaxed, normal conversations. On the left was the head's office, the door still ajar, the light still off.

I stepped lightly across the hall and slipped into the office.

My plan had been loose and vague: get in and get out. Rix had glanced at the desk when I'd asked about Petersen's whereabouts.

The light from the hall was sufficient so I quickly jemmied the desk drawer open and started to search for anything that looked like an address book.

I flicked through letters and brochures and then I stopped. The realization that I'd been on the wrong trail struck me at the same time as two other things happened. I spotted what looked like a neat little address book. The second thing was the sound of footsteps outside the office.

Heart pounding, I grabbed the address book and pulled my gun.

The door moved.

# FORTY-EIGHT

The office light went on but the person hesitated for some reason. By the time the door opened wider, I was behind it, ready to defend myself if need be.

I expected Rix but it wasn't him. The assistant stepped into the room.

Maybe she knew something was wrong because she took a sharp breath. Even as she turned towards me, I was moving. I put my gloved right hand over her mouth.

Her eyes went wide with shock and panic. I could feel her scream through the leather against my palm. Her body jerked and I wrapped my arm around her until the fight subsided.

Our eyes locked and I mouthed, "It's all right. I won't hurt you."

No response.

"I'm here to help you."

This time she nodded slightly.

I mouthed, "Don't make a sound."

She nodded again.

I eased my hand off her mouth. Her lungs filled ready to scream but I was ready for it. I clamped the hand back. My other hand wrapped quickly around her neck until I could put pressure on her carotid artery. I squeezed until the moment her body went limp.

I hate doing a chokehold but at least she'd wake up with a slight headache rather than a bruise from my pistol butt.

"Sorry," I whispered, as I dragged her body over between the desk and window.

I stuck the address book in my pocket, stepped into the hall and shut the door. Opposite, the other door was still closed and the voices still relaxed. And if it had stayed that way I would have been fine. However, as I reached the back door, I heard Rix distinctly and the door handle jerked down.

I barely had time to move, but I sidestepped into the plant by the door. If he looked my way, I'd be seen. He didn't.

Four long strides took him to the office door. I might have wondered why he knocked before entering but I didn't have time. As soon as he moved out of the hall, I was out of the back door. Only, I'd also snatched the key and turned it in the lock from the outside.

This time, I didn't crawl. I ran down the path and then veered off and found the place where I'd jumped down.

There was no rope.

Stevenson was supposed to have thrown the rope over so I could climb back. But it wasn't there.

And then I spotted the reason. There was another man, someone patrolling the perimeter. I figured Stevenson couldn't risk him spotting the rope.

I saw the guard's torchlight flash across the garden close by. He wasn't hurrying. He was coming my way, not because he'd seen me, but more out of curiosity, it seemed. Maybe he was used to hearing rats, squirrels and monkeys too.

I shrank against the wall, moving into the shadow of the building where the girl had gone. I could climb onto this building but the distance to the wall was too far to jump. Maybe I could take a vehicle from the garage and ram my way out. The only problem with that idea was that the approaching guard was between me and the garage.

I could try and scale the gates, although I'd have to deal with the dog if it was still there.

Before I needed to decide, I heard it: a shrill whistle. Not a bird. Not a monkey. Stevenson trying to get my attention.

The guard had disappeared behind my building, going around the back. I saw the wall light up only thirty feet away.

A crashing sound came from the house. Someone kicked the back door. The guard close by, startled by the noise, started to run to the school.

The back door crashed open and Rix appeared and was shouting. "Intruder!"

His second shout was aimed at the guard: "Not this way, you idiot!" Then he turned back to the house and shouted, "Lights! Get the lights on!"

The dog started barking again. The sound seemed to come from the front, so at least I knew where it was, and the gates now seemed my only option.

Just as I was about to run that way, the rope clattered over the wall.

I snatched it up and felt Stevenson's resistance on the other end.

I didn't look back, but I could hear more men in the garden now. Rix was still yelling for lights. And then he got them.

The world exploded with light all around me, much brighter than earlier. My shadow looked large and obvious on the pale grey wall.

I doubt anyone in the history of mankind has scaled a ten-foot wall as fast as I did that night. As I scrabbled onto the coat, the first bullet pinged close by. Then a volley of shots rang out, but I was already falling beyond the top.

I landed ignominiously on my backside. Stevenson yanked me to my feet and we started running. Would we reach the Land Rover in time? Would they guess where we'd gone? Could they circle around and meet us on the other side of the pig farm?

We burst out of the trees only yards away from our parked Land Rover.

As Stevenson kicked the jeep into life, I saw his hands shaking. But it wasn't through fear, because he shouted "Woohoo!" as we shot past the farm and down the hill.

I was still thinking about them coming at us from the other side.

"We've not got away yet," I shouted breathlessly into the rushing air.

"So which way?" he shouted back.

"Any way you like, but fast."

They may have expected us to head to the town, keeping to main roads. Because of this, Stevenson turned south as soon as he could, and then east and then south again.

We headed down a narrow sandy track before he pulled off and stopped.

I said, "Are we lost?"

"Not at all. This is a pretty spot. The straits are just over there." He pointed into the darkness. "I brought a girl here once."

We sat and listened. Stevenson smoked.

The air was full of animal noise; it almost always was. Occasionally we heard a far-off engine, but nothing came close.

I said, "So what happened to our plan?"

"The rope after you'd gone over? It was a rubbish plan." I saw him grinning at me in the dark, enjoying this.

"The guard?"

"Yes, the guard. Lucky for you, I climbed up a tree to watch and saw him patrolling. I reckoned he'd have seen the rope long before you came back out."

"So you waited." I was thinking that he could have at least thrown me the rope a bit sooner.

"More than that, College Cop. I saw to the hound."

"What?"

"The dog."

"I know a hound is a dog, for Christ's sake." He was baiting me but I played along. I'd been in and out without getting shot and I'd learned more than I could have hoped for. Although he didn't know that yet. So I said, "What do you mean you *saw to it*?"

"You wanted to know what was in the bag. Well it was beef stew and dumplings. Dogs love a bit of beef stew. I lured him to the gate and tied him up while he was eating the stew."

"Ingenious."

"I thought so."

I let him gloat for a minute.

"And the big question? Was it worth it? Breaking into the school and almost getting shot?"

I patted my pocket. "Get me to the hotel and we'll see."


Stevenson parked at the front of the King George and I went inside alone. My new clothes were soaked and dirty from crawling across the garden. As the receptionist handed me my room key, I made a big thing about being caught in the rain.

When he said, "Have a good night, Mr Carter," I was sure he'd remember my name.

Once in my room, I cleaned up and changed. Putting a pillow under the covers, I bunched up my bed like I was in it and then climbed out of the window.

I dropped into the backyard and found Stevenson waiting for me on the road. We walked into the town and caught the first taxi we found.

"What now?" he asked

"Drop me at the European and Oriental Hotel," I said. You can go back to base.

"You were going to tell me what you discovered at the school."

"And I will," I said. "But first I want some sleep. And then I want to think. Meet me in the morning for breakfast."

He grabbed my arm. "You're not getting away with that!"

I grinned. "All right, I'll tell you that I discovered that the name of the school is important. *Rafflesia* is a flower. I saw it on a letterhead, like a logo or something."

He wasn't happy with that explanation but it was all I would say. I shook his hand, thanked him for all his help and repeated: "Meet me in the morning for breakfast."

However, when I got up, it wasn't Stevenson in the hotel lobby but someone totally unexpected.

# FORTY-NINE

Jane Dobson was curled up asleep in an armchair.

"How long has she been here?" I asked a member of staff.

"About two hours, sir. She seemed unsure whether you were staying at the hotel."

Maybe she heard my voice because she opened her eyes, stretched and smiled uncertainly.

I stepped over and gave her a hug. "What the hell, Jane...?"

"You're cross with me."

"What are you doing here?"

She stretched again and I saw how tired she was. She said, "Let's have some coffee and I'll explain."

A few minutes later we were sitting at a table and she was on her second cup. Strong, black and sweet.

"I've been travelling since you left me in Penang," she began. "The ferry and then the train. I gambled that you were here. If not, my next step was Singapore."

"You were lucky," I said. "I almost stayed at a different hotel."

"I just couldn't sit and do nothing."

"What about your job?"

"This is more important."

I nodded, but I hadn't wanted her involved. I didn't know how this would play out and she had no idea of the risks.

"Well," she said, interrupting my thoughts. "What have you learned? What was Lipscombe up to?"

I explained about Turner and how he and Jeevan had history. "Turner was transporting the girls and handing them over to Petersen."

"The man from the adoption centre."

"Right. And I think I've seen the airstrip where he delivered them."

"What else did he tell you? Do you know where Laura is?"

"I couldn't get him to tell me anything. He's afraid of the person who killed his friend Jeevan. He called him the Man." And then I said, "I think I know who it is."

"Who?"

"The man who runs the boarding school to the west. It's called Rafflesia."

"Rafflesia—as in the flower?" She stared at me. "The poisonous flower!"

I nodded. That's one of the things I'd realized last night. I'd seen a brochure for the school with a flower logo. The girl who'd died in the Kuala Lumpur hospital hadn't said poisonous flower. I now suspected she'd said *Rafflesia* and the nurse had thought she meant she'd eaten a poisonous flower.

I told Jane about last night, how I'd broken in and taken documents from Major Rix's office. I was hoping to find Petersen's address but I'd found something much more damning.

"I thought I'd found a pocket address book at first, but it wasn't. It had names all right, but no addresses."

"Any names I'd know?"

"Monalisa Cardoso was in there."

She took a sharp breath. "And Laura?"

I hesitated. How should I explain? We were having this conversation much sooner than I could have imagined. I'd hoped to know more by the time Jane and I discussed Laura again.

I delayed. "I'll come to that."

She looked alarmed and I put my hand on hers.

"It's not necessarily bad. Let me explain first."

Jane sat back and waited.

"There are a hundred and fifty-two entries in there. The early ones are written in Japanese, but there's English names written there too. As far as I can tell, all one hundred and fifty-two are girls." I paused a beat before continuing: "I don't know about the Japanese, but the ones in English all have dates that range from four years ago to recently—three months ago."

She shook her head. "Dates?"

"They look like arrival dates. I've checked against the list we got from Lipscombe and all the names with ticks are there. The dates match when they left Penang."

"And Laura's was seven weeks ago?" Tears threatened to fill her eyes. "But you said the most recent was three months."

"Laura's doesn't have a date." I gripped her hand. "It could be good news."

"How?"

"She never arrived. That's my theory."

Tears flowed freely now. "Because something happened to her?"

"We don't know that. Maybe the notes haven't been updated." Even as I said it, I knew I didn't sound convincing.

I held her until she nodded and eased me away. As she wiped her eyes, I squatted by her chair, just in case, ready to hold her again. She took deep breaths and composed herself.

"How many girls are there?" Emotion crackled in her voice.

"That's the other thing. There are second dates and I suspect those are dates the girls leave the school." I no longer believed Rafflesia was really a school but the term was better than the alternative I had in my head. "Again, I can't tell about the early ones, but if I'm right there are sixteen girls remaining. Which would have been twenty including Laura and three crossed off."

"Monalisa Cardoso?"

"One of the three."

"And Laura's not crossed off?"

"No."

"Who are the other two?"

"Di Yang and Jakaterina Tiurina."

"Kate—Jakaterina called herself Kate. Lovely girl, but funny about her name."

I nodded but I was thinking. There was something else too. Against each one were other names. My gut told me what these were. I didn't recognize any but then I suspected they were aliases.

The girls with leaving dates also had a number. It looked like a price paid. A large price paid. Some girls seemed to get sold immediately. Their prices were lower than the ones who spent time at Rafflesia.

She was watching me, maybe guessing that I was holding back.

"So Rix is in partnership with Petersen, running a business on the side?" She swallowed as though the next words wouldn't come out straight away. "He's selling girls for the sex trade."

I said nothing.

"Not your theory?"

"Almost," I said quietly. "I think it's the school itself." I paused and she blinked.

"It's not a finishing school?"

"It's too heavily protected. There are the high walls and bars at the windows and the men have guns. But most of all because of the name—the poisonous flower."

I could see her mind working. She drank more coffee.

"So, Monalisa, Kate and Di escaped. If they were at the school and if the security is as good as you say, then how did they escape? How did three girls get out?"

"I don't know."

"Someone on the inside," she said.

It was a reasonable possibility. And that led her to ask me about the people I'd seen at the school. She was particularly interested in the lady. I said Rix had called his assistant Sarah.

Jane said, "And she was the only one unarmed."

"Rix didn't seem to have a gun and there may have been other employees I didn't see."

"What others?" Stevenson sat down at our table.

I introduced them to each other and told him about the flower on the brochure and the list of girls.

"Makes sense," he said.

"We were just talking about the number of people involved. There must be a gardener at least, but a business like that, you'd want to keep numbers to a minimum."

Jane said, "I think we're missing the point."

"Which is?"

"There are girls in there being held against their will. We need to report it." She must have seen my blank face because she added: "To the police."

Stevenson laughed. "I thought you were going to tell us to go in all-guns-blazing."

283

"No," I said, "that's what you wanted to hear. Jane is right. Breakfast first and then we present our case to the JB police."

We could smell the sea from the police station. The causeway was only a few hundred yards beyond the trees, and although it was overcast, the air was fresh and clear.

We walked around a courtyard, busy with vehicles and men on parade, which then hooked around to a long frontage.

After speaking to a desk sergeant, we were treated courteously, taken to a private waiting room and given water. A captain called McNaughton eventually joined us. He had a firm handshake and an easy smile.

McNaughton placed his police cap on the table and smoothed his buff-coloured suit as he sat. The whole move was practised and undoubtedly intended as a subliminal message: *I'm in charge here.*

He asked no questions after the preliminary introductions and confirmation of our statuses. I appreciated that we must have seemed an odd group: a nurse from Penang, an aid worker from Kota Tinggi, and me, the Singapore government man.

The captain's face was unreadable as I spoke. When I'd finished, he said, "Right, thank you for coming in." He placed a hand on his cap—another subliminal message. "We'll certainly investigate this."

"When?" Jane asked.

McNaughton bristled. "When we get round to it, young lady."

"But—"

"All I have heard is suspicion and conjecture. Ifs and maybes. You don't know the girls from Penang are at the school. You don't—"

"*Were* at the school," Jane cut in. "You should say *were* at the school. We know that at least one girl is dead."

McNaughton nodded as though understanding. However he said, "But you have no evidence that she was taken to the school. And therefore no evidence that she escaped from the school."

Jane started to complain but I placed a hand on her arm and she stopped.

"Look," he said, sounding apologetic or maybe just placatory, "I said we'll investigate the claims and we will. Rafflesia school... well it can't be as you say because the parents are extremely wealthy and powerful people. You mentioned high security. Of course there's high security. Just imagine if one of those girls was kidnapped!"

Jane said, "Imagine if three of them escaped and died."

McNaughton shook his head.

"You see, it's nonsense." He smiled as if he understood. "If three girls escaped and died then their parents would be here. Not you."

"But—"

He stood up and held out his hand. "Look, I'm sorry, it's been a tough morning—arson to worry about, it seems. I realize you think you're on to something but I'm sure it's all a misunderstanding."

I said, "Just tell me you'll investigate."

"I'll visit the school, personally."

"That's all we ask," I said, and shook his hand.

We were about to leave when a young police officer came into the room and handed McNaughton a slip of paper. The captain looked at me and then back at the paper.

"Well, well," he said. "I'm glad you've come to see us after all."

I waited for the explanation and he pointed to the chairs, expecting us to sit.

I remained standing.

"You stayed in the King George last night, correct?"

"I had a room."

"But didn't use it?"

"I didn't stay."

He nodded and looked at the paper again. "Mr Carter, I'm arresting you for wilful damage to the hotel."

"Wilful damage?"

"You're my arsonist," he said. "You tried to burn it down."

# FIFTY

The others were asked to leave and McNaughton wanted me to explain my movements of the night before. I decided against mentioning the school visit. Instead I told him I had checked into the King George and then spent the evening with a friend.

"The other chap?" McNaughton prompted, referring to Stevenson.

"Yes. We ate at the camp, saw a film and had a few drinks."

"And then what?"

"I had a bit too much I'm afraid." Mea culpa. I hoped my contrition was convincing. "You know... I had so much I forgot my hotel. I must have told the taxi driver the wrong one. I'd stayed in the European and Oriental before, so maybe that was why."

"So you checked into a different hotel."

"I did."

McNaughton nodded as though he believed me, but I knew the technique. He was encouraging me to talk, hoping I'd say something I shouldn't. But of course I was innocent.

I said, "Tell me what happened at the other hotel."

"If I call the European and Oriental, they'll have a room in your name?"

"Yes—and confirm my arrival time. What time was the fire?"

He stood up and left me then. The room was airless and I felt sweat prickle my scalp. I sipped my water and considered my options. There would be a guard outside the door but it wasn't locked. I suspected I could make my escape with little bother but then maybe McNaughton wanted that. Maybe McNaughton was in on this whole thing. Or was I becoming paranoid?

I decided to wait.

McNaughton gave me his easy smile when he came back twenty minutes later.

"You're sweating," he said.

"It's hot."

He smiled again. "I made two phone calls. Firstly I rang the E&O and confirmed your story. You checked in before the fire at the George and no one saw you leave."

I nodded.

He continued: "However you also checked into the George and no one saw you leave there either... And the receptionist at the E&O said you weren't drunk."

I shrugged. "I can't comment because I barely remember checking in."

"Tell me about the fire in your room at the George."

"I can't because this is the first I've heard about it."

"Why would you set fire to it?"

"I didn't."

"Why would someone else?"

I cocked an eyebrow. "Because they thought I was in it?"

He watched my eyes for a while. "What's your theory?"

"I told Major Rix at the school where I was staying."

"So you think Rix did it?"

"Or one of his cronies."

288

McNaughton sighed. "And that's because of this whole sex trade thing and escaping girls at the school?"

"Yes."

He said, "The second phone call was to your boss, Secretary Coates. He vouched for you..." He paused, like he was going to say more.

"Good," I said, and started to stand.

"He vouched for you but said you were in trouble."

I said nothing.

McNaughton watched me and I could tell he wanted me to explain. Eventually he gave up and said, "You are free to go but I want to know where you are staying—the genuine hotel."

I hesitated but then decided there was no point in lying to the captain. If he suspected I would move to a different hotel then I'd be brought in again. "The European and Oriental," I said.

He nodded. "Make sure you are. And there's something else. Your boss only vouched for you on the condition you call him. Now."

I was taken into another room and waited while someone somewhere connected the Johor Bahru police station to the Singapore government offices and then Secretary Coates.

McNaughton listened before handing me the receiver.

"Carter?" Coates said.

"Yes."

"What the hell are you doing?"

"I'm investigating that crime, the one that started on the causeway."

I heard his teeth click. "Is this an internal security issue?"

"It may be."

"No it isn't!" His teeth clicked again, and although his voice remained calm, I knew he was angry.

289

I said, "It's connected in some way to the abduction of girls for the sex trade."

"You have proof?"

"Not exactly, but—"

Now he raised his voice. "But nothing. You work for me. You are not a private investigator. If this is a JB police matter then let the JB police investigate."

"That's why I'm here."

I heard dead air for a moment as he processed this. "Right. Good. Then I'll expect you in the office shortly."

I said, "Yes, sir."

He said, "If you don't come back, you'll be fired. Understand?"

"Yes, sir."


Jane and Stevenson looked worried as I appeared in the station's reception area.

Stevenson said, "You're released?"

I nodded and Jane hugged me.

I said, "They tried to kill me last night. Set fire to my room."

Jane said, "So we have confirmation?"

"Oh yes, we do."

"What do we do next?" Stevenson asked. "Back to the hotel?"

"Let's get the Land Rover," I said. "At least then we'll have some wheels."

Outside, I scanned the street for a taxi but resorted to a trishaw. Jane and I got in. Stevenson flagged down another and we set off for the King George Hotel.

★ ★ ★

The RMP Land Rover was still there. A thin line of smoke rose up from the roof and I figured it came from the room I'd used.

There was no fire crew and no police cars but I could see a number of bobbies inside.

Following my instructions, our cyclist didn't stop. Instead, I signalled to Stevenson and saw that he understood.

We waited a street away and he picked us up in the jeep a few minutes later and drove to the European and Oriental.

Back in the other hotel lobby, Stevenson said, "Are we safe here?"

"As safe as anywhere," I said.

He shook his head. "Not as safe as at Kota Tinggi. We could go there."

"Are you serious? The security is a guardhouse and picket fence!" Normally, I would have laughed but my colleagues were in a sombre mood. The long uncertain wait for me to be released by McNaughton showed on both their faces.

I leaned back in a leather chair and said, "Secretary Coates wants me back in Singapore. He wants me off this case."

Jane shook her head. "The police captain isn't going to investigate, is he?"

"Probably. Eventually. He'll visit them. He'll ask Major Rix a bunch of questions and he'll go away again."

"Why?"

"Because he hasn't got a crime. All he's got is a theory from us."

Stevenson said, "But the body on the causeway?"

"Isn't his concern. Remember, it was in no man's land. If it'd been in JB, then I think he'd have a different attitude."

Jane said, "So if you're going back to Singapore, what are we going to do?"

"Don't worry," I said. "I'm not going back. Not just yet anyway."

# FIFTY-ONE

Avoid that which is strong and strike at what is weak. That was Sun Tzu's principle, but it created a problem for us. The school was strong. It was a fortress.

We'd bounced around ideas but I kept coming back to the school. We had to attack the school.

Jane's blinks became longer and longer and I thought she'd fall asleep at any moment. However, she drank another cup of coffee and waited until we'd convinced ourselves of the only option.

"But what about the girls?" she said. "If you start shooting in the school, anything could happen."

"We'll be careful," Stevenson said.

"You can't guarantee they won't get hurt."

"Maybe we won't need guns."

"Only a man who carries a gun ever needs one," I said, quoting the film we'd watched.

"What does that mean?" Jane asked.

"John Wayne," Stevenson scoffed. "In theory we don't need guns. But they're armed, and if we just go in with fists, we won't be coming out alive."

I nodded. "There's no alternative."

Jane shook her head. "You could get the girls out first."

Stevenson said, "And how would we do that?"

"I don't know, but we need a better plan." She yawned. "And as I understand it, we have plenty of time."

She was right. I wanted to go in at night and it still wasn't midday. Stevenson had argued for a daylight attack. Go now. But that increased the risk for the girls.

If we warned Rix we were coming, then we might hope he'd protect the girls, but there was also the possibility that they'd use them against us. More than a possibility.

Our best bet was a night-time attack. Even so, they would be expecting us. They knew I'd broken in. They'd tried to kill me by setting fire to my room at the wrong hotel. Yes, they knew I was coming, so how to surprise them? We needed an angle.

Jane yawned again. She'd been up for almost thirty hours and the coffee could no longer hold back the exhaustion.

We agreed that she shouldn't take my room—just in case Rix found out we were here. Taking no chances, she booked in under an assumed name and I said we would come back later.

"With a better plan," she said, and I agreed.


Lieutenant Cole stood outside by the Land Rover. There was another RMP vehicle with a driver and I figured one had arrived and two were going back.

I nodded a greeting like I was expecting him.

"I've come for the jeep," he said.

"Vernon sent you."

Cole nodded. "He's baying for your blood. Been complaining to your boss in the government too."

I'd figured as much.

He said, "How's it going? The investigation I mean."

"Making progress."

He climbed into the Land Rover and started her up.

"Look," he said, "I really am sorry about... you know, not telling you."

"Vernon?" I said.

"Right."

I said, "I'll find a way you can make amends."

He nodded. "Has RZ made any sense?"

I said nothing. My working theory was that R stood for Rafflesia and Z for Bukit Zarah. But why on the body and who was the body? I was no closer to understanding that piece of the puzzle.

As though reading my thoughts about the blue van, Cole said, "Did you find where that private ambulance went—with the dead girl?"

"No."

"You need to come up with something soon. Vernon won't let me hold Turner and Lipscombe very long with no evidence."

"How long have I got?"

"I can hold him off until tomorrow morning, I think. I hope."

I was still thinking about the blue van. "Any more news from Customs?"

"No. As you know, the investigation's over."

He turned the Land Rover around and signalled for the other driver to leave. Again he leaned towards me.

"We're having drinks for Hedge tonight. In his honour. You know, a kind of wake."

I said, "He was a good lad."

"Will you join us?"

I thought it unlikely but said I'd try.

He said, "Vernon insisted I bring you back."

I shook my head. No way was that going to happen. Stevenson stepped closer.

295

Cole grinned. "It's OK. I'll tell him you weren't here."

"You still owe me."

"I do," he said, as the Land Rover started to roll. "And good luck. I mean it."

Stevenson was watching me. "The wake…"

"No, I won't be going. Cole was in part warning me about Vernon. I show up, he'll probably arrest me. Plus we've got hours to finish this thing tonight."

"So what next?"

"We plan. But first we'll detour via the causeway."

"Going back to Singapore?"

"No, we're paying a visit to Customs."


A hot ten minutes later, our taxi stopped outside the Customs building. I'd used the time to think about what I knew. The blue van had been classed as a meat wagon and been one of the last vehicles across before the border closed for the night. Major Vernon had been one of the first on the scene and started the investigation. Lieutenant Cole had been assigned to lead, Doctor Thobhani had been called and Hegarty instructed to get me involved.

The blue van would have had to return at some point but I had no record of when. Maybe that would have helped. Maybe not. But that wasn't the most important question in my mind.

Between the body being positioned on the causeway and the investigation starting, the letters RZ had been changed. And then there were the chevrons. Someone had tried to remove them. If it was a warning, did it mean? And why remove the message?

In our taxi, Customs wouldn't have waved us through, but we had avoided the queue and I went inside alone.

I had no power, no right to see the records, but when I showed my ID, the desk clerk didn't hesitate. He pulled the file from the night before the body had been found and I glanced at the records. Then I asked for the following day.

As soon as I saw the first entry, I knew we'd made a huge assumption. An incorrect assumption. It didn't solve everything but it explained a lot.

"Why are you smiling," Stevenson asked as I climbed back into the taxi.

I said, "I've started to understand."

"Care to explain?"

"Not yet," I said. "That comes later. For now we need to plan how we get Rix."

# FIFTY-TWO

Back at the Kota Tinggi camp, Stevenson wanted to involve his men. "Like an army besieging a castle," he said. "That would have shock value."

I didn't like the idea. The more people involved, the less control I'd have and the greater the chance of something going wrong. However, I finally agreed to one additional man. It made sense for what we had planned.

We ate lunch with Stevenson's man, Cranfield, who reminded me a bit of Hegarty, full of life and humour. Stevenson said he trusted him with his life. Which Cranfield found hilarious.

I told him what was going on and that we planned an attack on the school.

"This needs to be controlled," I said.

Cranfield nodded.

I said, "When I tell you what to do, you do it."

"We're soldiers," Cranfield said with a grin. It wasn't strictly true. They'd been soldiers once. They were military, yes, but now they were aid workers. Sidelined. Cranfield showed no sign of being lame or sick so he was probably in the lazy category. Some CO somewhere had wanted shot of him and now he was in my team.

I drew a map of the school: the perimeter wall, the garage, the outbuilding, and the school house. I pointed to the outbuilding and said I expected the girls would be there. Then I drew the layout of the school house as best I could. I hadn't seen the upper floor and again said there could be innocents up there.

I explained that all of the windows had bars and that there was just a front entrance and a back door. The perimeter wall was ten feet tall and intact the whole way round. The only easy way in or out was through the main gates.

Cranfield asked some good questions and when he was done, I said, "Here's what I want you to do."

After I'd given him a shopping list, he asked, "What about guns?"

Stevenson and I had discussed this. I was uncomfortable with his plan, but the alternative was a single Beretta between the four of us.

"Don't you worry," Stevenson said. "It'll be sorted."


We took the humanitarian aid Land Rover and first stopped off at the hotel. I knocked lightly on Jane's bedroom door and got no response, so I left a note at reception so that she'd know I'd checked on her. Then I directed Stevenson back to Bukit Zarah and reconnoitred the area.

We'd found the pig farm without difficulty last night, but north of the hill the roads had been hidden beneath the canopy when I'd flown over in the Auster.

We got a sense of their complexity before leaving the area and taking the road to Kluang. After a couple of miles I decided we should turn left and take a route heading north-west.

The road narrowed and we passed through jungle that was broken with huge swathes given up to rubber plantations.

I drew my Beretta.

Stevenson looked at me and nodded. "This is the Yong Peng road, isn't it?"

Yong Peng had been notorious for bandit activity earlier in the year. Ex-plantation workers had ambushed vehicles and killed civilians and soldiers alike.

Stevenson drove fast and laterite stones kicked up and rattled under the wheel arches. Occasionally, I spotted tappers bleeding trees, but no one paid us any heed.

The jungle closed in once more until we rounded a hillock and dropped into a shallow valley. I pictured the area from above and was sure we were close.

After another mile and a half I told Stevenson to stop and back up. The track was overgrown and rutted, but between the trees I could see daylight and a minute later we were in a field.

"The airstrip," I explained. This was the narrow swathe cut through the trees that I'd seen from the air. "This is where the transfer happened. Turner flew the girls here and handed them over to Petersen."

We drove along the field, which was about two wingspans wide and two hundred yards long. We could see no planes, no hangar, but there was a shed and fuel drums at the far end.

Stevenson parked and I opened the shed door. It was more like a workshop, with an array of pristine tools on the wall. In the middle of the room was a small generator.

The metal was cold to my touch.

"In use but not recent," I said.

Stevenson walked past me and kicked a wooden box.

"You were spot on," he said. "Come and look."

There among the crates was one with holes drilled in the side. Air holes.

"That's what they shipped them in," he said unnecessarily. "Poor kids."

I lifted the lid and looked at the confined space. No way was anyone getting in there voluntarily.

"Must have drugged them," I said.

He nodded, and I could see in his eyes that this was now much more than revenge for Jeevan's murder.

We went back into the daylight and I walked along the airstrip. I could see the tracks and indentations. I could see where planes had landed and taken off. How many times? Was this just one operation or many?

And then I saw them: the faintest of faint tracks. They veered off into the bushes.

I followed and saw that the bushes were in fact cut branches. Stevenson helped me pull the camouflage away to reveal a wooden fence. I tugged and the front panels moved. Behind the fence, covered by tarpaulin, was a light aircraft.

Stevenson looked along the side. "Cessna 140," he said. "Two man. Not fast, but handy if you need to get away."

I looked at him, impressed. "How do you...?"

"Don't ask." He grinned. "Though maybe I'll tell you one day, when I'm sure you won't shop me."

I checked the plane over.

"How can we disable it?"

"Fuel line. Easy," he said.

He pulled out a penknife and quickly slashed a hose in two. The smell of aviation fuel rose up and filled my nostrils.

We replaced the tarpaulin, the fence and then the bushes and drove away. One thing I'd learned from my spell in the Middle East: when it comes to a fight, the man who knows the lay of the land has the upper hand. Rix knew this country better than me. But I'd familiarized myself with the school, I'd assessed the surroundings and roads, and now I had another piece of the puzzle. If Rix had an escape plan, then I reckoned we'd just scuppered it.

On the way back, Stevenson hummed a tune and it reminded me of Hegarty's annoying habit.

"What is that?" I asked.

"'Ten Green Bottles'. You know, *hanging on a wall.*"

"The kids' song."

"Nothing wrong with kids' songs, although you'd probably prefer the *ten sticks of dynamite* version."

"Why?"

"Because after one falls, there's no bloody wall."

"Ah. That would solve our problem with the school, but we haven't got dynamite," I said. "More's the pity."

And then Stevenson said something that surprised me. "You're not so bad," he said.

"What?"

"I was just thinking about the John Wayne film. He's the bad man but isn't in the end." He looked at me in all seriousness. "That's like you."

"What?" I said again. "You're saying I'm the bad one?"

"Well you're the cop. An ex-cop at least. I had you down as the bad man, but you're all right really. Just goes to show that leopards can change their spots."

I shook my head. I'd pegged Stevenson as the bad guy. I guess it's just perspective. There probably aren't many people who'd think they're bad. I suppose even criminals justify their actions.

I said, "Maybe nothing is as black and white as we'd like to believe."

"Are you having doubts about Rix?"

"Hell no," I said. "Hell no."

# FIFTY-THREE

We returned to the hotel expecting to find Jane but she'd gone. She'd left me a message about visiting the orphanage. There was an important part of our loose plan that we'd overlooked, according to her. What were we going to do with the girls? This was as much about rescuing them as it was capturing Rix.

My change of clothes had gone up in flames at the other hotel so Stevenson and I walked towards the centre and found the same clothes shop I'd been to before.

The Indian shopkeeper recognized me. Buying the same black clothes two days running must have seemed strange. But I figured a sale is a sale. He grinned as I paid but didn't comment. However, when Stevenson bought two of the tops—one large for himself and one medium for Cranfield—I could see the shopkeeper's mind whirring.

"I can get more," he said. "Lots more. Come back tomorrow. Bring more friends."

We thanked him and made our way back to the hotel.

"What are you going to do about Jane?" Stevenson asked as we approached. "She can't come with us."

"No," I said, "she can't." I wasn't sure what she expected, but based on her appearance this morning, she needed some involvement. The orphanage idea appeared a good distraction and I half hoped she wouldn't be at the hotel when we returned.

She wasn't. I checked for messages and was surprised by a call from McNaughton.

I rang the police station and got put through to him.

"Mr Carter," he said, "I have news."

"Have you been to the school yet?"

"No."

"That's the only news I want from you."

He said nothing for a moment and I wondered if he was considering whether to tell me. Finally he said, "Another girl has turned up."

"Go on," I said, "I'm listening."

"At the KL hospital. They've got another girl in similar condition to the first one—Monalisa Cardoso—if I have the name right. Well, this one says her name is Jakaterina Tiurina."

"Hard name to say."

"I have it written down. I'm just passing this on."

"OK, why do you think I'll be interested?"

"She's half-caste," he said, "and alive."

"So she can talk—she can tell me what happened?"

"I guess so. The reason I mention it is because she asked about two other girls and one of those was the Cardoso girl, so I reckon they are connected."

I said, "So now you'll take my claim seriously? Two girls from the same school."

He took a long breath. "I'm telling you this as a courtesy, Mr Carter. This new girl is connected to the one you said was important. I'm not saying it validates your theory about the Rafflesia school."

"What did she say about the school?"

"I don't know. I haven't spoken to her and the hospital says she's delirious. Like the other one was. I don't think she'll do much talking over the telephone."

I looked at my watch. I said, "I could be at the hospital by seven o'clock."

"What you do next is totally up to you," he said. "I'm just calling as a courtesy."

I thanked him and put the phone down. Stevenson had been leaning close, trying to hear. I told him about the second girl, Jakaterina Tiurina.

He said, "Was she on the list?"

"In the notebook and from Penang," I said. "She's definitely one of the three who escaped."

I could see him thinking about the information. Did that change things?

"What do we do now?" he asked.

I held up a hand and asked the receptionist for a pen and paper. I scribbled a quick note to Jane and said I was returning to KL hospital to interview another runaway.

Outside the hotel, Stevenson shook his head. "This will delay everything. Are you sure...?"

"Let's just go," I said. But once we were outside the town I asked him to take us back to Kota Tinggi.

Again I saw Stevenson shake his head.

"We needed an angle with Rix," I explained. "And I think he's just given us one."

# FIFTY-FOUR

Jane's meeting with Lady Hage-Dando at the orphanage had gone well. The elderly lady had given her tea and cucumber sandwiches followed by fruit cake and listened intently. At times, Jane thought Lady Hage-Dando didn't really understand. She mentioned the sale of babies at the Johor Bahru hospital, which seemed her biggest concern.

"These girls aren't babies," Jane had said.

"I know, dear. I know."

"They're teenagers... maybe a bit older... I don't really know."

Then Lady Hage-Dando had smiled and nodded. "They will be welcome here," she'd said, and pointed to the young woman who had served tea. "If they're too old to be found homes, then perhaps they will help run the orphanage and teach the children."

Jane returned to the hotel in good spirits. The trip had taken much longer than she'd anticipated, mainly because of the time it had taken with the old lady.

The receptionist passed her the message Ash had left and she returned to her room. An hour later, frustration took her back downstairs and a walk outside.

An attractive tall woman stood in the lobby.

"Jane Dobson?"

"Yes."

"I'm Sarah. Can we talk?" She pointed to an armchair and guided Jane towards it.

"What's this about?"

"I'm from the school." The woman held out her hand and Jane instinctively took it, feeling the cool smoothness of the other's elegant fingers.

Jane said nothing. This woman was Rix's assistant from Rafflesia. Rix was the enemy and so by extension…

The woman broke into Jane's scattered thoughts. "You've got it wrong," she said.

Now Jane found her voice. "What, wrong about the abduction of girls? Keeping them against their will?"

The woman looked around, maybe feeling awkward because of Jane's raised voice.

Jane felt her chest constrict. "The school is a cover for the sex trade."

And then the woman's face creased with concern. "You've got it all wrong," she said.

Jane shook her head. She desperately wanted to say something about rescuing the girls but instead managed: "We've been to the police."

Now the woman shook her head and smiled kindly. "My sweet girl, you have it all wrong. Really you do."

"I don't think so."

"The police won't do anything… because we've done nothing wrong."

"What about abduction—?"

"Let me explain." The woman reached forward to touch Jane's arm but Jane shrank back into the chair. "We take girls in."

"Abduct them."

"They are free to leave at any time. Yes, we take in girls—and many of them are orphans—but Rafflesia is a respected finishing school. We've been established for over fifty years. In fact, I was once a pupil there. I was also an orphan so I know the importance of the school. This is a once in a lifetime opportunity for a handful of girls to better themselves, better their prospects."

Now the woman called Sarah touched Jane's arm. "Honestly. Like I say, I was once given the same opportunity and I see this as my duty to provide the same for other girls."

Jane blinked rapidly. She'd slept for a few hours but her head hurt. She couldn't think straight. Could this be right? Could the whole thing have been a misunderstanding? And then she realized the problem with the story.

"What about the girls who escaped?"

Sarah nodded. Her face dropped. "Tragic," she said. "But they didn't escape. Not at all. Three girls wanted to leave and they were allowed to. It's the first time in our history that someone has done that and there were the three of them together. It was like they worked themselves up—convinced themselves that they would have a better life if they left. It was ridiculous and we handled it badly." She paused.

"Yes?"

"We just let them walk out. I listened to Major Rix and let them just walk out. I blame myself, but the major said they would realize their mistake and come back. He said we shouldn't give them anything or take them anywhere." Tears welled. "It won't happen again. Next time we will make sure they have travel plans, that they are taken to the station in JB at least."

Jane didn't say anything for a while and Sarah seemed to stare into the distance, maybe thinking about the girls she'd let go.

Jane said, "What about Laura?"

"Laura?" Sarah's focus came back.

"Laura van Loon. She left Penang seven weeks ago. A man called Turner took her in his plane and handed her over to someone called Petersen."

Sarah shook her head. "I don't know about the arrangements. I leave that for others. I just make sure the girls get proper training. You know, some of the girls have gone on to marry wealthy gentlemen. They couldn't have done that without learning how to be a lady."

Jane said, "What happened to Laura?"

"I don't know," Sarah repeated. "I really don't know."

"Where is Petersen?"

Sarah didn't answer straight away. Then she said, "Why don't you come back with me. Visit the school. Speak to the girls. You'll soon realize you're mistaken. And I'll introduce you to the major. I'd also like to know why Laura didn't come to the school. Perhaps he knows what his friend Petersen did with her."

Jane thought the car parked outside the hotel was a light grey Rolls Royce. She realized it wasn't when she spotted the silver cat on the bonnet.

A driver opened the door for her. She climbed into the rear with Sarah and settled into the luxury leather seat. It had a Motorola radio. She hadn't seen a car radio before and Sarah asked the driver to turn it on.

As they drove, Sarah asked Jane about Penang and her work.

"So you aren't in the army," Sarah said when Jane told her she was a nurse.

"Oh no! Queen Alexandra's Royal Army Nursing Corps." She laughed. "Just doing my bit."

"Then you know what it's like to care for others. Medicine is such an honourable profession."

309

They left the town and continued west. Sarah asked more questions, about England and home, and Jane watched the trees and elephant grass as they sped past.

Up a hill and around a bend and then the school walls appeared, cold and incongruous. The gates were closed and she saw the eagles either side, looking down as though judging her. It had been so easy to assume the worst. Laura was missing but it now seemed foolish to have put two and two together. Sarah was nice and friendly. She really wanted to help these girls. It was just the way they arrived here that was off.

The Jaguar barely slowed as the gates were opened before them and Jane saw the immaculate gardens and stunning house.

"Impressive, isn't it?" Sarah said. "Used to be a royal house a long time ago. Then it became a high-end school."

The Jaguar pulled up alongside steps to an entrance door and Sarah got out. Jane stepped out of her side and the Jaguar rolled forward towards a garage.

Jane said, "It's a school now, but what happened during the occupation?" She glanced up at the ornate arches and spotted the window bars that had mentioned. "Sarah?"

Sarah wasn't listening. She opened the door and stepped inside.

Jane followed, but when she looked around the entrance hall, Sarah wasn't there.

A man came out of a room to her right.

"Welcome," he said. He had a disarming smile and offered his hand.

As she was about to greet him, Jane heard a noise. She turned just in time to see something rush towards her.

And a burst of stars preceded utter darkness.

# FIFTY-FIVE

We waited at Kota Tinggi. The night closed in quickly from the east and the camp was soon in darkness except for the central area and scattered, burning hurricane lamps. I found the communications office and persuaded them to let me use the phone.

I called the Penang switchboard and asked for Deborah.

"Ash Carter," I said when the woman came on the line. "You placed a call for me three nights ago, remember?"

"Hmmm."

"I called the RMP in Singapore and Camp Kota Tinggi in JB."

She laughed like the faint tinkling of a bell. "Of course I remember you, sweetheart. You've got the nice voice."

"Short, fat and ugly," I said.

"My type."

"I need a favour."

"Anything, sweetheart."

Two minutes later she was calling the Rafflesia school in Bukit Zarah.

I heard her say, "This is the KL switchboard. I have a Mr Carter calling for a Major Rix." I heard a click and then I was through.

"Yes?" It was Rix.

"I'm at the hospital," I said. "Good trick."

"Expecting Miss Tiurina were you, Carter?" I could hear the smile in his voice.

I said, "I'm coming for you, Rix."

And then he surprised me by saying, "I don't think so."

"I'm coming back there and I'm taking your fake school down, brick by brick if I have to."

"Really?" he said, the smile still there.

"You'd better prepare," I said, feeling increasingly uncertain by his relaxed attitude. Yes he was in a fortress, but all he'd done was buy himself more time.

He said, "Jane Dobson."

The words were like a belt tightening around my chest. "What about her?"

"She's here," he said, paused, then added: "Although she's sleeping at the moment."

I said nothing.

"Oh, when I say sleeping, I mean when she wakes up she'll have quite a headache."

I gritted my teeth. "You've just made it worse for yourself, Rix. A hundred times worse. Like I said, I'm coming for you."

"You and whose army?"

"The Royal Military Police."

He laughed then. "Listen, Carter, come here and we'll talk. I can be a reasonable man. I'm sure you are too."

I said nothing.

"Just charging in here, being stupid, will get you killed. It'll get your girlfriend killed. We can talk."

There was silence as he thought, then he said, "Get here as soon as you can. Be sensible and your little girlfriend will be fine. We'll talk. We'll come to an arrangement."

I put the phone down.

"What's up?" Stevenson was sitting on the wall outside the comms room.

I told him and added: "We'd better move. Our advantage is time. He thinks he's got three to four hours, we're going to be there in one."

Stevenson nodded. "Then we'd better go get those guns."

# FIFTY-SIX

The Bedford truck bounced over the rough terrain in the darkness. Cranfield drove with the lights off. Ahead, we could see the Jungle Training Corps area.

We stopped forty yards away. There were lights on in one of the Nissen huts and it was quiet.

"Just one nightwatchman," Stevenson said as he got out.

I moved to follow him.

"No," he said. "You stay here. You don't want to be involved in what we're about to do."

I was about to disagree but he raised a hand. "Seriously, Ash, stay here."

Their dark forms disappeared in the gloom and then a minute later the Nissen hut door opened. They went inside.

I watched and waited.

Cranfield was the first to reappear. He ran out of the hut carrying a couple of rifles and a bag. Stevenson followed seconds later carrying something much bigger. It wasn't until he was back at the truck that I realized he had a Bren gun strapped across his chest.

"We can't risk that!" I said, getting out.

"I'll be careful." I could see his teeth as he grinned at me in the dark. He didn't stop and it clunked as its twenty-three pound weight met the metal of the load bed. He climbed in after it and reached out for me.

I took his hand and joined him in the back.

With our torches we surveyed our provisions. In addition to the arms, we had four ladders, three crates of the hooch, two flare guns, hurricane lamps, four petrol canisters and some butane bottles.

He turned his light on me. "Ready?"

"Let's go," I said.


"What did you do back there?" I asked as we headed down Route Three.

Stevenson said, "Just persuaded the guard to lend me the guns."

"How?"

"Cranny gave him a few bottles of hooch earlier. He couldn't resist, so providing he gets the weapons back he won't be telling anyone."

"And if he doesn't get them back."

"Then I probably don't need to worry about it, do I?" He laughed. "Seriously though, I knocked him out and tied him up so it looks like a burglary. About time they improved security around here!"

Although we'd now been over it many times, we talked through the plan again and I insisted that Stevenson only fired the Bren at the ground.

"Don't trust me with it?" he grumbled.

"No, I don't."

We skirted around the hill and parked where we had the previous night. I reckoned Rix would have set up a sentry. Someone would be the lookout, to pick us off before we even reached the gates. That's what I would have done. I would have also set an ambush on Route One—catch me on the way back from Kuala Lumpur.

315

I hoped he'd done that. If so, we were probably up against three men instead of four.

Stevenson and I split up and eased our way through the undergrowth. The loudest period of the cicadas had passed but there was still the insect hum and other jungle sounds that covered the noise of our footsteps.

I circled around the perimeter wall and came out near the gates. I flicked my torch on and off so that Stevenson would know I was there. He flashed back.

The lookout would either be at the bottom of the hill or, more likely, close to the gates. Maybe Rix would assume I'd just drive up to the gates and be an easy target.

The lookout wasn't near the gates. He was round the bend about a hundred and fifty yards away with a good line of sight for another fifty yards or so.

The idiot was smoking a cigarette and I saw the red glow as he inhaled. No doubt he thought he had plenty of time before I arrived.

But he wasn't on my side of the road. I saw the glow and then a grunt. A second later, Stevenson flashed his torch. I flashed back.

We continued down the hill, picking our way on either side of the road, and found no one else.

We joined up and returned to the lookout guy. I flicked on my torch. He was sprawled on the ground, face up, neck broken. It was the Brit I'd spoken to, which figured. The Aussies were probably closer to the boss and let the outsider be the sentry.

"One down." Stevenson grinned at me.

"Three to go," I said. "Where's the dog?"

"Don't know. Not in the kennel. I left the food by the gate but he could be anywhere."

We made our way back up the hill then cut through to the truck. I could smell the hooch ten yards away.

"You better not be drinking, you scum!" Stevenson whispered.

Cranfield chuckled. "Almost done," he said. "Thirty-six Molotov cocktails."

Stevenson and I took a ladder each and made our way to the perimeter, close to the outbuilding. I carried my Beretta and he had a rifle over one shoulder and the jemmy tucked into his belt.

I climbed up and checked for guards. Like before, I could see lights on in the garage and also one in the main building. It was the window where I'd seen Rix and his men last night. I saw movement inside and wondered whether they were in there planning and preparing.

I nodded down at Stevenson and he hauled up the second ladder. I placed it on the far side of the wall.

It wasn't for me. We'd talked about the girls, and the plan was to get them away before any shooting started. Stevenson handed me the jemmy and I dropped down on the grass and jogged over to the outbuilding wall. Again I waited, watched and listened.

After a few seconds punctuated only by distant animal cries, I moved around to the front. Now I could see a finger of light through the crack of the door. But I'd expected it to be locked, probably padlocked. That's why I had the jemmy. The girls were in here, and after three escaped, I figured the security would have been enhanced. But it wasn't.

No padlock. No bolt. Not even a keyhole.

I held the jemmy as a weapon and eased the door handle down. I paused and then moved it inwards. For a second I was bathed in light, so I stepped through and shut the door behind me.

It was a small room, smaller than I'd expected from the outside. There were dormitory beds but not twenty or sixteen. There were five.

The rest of the building was made up of a kitchen, a lounge and toilets. I'd guessed wrongly. This wasn't a girls' dorm. This was the staff quarters.

I slipped back outside and to the wall.

Stevenson was looking over the top.

"Not there," I whispered.

"Shit!"

I said, "Give me ten minutes." I could have added "Get everything ready", but he knew.

I dropped the jemmy and slunk along the wall, my Beretta at the ready. My biggest concern now was the dog. If it was roaming free in the grounds, I might not see it soon enough.

I made it to the garage without a sign of anyone or the dog.

Through the door I thought I heard a noise—like a quiet clang, but as I strained to hear, I heard nothing more.

I checked my watch. Two minutes gone.

The door creaked as I opened it but there was no one inside. It was a workshop with tools and sawdust on the floor. A cricket bat leaned against one wall. I walked on, through a door into the garage itself. It smelled of old oil and was empty except for four vehicles.

A sleek light grey Jaguar Mk II was the first. Then a small black car that I didn't recognize, a Ford probably. Then a Land Rover, plain and cream.

The final vehicle was a van. A dark blue van.

# FIFTY-SEVEN

Almost four minutes gone. I slipped outside and heard the dog for the first time. Which was a good thing. It's bark told me it was over by the staff outbuilding.

There were people in the downstairs room with the light on. But there was probably someone—maybe more than one—in an upstairs room, watching in the dark. That's what I would have done. If they were expecting me yet. I still hoped they thought I was two and a half hours away. Plenty of time to relax. Plenty of time to prepare.

I went onto all fours and began to crawl towards the main building, using the hedges as a shield.

When I reached the back door, I stood to one side. The frame was broken where they'd kicked their way out yesterday after I'd locked it. The hallway was dark and empty.

I glanced towards where I guessed the dog was sniffing the ladder, and then I went inside.

If Rix and his remaining men were in the room on the right again, we could have followed Stevenson's idea: all-guns-blazing. But with the dog outside I couldn't risk Stevenson joining me. I also needed to find those girls.

Inside, I could again hear the mumble of voices through the closed door. I stepped quietly along the carpet and noted that all the other doors were open. No

319

lights were on. Which led me to assume the girls were being held upstairs.

I tried to take the stairs lightly but they creaked and groaned as I moved up them. At the top, seven doors led off from the long landing. If there was a sniper, he would be at the front, so I checked the rear rooms. The first room was a bedroom, dark and otherwise empty. I noted a four-poster bed and plush furnishings: lace and velvet and maybe something like chiffon hanging down. I'd seen similar in my career as an MP, although never this fine. My instinct said brothel. High-end and luxury, but a room designed for sexual pleasure.

The second room was the same. The third looked like a typical classroom—certainly not what I'd seen in any brothel before. There was a small room at the end of the corridor that turned out to be a bathroom.

Three rooms remaining. One minute remaining.

I figured one sniper, one room. Odds of one in three. I chose the nearest door, the one furthest from the gates, furthest from where a sniper would want to be.

I turned the handle and stepped inside.

# FIFTY-EIGHT

Another classroom, dark and empty. I strode to the windows that opened onto a balcony, checked my watch and waited.

A number of things happened almost simultaneously. To the left of the gates a Molotov cocktail crashed against the wall and flames whooshed upwards. A split second later, a flare shot from left to right and ignited gas from a butane bottle that had been lobbed over the wall on the right. As the gas bottle exploded, so did a string of bottles hanging from the left-hand wall. *Ten green bottles hanging on a wall.*

There were flashes to the left and right and the gates burst apart. Stevenson had hit them dead centre with the Bedford with his foot to the floor.

We'd gone for a shock impact and I think we achieved it: an explosion of light and noise like the walls were coming down.

The truck slewed into the garden as Stevenson slammed on the brakes. He was out of the cab before a sniper could open fire.

In the noise and confusion, I stepped onto the balcony and saw a man at the far end. He made only a handful of shots at Stevenson before I took him down.

I flashed my torch three times to let them know it was now me up here but I still didn't know where the girls were. I repeated the signal and dashed back inside.

When I reached the top of the stairs, I could hear Stevenson open up with the Bren. He would be in the back of the Bedford now, behind the cab. I hoped he and Cranfield were following instructions: don't shoot at the school, just make a lot of noise.

Two men were already running along the hallway to the front. I shot one before he reached the end. The second turned in surprise and I shot him before his gun came up.

Neither was Rix. Four men were down, which hopefully meant just one to go.

The noise outside continued and I waited on the stairs. But no one appeared. I heard a door close somewhere downstairs but no one appeared beneath me.

The shooting outside stopped and I listened hard. All I could hear was a moan coming from one of the men sprawled on the floor below.

I edged down the staircase. At the bottom, I scooted across the hallway and checked the two fallen guys. One was dead, the other dying. I put him out of his misery. At the window I gave three flashes again: *I still haven't found the girls.*

"Rix!" I shouted. "It's over, Rix."

No response.

I started checking rooms, kicking the doors wide open, flicking on the lights. I passed two empty ones before I heard him.

"In here," he said. He didn't sound defeated, but then he didn't sound aggressive. It was like a friend telling me where they were.

I figured his voice came from the back—from the headmaster's office, the one with the Japanese artefacts.

322

Walking cautiously, I approached the door. Then a noise behind me made me turn and look at the entrance. Stevenson was there. He had the big gun in both hands and he was grinning.

He said, "Still no girls?"

I said, "Check all the rooms. They have to be here somewhere."

"You?"

"Rix is in his office," I said. I didn't mention that I expected to find Jane in there too. He was calm because he had a hostage. Someone who meant even more to me than saving the lives of schoolgirls—if I had to make a choice.

Fortunately I didn't.

I kicked open the door and could see him standing beside the desk. He was alone and had a revolver in his hand.

I noticed that the kimono was still in place but the samurai sword was on the desk and other artefacts were missing. My back brain processed this as we aimed our guns at each other.

"Where's Jane," I asked.

"Safe," he said. "But before we talk, I want to make a deal."

I shook my head. "Was your plan to have me picked up by the police?"

"They're on their way," he said, but I heard bluff in his voice.

"I got here before you were ready," I said. "McNaughton's not coming." For a second I saw doubt in his eyes. Not McNaughton then. "Who are you expecting?"

He shook his head. "You've got it all wrong."

"What do you mean?"

"I'll turn evidence."

I said, "Put the gun down."

He dropped it at his feet and placed a hand on the desk.

He said, "There you are. I'm showing good faith."

"Is that what you showed the guy you killed and decapitated—the man on the causeway?"

"I was following orders," he said. "Deal and I'll explain."

"Explain and I'll consider it," I said.

"All right. I'm not in charge here."

I shook my head. "You beat someone to death with a cricket bat and then you took off his head and hands. You didn't want him recognized—because that wasn't the purpose. You used him as a threat to warn off someone else."

Now he shook his head, although his eyes never left mine.

I said, "You used that sword and it cut cleanly."

"But that doesn't make me the boss."

"So who's the boss?"

He smiled with his mouth but not with his eyes. "I thought you'd spotted it. When you were in here before. I thought you saw the signature on the bottom of the letter. The one on the desk. RZ."

"RZ."

"She liked to call herself Rafflesia Zarah. She liked the power, liked men to be afraid of her. She was here during the war, you know. And at the end she killed three of the Japanese officers who had kept her here. She tortured them for days. She's a hard woman. Yes I used the sword, but I didn't beat him to death. That was her. She went crazy because he betrayed us. He let those girls escape."

I said, "Where are the girls."

"Deal?"

"All right. You help us get Sarah, you have a deal. Where is she?"

"Right now? Beneath us."

I must have involuntarily followed his gaze, because I didn't see his initial move. The next second he had the sword in his hand and lunged for me.

The sound of the Bren gun pummelled the air. Rix's arms went up and he danced briefly like a marionette. And then his body went down but kept jerking despite him being dead.

Stevenson stood beside me.

"Bastard," he said.

"There must be a cellar," I said. "The girls are down there and the woman probably has them held hostage."

It took us a few minutes to find the hidden door in the panelling beneath the staircase.

I kicked it open and found a light switch. The smell of fear assaulted my nostrils as I moved down, step by step, gun ready. But when I reached the bottom I was surprised at what I saw. It was like a dorm room with twenty basic cots. At the end was a cage were young women and girls huddled together, with tape around their mouths. Their hands were also bound.

We quickly opened it up and they spilled out, nervous and uncertain. They clustered by the nearest bed.

I eased forward and removed the first gag. The girl looked Eurasian and was maybe sixteen.

"Where is she?" I said.

"Sarah?" she said, hoarse with nerves, and pointed towards the far end of the room where there appeared to be a hole in the wall leading into a tunnel.

"And the other woman—Jane?"

The girl nodded again.

"Help them," I said to Stevenson, meaning the girls from the cage. I shone my torch and proceeded along the tunnel. It was barely wide enough for one person, with a rounded ceiling that made me duck. There were no doors and, after fifty yards, it seemed to be a dead end.

But it wasn't. When I got there I saw it was a turn, and then a few yards later a four-rung metal ladder went upwards.

The hatch moved easily and I poked it open before risking climbing up.

I was in the garage.

The doors were open and the black Ford was gone.

# FIFTY-NINE

The front garden, wall and broken gates glowed orange. Fires burned where Molotov cocktails had been thrown. Cranfield crunched down the drive, weapon at the ready.

I called to him and we met halfway.

"Black car," I said. "Did you see it?"

"Yeah, she got away," Cranfield said.

"Young woman with black hair?" I asked.

"No. A little old woman. I let her through." Doubt creased his forehead. "She *was* escaping, right?"

I didn't answer. I was already running back to the garage.

Sarah pulled off the grey wig and tossed it into the footwell. Jane was in the boot and she could hear the bangs as the feisty girl thrashed about. If that stupid soldier in the drive had listened he would have surely heard, but he hadn't. He was too anxious to worry about an old woman.

It was over. She'd hoped that the decapitation and extreme treatment of Jeevan would shock the others into line. They should have killed Carter when they had the chance but that was now in the past. The future lay in Sumatra. That was her contingency plan and she'd been ready. She had plenty of money and taken a few of her most precious artefacts.

And she had the girl as a hostage.

Sarah would lie low for a few weeks in Sumatra and then fly to the Philippines. She had heard that Manila was becoming like Singapore city. There would be plenty of opportunity to re-establish her business. She would find a town close but not too close, and the men would come—they always did.

Once out of Bukit Zarah, Sarah drove much faster. She took the laterite-covered lane into the jungle, her headlights bouncing due to the uneven ground. It was narrow and treacherous in places, but it was a shorter route to the airfield.

After twenty-five minutes she reached the left turning she was looking for. She slowed and took it carefully and then stopped.

Standing in the middle of the road was a man with a rifle. In the headlights she could see a Chinese face, a light green uniform and the cap of a communist. He was dirty and tired and thin.

The surprise on his face told her it was a chance confrontation. She was on a remote track and he was crossing it.

The communist's rifle came up and he advanced. His eyes were wide and scared. She guessed he was young and inexperienced. Most of the insurgents had been plantation labourers. They joined the MRLA—the liberation army—expecting money, food and women. The reality was quite different, and most of them looked starved.

Sarah wound down the window.

"I am Chinese," she said in fluent Mandarin. She repeated it in the Hokkien dialect.

The soldier hesitated but kept the gun raised. He stepped forward until he was within reach.

"Do you have food?" he said in Hokkien.

"No."

He looked into the car and focused on the bags on the back seat. With a jerk he had the door open and one of the bags out. It contained her clothes and artefacts. As he tossed the pagoda paperweight aside, a thump came from the rear.

"What do you have in the boot?" he asked.

"A pig," she said, and even as the words came out of her mouth, she realized her mistake. Honesty would have been better than the lure of food.

He walked around the car. As she got out he swivelled his gun towards her.

"I'm not a threat. I am just a schoolteacher," she said and smiled. "You can have the pig."

His attention turned back to the rear of the Ford. He placed his hand on the latch and opened the boot. For a second, the surprise of finding a bound woman made him freeze.

Sarah was already moving. She dropped her shoulder and charged, hitting the communist sideways. The rifle went off, a sound that echoed through the close trees. The man fell to the floor still holding his gun. He tried to swing it up, but Sarah was too close. She kicked the man's arm and then stamped on his chest.

Another gunshot sounded, not far away. The communist wasn't alone after all. She heard voices in the jungle and the sound of men running through undergrowth.

Sarah slammed the boot shut and jumped back into the driver's seat. There was a shout and a volley of shots.

The engine was still running and the wheels spun as she stamped her foot on the accelerator. The car lurched forward, slewing one way and then the other as she fought for control.

Twenty feet, then thirty feet away. Bullets pinged off the metalwork and the rear window shattered. She kept her foot down until the sound of gunfire faded and then stopped.

She cursed her bad luck and the loss of her bag and artefacts. Then she cursed the car. It was getting increasingly hard to control and the offside rear wheel hit every bump hard.

A puncture and no spare. But she wasn't going to stop again. The car was still drivable providing she slowed. She dropped the speed to under twenty and less noise brought back her composure. Now she realized that she could no longer hear Jane banging about. Had a stray shot killed her? No matter. She was well away and almost at the airfield.

She saw the final turn and cut through from the lane to the field. She followed the track around the perimeter to the buildings and stopped at the workshop.

Bullet holes peppered the bodywork, but when she opened the boot, Jane was still alive. Unhurt.

Sarah pulled her out and she flopped, dazed, onto the ground. Then she dragged her by the arms to the shed and opened the doors. She started the generator, threw the power switch and bright lights flooded the inside.

She tied Jane to a workbench and touched her hair. It wasn't red but it was close enough. She was more than a hostage. With her pretty face and hair, the girl would fetch a good price in Sumatra. Or maybe she'd keep her and be the start of the new business. Good always came from bad, and this was the start of a new beginning.

She opened the back doors to the shed and walked straight to the trees.

★ ★ ★

Jane's head hurt from where she'd been hit and from being thrown about in the boot.

She would need to focus if she were to survive this, but it was hard. She just wanted to close her eyes and sleep and wake up in a comfortable bed, like this was all a bad dream. But it wasn't. It was real. She'd fallen for this woman's charm and trusted her.

She felt sick as the woman caressed her face and hair, but she continued to act as if she was half-conscious. She had to wait for her chance.

Sarah walked towards the trees and then started to pull away the bushes. While she was occupied, Jane scanned around for something, anything to cut her bonds.

There were tools neatly attached to the wall above the workbench. She managed to stand and raised a leg over the bench. It just reached the wall, so she flicked her foot and made contact with a file. On the third attempt it dislodged and fell. With more manoeuvring she got it close enough to reach. Then, holding it in one hand and with just a little play in the bindings, she began to saw at the rope.

Jane watched the woman again and abruptly stopped sawing. Sarah had cleared the undergrowth and a palm-fence to reveal a small aircraft. Now she was coming back.

She walked into the workshop and picked up a hook on the end of a cable. Then she returned to the plane, reeling out the cable as she went. Once there, she attached the hook above the front wheel. Then she returned and switched on a motor and pulled a lever. The cable was a winch that tightened and rewound itself.

The plane began to move slowly. It rolled forward twelve yards, clear of the undergrowth, and Sarah

331

pushed the lever and the winch stopped. She returned to the plane, disconnected the hook and went back to the motor and switched it off.

She climbed up on the plane's wing and opened the door to the cockpit. She got in, and Jane saw what looked like confusion on the other woman's face.

She heard the plane's engine turn and choke and die.

Sarah yelled inside the cockpit and pounded the instrument panel. She went quiet for a moment and then climbed out.

In the workshop once more, she wheeled out a fuel tank and connected a hose.

The smell of aviation fuel filled the air and made Jane's eyes water. Each time Sarah looked at her she stopped sawing at the ropes. Now she felt one start to fray.

Sarah yelled again—frustration and anger. Jane stopped and watched her. Fluid was running under the belly of the plane and onto the ground. And then Jane got it: the fuel line had been severed. Sabotaged maybe? She hoped so.

Sarah calmed herself and searched the workshop, presumably for something to mend the leak. She scrabbled a hand over the workbench.

Jane dropped her head, subdued, no threat. If Sarah spotted the missing file… but she didn't. She moved away, and through half-open eyelids, Jane saw her find what she was looking for and hurry back to the plane.

The first cord snapped and her right hand moved more freely. She started sawing at the next cord.

Sarah connected a new tube and immediately began to fill the tank again. A few minutes later, she disconnected the fuel line and climbed into the cockpit.

The engine fired on the third attempt and the propeller started to turn, slowly at first and then faster.

She released the brakes and taxied round the buildings and to the start of the strip.

For a moment Jane thought the woman was going to take off, but the propeller speed dropped again and Sarah climbed out. From the Ford she fetched a bag and threw it into the plane. Then she headed back to the workshop.

Jane kept her head down but kept watching.

Sarah suddenly had a knife.

"OK, time to go," she said, and placed a hand on Jane's shoulder, ready to cut the ties.

In one movement Jane jerked her head upwards and pushed up with her feet. The top of her head struck Sarah under the chin as she bent down.

The woman didn't howl. She just jolted up and backwards like a felled tree. She lay flat on her back and seemed out cold. Blood on the light concrete looked stark around her head. Her hair looked sticky with it.

Jane's head hurt like hell where she'd connected with Sarah's jaw, but she ignored the pain. She kicked away the dropped knife and felt in the woman's pocket. Her fingers closed around a key—the car key—and she gripped it like it was salvation itself. Then she started for the car. Her legs were weak and her hands shaking as she pulled the driver's door open and slid into the seat.

She put the key in the ignition. The engine turned over once and stopped. Fear and instinct made her glance in the rear-view mirror. The interior of the workshop was clearly visible. And Sarah was no longer on the floor.

# SIXTY

*Just go!* Jane forced herself to turn back and fumble with the ignition key. And then she screamed.

Sarah's face loomed large through the windscreen. Blood edged her hair and left tracks on her neck. Both of her hands were pressed on the bonnet as though stopping the car from moving.

*Focus!* Jane screamed to herself. Her trembling hand took hold of the key and turned it once more. The engine started. She hit the accelerator and heard a reassuring roar of power. Then she jammed the gearstick into first. But she forgot the clutch and the car lurched and stalled.

Sarah pulled open the door.

Jane started to turn the key but Sarah grabbed her right arm and pulled. Another jerk and Jane found herself falling from the car. And Sarah didn't let go. She kept on pulling, dragging Jane by her arm towards the plane.

Sarah had something in her other hand, and as Jane fought, it was brought down hard onto her shoulder.

The acute pain made her head swim. Her arm was useless. Her collarbone felt broken. Jane fought against blacking out but the fight was gone. Sarah pulled harder and Jane howled with the searing pain. It was like her arm was being torn off. She had no choice but to go where Sarah pulled her.

They were heading for the plane. Her ears rang but above the noise in her head she could hear the propellers continuing their lazy rotation. Then she thought there was something else. Another machine.

Sarah switched direction, as though she'd changed her mind. Now Jane was being tugged towards the workshop and there was panic in Sarah's face.

She glanced back, again and again. And then Jane saw them: lights bouncing towards them along the runway. Headlights. A car's headlights.

"Ash!" Jane yelled, although her voice was faint and lost.


I had been driving like a maniac for almost forty minutes. I'd hared along the route I'd driven with Stevenson but faster. It was dark and dangerous but desperation and intense focus had kept me on the road.

I'd figured Sarah would have taken a shorter route and she had a head start. A growing ache in my gut told me I was too late.

As I burst out onto the runway my spirits rose. I saw the plane lit by the workshop lights. I drove straight at it in case Sarah tried to take off, but then I saw two people struggling in the field behind it.

I closed the gap and realized Sarah was dragging Jane. She pulled her into the workshop and looped an arm around Jane's neck. There was something in her other hand.

I passed the Ford, skidded to a halt ten yards out and dived out of the jeep. Using it as cover, I aimed my gun.

"Game's up!" I shouted.

Sarah was holding Jane in front of her like a shield. In her free hand she held a crowbar, not a gun.

I stood and walked towards the workshop. Sarah pulled Jane backwards until they could go no further.

Then she swung the crowbar under Jane's chin and pulled hard.

Jane fought, but she was stopped as the metal pressed into her soft throat. I could see Sarah speaking to her, threatening.

I shouted, "Stop!"

I entered the workshop, the sound of the generator beating against the wooden walls.

Sarah said, "Take another step and she'll never speak again. Take two and she'll die." Her voice came out like an animal's snarl.

I didn't move.

Sarah said, "Now drop the gun."

I paused and then placed it at my feet.

"Good man. Now kick it over to me," Sarah said, her voice gaining in confidence.

I kicked the gun but aimed it short. I figured Sarah would want it. She looked at me with cold eyes and then shuffled forward. One pace. Two. It was almost within her reach. As soon as her eyes left mine and flicked to the gun, I lunged.

Sarah stepped back, the gun still between us. I could feel the hum of the electricity from the generator. It was behind me now.

I saw something flash across Jane's eyes, and then she did a slow blink. One. Two. Three. On three she became a dead weight, dropping an inch or so and startling Sarah. At the same instant she dug her left elbow into the woman's gut and stamped down and back with her left foot. The elbow made good contact and the foot scraped down her shin.

Sarah fell back and must have released her grip on the bar because Jane squirmed free and dived for the floor.

I was already moving. I closed the gap and made a grab for the crowbar.

Sarah saw the move and swung it at me.

I leaned back, like avoiding a punch, and the crowbar whooshed past. Then I stepped in to counterpunch. But the woman was fast. She sidestepped, jabbed out with the crowbar and caught the meat of my right arm.

For a second my arm felt paralyzed. Sarah saw an opening and advanced, jabbing and jabbing. I dodged and weaved and backed up.

She caught me again. Same arm, although less pain this time. But I made it look bad. I staggered and went on one knee.

The generator was right behind me now, but the noise was forgotten in the excitement. Sarah was like a hunter who had closed in for the kill. Her eyes had a wild look and an insane grin split her face.

"Goodbye, scum!" she said, and she swept the crowbar overarm towards my head. At the last moment I dived away. Momentum carried the crowbar into the space where I'd been and beyond. There was no way to change the course.

The smart thing would have been to let go. But it was a split-second thing and the realization of her error came too late.

The crowbar struck the electrical terminals of the generator in a shower of sparks. Sarah was hit by the full force of the electrical current discharging to earth. Her body jiggled and she screamed. It seemed to go on a long time but the noise was just the echo against the walls and jungle beyond.

# SIXTY-ONE

I checked Jane's collarbone in case it was broken but found no damage just tenderness. At first, she held herself up, apparently stoic. But this was shock. I put my arms round her and she collapsed into me. The emotion finally came out. She cried hard and let me take her weight.

Maybe five minutes passed before she eased herself away and wiped her eyes.

"I'm all right," she said.

"Yes, you did well."

She started to apologize for her stupidity but I waved it away and guided her to the Land Rover and drove. The generator still hummed but it soon became lost in the rumble of the jeep and the buzz of the jungle.

I went back to our hotel and stayed with her as she had a bath. She knew about the girls in the cellar because she'd been taken past them. What she didn't know was that Stevenson had agreed to take them in the Bedford to the orphanage.

I tucked her into bed and told her I had things to do.

Concern creased her face. "More trouble?"

"No," I said. "Just things I need to wrap up. Get some sleep and wait for me here."

I made her promise this time. No more heading out on her own. I needed to do two things. There was an outstanding matter regarding the body on the causeway, plus I wanted the truth about Laura van Loon.

# SIXTY-TWO

It was still dark when I arrived at the Kota Tinggi camp. The boom was raised for a troop carrier leaving the base. I nodded to the guards by their picket fence and they waved me through.

The central block of buildings—the NAAFI, the canteen, the cinema—were all in darkness except for the odd outside light. I turned left and bumped over the rough ground towards the humanitarian aid tents.

I could see a string of hurricane lamps and two trucks. People were up and Stevenson was back.

There was a light on in their mess tent and I could smell sausages. Stevenson sat with Cranfield at a bench inside. Both of them had the same glow, the same fixed grin.

Stevenson waved and pointed to his plate, piled high with eggs, sausages and beans.

"Breakfast?" he asked.

"Tea would be good."

The sergeant bellowed and a very tired-looking private rushed a mug of tea to the table. I guessed he'd been dragged out in the middle of the night just to get Stevenson a very early breakfast.

"How are the girls?" I asked, after telling them I'd rescued Jane and that Sarah was dead.

"At the orphanage," Stevenson said. "That Lady Dandy—or whatever—is a strange old bird."

I nodded.

"But she was ready and had blankets and fruit cake ready for them."

"Fruit cake!" Cranfield laughed and I figured he was talking about Lady Hage-Dando.

I said, "JTC?"

"Not a problem," Stevenson said. "We took the guns back and untied the poor bastard. Yes they're missing quite a few bullets, but... well you can guess a lot of bullets can get used up and lost."

I nodded.

Cranfield said, "Sorry I let the old lady escape."

"She was wearing a wig," I explained. "That was Sarah."

"Ah," he said, finally getting it. Then he grinned. "But I'm very proud of my shot—the flare hit the target first time."

I was looking at Stevenson. "Rix..." I prompted.

He smiled. "Overkill, you think?"

"You blasted him to bits with that Bren!"

"I was angry. The dog came at me so I had to shoot him."

"And that made you angry with Rix?"

"I like dogs. It wasn't the dog's fault. If it hadn't been let loose... Anyway I figured Rix was to blame."

I nodded. "What about the bodies?"

Cranfield said, "What bodies?" and they both laughed.

Stevenson explained: "We dumped them in the outbuilding and used the remaining petrol."

They ate and I drank my tea.

"What's next?" Stevenson asked as he finished his last mouthful. "For you, I mean."

"It's over, right?" Cranfield added.

"It's not over."

I could see their minds processing this, trying to figure out what I meant.

"The body on the causeway," I said.

"You need to know who did it." Stevenson nodded, like he understood how a cop's mind worked.

"It doesn't matter which of them did it, though I suspect Rix was telling the truth. She beat him to death with a cricket bat and then later got Rix to remove the head and hands."

Stevenson nodded. "You want to know who the man was."

I said, "Partly, but this is more about why."

"Why?"

"It was a warning. Like the death threat I received at the hotel—the Chinese note. I ignored it and they attacked my hotel. I thought there was a woman in my room and I now think it was Sarah."

Stevenson shook his head.

I explained: "The headless body leads to the *who*. Who was being warned off?"

"And you know?"

"I think so."

"Who then?" Cranfield asked.

I said, "I'll find out very soon."


I stayed with them until daybreak, thanked them again for their help and left. But I only went as far as the comms room and made three phone calls.

My first was to Captain McNaughton at the JB police station.

When I was put through, I said, "You tried to set me up. I want to speak to you, face to face."

"Fine," he said gruffly, "but first explain."

"You called about a girl at the KL hospital. There was no girl. That call was to get me out of the way. Maybe someone was waiting for me there. But I didn't go."

"Why did you think there was no girl?"

"You said her name was Jakaterina. I knew she called herself Kate. If she told someone her name in hospital, no way would she say Jakaterina."

"I was just reading a message."

"Face to face," I said.

"Fine," he said again. "Where do you want to meet?"

"The school," I said, and ended the call. Then I asked the operator to put me through to Gillman Barracks and Lieutenant Cole.

When he picked up, I said, "I've worked it out, Jim. This whole thing with the body and the code. The misdirection of 221. I know why it all happened."

"Go on."

"It was a warning about the Rafflesia school. RZ referred to Sarah, the woman in charge. Everyone was afraid of her. She killed that pilot, threatened me and set fire to my hotel room. She also killed the man on the causeway."

"OK," he said.

"But this is now about a list."

"A list?"

"The list of clients who used her services. Important people. Men who would do anything to hide their involvement in what was effectively a sex trade involving young girls held against their will."

"God!" he said.

"This is where you can help me. I know roughly where the list is—the list of clients—the RZ List." I emphasized this and hoped I'd got it right.

"OK."

"I need help searching for it."

"Where?"

"At the school. Meet me there with a squad of men so we can pull the place apart and find that evidence."

"Evidence," he repeated.

"Yes."

"I'll do what I can, Ash."

I ended the call and asked for Secretary Coates at the government house.

He said, "I told you to come back. What do you think you're playing at, Carter?"

I said, "This is too important. I don't know who has been involved but I need to find out. I will find out."

"Stop now and come back to work or you are fired."

"There's a list," I said, ignoring him. "The RZ list of clients of the school. We need to know who's on it. They are senior figures, sir. There could be people in the government."

"Are you implying—?"

"I'm not implying anything. I'm just explaining why that list is so important. I'm going to the school and I'm going to resolve this now."

He said something else but I was already replacing the receiver.

# SIXTY-THREE

A large black Ford drove between the twisted gates and edged down the driveway. The walls were blackened and large patches of the garden still smouldered.

I was looking out of a front window and watched the car disappear down the side of the building. Then I took up my position in time to hear the front door squeak open.

"I'm in the last office on the right," I shouted. "The headmaster's office."

Heavy footsteps came towards me and the door opened. Major Vernon.

I was sitting at the desk and he scowled down at me.

"Carter," he said, in his best bellicose voice, "you are under arrest."

I inclined my head. "For what?"

"A whole list of things but mostly for wasting military police time. Now stand up."

I didn't move and it unnerved him.

I said, "Where is Lieutenant Cole?"

"Not coming. I caught wind of your little plan and stopped it. I don't know what you are doing here but it's not a military police issue."

I said, "Let me tell you about the body on the causeway. You'll agree that the body was a military police issue."

He said nothing.

"The body had the letters RZ on it for Rafflesia Zarah. It was a warning for someone, someone specific. Someone who would know it was for them and what it was about."

His hand rested on the service revolver at his side but he still said nothing.

"Draw your gun," I said. I lifted my Beretta from my lap and placed it in front of me. "Please give me an excuse to shoot you."

He dropped his hand by his side but there was still tension in the arm.

"The body and the threat," I said. "I don't think the intended target liked being in that position. I think they wanted to give a message back. He tried to wash off the RZ and change it. Upside down it looked like 221. Then the RMP—or rather me with a bit of RMP support—investigated. The drugs issue was old news. The colonel at Majidi Barracks had complained for months."

Vernon said, "Lieutenant Colonel Underwood is an idiot."

"You think we're all idiots," I said.

He glared at me.

"Doctor Thobhani spotted some other blood marks that had been washed off. Two chevrons—arrows—one up and one down. Only they weren't arrows, were they, Anthony?"

"Tony," he said, cautious now. "My name is Tony."

"Anthony Vernon," I said. "AV—like up and down arrows if you can't see the cross on the A."

He shook his head.

"The body on the causeway was a message for you. A warning that you could be next. You washed off the blood and replaced it with your own."

"You're guessing," he said.

346

"How's your finger now? When I saw you after you found the body, you'd cut your fingers, deliberately, to write 221."

"Rubbish!"

"You arrived on the scene after the body had been discovered and then you had Cole take over the case. In fact, you prompted Cole that the blood said 221."

"Exactly!" he scoffed. "The important phrase there was 'after the body had been discovered'. I wasn't there first. I didn't have the opportunity."

"The opportunity threw me for a long time," I said. "I'd assumed you'd been travelling into Malaysia in the morning, but you weren't. And you were in the Ford that you've just arrived in. How do I know? Because Customs noted you as the third to cross in the morning. You probably jumped the queue. Not too early, not too late, so that someone else could have started the investigation."

"So?"

"So you were crossing *back*. You had to cross to Malaya at some point. You weren't recorded by Customs because you went through Woodlands Crossing at night. The guards would have recognized you and let you pass. They did it for me when I was with Sergeant Hegarty. RZ—Sarah—knew you were coming and made sure you'd see the body. And you did. You had plenty of time to wash off the message, cut yourself and write 221. You must have been so smug. Send a message right back at her. A threat of your own."

He shook his head. "All just speculation."

I said, "If you hadn't sent us on the wild goose chase, Dave Hegarty would still be alive today."

"Don't blame that on me!"

Keeping my eyes on Vernon, I opened the desk draw and pulled out a black pocket book.

"What's that?"

"The RZ list. The names of all the clients this so-called school has ever had."

I saw his face whiten and his teeth clench. He held out a hand—his left, so that he could still go for the revolver.

I placed the book on the desk, next to my gun, with my hand over it.

"So it's not just speculation," I said.

"Let me explain."

"Please do."

"I was a client when it was legitimate. They were training the girls to be young ladies. I expected I'd marry one someday."

I looked dubious.

"All right, I'll be honest, I expected I'd have one as a mistress. An attractive girl on my arm. One who knew how to behave and be discreet. But the girls got younger and I expressed concern."

"Then some girls escaped."

"Yes!"

I shook my head. "Didn't it trouble you that they were held captive here?"

He looked pleadingly at me. "I didn't know!"

"But you had sexual relations with them."

"Yes, but never—"

"Never what?"

"Against their will."

He said, "Look, I complained and they threatened me. She threatened me. They were nice and friendly but then the body turned up with my initials and I knew what she was saying. I had to protect myself."

"You misdirected an investigation for your own ends. And Hedge got killed."

He said, "Let me have the list. I'll make sure all those men are brought to justice."

"You don't know who they are?"

"Just one."

"Your chum Commander Alldritt."

He nodded. He was offering up his friend in an attempt to convince me of his good intentions.

I said, "Who else?"

"I don't know, honestly. We could only come at scheduled times. I knew there were senior people involved but never who."

And then the realization hit him. "Hold on," he said. "You have the list. You said you have the list."

I skimmed the black book across the desk towards him. He caught it and flicked through.

The pages were blank. When he looked up, my gun was aimed at him.

"You're not going to kill me," he said.

"No. I'm going to see you suffer the disgrace of a court martial."

"You're way outside your jurisdiction." He laughed but it was hollow.

I said, "They were clever with the body. The causeway was your jurisdiction and the crime was committed here. I found the murder weapon in the garage. Rafflesia Zarah—Sarah—beat him to death with a cricket bat. There were bloodstains in the garage workshop under the sawdust. He was killed there and then his head and hands were removed with a samurai sword. They were probably fed to the local pigs. They kept his body on ice—"

"I don't know who it was."

"Doesn't matter. Who he was didn't matter to you or them. In fact, his anonymity was important. It wasn't a murder investigation, it was just a message. But it was a murder nonetheless."

Again he said, "Outside your jurisdiction."

"But not mine!" Another man stepped into the room. Captain McNaughton. He'd convinced me he had just been the messenger about a second girl. After I'd called him, McNaughton confirmed with the hospital in Kuala Lumpur that no second girl had been found. Then he confronted the lieutenant who had passed on the message. The man confessed he'd been another customer of the school. He'd also been instrumental in deflecting any investigation into the school.

McNaughton snapped handcuffs onto Vernon and removed his revolver.

"Think yourself lucky," I said to Vernon as he was led away. "I wanted to shoot you."

# SIXTY-FOUR

Su Ling took a long time to answer my call but I stayed on the line until I was put through.

"Yes?" she said, without a pleasantry or explanation for the delay.

I said, "I need a favour. I need an address."

Her tone was cold. "Why should I help you?"

"Because of what we have... what we had."

She didn't say anything for a minute. I heard a door close and guessed she was in an office and didn't want anyone to overhear.

"I never really loved you," she said when she came back on the line. "You know that. It was just physical."

"OK," I said, but I thought she was trying to convince herself as much as me.

She said, "You could never accept me for who I am. Who I work for."

"I did."

"No you didn't. Otherwise you wouldn't have suspected me of sending that death threat."

"I didn't—"

"You did!"

I let a silence grow on the line, like it was pushing us apart. I thought about the John Wayne film. Su Ling and I came from different worlds. The silver screen wasn't reality. A gunslinger couldn't marry an angelic Quaker.

A cop couldn't be with the mistress of a criminal. If that was what she was. If that's what Yipp was.

Finally, I said, "I'm sorry. It was just—"

"Accept it, Ash. We used one another and you just demonstrated it again when you asked me to help. You got information from me. I got information from you."

"Just spies," I said, reflecting what Andrew Yipp had said to me about *The Art of War*.

She said nothing.

I said, "I just need your help one more time."

"And then you will leave us alone."

*Us*. I figured she was now including her boss.

I said, "I can't influence what Secretary Coates does but I will give you my assurance that I won't pursue Mr Yipp."

"Or me."

"Or you."

I said, "What do you know about the business they were running at Rafflesia school?"

"Is that what this is about?" She sounded surprised.

"Maybe. Was Mr Yipp involved in any way?"

"I don't know," she said, and I believed her.

"There must have been a client list."

"Probably. There usually is. You know it used to be a finishing school. Then the Japanese officers used it and there were rumours that they kept young women there. For their pleasure."

I said, "Sarah?"

"Zarah," she said. "That isn't her real name. I believe she was once a girl there—in the time of the occupation."

"She was in charge. Did you know that?"

"Yes."

"Why wouldn't Mr Yipp be involved? He runs brothels."

"Too niche for him. And other reasons."

"Other reasons?"

"I don't know everything, Ash. Maybe he didn't like the Australian connection. But more likely it was the age of the girls."

"What about Yiqing Liang?"

"What about her?"

"She used to run the adoption unit at the hospital. And I know about that department."

She didn't comment.

I said, "They take babies and sell them. Your boss is involved in that business, so he knows Miss Liang."

Again silence.

I said, "I need to talk to her?"

"Why?" Now she sounded suspicious, but I wasn't trying to trap her or her boss.

"I need to understand something and I think she knows."

"Knows what?"

"Where Petersen is—the man who handed the girls over to the school. The man who was the last to see a young girl called Laura van Loon."

"And that's it?"

"I want to know what happened to the girl—for a friend." I wished we were looking at one another. Wished she could see the desperation in my eyes, the need to know for Jane's sake. "Please."

She took a long breath. "And this is the last thing. You promise?"

"Yes."

"Say you promise."

"I promise."

She said, "Give me half an hour and I'll call you back."

353

It was only ten minutes later when the hotel receptionist called me to the phone. But it wasn't Su Ling. She had an assistant, an awkward-sounding young man, call me. He confirmed it was me and then gave me an address in Johor Bahru.

The address for Yiqing Liang.

# SIXTY-FIVE

I'd passed the house many times since it was on the road between the European and Oriental Hotel and the centre of the town.

It was a typical shop-house: downstairs a retail outlet or service, upstairs living accommodation. This particular shop was half vegetables and half hardware. I didn't stop to consider the odd combination. Instead I walked straight through towards the elderly Malay shopkeeper. He just watched me. Initially his face lit with the expectation of business, then concern as I strode directly up to him.

"I'm looking for Yiqing Liang," I said.

He turned away and busied himself with some tools. I figured he was a smart man and knew how to protect himself if need be.

I said, "I need her help. I'm looking for somebody and she can help."

"You shouldn't come here," he said, turning back to me but with a hand still inside a toolbox, gripping a hammer probably.

I wondered now whether I should have allowed Jane to come with me.

"You should stay here and rest," I'd said to her in the bedroom.

"I want to know." She pulled the face that I'd grown to know as her intransigent look. "I need to know what happened to Laura."

"And you will," I said, "but it could still be dangerous. This woman is likely to have been involved."

If I'd been accompanied by Jane, maybe this shopkeeper would have been less suspicious. I moved quickly and gripped his arm—the one inside the toolbox. He held a claw hammer briefly and then let go.

"It's over," I said, gambling. "The trouble is over. I just need to speak to her now."

I could see his eyes assessing me and figured I'd been right. He was worried for her and assumed I was here for trouble—to hurt her.

I let go of his arm. "Sorry, I just need a minute of her time. Where is Yiqing?"

And then he did that classic thing of thinking about her location and giving it away by the flick of his rheumy eyes. Upstairs.

I stepped away from him and made sure he wasn't going to come at me with the hammer before I turned and opened the rear door. It took me out into an enclosed courtyard, filled with boxes and detritus. A metal staircase ran up to the first floor and I mounted them swiftly.

I knocked on the door and stepped close to the wall, hidden from the rear window.

Miss Liang froze for a second as she pulled the door wide enough to see me. Then she tried to close it again but I'd already stepped forward.

"What happened?" I said, walking into the room as she back-pedalled.

She stopped when she could go no further. She placed her hands on the wall and a window pressed at her back.

"You know what happened. Tell me!"

Miss Liang shook her head.

I said, "It's over. Rix is dead."

She looked uncertain. "What about Zarah—the woman?" Her voice was quiet and afraid.

"She's dead too."

Miss Liang's left hand relaxed from the wall.

"You're sure?"

"Yes. I saw them both die."

Relief flushed through Miss Liang's body then. I thought she would collapse but she didn't. She took a few seconds to regain her composure and nod.

"Thank God." Her voice was more confident now, though still not the harsh tones of when I'd met her before at the adoption centre. She pointed to chairs around a table and we sat.

Now it was her turn to say, "What happened?"

I told her about the gunfight at the school and then chasing Zarah to the airstrip.

"Thank God," she said again when I finished. "She was a terrible woman. Everyone was afraid of her, although no one ever saw her do it. Poor old Dan."

"Dan?"

"Dan Petersen."

I already suspected the truth. It all made sense. The final piece of the puzzle that I really didn't want to fall into place. Petersen was my connection to Laura.

I said, "Petersen was the body on the causeway, wasn't he?"

Miss Liang nodded. "I think so."

"Why?" I said. "I thought he was Rix's friend."

"They had history," she said. "But Dan was never totally on board with it. I don't know why he was duty-bound, but he said he had to help Rix."

"That still doesn't explain why."

"The business changed. He told me he wasn't happy. I think it was originally about providing young ladies for wealthy gentlemen."

"For sex."

"Not initially. Well not really. It was giving the young women... what do you call it... class, perhaps. I think Zarah intended them as potential wives for rich bachelors. Only it became clear that the men with the money wanted a mistress more than a wife. Having a maid who performed other services and knew how to be discreet was an attractive prospect, it seems."

"But the girls were taken—"

"And given a chance at a better life. Whether they knew about the likelihood of marriage, I can't say."

"And Petersen objected?"

"Not at that. Not even at the way the school started to let the men... hmm... sample the goods, you would say."

"So it became more of a brothel."

"They didn't see it that way, but of course it was. The difference was that the girls were supposed to be exclusive to their gentleman."

I figured that made sense. It also explained the luxury bedrooms I'd seen upstairs in the school as well as the classrooms for legitimate instruction.

She said, "But that wasn't what Petersen objected to. The girls were getting younger. And then they had a girl who was only twelve."

"Laura," I said.

"Yes, Laura."

I was relieved Jane wasn't here.

Quietly, I said, "Tell me what happened to Laura."

"Petersen didn't take her to the school. He hid her."

"Hid her?"

"He told them she'd been delayed, and for a few days they believed him. I spoke to him then and he said he'd

358

had enough—couldn't live with it anymore. He might have got away with it but he did more. He helped the other younger girls escape."

"You aren't telling me about Laura. What did he do with Laura?"

Miss Liang looked down and seemed to consider her next words carefully.

"Laura..." she started, but stopped.

"Yes?"

"Laura... It's better I show you rather than say."

# SIXTY-SIX

I had acquired the Land Rover from the school and drove. Miss Liang sat in the passenger seat. She didn't say much at first except to give me occasional directions.

I didn't totally trust her and made it obvious when I placed my Beretta alongside my thigh. Just in case.

When we turned on to Route One, she said, "Do you realize how persecuted the Chinese have been under the British?"

I said, "It's a guerrilla war and mostly Chinese."

"But not all. Tens of thousands have been interred into camps or shipped out. Forced repatriation it's called. It's not repatriation if you come from Malaya. Is it a wonder that people turn against you? And those who don't, live in fear and poverty."

"Not you though. You had a job at the hospital and now run the adoption centre."

"I am lucky, but I still have constant worries."

I glanced at her. "Are you trying to justify your actions?"

She looked straight ahead and then pointed. "Turn right, here."

We entered a town called Kulai, just north of Johor Bahru. There was a small hotel close to the highway and then a main street with shops. She asked me to stop and went to a vendor selling vegetables. I watched and wondered what she was doing but she just bought vegetables. She returned with a full bag and asked me to continue.

"Almost there," she said.

A hundred yards later, we turned off down a muddy street and passed row upon row of run-down buildings, originally brick but now supported by corrugated sheets, mud and palm fronds. The smell of sewage rose up as we approached the heart of the slum.

She told me to stop again.

"This was the old Chinese quarter," she said, and I heard sadness in her voice. "Destroyed by the Japanese and left to rot by the British."

I said, "Why are we here?"

"This is where I was brought up. My mother and my family still live here."

We got out of the jeep and she took me into a house with no door. There were people sitting on the floor, all women. They looked wary but bowed their heads in greeting.

Miss Liang approached an elderly lady who struggled to stand. They hugged and Miss Liang handed over the bag of vegetables before saying something I could barely hear.

The old woman pointed to the rear and I followed Miss Liang into the darkness. There were rooms back there with mats on the floor. The farthest room had windows and children were playing a game like marbles but with stones. They stopped their game and stared at me.

Miss Liang spoke and one child spoke softly in return.

I said, "Where is she?"

We continued on through the back of the property and out into a dirt yard. There was a path and then a cluster of huts. The stink suggested toilets. My eyes were drawn to a pile of earth, maybe child-size.

I started to walk towards it.

"No," Miss Liang said. "Wait."

She stepped over to a hut and knocked on the closed door. She pushed it open and inside I could see a young girl cowering in the shadow.

"You know me," Miss Liang said in English. "There's no need to hide. And this man is a friend."

We waited and Miss Liang repeated herself. Then the child stepped forward into the light. She had dirty clothes, dirty skin and dirty hair. Her hair was cropped Chinese-style but it had once been fair and her bone structure suggested European blood.

I squatted and smiled. "Laura? Is that you?"

The girl's dirty cheeks streaked with tears.

I wanted to scoop her up and hug her fragile frame and tell her everything would be all right, but I was a man and she was still wary.

And then she surprised me by holding out her hand. "Hello, sir."

I shook it. "You're safe now, Laura."

She gave a small nod and followed us back along the path and into the house. While she was saying goodbye to the people she'd lived with for the past seven weeks, I spoke to Miss Liang.

I said, "Why didn't you tell me before."

She looked at me, hard. "How could I know if I could trust you? There are many people involved and I don't know them. You could easily have been working for them. They killed Dan Petersen, so I'm sure they wouldn't have hesitated to kill me."

I nodded. It seemed that everyone was afraid, whether they thought it was Sarah or Rix.

"What about the orphanage at Pasir Gudang?"

"Take her to Lady Hage-Dando? That woman confronted me at the hospital. She called me the devil. There's no way I could have asked her for help."

I said, "Then you could have sent Laura back to Penang?" Even as I said it, I realized my mistake. She didn't know Jane—didn't know that she would have protected the girl.

"And risk her returning to the people who sent her in the first place?"

I nodded again.

She said, "What now?"

I said, "Now I ring someone."


We left Miss Liang in the slum house and stopped at the hotel on the edge of the village. I checked they had a telephone and a bath. They had both, although only one bath for all the guests, which was fine. I paid for a room and took Laura up and told her to take her time.

While she used the bathroom, I first made a quick call and then walked along the high street where I found a shop selling children's clothes. I had to ask the shopkeeper for advice on the size and I figured the flowery dress that I bought looked European rather than Asian.

I left the clothes on the bed for the girl and waited in the hotel lobby.

She came down thirty minutes later. Her blonde hair was still damp and hanging loose. The shoulders of the new dress were wet but it fitted and looked good.

"Hungry?" I asked.

"Could I have English food?"

I smiled and guessed she'd been eating Chinese cuisine for the past few weeks.

"Sure," I said. "If we can find somewhere."

363

The receptionist told us where to go and she chose a simple ham and cheese sandwich and a Coke. It didn't look great but she said it was the best she'd ever tasted.

When we got back to the hotel, there was a car outside that I recognized: a light grey Jaguar Mk II. Jane must have been waiting at a window because she came running outside.

Laura missed a step as she saw her and then started running. She jumped into Jane's arms and the two spun around, laughing and shrieking. And when they stopped spinning, they were both crying. Jane hugged the girl like she was afraid to let go.

I kept back. I leaned against the Jaguar and enjoyed the sunlight that had broken through the clouds.

Eventually Jane held Laura's hand and walked over to me.

"Thank you!" She kissed me and cupped my chin briefly. Although her face was radiant with happiness, there was sadness in her eyes.

I said, "You're going back."

"To Penang," she said. "Yes. I'm taking Laura back with me."

"Back to an orphanage?"

"No. I'm going to take her home. England." She held my hand. "I don't suppose…"

"Come back to England?"

"Yes." She smiled but I could see she already knew the answer. I wasn't ready to settle down. Also, I wasn't ready to leave Singapore.

I said, "I'll come and visit one day."

"Come now—no commitment. Spend a few days with us in Penang."

"That would be nice," I said, "but I have things to do."

She nodded and then they got into the big car.

"No long goodbyes," she said.

"Drive carefully."

I just stood there and watched as Jane turned the car around. I could see Laura fiddling with something on the dashboard. As they pulled away, I could hear music, loud and tinny. Johnnie Ray, I think.

Both girls were smiling.

They waved and were gone.

# SIXTY-SEVEN

Inspector McNaughton worked diligently on the case. He believed there were as many as forty men involved with the brothel-school but only managed to identify seventeen. Major Vernon received an honourable discharge and was subsequently replaced by a much better CO. Commander Alldritt provided three other names and retired quietly without an official blemish to his reputation.

McNaughton interviewed the girls who had remained at Lady Hage-Dando's orphanage and got some more names. He charged the colleague who had provided him with the false information about the girl in the Kuala Lumpur hospital. He also suspected at least one superior officer of being involved but couldn't prove it. It seemed that many of the men didn't reveal their names to the girls at the school.

But he did find success with a number of wealthy civilians and two politicians in the Singapore legislature. I didn't know either of them.

Some of those involved were single but most were married. They were fairly wealthy and senior. And they were all white.

For months after, I found myself wondering if anyone I met was involved. And if they were I hoped they feared that one day they'd be found out.

McNaughton also tried to trace the girls who had been taken but not into the school. He learned that Sarah was highly selective and would sell on any girl she thought unsuitable. The inspector had the names from the address book but he didn't locate one. We also never found out what happened to Di Yang and Kate Tiurina—the two who had escaped with Monalisa Cardoso.

Jane returned to her home town of Hastings and became a civilian nurse. She formally adopted Laura, and the last I heard, the girl was doing academically well and played hockey for the school.

Stevenson's men were released while Turner and Lipscombe received lengthy sentences for child abduction. I found it ironic that Alldritt and Vernon got off lightly in comparison.

Sergeant Dave "Hedge" Hegarty received a posthumous award—a DSO—for his role in the discovery of the illegal drugs operation by communist terrorists. It was a small thing that gave me most satisfaction.

But that was all in the future.

After discovering Laura, I returned to Singapore, got cleaned up and knocked on the door of the house in the government sector. The Malay butler answered and ushered me into the library-styled room.

Coates was there, blue smoke swirling above his armchair. He looked surprised to see me, like he never expected to see me again. He put down a thick cigar and stood up, his fake leg causing more awkwardness than usual.

"What have you got to say for yourself?" he said, like a headmaster about to scold a pupil.

I smiled. "I've had a good morning."

"You've not been at your post."

"I found the missing girl and I solved the murder of the man on the causeway."

He waited for me to say more, but I was watching his reaction, trying to read him.

Eventually he said, "How is Major Vernon?"

"Indisposed."

He looked at me askance.

I said, "Did you get my message about the client list?"

"You're talking in riddles."

"Did you get it?"

"Yes, but I didn't understand. I still don't understand. All I know is you are this close"—he showed a small gap between his thumb and index finger—"to being fired. And you don't want that, do you!"

I nodded. He was threatening me with disclosure of what he thought he knew about my past. Maybe he did. Maybe he didn't.

I said, "Vernon has been arrested and the JB police will find out who the other men are—the men who were complicit in a sex-slave business at a school." I watched his eyes. "Including underage girls."

His eyes narrowed. I wondered if he'd become defensive, but instead he was thinking. He said, "Could Yipp be on that list?"

"No," I said, and was certain of it.

"OK, how can we use this?" He waved me over to a chair and sat opposite. "Could Yipp be involved in running the school?"

"No."

"But what if he were? I mean, can we show a connection somehow?"

"He's not connected," I said.

"Do you have proof?"

"No."

"You have a lot to learn," he said, shaking his head again in the teacher mode. "You don't have proof either way. You can't prove he wasn't involved."

I said nothing.

"This is the way for you to save your job, Carter. Do this and I'll overlook your insubordination."

I said, "Even if he were involved, it's not a security issue."

He smiled mirthlessly and we both knew this was personal. Coates knew Yipp wasn't a communist, knew he wasn't really a threat.

I said, "You'd have more luck looking into the maternity ward at a hospital in JB—the Sultana Aminah Hospital."

"Why?"

"Because there's a trade in babies going on there. And Yipp is definitely involved in that."

Now his eyes went bright.

I added: "And speak to Lady Hage-Dando—she runs the orphanage. She'll give you plenty of detail about the baby trade."

"I want you to do it—make amends."

"Later," I said. "I've just got back and I've things to sort out."

For a moment I thought he would argue, but he just waved me away. Before the door closed behind me I heard him on the telephone, probably to the police commissioner. Probably mobilizing things against Yipp.

I doubted he'd get anywhere. Yipp was too careful. I'd seen that in the records I'd had to go over and over again. He was an investor and on the board of the hospital. Yes, there was the adoption of babies, but proving the mothers were coerced, proving that Yipp made money at their expense, would be nigh impossible.

369

And as for Lady Hage-Dando? As lovely and kind as she was, any evidence she provided would be nonsense.

When I arrived at my desk, I sat down and wrote two letters. The first was to Sergeant Hegarty's parents. I knew that nothing I could write would make them feel any better about losing their son, but I wanted them to know what a great guy he was. He had helped me when others wouldn't, even at considerable personal cost. I told them about tracking down the Chinese gang in the jungle and that he was a hero. He had died instantly from the gunshot and hadn't suffered.

My final point to his parents was that I would always remember his humour, his smile and his eyebrows. Most of all I'd think of him whenever I heard a cliché or phrase, especially "silence is golden". I found this one ironic since he liked to talk so much.

I wrote a second letter and then pulled out the police records and my notes. While I'd been killing time with Stevenson, waiting to attack the school, I'd thought about the police reports. It wasn't the obvious. It wasn't what was said. The important thing was what wasn't said.

Yipp wasn't a security threat; he was a threat to the British power base. He effectively owned large sectors of the city. You could call it protection or you could call it internal security. Yipp and Coates were two sides of the same coin.

I took a map and drew the areas of Yipp's implied control. There were two sectors that stood out, small areas that appeared to be islands surrounded by Yipp's influence. One included the building from where we followed the men to Singorah airfield. They had been working for him even if they denied it. That location was a distraction from the other.

I picked up a satchel and stuffed my map in it followed by a handful of the police reports—including the Singorah one. The rest of the reports, I returned to their boxes.

Then I stood up and walked out.


The wind blew hard across Fullerton Square as I strode over to the General Post Office. In my hand were two letters: one for the Hegartys and the second for Secretary Coates. My resignation.

I had a third letter in my pocket, burning a hole. It was the one that Gary Bender had given me as he sat dying in the Land Rover.

I hadn't thrown it away. I couldn't.

Bender may not have deserved it, but a mother is a mother after all. So I posted it along with the other two.

I crossed the Cavenagh Bridge and walked along the Esplanade. Cars and buses came into the centre and left the centre. People walked purposefully and strolled around the Padang. The rugby posts were being erected. Singapore life continued. It always would, whether I was here or not.

On Beach Road I stopped briefly to watch a thunderstorm out over the South China Sea. I thought about my job—my ex-job—generally, about Andrew Yipp specifically. And then I made my decision.

I tossed my satchel over the sea wall and watched it sink beneath the waves. A weight was lifted. I was free of Coates and now I was free of Yipp. No more political games and manoeuvres.

I strode along the coast, the sun on my back, and wondered what I'd do next.

## Acknowledgements

Once again I must thank my father, David Bailey, and Ian Johnson for their stories on Singapore in the 1950s. I would also like to thank Ray Theobald who provided considerable help (including photographs) that brought the Kota Tinggi camp and the BVD to life.

I'm grateful to my sister, Dr Kerry Bailey-Jones, for assisting with all things medical. Also to Di Yang for help with the Chinese warning note. Thanks to my early reviewers, my wife and Pete Tonkin, for their feedback and helping me with the reader's perspective. I'm also grateful to my excellent editor, Richard Sheehan. How you do it is a mystery to me.

My final thanks go to the lovely people of Neyber, the financial wellbeing company. With permission I have used some of their names for many of the characters as a thank you for encouragement and support.

Want to know what happens next?

Exclusively read the first four chapters of Ash Carter's
next adventure:

# Singapore Boxer

# ONE

All they had to do was last three minutes in the ring with me. A knockout was classed as a hand or knee touching the canvas. If they were lucky they could remain standing and get their money back. But they wanted the big prize. Knock me down and win fifty pounds.

I'd been a prize fighter at the New World Amusement Park for a month and no one had put me down. Not even close.

I sidestepped the latest wild punch and connected a roundhouse to the young pretender's cheek. He staggered sideways, looked bemused that something had hit him, and then dropped to his knees.

The crowd cheered. Although I have to confess I'd grown used to the sound, that was more of an appreciation of another's misfortune than support for me: a sarcastic *whoop!* rather than a cheer.

He was helped out of the ring and I prepared for the next lad. Maybe they were reasonable brawlers but very few of them knew how to box properly. Since we were surrounded by entertainment and alcohol, most of the bravado was also fuelled by booze. Peer pressure also encouraged the foolhardy to have a go.

The prize fighting took place five days a week between 5 and 7pm. There was no point in fighting after seven since the park became out of bounds to soldiers. And most of the customers were men on shore leave, enjoying the exotic dancers, striptease and sideshows that New World offered over a site the size of a football pitch.

There were three prize fighters and we usually took it in turns. I'd fought three bouts this evening and I had two more to go. Neither of my colleagues had turned up. The astute men in the crowd would be watching and waiting. Why have a go when I'm fresh? The best time to challenge would be on my last fight.

I could see three likely contenders. Two were soldiers surrounded by their mates. Their eyes tracked my moves hoping to spot a weakness. Hoping to learn my instinctive combinations.

Then there was a third man. I'd seen him the previous day, watching, assessing. He wasn't in uniform—he wore a grey suit—and he didn't look like a fighter. He didn't look like a heavyweight but I assessed his height to be similar to my six two. I'd heard of Thai fighters whose looks were deceptive. But this was no Thai. This guy was white and very British. His stance spoke of confidence, maybe even arrogance, and his face was inscrutable.

One of the army lads clambered into the ring. He was big. His oversize face was like a sunburnt moon on a heavy frame.

The bell rang and we touched gloves. He stepped forward, left glove up by his giant face, right hand jabbing.

I stepped back and let him jab. I glanced down at the promoter and he shook his head at me. I was asking permission to end this quickly. I knew the drill. Make it too quick and you put off the others. Draw it out; make the challengers think they have a chance. That's what the promoter wanted. Better for business that way.

I traded a few blows and moved around the ring. The guy followed. His mates cheered loudly each time he made contact, although no judge would have given him points.

2

He wasn't bad, maybe a bit obvious. His right jab was OK, but when he shielded with his right glove, half his massive face was exposed.

I glanced at the promoter again. Surely we could end this? I got a shrug.

The next time my opponent threw a left, I stepped right and slammed my right into the side of his nose. He did a nice pirouette before collapsing on the ropes.

The crowd did their whoop and Moonface was pulled out of the ring.

I walked to my corner and took water and a towel.

The white guy in a suit watched me.

The squaddie in the second group shrugged his mates aside and handed over his five shillings.

He had hard eyes and a better stance than the last guy. He also had three or four inches on me and solid-looking muscles. His biceps were almost as big as my thighs.

"The bigger they are the harder they fall!" my father used to say in my early years playing school rugby. Better advice came from my first boxing coach. He used to say, "The bigger they are the longer their reach."

Estimating a man's reach could be the difference between clear air and a punch in the face.

The bell sounded, and because he'd been watching, he didn't come for me. He knew I liked to counterpunch. So he stepped back and grinned. He dropped his hands as though encouraging me to attack. Encouraging me to come within range of his longer arms. I decided to see what he'd got, so I obliged. It was more fun that way.

I skipped forward and jabbed and moved. He landed a couple of heavy blows on my arms. Strong but slow. He probably worked out. Large muscles, good for intimidation, not so good for fast punches.

"Fought before?" I asked as we moved around the ring.

"A bit," he said, and took a punch in the mouth.

3

He spat blood and his eyes narrowed more. Then he surprised me with a combination that first took my breath and ended with a blow to my eye. I rolled with most of it but it was still a good shot.

His mates went crazy as I back-pedalled briefly.

I wanted him to come after me then so I could counterpunch but he didn't. He stepped back and dropped his hands like he'd done at the start. Maybe he thought he was taunting me but this was against the clock. We moved in again and traded blows. Most of his missed, but he made contact with a couple that felt like sledgehammers.

When the final bell rang, he blinked sweat from his eyes and staggered back to the ropes. He'd done well and deserved his five shillings back.

I gave him a respectful nod.

"Lucky it wasn't two or three rounds," he said between ragged breaths, "I'd have got you eventually."

I smiled. He wouldn't have lasted another round. The guy had given everything he had in that three-minute burst. "Tomorrow. I'm back tomorrow," I said.

My second put a robe over my shoulders and I climbed through the ropes. That's when I saw the guy in the suit again. He was right in front of me. Same rigid posture. Same lack of expression.

He stepped towards me.

"Didn't fancy your chances?" I said.

"I was just watching."

I took a swig of water.

He said, "Why do you do it?"

"Entertainment."

"Really?" For the first time, his face made an expression. It seemed to be somewhere between disapproval and doubt.

I started to walk towards the tent where I could get changed.

The strange man kept pace with me.

4

"Can I help you?"

"After watching that," he said, "I was thinking perhaps I could help you, sir."

I stopped.

He said, "You're Captain Ash Carter, ex-Royal Military Police, ex-Special Investigations Branch."

I said nothing. Was this the moment I'd been waiting for? The moment that my past caught up with me?

He said, "Boxing for money is a bit beneath you, isn't it?"

"Apparently not."

"I beg to differ." He lowered his voice. "I have a job for you."

# TWO

I figured the guy in the suit was a government man. I'd worked for the government and I'd had enough. Politics wasn't for me. Working for a politician also wasn't for me.

I'd shaken my head and walked away. After washing and dressing, I came out of our changing room. I expected him to be outside, waiting. But he wasn't.

The crowds were thin now that the 7pm watershed had passed. The food stalls stayed open for a few more hours and there would be a film at the cinema, but the soldiers had left. MPs would do a quick patrol of the grounds and any soldier within the out of bounds sector would soon find themselves in the clink.

There were plenty of bars outside the three "Worlds"— the amusement parks—where a man could burn his shore leave money. Spending your last hours of freedom behind bars was enough to deter all but the foolhardy.

5

I walked under the white stone arch onto Jalan Besar. My apartment on Beach Road was only a few minutes' walk away. West towards the city centre and then south to the coast.

Night had already fallen and the streets were much darker than New World had been. Despite the gloom I still spotted them straight away. They were on the corner by Kitchener Road, standing under a street light, looking anything but innocent.

I was on the opposite side of the road and kept walking.

"Oi!" Hard-eyes shouted across to me. He stepped into the road and his men formed a phalanx behind him. I counted eight of them. They looked like kids in a schoolyard, itching for a fight. In fact, they looked little older than schoolkids.

I raised a friendly hand. "See you tomorrow. I'll look forward to it."

Hard-eyes waited for a car to pass and then marched across towards me. His men strung out behind him, identifying three that were braver than the others. If there was a fight I figured those three would join in quickly. The others would wait until I was subdued, probably on the floor and safe to kick.

I stopped and faced them as Hard-eyes stepped onto my pavement.

I said, "I leave my fighting to the ring."

He puffed up his chest. "I'm leaving in the morning."

"Shame then." I made to walk past him but he stepped in my way.

Again I said, "I leave my fighting to the ring. And there are better things to do with your last hours. There are lots of good bars. And if you're looking for girls…"

"I've found a girl." He laughed. "It's you! You're too girly to fight without gloves."

One of his men blew me a kiss and the others joined in with the laughter.

6

I was still calm and said, "You know MPs patrol this area. You get caught fighting and you'll be in the clink."

Hard-eyes tensed up. I could see him planning his attack, assessing my counters. He was still more than an arm's reach away, standing square on. A big and threatening pose. A mistake.

I said, "Marquess of Queensbury rules."

He laughed again. "You've got to be—?"

I kicked him between the legs. Hard.

He buckled and howled. The explosive, surprise attack gave me a second. I could have followed through and taken out a couple of his lieutenants before they realized what was going on. But I didn't.

I stepped back and crouched. When I stood again, I was holding my gun—a Beretta I wore on my left ankle. I didn't aim it at them. I didn't need to. They started easing backwards. Two of the lieutenants pulled their leader to his feet.

"Consider yourselves lucky," I said. "You pick the wrong man and you'll end up dead."

Hard-eyes spat.

"Now go back into town"—with the gun, I pointed down the road towards the city—"and have some fun. But if you ever threaten me again, I won't hesitate to use this." I aimed the Berretta at Hard-eyes. "Now scoot!"

I crossed over to where they had been waiting for me and walked down Kitchener. I heard nothing behind me and I didn't turn around until I reached Beach Road. Thankfully they had taken my advice.

There was a fresh breeze blowing off the South China Sea. I walked half the way towards my apartment and stopped. I stood by the sea wall and looked out at the inky blackness, peppered with flickering lights. There were many cargo ships out there moored up for the night.

7

I loved Singapore: the juxtaposition of jungle and first world city, its energy, its vitality and the exotic. The only thing I lacked was the intellectual challenge.

There was more traffic on Beach Road than on the route I'd walked, but I also liked the fact that I could stand there and feel as though I was the only person in the world. I used to enjoy standing on the bridges over Singapore River and breathing in the spice and rubber smells and thinking. Daydreaming or relaxing or internalizing. Call it what you will, but it was as though you could escape the hustle and bustle at any time.

And then a voice beside me brought me back to the present.

"Rain is coming."

It was the guy in the suit.

"Rain is always coming," I said. "But then it's always warm and the rain is refreshing."

He said, "Hear me out and then decide."

"About your job? I don't work for the government anymore."

"Neither do I."

I looked at him. "What are you then?"

"I'd rather my job didn't define me. My name is Edward Symes."

"And you don't work for the government."

"No. I work for Lloyds."

"The bank?"

"The insurer."

"You're a long way from London."

He inclined his head. "We have an office in KL."

I said nothing and he looked out to sea.

"Maybe we should relocate to Singapore," he said.

I looked at him. "What's the job?"

For the first time, his impassive face showed a hint of a smile. He'd been teasing me, waiting for me to take the bait. "Do you know Perak—the region?"

8

"I've driven through it."

"Very industrial. Tin mines, smelting works, big power station and rubber plantations."

"Tin mines and rubber plantations all over Malaya."

"Eighty percent of the country is still jungle. The Perak region is the most industrial."

"OK. How does that involve Lloyds of London?"

"Insurance claims."

I knew about the insurance situation. The British government called the Malayan war an Emergency. Wars invalidate insurance so the classification protected businesses. Many of those business owners were of course British.

I said, "Are you an assessor?"

"I'm an actuary, but we have assessors out in the field. In fact, that's the job."

"I'm not going to assess an insurance claim for you."

"Hear me out first."

I looked at him.

He said, "A rubber plantation had its payroll stolen. The owner was lucky. He was on his way back from the bank when he was attacked."

"That's lucky?"

"To be alive. The claim is for the lost cash."

"Sounds straightforward."

"That's what we thought. Our assessor went in and never came back."

"What happened?"

"Murdered."

"Sounds like a job for the police."

"It should be but they've got nowhere. So we have a problem. Not only do we have a claim that needs assessing but we have a colleague whose murder needs to be solved."

"And you're speaking to me because...?"

"Because once an investigator, always an investigator."

He was right about that at least.

9

# THREE

Two days later, I stepped off the passenger train at Kuala Lumpur and waited an hour until a freight train came by. It didn't stop but was travelling slow enough that I could run alongside and jump onto a truck. I wasn't the only one taking the free ride north. The train of twenty empty wooden trucks must have had over a hundred men clinging to the sides. I was the only white man and figured they were looking for or travelling to work.

Each time we passed through a station, some men jumped off and some jumped on. We didn't stop though until we came into a town called Kampar. The train took a branch line, I assumed to some industrial site, and I got off.

I stood on the concrete platform. There was a green wooden hut, probably for railway staff, and a covered area, presumably for passengers when it rained. To the east was a hill; maybe it was a mountain. I found height difficult to gauge since everything was covered in trees, but it was below the clouds so I figured just a hill. The mountains were probably further east.

The west was also jungle but flatter and I knew there was a river and lakes out there. The trees were less dense and to the west and north I could see signs of industry. Odd grey buildings jutted above the canopy and thin lines of smoke reached up in the still air like stilts holding up the clouds.

Kampar, like most small towns and villages, was a ribbon development. It ran north–south along Route One, the main road from Singapore to Thailand.

I walked out onto the road. Most of the traffic was travelling through. I saw heavy trucks, light trucks, civilian cars and an occasional army truck. But most of all I saw bicycles. Hundreds of them.

The buildings were all two-storey except for one. It was the colour of cooked salmon and it stood out. It needed to. It was a hotel. If you needed to stay in Kampar then this was the only option. And based on how quiet it was, I guessed there weren't many people who wanted to stay in Kampar.

I paid for a room, dropped off my things and found the bathroom—the one shared by all twenty bedrooms. It had an old chipped tub but the water was hot and clean.

I freshened up but left the two days of facial hair. I also re-dressed in my travelling clothes. They were grimy from the train ride and smelled of coal dust. Perfect. The last thing I wanted was to look clean and respectable. I was going for an edge of roughness because I was about to play a role.

Edward Symes the actuary had asked me to find out what had happened to his man. He also wanted a view on the legitimacy of the insurance claim. He said Lloyds could have sent someone else in. Officially. But they were worried. They'd lost one man and didn't want to lose another.

"But you don't mind risking my life," I'd said.

"You're different," he'd said. "You do this type of thing. And we want you undercover."

It made sense. He also said that they'd pay me no matter what. Whether I discovered what was going on or not.

"We just need to investigate," he'd explained with a shrug. "You know, compliance with policy."

I found the bar he'd told me about. There was a jumble of bicycles outside and a similar jumble of men inside. I'd visited a zoo once and the noise here was worse than feeding time in the monkey house. Everyone was talking

11

over everyone else and it was accompanied by the clatter of beer glasses and cutlery. The zoo analogy didn't end there, because, beneath the odour of beer, there was a smell akin to elephant dung. And yet this was clearly the most popular place in town.

As it was dinnertime, I suspected most of these men had finished their shifts for the day and were here to blow off steam.

I ordered a Tiger Beer, a glass of water and a sandwich and found a spare table at the rear. I sat with my back to the wall and had a good view of the entire room as well as the entrance.

The bar was a real melting pot of nationalities. The one thing they all had in common was that they looked like workers. There was no one in a suit. No one looked superior to anyone else, except perhaps me. Even in my dirty state, I knew I didn't look like a labourer.

I could imagine this bar set in the American Wild West if there had been Malays and Chinese and Thais and only a handful of whites. And there were no cowboy hats or a piano. Apart from that it was exactly how I pictured it.

I left the beer in front of me and drank the water with my sandwich. It was Spam. It didn't taste like any specific meat but was allegedly nutritious. If I was going to be here for the two weeks Symes would pay me for, I prayed that I'd find something better to eat.

After half an hour I took out a pack of playing cards and began to shuffle. Within minutes I had three new friends at the table all wanting to play a variant of poker called five-card stud.

We wagered small and they played well. The guy to my right was a Malay. He had quick eyes and a quicker hand. I knew he was cheating but the money I was losing amounted to pennies so I turned a blind eye.

There were other games going on in the bar, but ours eventually encouraged the largest crowd. Occasionally one

12

of our table would drop out and his seat would be immediately filled. The Malay with the quick eyes kept on playing, kept subtly cheating just enough to matter, not too often to stand out. And his pot grew to a couple of pounds.

At eight o'clock I noticed a policeman enter the bar. He stood in the doorway as if to say, "Look, I'm here, so carry on behaving yourself." He wasn't tall but had a natural air of authority about him.

Two men at our table glanced at the cop. The Malay guy slipped a card from the bottom of the deck.

I yelled, "Cheat!" and punched him in the mouth.

The table went over. My full glass of beer emptied over the man to my left. The money went into the air. It was as if a starter's pistol had been fired. The crowd around the table dived for the cash. The man to my right took a swing at me and missed. The cheating Malay guy lifted his chair as though to throw it at me. But he was too obvious and slow and I hit him again.

And then the money seemed to be forgotten and we were in a full-scale bar brawl.

# FOUR

I spent the night in the Kampar police cell.

"Why me?" I said to the arresting police officer when he closed the cell door.

"Because you were fighting."

I shook my head. "No, I mean, why just me. I wasn't the only one in that fight."

He took a long breath and pursed his lips. Maybe he delayed because he was wondering about whether to tell the truth or not. Then maybe he decided what the hell. "You're the outsider," he said.

"And that makes me guilty?"

"That makes you the problem."

He left me there to stew overnight. The air didn't move and had a strange metallic tang. There was a desk clerk but he ignored me when I called out for water.

I curled up on the small bench and tried to sleep. I'd been dismissive of the grubby salmon-pink hotel but suspected the bed would have been a hundred times more comfortable than this bench. And at least I could have a drink of water.

It was still dark when the arresting officer returned. I heard cockerels crowing for a sunrise that was probably two hours distant.

He handed me a cup of lukewarm tea through the bars.

"Sleep off the beer?" he asked. "How's the hangover."

"I didn't drink any alcohol," I said.

"Oh," he said, not really listening. He had a ledger and a pen. "So a few questions, if you will."

I waited.

"Name."

"Ash Burton." It was the name I'd agreed with Symes, just in case anyone had heard of my real name and past.

The officer wrote it in the book. He was a lefty like me, although he held his pen more awkwardly, like he was writing upside down.

"Occupation?"

"Travelling through."

"None then."

"Right."

"Address?"

I gave him the address of the hotel.

He wrote it down with a smile. "I know, just travelling through."

"Right."

"Moving on today?" I could see him wondering if I was going to continue to be a problem.

I shook my head. "I don't know. I kind of like it here."

He said nothing for a while. Took my empty cup.

When he spoke again it was less of an interrogation and more conversational. "Ex-army?"

"Yes."

"Thought so."

I said, "What's that funny smell?"

"Joss sticks," he said. "It's supposed to make it smell better in here. You'd like it much less without them."

"That's thoughtful."

"It's not for your benefit. It's for the staff."

I smiled. I was beginning to warm to this little guy.

He said, "Are you looking for work?"

"Maybe." I showed him my palms. "As long as it's not labouring."

He unlocked the cell door and swung it open like I'd passed the test and was free to go. He said, "I may have something for you. Where will you be later?"

"In the bar."

"No you won't. You'll wait at the hotel."

"Fine," I said.

"If he's interested, the general will find you there."

"And if he's not?"

"I'd appreciate it if you leave town tomorrow."


I caught up on sleep for most of the morning. When the man came through the hotel door, I guessed at once who it was. The policeman had called him "The General". He wore army fatigues with a jungle pattern and had a rifle slung over one shoulder.

He strode towards me like he ran the hotel, maybe ran the whole town. He was tall and charismatic with a shock of

15

steel-grey hair, big moustache and tanned skin. Before he opened his mouth I guessed eastern European.

"Maxim," he said, looking down at me in my comfortable chair. "You must be Burton."

I stood and thought of offering a hand but decided against. He looked the sort that would ignore the gesture.

He appraised me with intelligent brown eyes under bushy eyebrows. It was like he was sighting a rifle. Like he was a hidden sniper and I was his target.

"Rank? Unit?"

I said, "Sergeant," and gave him a squad I'd dealt with in the Middle East.

"Seen action?"

I'd joined up a few months before the end of the Second World War. I was still in officer training at Sandhurst when the H-bomb was dropped. But he'd figure from my age and status that I must have been called up earlier. Conscription at the age of eighteen.

"No," I said. "It's been the biggest frustration. Everywhere I was deployed, it was too late."

He nodded and I could see he was ready to hear the story.

"That's why I left. You can't choose where you go unless you're a free man. The Middle East was too dull."

"There's the SAS. You should have tried them."

"I didn't get the chance."

"Korea?"

"Malaya seemed a better option." I grinned and he nodded again. "I don't fancy fighting a whole army."

"I have an opening for a good man," he said.

"I'm not a labourer."

"No. I'm looking for a soldier." He pointed to a circular badge on his left arm. "Perak Protection."

"I've not heard of them."

"Private. Small. I have eight men." He shrugged. "Seven men and one vacancy."

16

"One of your men left?"

"Died." He grinned. "No point in pretending to take the risk. If you don't risk death then you are just playing at soldiering. Are you just playing, Burton?"

"No, sir," I said.

"You have a gun?"

"Of course. I acquired a Browning revolver." I didn't mention my hidden Beretta.

"Where is it?"

"Safe. In my room."

"Follow me," he said, did a one-eighty turn and marched through the back of the hotel. He led me outside and kept walking until he reached a wall of trees. He took an envelope from an inside pocket and tacked it to the nearest tree, chest height. Then he paced thirty yards back and stopped.

"Much of a shot?"

"I'm all right, though I wouldn't class myself as a sharpshooter."

He swung the rifle off his shoulder and handed it to me. "Used one of these before?"

It was a Springfield M1903. Bolt action. Old but reliable. A model that had seen action for almost fifty years.

"Seen them but never fired one," I said, feeling its weight.

He handed me a single bullet.

"You hit the target, you've got the job," he said.

I pulled back the bolt and loaded the bullet and took up my stance.

"Left-handed," he said.

"Is that a problem?"

"Not at all." He chuckled. "Unless you can't hit the paper."

I lined up the sights. Without a wind, this should be straightforward, but then the sights could be off. With an unknown gun, I might take three shots to work out the compensation. But I only had one bullet and this guy wasn't going to hear any excuses.

I calmed my heart, held my breath and fired.

My bullet clipped the bottom right-hand corner of the paper.

Without a comment, Maxim took the rifle from me and then, with blistering speed, loaded, aimed and fired. From this distance the new hole appeared dead centre.

He grunted like it was an acceptable shot, but I could see he was pleased. He was happy with me and satisfied he'd proved himself my superior.

"Consider yourself hired."

We walked back to the hotel. I said, "What if I don't want the job?"

"You want the job."

"What's the pay?"

"Forty shillings and six pence a week."

I didn't comment. It was more than army pay but less than I'd been getting in my previous job.

"Food and lodgings?" I asked.

He inclined his head. "Of course. Now get your things and meet me outside."

When I came down with my bag, Maxim was sitting in the passenger seat of a Land Rover. It was painted with a camouflage pattern and had Perak Protection stencilled on the side. He pointed and I climbed into the passenger seat.

We went north along Route One. When I tried to make conversation he put me in my place.

"Now you're one of my men," he said gruffly, "you treat me as the officer. You only speak when spoken to, got it?"

"Yes, sir," I said with appropriate deference. That would be a nuisance. If I was to do the job that Edward Symes had commissioned me for, I needed to talk to people, and Maxim was my initial contact.

We reached the state town of Perak and Maxim went into a bank. He returned with a tin the size of a large book. It had a metal handle and lock. It didn't look very secure but then I figured Maxim didn't worry about such things.

From Perak we turned south-west on a road that took us through wetlands and along the route of the Kinta River.

On the outskirts of a town called Batu Gajah we parked by a long timber shed. The wood was shiplapped and I guessed it had once been a sawmill. There was another identical Land Rover parked outside.

The militia logo was painted on the side of the hut and I knew this would be home for at least a week, maybe two if Symes was right.

My first objective was to find out what had happened to a chap called Sid Wilding. He was the dead guy, the assessor sent to find out about the stolen money.

The Perak Protection Force had recently lost a soldier. I wondered whether this was my man, whether Wilding had gone undercover like me.

I soon learned this was something else altogether.